Michael Parker was born in We[...] a Senior Lecturer in English at t[...] Education, and has taught full-time at the University of Łódź in Poland, and part-time at the universities of Liverpool and Manchester, contributing to courses on modern Irish literature. His interest in writing from the north of Ireland began in the early 1980s, and he has published a best-selling study of the poetry of Seamus Heaney, *Seamus Heaney: The Making of the Poet* (Macmillan, 1993), and is co-editor of *Postcolonial Literature* (Macmillan, 1995). He has reviewed for the *Guardian*, the *Times Literary Supplement* and the *Honest Ulsterman*, and is currently working on a study of writers and the Troubles, which will examine drama, fiction and poetry from Northern Ireland in the period from 1968 to 1994.

Michael Parker lives in Warrington, Cheshire.

THE
HURT WORLD

SHORT STORIES OF THE TROUBLES

Edited by
MICHAEL PARKER

THE
BLACKSTAFF
PRESS

First published in 1995 by
The Blackstaff Press Limited
3 Galway Park, Dundonald, Belfast BT16 0AN, Northern Ireland
with the assistance of
The Arts Council of Northern Ireland

© Selection, Introduction and Notes, Michael Parker, 1995
The acknowledgements on pp. 362–3 constitute
an extension of this copyright page

Typeset by Paragon Typesetters, Queensferry, Clwyd

Printed in England by The Cromwell Press Limited

A CIP catalogue record for this book
is available from the British Library

ISBN 0-85640-557-4

for
Michael Longley
and
Frank Ormsby

The editor would particularly like to thank David Marcus,
Ruth Hooley, Robert Bell and Richard Haslam for their generous
help and advice in putting together this collection of stories.

CONTENTS

INTRODUCTION

Between tall houses down the blackened street;
the hurled stones pour, hurt-instinct aims to hurt . . .
JOHN HEWITT, 'Bogside, Derry, 1971'

In that bower, closed off from the hurt of the hurt world,
Denver's imagination produced its own hunger and its own food.
TONI MORRISON, *Beloved*

This book is intended both as a celebration and a commemoration. In response to a continuingly dislocating narrative of appalling violence, injustice and suffering over the last twenty-five years, writers from the north of Ireland have struggled to find a language and create forms which might in some way contain their own and a generation's horror, anger, grief, and bewilderment. Without the benefit of a bower or retreat to a 'place out of time' (Derek Mahon, 'Last of the Fire Kings') – for even those who physically left the North did not and could not leave in another sense – these writers have endeavoured to address what Edna Longley has termed the 'cultural dynamic underlying the conflict', and to fashion in their fictions, with as much integrity and compassion as they could muster, objective correlatives for the brutal experiences endured by ordinary people repeatedly hurt in an uncivil war.

'Confusion is not an ignoble condition,' says Brian Friel's schoolmaster at the end of *Translations*; nor is an acute sense of others' and one's own vulnerability. Not surprisingly, these basic human feelings of fear and disorientation manifest themselves within the characterisation and focalisation in the stories, and occasionally, as in the case of 'Naming the Names', within narrative structures. Frequently, as in Michael McLaverty's 'Pigeons', Shane Connaughton's 'Beatrice' and David Park's 'Killing a Brit', children are the central characters and focalisers, or, like the narrator of 'Oranges from Spain', Joe and Colette in Una Woods's 'The Dark Hole Days', and Finnula in Anne Devlin's 'Naming the Names', young people on the verge of adulthood or in their early twenties, who are forced by their experiences to know again what D.H. Lawrence calls 'the painful terrified helplessness of childhood', to feel like the young IRA volunteer in Frank O'Connor's 'Guests of the Nation', 'very lost and lonely like a child astray in the snow'. Attempts to suppress the memory of pain and the pain of memory inevitably fail, such as when the adult narrative voice at the beginning of 'Oranges from Spain' confesses to the reader that 'I stopped telling anyone about the nightmares and kept them strictly private. They don't come very often now, but when they do only my wife knows. Sometimes she cradles me in her arms like a child until I fall asleep again.'

In these stories, and in the ones with older protagonists, such as Mary Beckett's 'A Belfast Woman' or William Trevor's 'The Distant Past', the concepts of personal choice and authority have all but disappeared, and one is constantly presented with figures whose lives seem totally determined by others. Significantly, both the unemployed teenagers in Una Woods's novella keep diaries, endeavour to construct their lives into a defining narrative: whereas the young woman envisions the very act of writing as a way of opening up possibilities, asserting her presence in the face of constraining domestic loyalties, Joe uses his text to record his increasing loss of self in a paramilitary fiction, with its myth of a cleansing, liberating violence, which makes him feel 'part of something', with 'friends and important thoughts about history and the country'.

Unlike those people on both sides of the Irish Sea who have implied that there is a single version of the 'truth' and of 'history', and merely recycled myths about 'the other side' in order to maintain a solidarity bred on fear and ignorance, the best writers from both traditions have in the main avoided the temptation to massage collective feelings, to use a phrase of Seamus Heaney's. In fact, the Troubles experience has often led to texts in which the writers' own communities and their value systems have been subjected to a rigorous scrutiny. The nucleus of John Montague's 1963 story 'The Cry' is an incident in which a Catholic teenage boy is beaten up by four B Specials. However, when Peter, a young Irish journalist, determines to expose the case in the English press, he quickly comes up against fierce opposition from his own people, including the victim's family. Peter's mother speaks for all of them, perhaps, when she counsels a path of resignation: 'They're a bad lot . . . But we have to live with them . . . Why else did God put them there?' Although Montague is clearly condemning the gross abuse of power within what Michael Farrell terms 'the Orange State', his narrative also articulates the frustrations of the younger genera- tion with the pre-civil rights Nationalist Party position, en- dorsed by the Catholic Church, that it is meet and fitting to suffer silently.

Many of the other stories exhibit their female characters' increasing impatience with, and resistance to, male readings and patriarchal order, and illustrate the point that 'Troubles liter- ature' – or rather, contemporary Northern Irish writing – is not just concerned with bombs and bullets, but with many other issues of power. The 'abandoned' wife in Mary Beckett's 'The Master and the Bombs' makes no bones about the resentment she feels towards her activist husband and the mythic status surrounding those on political charges. An acerbic portrait of male-reverencing bourgeois Protestantism is provided in Linda

Anderson's 'The Death of Men', which, to switch metaphors, makes easy meat of its men. The passing-on of one ineffectual patriarch on Christmas Day, only to be 'upstaged by a turkey', prompts the narrator to recall the death of her own father; another equally 'joyless and forbidding' man, he was only reduced to tenderness by the effects of cancer. It is obviously no accident that the ill-used central character, Liz O'Prey, in Bernard Mac Laverty's 'The Daily Woman', bears the surname she has, along with the bruises.

Complementary to these texts in some ways is Anne-Marie Reilly's beautifully succinct and ironic tale, 'Leaving'. At first sight the principal target again seems to be male self-centredness, with the narrator perhaps shifting between an echoed restatement of her mother's convictions and her own adult reading of the situation: 'My father, as usual, was the problem. He was frightened of the responsibility of buying a house. He might have to sacrifice his social life and he wasn't prepared to do that . . . *He had all he wanted, he could not understand her need'* (my italics). The second half of the story, however, sees the mother's bourgeois social aspirations to move up the road and 'better' herself and her daughters being mocked by external events. Although the narrator struggles to distance herself from her mother's 'defeat' and the lifetime of unfulfilled longing endured by her mother's generation, she recognises that a determination to will a different outcome for herself may not be enough. Sometimes, as Devlin's 'The Way-paver' suggests, the risk just has to be taken to separate oneself, to metamorphose, to be a gull or become 'that stray seal'.

That male-chained politics will not suffer contradiction is shown, for example, in Fiona Barr's 'The Wall-reader' and in Brenda Murphy's ironically titled 'A Social Call'. The latter story questions macho republicanism, and its system of justice, and asks how the beating of women and the kneecapping of sixteen-year-olds furthers 'the Cause'. Barr's story similarly centres upon the experience of a young mother and wife. An intrigued reader of Belfast graffiti, trapped in routine, she longs for a script which would provide 'evidence she was having impact on others'. Just as in the grimmest fairy tales, wishes have a way of rebounding on the wishers. 'The Wall-reader' warns of the consequences of talking to strangers, and what can happen to your house if you talk to the Beast.

Within much of the collection there is an underlying dismay at the way competing ideologies – republican, loyalist and British – construct 'the enemy', and a common abhorrence when individual human beings are translated into 'legitimate targets'. One might cite characterisations such as the paramilitary snatch squad in Bernard Mac Laverty's 'Walking the Dog' who are driving around the streets seeking out somebody from the other 'persuasion' in order to make them any body, or Corporal Jessop in Maurice Leitch's 'Green Roads', whose loathing and self-loathing are triggered on hearing a soft Irish accent while on leave in a Swindon pub; he waits in the car park until the unoffending man leaves, in order to give him a comprehensive beating, 'for the corporal had been trained to inflict the utmost damage as speedily and as effectively as possible'.

In 'An Irish Answer', written for the *Guardian*, on 16 July 1994, Ronan Bennett has claimed:

> The conflict is too insistent to be kept entirely out of the arts, but when it enters it tends to be neutral, apolitical, disengaged . . . In other words the mainstream artistic mediators of the conflict have tended to opt, like the largely middle-class audience they serve, for an apolitical vision. Theirs is the culture of aloofness, of 'being above it all', of distance from the two sets of proletarian tribes fighting out their bloody atavistic war . . . Speculation on the causes of the conflict is territory most novelists resolutely refuse to cross.

However, the evidence of my reading for this collection and more broadly into Northern literature does not bear out Bennett's charges. Serious writers from the North have not in fact been apolitical, or shirked from showing the injustices and incomprehensions which gave rise to and sustained the violence. When at the opening of 'A Belfast Woman' the main character opens an envelope containing the message 'Get out or we'll burn you out', it immediately sets in motion two earlier narratives, as she recalls similar texts from previous pogrom years, 1921 and 1935. The web in Anne Devlin's 'Naming the Names', similarly, is made up of interlinking threads of fictional and real life experiences; symbolic episodes such as Finnula's recurring nightmare about an old woman – Cathleen ni Houlihan, one presumes – who 'grasped my hand and . . . would not let me go', merge with actual historical events such as the burning out of Conway Street and other Catholic streets in Belfast and the arrival of British troops in 1969, and the disastrous introduction of internment in August 1971. ('A "terrorist",' notes Edna Longley in *The Living Stream*, 'is no psychopathic aberration, but produced by the codes, curriculum and pathology of a whole community' – and also 'of an unwhole state', I would suggest.) The institutionalised discrimination of successive Stormont governments from 1922 to 1969 against Catholics is reflected in the patronising attitude of the judge's son towards Finnula in the same story and within the predatory character of Mr Henderson in Bernard Mac Laverty's 'The Daily Woman'. A future lord mayor of Belfast, or so he thinks, in public he talks about building bridges between the communities; in private, however, he repeatedly propositions his Catholic cleaning lady. When she finally submits, he speaks to her 'as if she wasn't there', inspects her, curious as her Creator, 'fascinated by her bruises . . . praised her thinness, her each rib'.

A reminder, if it were needed, that injustice and prejudice are not confined to one state or religious affiliation comes in the person of the father in Shane Connaughton's 'Beatrice' and in the fate of the ageing eccentric couple in William Trevor's 'The Distant Past'. The Middletons, a brother and sister, are Protestant casualties of the border, marooned in the Republic, holding on 'instinctively' to a house and a history which 'ceased to afford protection'. With the onset of the latest Troubles and the consequent decline in trade and tourism, almost overnight the tolerance of decades ebbs away; the pair are boycotted by their Catholic neighbours, fixed in an equation, left 'to face the silence that would sourly thicken as their own two deaths came closer and death increased in another part of their island'. In Ireland, as in any other colonised or newly independent country, narratives about the past defy closure, and history can never be safely distant; hence the inclusion in this collection of four stories which pre-date 1968 in their composition, 'Guests of the Nation', 'Pigeons', 'The Cry', and 'The Master and the Bombs', and of stories written from outside the old divisions of Ulster.

The polarisation in politics in the North over the past twenty-five years has placed such enormous pressure on in-dividuals within communities to keep faith with the collective historical experience, and on writers to bear witness, that at times the fact has been obscured that they possess not just one single homogeneous cultural tradition, but rather a much more complex, multiple cultural and linguistic heritage. A 'dramatic-ally broken history', in the words of Seamus Deane, may have left 'artists caught between identities' ('The Artist and the Troubles', *Ireland and the Arts*), but has also established oppor-tunities to scrutinise the ambivalences within origins – those 'hurled stones', that 'hurt-instinct' – and in the process to employ a diverse range of cultural and historical perspectives, aesthetic strategies. What has been achieved individually and collectively, as these stories I hope demonstrate, has been an art that constantly 'changes the perceptual angle' (Edna Longley) within texts, between texts, within and between people.

MICHAEL PARKER

THELWALL, WARRINGTON
DECEMBER 1994

GUESTS OF THE NATION

FRANK O'CONNOR

I

At dusk the big Englishman, Belcher, would shift his long legs out of the ashes and say, 'Well, chums, what about it?' and Noble and myself would say, 'All right, chum' (for we had picked up some of their curious expressions), and the little Englishman, Hawkins, would light the lamp and bring out the cards. Sometimes Jeremiah Donovan would come up and supervise the game, and get excited over Hawkins's cards, which he always played badly, and shout at him, as if he was one of our own, 'Ah, you divil, why didn't you play the tray?'

But ordinarily Jeremiah was a sober and contented poor devil like the big Englishman, Belcher, and was looked up to only because he was a fair hand at documents, though he was slow even with them. He wore a small cloth hat and big gaiters over his long pants, and you seldom saw him with his hands out of his pockets. He reddened when you talked to him, tilting from toe to heel and back, and looking down all the time at his big farmer's feet. Noble and myself used to make fun of his broad accent, because we were both from the town.

I could not at the time see the point of myself and Noble guarding Belcher and Hawkins at all, for it was my belief that you could have planted that pair down anywhere from this to Claregalway and they'd have taken root there like a native weed. I never in my short experience saw two men take to the country as they did.

They were passed on to us by the Second Battalion when the search for them became too hot, and Noble and myself, being young, took them over with a natural feeling of responsibility, but Hawkins made us look like fools when he showed that he knew the country better than we did.

'You're the bloke they call Bonaparte,' he says to me. 'Mary Brigid O'Connell told me to ask what you'd done with the pair of her brother's socks you borrowed.'

For it seemed, as they explained it, that the Second had little evenings, and some of the girls of the neighbourhood turned up, and, seeing they were such decent chaps, our fellows could not leave the two Englishmen out. Hawkins learned to dance 'The Walls of Limerick', 'The Siege of Ennis' and 'The Waves of Tory' as well as any of them, though he could not return the compliment, because our lads at that time did not dance foreign dances on principle.

So whatever privileges Belcher and Hawkins had with the Second they just took naturally with us, and after the first couple of days we gave up all pretence of keeping an eye on them. Not that they could have got far, because they had accents you could cut with a knife, and wore khaki tunics and overcoats with civilian pants and boots, but I believe myself they never had any idea of escaping and were quite content to be where they were.

It was a treat to see how Belcher got off with the old woman in the house where we were staying. She was a great warrant to scold, and cranky even with us, but before ever she had a chance of giving our guests, as I may call them, a lick of her tongue, Belcher had made her his friend for life. She was breaking sticks, and Belcher, who had not been more than ten minutes in the house, jumped up and went over to her.

'Allow me, madam,' he said, smiling his queer little smile. 'Please allow me', and he took the hatchet from her. She was too surprised to speak, and after that, Belcher would be at her heels, carrying a bucket, a basket or a load of turf. As Noble said, he got into looking before she leapt, and hot water, or any little thing she wanted, Belcher would have ready for her. For such a huge man (and though I am five foot ten myself I had to look up at him) he had an uncommon lack of speech. It took us a little while to get used to him, walking in and out like a ghost, without speaking. Especially because Hawkins talked enough for a platoon, it was strange to hear Belcher with his toes in the ashes come out with a solitary 'Excuse me, chum', or 'That's right, chum'. His one and only passion was cards, and he was a remarkably good card player. He could have skinned myself and Noble, but whatever we lost to him, Hawkins lost to us, and Hawkins only played with the money Belcher gave him.

Hawkins lost to us because he had too much old gab, and we probably lost to Belcher for the same reason. Hawkins and Noble argued about religion into the early hours of the morning, and Hawkins worried the life out of Noble, who had a brother a priest, with a string of questions that would puzzle a cardinal. Even in treating of holy subjects, Hawkins had a deplorable tongue. I never met a man who could mix such a variety of cursing and bad language into any argument. He was a terrible man, and a fright to argue. He never did a stroke of work, and when he had no one else to argue with, he got stuck in the old woman.

He met his match in her, for when he tried to get her to complain profanely of the drought she gave him a great come-down by blaming it entirely on Jupiter Pluvius (a deity neither Hawkins nor I had ever heard of, though Noble said that among the pagans it was believed that he had something to do with the rain). Another day he was swearing at the capitalists for starting the German war when the old lady laid down her iron, puckered up her little crab's mouth and said: 'Mr Hawkins, you can say what you like about the war, and think you'll deceive me because I'm only a simple poor countrywoman, but I know what started the war. It was the Italian count that stole the heathen divinity out of the temple of Japan. Believe me, Mr Hawkins, nothing but sorrow and want can follow people who disturb the hidden powers.'

A queer old girl, all right.

II

One evening we had our tea and Hawkins lit the lamp and we all sat into cards. Jeremiah Donovan came in too, and sat and watched us for a while, and it suddenly struck me that he had no great love for the two Englishmen. It came as a surprise to me because I had noticed nothing of it before.

Late in the evening a really terrible argument blew up between Hawkins and Noble about capitalists and priests and love of country.

'The capitalists pay the priests to tell you about the next world so that you won't notice what the bastards are up to in this,' said Hawkins.

'Nonsense, man!' said Noble, losing his temper. 'Before ever a capitalist was thought of people believed in the next world.'

Hawkins stood up as though he was preaching.

'Oh, they did, did they?' he said with a sneer. 'They believed all the things you believe – isn't that what you mean? And you believe God created Adam, and Adam created Shem, and Shem created Jehashophat. You believe all that silly old fairy tale about Eve and Eden and the apple. Well listen to me, chum! If you're entitled to a silly belief like that, I'm entitled to my own silly belief – which is that the first thing your God created was a bleeding capitalist, with morality and a Rolls-Royce complete. Am I right, chum?' he says to Belcher.

'You're right, chum,' says Belcher with a smile, and he got up from the table to stretch his long legs into the fire and stroke his moustache. So, seeing that Jeremiah Donovan was going, and that there was no knowing when the argument about religion would be over, I went out with him. We strolled down to the village together, and then he stopped, blushing and mumbling, and said I should be behind, keeping guard. I didn't like the tone he took with me, and anyway I was bored with life in the cottage, so I replied by asking what the hell we wanted to guard them for at all.

He looked at me in surprise and said: 'I thought you knew we were keeping them as hostages.'

'Hostages?' I said.

'The enemy have prisoners belonging to us, and now they're talking of shooting them,' he said. 'If they shoot our prisoners, we'll shoot theirs.'

'Shoot Belcher and Hawkins?' I said.

'What else did you think we were keeping them for?' he said.

'Wasn't it very unforeseen of you not to warn Noble and myself of that in the beginning?' I said.

'How was it?' he said. 'You might have known that much.'

'We could not know it, Jeremiah Donovan,' I said. 'How could we when they were on our hands so long?'

'The enemy have our prisoners as long and longer,' he said.

'That's not the same thing at all,' said I.

'What difference is there?' said he.

I couldn't tell him, because I knew he wouldn't understand. If it was only an old dog that you had to take to the vet's, you'd try and not get too fond of him, but Jeremiah Donovan was not a man who would ever be in danger of that.

'And when is this to be decided?' I said.

'We might hear tonight,' he said. 'Or tomorrow or the next day at latest. So if it's only hanging round that's a trouble to you, you'll be free soon enough.'

It was not the hanging round that was a trouble to me at all by this time. I had worse things to worry about. When I got back to the cottage the argument was still on. Hawkins was holding forth in his best style, maintaining that there was no next world, and Noble saying that there was; but I could see that Hawkins had had the best of it.

'Do you know what, chum?' he was saying with a saucy smile. 'I think you're just as big a bleeding unbeliever as I am. You say you believe in the next world, and you know just as much about the next world as I do, which is sweet damn all. What's heaven? You don't know. Where's heaven? You don't know. You know sweet damn all! I ask you again, do they wear wings?'

'Very well, then,' said Noble. 'They do. Is that enough for you? They do wear wings.'

'Where do they get them then? Who makes them? Have they a factory for wings? Have they a sort of store where you hand in your chit and take your bleeding wings?'

'You're an impossible man to argue with,' said Noble. 'Now, listen to me –' And they were off again.

It was long after midnight when we locked up and went to bed. As I blew out the candle I told Noble. He took it very quietly. When we'd been in bed about an hour he asked if I thought we should tell the Englishmen. I didn't, because I doubted if the English would shoot our men. Even if they did, the Brigade officers, who were always up and down to the Second Battalion and knew the Englishmen well, would hardly want to see them plugged. 'I think so too,' said Noble. 'It would be great cruelty to put the wind up them now.'

'It was very unforeseen of Jeremiah Donovan, anyhow,' said I.

It was next morning that we found it so hard to face Belcher and Hawkins. We went about the house all day, scarcely saying a word. Belcher didn't seem to notice; he was stretched into the ashes as usual, with his usual look of waiting in quietness for something unforeseen to happen, but Hawkins noticed it and put it down to Noble being beaten in the argument of the night before.

'Why can't you take the discussion in the proper spirit?' he said severely. 'You and your Adam and Eve! I'm a Communist, that's what I am. Communist or anarchist, it all comes to much the same thing.' And he went round the house, muttering when the fit took him: 'Adam and Eve! Adam and Eve! Nothing better to do with their time than pick bleeding apples!'

III

I don't know how we got through that day, but I was very glad when it was over, the tea things were cleared away, and Belcher said in his peaceable way: 'Well, chums, what about it?' We sat round the table and Hawkins took out the cards, and just then I heard Jeremiah Donovan's footsteps on the path and a dark presentiment crossed my mind. I rose from the table and caught him before he reached the door.

'What do you want?' I asked.

'I want those two soldier friends of yours,' he said, getting red.

'Is that the way, Jeremiah Donovan?' I asked.

'That's the way. There were four of our lads shot this morning, one of them a boy of sixteen.'

'That's bad,' I said.

At that moment Noble followed me out, and the three of us

walked down the path together, talking in whispers. Feeney, the local intelligence officer, was standing by the gate.

'What are you going to do about it?' I asked Jeremiah Donovan.

'I want you and Noble to get them out; tell them they're being shifted again; that'll be the quietest way.'

'Leave me out of that,' said Noble, under his breath.

Jeremiah Donovan looked at him hard.

'All right,' he says. 'You and Feeney get a few tools from the shed and dig a hole by the far end of the bog. Bonaparte and myself will be after you. Don't let anyone see you with the tools. I wouldn't like it to go beyond ourselves.'

We saw Feeney and Noble go round to the shed and went in ourselves. I left Jeremiah Donovan to do the explanations. He told them that he had orders to send them back to the Second Battalion. Hawkins let out a mouthful of curses, and you could see that though Belcher didn't say anything, he was a bit upset too. The old woman was for having them stay in spite of us, and she didn't stop advising them until Jeremiah Donovan lost his temper and turned on her. He had a nasty temper, I noticed. It was pitch dark in the cottage by this time, but no one thought of lighting the lamp, and in the darkness the two Englishmen fetched their topcoats and said goodbye to the old woman.

'Just as a man makes a home of a bleeding place, some bastard at headquarters thinks you're too cushy and shunts you off,' said Hawkins, shaking her hand.

'A thousand thanks, madam,' said Belcher. 'A thousand thanks for everything' – as though he'd made it up.

We went round to the back of the house and down towards the bog. It was only then that Jeremiah Donovan told them. He was shaking with excitement.

'There were four of our fellows shot in Cork this morning and now you are to be shot as a reprisal.'

'What are you talking about?' snaps Hawkins. 'It's bad enough being mucked about as we are without having to put up with your funny jokes.'

'It isn't a joke,' said Donovan. 'I'm sorry, Hawkins, but it's true', and begins on the usual rigmarole about duty and how unpleasant it is. I never noticed that people who talk a lot about duty find it much of a trouble to them.

'Oh, cut it out!' said Hawkins.

'Ask Bonaparte,' said Donovan, seeing that Hawkins wasn't taking him seriously. 'Isn't it true, Bonaparte?'

'It is,' I said, and Hawkins stopped.

'Ah, for Christ's sake, chum!'

'I mean it, chum,' I said.

'You don't sound as if you meant it.'

'If he doesn't mean it, I do,' said Donovan, working himself up.

'What have you against me, Jeremiah Donovan?'

'I never said I had anything against you. But why did your people take out four of your prisoners and shoot them in cold blood?'

He took Hawkins by the arm and dragged him on, but it was impossible to make him understand that we were in earnest. I had the Smith and Wesson in my pocket and I kept fingering it and wondering what I'd do if they put up a fight for it or ran, and wishing to God they'd do one or the other. I knew if they did run for it, that I'd never fire on them. Hawkins wanted to know was Noble in it, and when we said yes, he asked us why Noble wanted to plug him. Why did any of us want to plug him? What had he done to us? Weren't we all chums? Didn't we understand him and didn't he understand us? Did we imagine for an instant that he'd shoot us for all the so-and-so officers in the so-and-so British Army?

By this time we'd reached the bog, and I was so sick I

couldn't even answer him. We walked along the edge of it in the darkness, and every now and then Hawkins would call a halt and begin all over again, as if he was wound up, about our being chums, and I knew that nothing but the sight of the grave would convince him that we had to do it. And all the time I was hoping that something would happen; that they'd run for it or that Noble would take over the responsibility from me. I had the feeling that it was worse on Noble than on me.

IV

At last we saw the lantern in the distance and made towards it. Noble was carrying it, and Feeney was standing somewhere in the darkness behind him, and the picture of them so still and silent in the bogland brought it home to me that we were in earnest, and banished the last bit of hope I had.

Belcher, on recognising Noble, said: 'Hallo, chum', in his quiet way, but Hawkins flew at him at once, and the argument began all over again, only this time Noble had nothing to say for himself and stood with his head down, holding the lantern between his legs.

It was Jeremiah Donovan who did the answering. For the twentieth time, as though it was haunting his mind, Hawkins asked if anybody thought he'd shoot Noble.

'Yes, you would,' said Jeremiah Donovan.

'No, I wouldn't, damn you!'

'You would, because you'd know you'd be shot for not doing it.'

'I wouldn't, not if I was to be shot twenty times over. I wouldn't shoot a pal. And Belcher wouldn't – isn't that right, Belcher?'

'That's right, chum,' Belcher said, but more by way of answering the question than of joining in the argument. Belcher sounded as though whatever unforeseen thing he'd always been waiting for had come at last.

'Anyway, who says Noble would be shot if I wasn't? What do you think I'd do if I was in his place, out in the middle of a blasted bog?'

'What would you do?' asked Donovan.

'I'd go with him wherever he was going, of course. Share my last bob with him and stick by him through thick and thin. No one can ever say of me that I let down a pal.'

'We've had enough of this,' said Jeremiah Donovan, cocking his revolver. 'Is there any message you want to send?'

'No, there isn't.'

'Do you want to say your prayers?'

Hawkins came out with a cold-blooded remark that even shocked me and turned on Noble again.

'Listen to me, Noble,' he said. 'You and me are chums. You can't come over to my side, so I'll come over to your side. That show you I mean what I say? Give me a rifle and I'll go along with you and the other lads.'

Noble answered him. We knew that was no way out.

'Hear what I'm saying?' he said. 'I'm through with it. I'm a deserter or anything else you like. I don't believe in your stuff, but it's no worse than mine. That satisfy you?'

Noble raised his head, but Donovan began to speak and he lowered it again without replying.

'For the last time, have you any messages to send?' said Donovan in a cold, excited sort of voice.

'Shut up, Donovan! You don't understand me, but these lads do. They're not the sort to make a pal and kill a pal. They're not the tools of any capitalist.'

I alone of the crowd saw Donovan raise his Webley to the back of Hawkins's neck, and as he did so I shut my eyes and tried to pray. Hawkins had begun to say something else when

Donovan fired, and as I opened my eyes at the bang, I saw Hawkins stagger at the knees and lie out flat at Noble's feet, slowly and as quiet as a kid falling asleep, with the lantern-light on his lean legs and bright farmer's boots. We all stood very still, watching him settle out in the last agony.

Then Belcher took out a handkerchief and began to tie it about his own eyes (in our excitement we'd forgotten to do the same for Hawkins), and, seeing it wasn't big enough, turned and asked for the loan of mine. I gave it to him, and he knotted the two together and pointed with his foot at Hawkins.

'He's not quite dead,' he said. 'Better give him another.'

Sure enough, Hawkins's left knee was beginning to rise. I bent down and put my gun to his head; then recollecting myself, I got up again. Belcher understood what was in my mind.

'Give him his first,' he said. 'I don't mind. Poor bastard, we don't know what's happening to him now.'

I knelt and fired. By this time I didn't seem to know what I was doing. Belcher, who was fumbling a bit awkwardly with the handkerchiefs, came out with a laugh as he heard the shot. It was the first time I had heard him laugh and it sent a shudder down my back; it sounded so unnatural.

'Poor bugger!' he said quietly. 'And last night he was so curious about it all. It's very queer, chums, I always think. Now he knows as much about it as they'll ever let him know, and last night he was all in the dark.'

Donovan helped him to tie the handkerchiefs about his eyes. 'Thanks, chum,' he said. Donovan asked if there were any messages he wanted sent.

'No, chum,' he said. 'Not for me. If any of you would like to write to Hawkins's mother, you'll find a letter from her in his pocket. He and his mother were great chums. But my missus left me eight years ago. Went away with another fellow and took the kid with her. I like the feeling of a home, as you may have noticed, but I couldn't start another again after that.'

It was an extraordinary thing, but in those few minutes Belcher said more than in all the weeks before. It was just as if the sound of the shot had started a flood of talk in him and he could go on the whole night like that, quite happily, talking about himself. We stood around like fools now that he couldn't see us any longer. Donovan looked at Noble, and Noble shook his head. Then Donovan raised his Webley, and at that moment Belcher gave his queer laugh again. He may have thought we were talking about him, or perhaps he noticed the same thing I'd noticed and couldn't understand it.

'Excuse me, chums,' he said. 'I feel I'm talking the hell of a lot, and so silly, about my being so handy about a house and things like that. But this thing came on me suddenly. You'll forgive me, I'm sure.'

'You don't want to say a prayer?' asked Donovan.

'No, chum,' he said. 'I don't think it would help. I'm ready, and you boys want to get it over.'

'You understand that we're only doing our duty?' said Donovan.

Belcher's head was raised like a blind man's, so that you could only see his chin and the top of his nose in the lantern-light.

'I never could make out what duty was myself,' he said. 'I think you're all good lads, if that's what you mean. I'm not complaining.'

Noble, just as if he couldn't bear any more of it, raised his fist at Donovan, and in a flash Donovan raised his gun and fired. The big man went over like a sack of meal, and this time there was no need for a second shot.

I don't remember much about the burying, but that it was worse than all the rest because we had to carry them to the grave. It was all mad lonely with nothing but a patch of lantern-light between ourselves and the dark, and birds hooting and screeching all round, disturbed by the guns. Noble went through Hawkins's belongings to find the letter from his mother, and then joined his hands together. He did the same with Belcher. Then, when we'd filled in the grave, we separated from Jeremiah Donovan and Feeney and took our tools back to the shed. All the way we didn't speak a word. The kitchen was dark and cold as we'd left it, and the old woman was sitting over the hearth, saying her beads. We walked past her into the room, and Noble struck a match to light the lamp. She rose quietly and came to the doorway with all her cantankerousness gone.

'What did ye do with them?' she asked in a whisper, and Noble started so that the match went out in his hand.

'What's that?' he asked without turning round.

'I heard ye,' she said.

'What did you hear?' asked Noble.

'I heard ye. Do you think I didn't hear ye, putting the spade back in the houseen?'

Noble struck another match and this time the lamp lit for him.

'Was that what ye did to them?' she asked.

Then, by God, in the very doorway, she fell on her knees and began praying, and after looking at her for a minute or two Noble did the same by the fireplace. I pushed my way out past her and left them at it. I stood at the door, watching the stars and listening to the shrieking of the birds dying out over the bogs. It is so strange what you feel at times like that that you can't describe it. Noble says he saw everything ten times the size, as though there were nothing in the whole world but that little patch of bog with the two Englishmen stiffening into it, but with me it was as if the patch of bog where the Englishmen were was a million miles away, and even Noble and the old woman, mumbling behind me, and the birds and the bloody stars were all far away, and I was somehow very small and very lost and lonely like a child astray in the snow. And anything that happened to me afterwards, I never felt the same about again.

LONELY HEART

JOHN MORROW

One blacked-out evening in January 1944 a jeep-load of drunk Yanks mounted the pavement alongside the one-and-ninepenny queue at the Ritz cinema and squashed him dead against a blind lamppost. At the moment it happened the one-and-ninepennies began to move in, so when a joint patrol of Yank MPs and British red-caps came on the scene minutes later there were no witnesses bar the jeep's cargo, and they were paralytic. When the British red-caps saw, by flashlight, that the broken heap lying at the base of the bent lamp wore a khaki greatcoat with a British lancejack's stripe on the sleeve, they wanted to kill the cargo, or at least the driver, there and then. The Yank MPs, naturally, wouldn't hear tell of it. Angry words were exchanged, lead-loaded flashlights brandished, gun butts fondled in dark confusion. Only the arrival of a civilian policeman saved the incident from developing into something really nasty. Turning the heap over with his toe, he said: 'Och sure, it's only oul Lonely Heart. He's a busker, a shell-shock case.' And they saw then that the greatcoat was faded and threadbare, and that the right hand still clutched a battered mouth organ. One of the red-caps, a long service man, noted that the few remaining buttons on the greatcoat bore the insignia of the Horse Artillery and remarked to himself the incongruity between this and the crossed rifles of a marksman on one sleeve: damn few of those in the Horse Guns.

The legally necessary postmortem on the remains of Thomas Woods, known as Lonely Heart to generations of cinemagoers, was held the next day. One thing brought to light was a fragment of a German dumdum bullet which had been wandering around in his puddings for twenty-eight years. Giving evidence at the coroner's inquest, the city pathologist said that the deceased must have lived in almost continual torment. The coroner declared that it showed again just how beastly the Boche were, recorded a verdict of accidental death, and the one hungover newsman present came away with the impression that Lonely Heart, writhing in agony, had fallen in front of the jeep. Those responsible for inter-allied harmony in the city heaved a sigh of relief.

People read about his death, and about the dumdum nagging away all those years, like a grain of sand in a barren oyster, and their sadness was tinged with remorse. Lonely Heart had been a case, a character on a par with 'Andy Gump', 'Oily Boke', 'Skin-the-goat'; all tattered derelicts who prowled the city, minds turned by war, drink, love or, in the case of one who lectured pigeons on the Custom House steps, 'The Books'. They'd called him Lonely Heart because he had never been known to play anything other than the mournful dirge 'I wandered today to the hills, Maggie', his appearance at the head of a cinema queue the signal for a chorus of cheerful abuse and a barrage of small missiles. And through it all he had played his dirge, the mouth organ in one hand and his extended cap, clinking, in the other.

His funeral column was the longest in living memory in his home district. At the cemetery the laid-out wreaths covered a dozen graves on either side of the waiting pit, most of them from people who had never known his proper name... 'For Lonely Heart – from the girls in Murray's snuff room'.

But there was one other, a small spray placed far back and

almost hidden behind a neighbouring headstone, which puzzled those few of the mourners who noticed it when, after the service, they made the traditional tour of the tributes to make sure their florist hadn't welshed.

'For Shooter,' the card on the spray said. '*Quis Separabit.*'

Tommy Woods had been a gunner in the Horse Artillery. Unlike most of his Belfast contemporaries in the Ulster Volunteers (Carson's Army) – Hostilities Only men – he was a regular and had been one of the first on French soil in 1914, retreating from Mons almost as fast as the contemptible Field Marshal French himself. When the armies were bogged down in trench warfare in 1915 Tommy was unhorsed and given a rifle, and it was as an infantryman near Ypres in early 1916 that he stopped the German dumdum with his guts. They managed to extract most of the fragments in the field hospital, after which Tommy was sent to a rest camp near Abbeville to convalesce.

He had been courting a girl called Aggie Gamble on and off since they had been half-timers at the mill school together, and they had corresponded regularly since his enlistment. They had talked of marriage, but always as a postwar happening – until the wound. Aggie's letters suddenly became very torrid and peremptory: all her friends were getting married; she was nearly twenty – she'd be left on the shelf; she'd heard of 'Blighty wounds' – surely Tommy's was one; an Easter wedding would be nice . . . Tommy applied for leave in February, it was granted on the first week in March and Aggie set in train arrangements for them to be married on the Thursday of Easter Week.

And so, in the early morning of Tuesday the twenty-fifth of April, 1916, Tommy Woods stood in a crowd of other happy 'Blighty Ones' at the rail of the Holyhead–Kingstown ferry as the gangplank thumped onto Irish cobbles. He could see the Belfast train lying just up the wharf, steaming on the leash, welcoming doors gaping. He also noticed a hobnailed scurry of military activity on and around the wharf – but being wartime, that was only to be expected. One of the returning warriors made a joke about 'Fireside Fusiliers' and Tommy, full of beery euphoria, was still laughing as he clattered down the gangplank... his last laugh ever. He had one foot on the cobbles when a hand fell on his shoulder. Its owner was a middle-aged sergeant of the Dublin Fusiliers, very white-faced and nervous. 'Thanks be to Christ, an artilleryman!' he cried, thumping Tommy's shoulder. 'Tell us, do you know anything about eighteen-pounders?'

'Aye, but what...' Tommy stuttered.

'Never mind,' said the sergeant. 'Come with me.'

He started to drag Tommy by the arm across the wharf in the direction of some army lorries. The Belfast train made shunting noises, its doors banging impatiently. Tommy found his tongue. 'Here... hi... that's my train,' he fairly yelled, wrenching free from the sergeant and hoking in his tunic pocket for pay book and leave pass. 'I'm getting married the day after –'

The sergeant took hold of Tommy by the webbing with one hand and half-drew a revolver from its holster on his belt with the other. 'She'll have to wait,' he said through his teeth, close to Tommy's face. 'Everything'll have to wait. If Christ himself walked up that harbour this minute and knew one end of an eighteen-pounder from the other he'd be up on that wagon double quick or I'd blow his fuckin' head off. Jump!'

Tommy jumped. He had seen men like the sergeant at that stage of hysteria before and he knew it was either jump or be crippled. The authority of such men rested on sincere presentation of stark choices.

For part of the way along the Dublin road the lorry ran abreast of the Belfast train. Then road and line parted company and Tommy felt as though his stomach was about to fall out.

'Cheer up,' said the sergeant, shoving a lit Woodbine between Tommy's lips. 'The day after tomorrow, is it? Sure you could be on the evening train. They brought up four eighteen-pounders from Athlone this morning. They'll soon winkle the bastards out.'

He took it for granted that Tommy had heard of the Sinn Féin rising, which he hadn't. It wasn't until long after the event that its true nature dawned on him, and then only as part of the long dream sequence his past life had become, a brief illumination in the fog behind him, quickly snuffed.

As the lorry clattered through deserted suburban streets and the familiar boom of eighteen-pounders and the fitful sparkle of small arms grew louder, Tommy barely noticed. He was thinking of Aggie. She'd be leaving work today. The girls in the mill would truss her up with hanks of flax, daub her face with loom grease and wheel her around the streets in a trolley, chanting:

> Here comes the bride,
> Forty inches wide.
> See how she wobbles
> Her big backside . . .

The lorry stopped close to the roar of guns. The sergeant screamed: 'Out!' and they dropped off the tailboard and ran crouching behind a wall beside a river. Two eighteen-pounders at either flank of a wide bridge . . . black-faced gunners training and laying. As Tommy and the sergeant reached the nearest gun it fired. Tommy swivelled to look and saw a wide street of tall buildings with, in the centre, tallest of all, a thin pillar, masonry crumbling. 'Close, fuck yis,' howled a bombardier. 'Mind what the general said, knock the one-eyed matelot down an' yis are all on a fizzer!'

The sergeant thrust Tommy forward and shouted into the bombardier's ear. The bombardier glared at Tommy's cap badge and growled: 'Christ! The galloping peashooters, that's all I needed. Come on, King Billy – at least you'll be no worse than that huer on the breech. I've been waitin' for his sporran an' bollocks to go scatterin' up Sackville Street.' A private of the Black Watch staggered to the rear and Tommy took his place. 'Prime . . . load . . . brush . . . fire!' And so began the waking nightmare of Tommy's life.

For two days he stoked the gun, with brief respites for bully and char and, once, champagne and cold chicken from the kitchen of a wrecked hotel. The air was still and the smoke and fumes hung around them, growing thicker by the hour, turning day into night and night into a small room containing the gun and themselves, lit spasmodically by muzzle flame.

Once, during a lull whilst ammunition was brought up, Tommy wandered out of the stour and over to the parapet of the river bank. It was night-time. Across the stretch of flame-tinted water the big street burnt. A four-storeyed shell glowed like a Hallowe'en turnip and then, as he watched, collapsed like an old gas mantle. But the one-eyed matelot still posed on his pillar, and that was all the bombardier cared about. 'Come away ar' that, King Billy, and lave that river alone.'

The rest spells became more frequent throughout Wednesday, and at dusk the word came to stand down – they'd run out of ammo. Most of the crews dropped where they stood, asleep before they hit the ground. The bombardier came across Tommy sitting on a shell box, curled up in a knot, heaving silently, holding what had been a khaki handkerchief over his mouth; it was now sopping red. 'Jasus! Is it the lung rot ye have?' asked the bombardier, slapping his back. 'You should have spoke up. That cordite's a bastard.'

Tommy managed to explain that the blood was from his stomach, not his lungs; they'd told him this might happen, and not to worry. The bombardier went away and came back with two thick horse blankets. He wrapped Tommy from head to toe like a cigar and, lifting him bodily, carried him to one of the waiting lorries. Stretched in the back, blanket-cowled head on his pack, Tommy didn't hear the engine start up or feel one jolt of the cobbled journey.

He awoke in familiar surroundings. He lay on a low camp-cot between two high hospital beds, all around him the muted hubbub of an early morning ward: a steady base of groaning and coughing overlaid by the clanking of utensils, the scurry and squeak of orderlies' feet, the raised voices of nurses. An RAMC stretcher party picked its way through rows of cots down the centre of the ward. For a dazed moment Tommy thought he was back in Abbeville; then everything came back to him . . . Aggie.

'How are ye now, Rip Van Winkle?'

A Belfast voice, issuing from a hairy face with Woodbine attached, framed in bandages, glaring over the edge of the bed to his right.

'What time is it?' asked Tommy.

'Eight o'clock or thereabouts. The way you've been snorin' you should be askin' the day, not the time.'

Tommy thought back frantically, heart in mouth. 'It's Thursday,' he said.

The man wheezed joyfully. 'There y'are! . . . Rip Van Winkle. They gave you a quare doze of somethin' when they carted you in. You've slep the clock roun' an' then some. It's bloody Friday mornin', an' if you don't believe me, just take a whiff . . . bloody fish! They start boilin' it at the scrake of dawn so's all the good'll be out of it by dinner hour. Fenian bastards! Here, where are you off to?'

Tommy was pulling on his trousers. Luckily they had piled his clothes and pack, army fashion, beside the cot. 'Home,' he replied, 'as soon as I can get a train.'

'They'll niver let ye.'

'They'll never notice, if I know anything about these places.'

Neither they did, all their attention being taken up at that moment with an intake of wounded from the field stations. Tommy pushed his way through a jam of bearers and stretchers and cadged a lift in an ambulance that left him off not far from Amiens Street station.

The city lay under a haze of smoke from the fires of Sackville Street. From there still arose an incessant rattle of machine-gun and rifle fire. But the vicinity of Amiens Street was quiet enough as Tommy hurried towards the station. In the almost deserted entrance hall he asked a railwayman about trains for Belfast. 'No civvies or leave men,' was the reply, 'only goods and troops-in-transit.'

Nevertheless, Tommy ran towards the platforms – and into the Dubliner sergeant, who now wore the red armband of an RTO . . . 'King Billy! I heard you were in hospital. When's that weddin' of yours?'

'Yesterday,' said Tommy. 'And I want home as soon as I can get. They say it's all troops-in-transit.'

The sergeant, suddenly grim-faced, again laid hold of Tommy by the webbing and started running him towards a train that was making its first jerky shunts out of platform one. He shouted in Tommy's ear: 'Say you're attached to the Sherwoods. Give my name . . . McKenna.'

Sergeant McKenna wrenched open the door of the last carriage and heaved Tommy in and across the legs of twelve tired Sherwood Foresters. They cursed, but none queried him and he settled on the floor for the long journey home. He tried to think. Aggie, the whole thing a bloody shambles. What'll her people say? But no matter how hard he tried he couldn't grasp the fragments, and the harder he tried the worse his guts ached;

like ducking for apples in a bucket; wits gun-scrambled. He'd seen it too often in others.

It was late afternoon when Tommy marched up Railway Street to his own house. The train had crawled all the way because of the danger of derailment by the rebels. In the hallway of the house he met two of Aggie's six brothers coming out, one a sailor on leave, the other a shipyardman. Without speaking they launched themselves at Tommy, knocking him back through the front door. The neighbours, who had been watching from behind curtains, swarmed into the street and managed to drag the berserk brothers off him, but not before the sailor had cracked the toe of his boot on Tommy's ear and the shipyardman had planted his clog, several times, in his gut.

His father and brother carried Tommy into the house while the neighbours saw off the still belligerent Gambles. Tommy's guts were on fire and the blood started coming again. The doctor was sent for, and being ex-army himself and knowing something of the ways of wandering foreign bodies, he prescribed coagulant and a sleeping draught. In the meantime Tommy had been told that Aggie, ashamed to face her mates at the mill, had left on the Liverpool boat the previous night. Mercifully, the draught combined with the residue of that given to him in Dublin knocked him out almost immediately.

On Saturday Tommy awoke as the person he was to be for the rest of his days. The family were puzzled. He talked to them quite cogently, about France, about his wound – but never a mention of Aggie, or of the happenings in Dublin. Still, he seemed to be well enough physically considering, and very placid in himself, so they thought it a 'wee kink' that would pass.

Tommy stayed in bed, sleeping most of the time, until Tuesday morning. Then he got up, washed, shaved and polished his boots. His ten-day pass included travelling time, so his return

warrant was made out for the five-thirty train to Dublin that day
(though there would be no connecting boat from Kingstown
until Wednesday morning). At two o'clock his father and
brother accompanied him to the Crown Bar opposite the
station, and between then and train time all three made fair
inroads on Tommy's wedding money – so much so that when
train time came the da, footless and maudlin, was unable to cross
the road to see Tommy off, and the brother wasn't far behind
him. Tommy had matched them drink for drink, but he
marched to the train stone sober. Throughout the drunken gar-
rulity of the afternoon no mention had been made of Aggie or
the wedding. Afterwards, the brother said that Tommy had
been so strangely calm he had been afraid to say or do anything
that might draw blood.

Before the train drew to a halt in Amiens Street Tommy saw
Sergeant McKenna on the platform. He appeared to be on the
lookout for someone, scanning faces at the window of each
carriage as it passed. He spotted Tommy. 'How's me oul son?
Come on down an' have a cuppa char. You've plenty of time,
there's no boat the night.'

Tommy followed the sergeant to an RTO hut at the end of
the platform. They had the place to themselves. The sergeant
put a kettle on a coke stove and said: 'I've been wondering how
you got on. What about the weddin'?'

At this point he had his back to Tommy, poking the stove
to get a flame. When no reply came he turned and faced him.
At first Tommy looked puzzled, then his eyes closed tightly and
he moved his head slowly from side to side. He held his big
square hands clasped to front, the thumbs circling one another
frantically, clockwise then counter clockwise. They reminded
the sergeant of mice on a treadmill.

The tea when it came was twenty-five per cent Power's
whiskey, causing Tommy's guts to burn pleasurably. 'Rest

easy, lad,' said the sergeant. 'I've a billet for you the night and we'll get you down to Kingstown in good time for the morning boat.'

After the tea they went to a nearby pub and the sergeant ordered hot whiskeys. The place was packed with troops, a ragtag and bobtail of all the units in Ireland plus a few press-gang jobs like Tommy. Tommy sat at the bar while the sergeant circulated, quartering the company with an appraising eye. When he rejoined Tommy there were two men with him, one an elderly corporal of the South Staffords and the other a youthful private in the Irish Rifles who hailed from Cullybackey, a raw-looking ganch.

More hot whiskeys, which the Cullybackey man threw into the flat remains of his pint. The sergeant went off on another tour, and after they'd been talking for a while Tommy noticed that both men wore crossed rifles on the sleeves of their tunics, the insignia of a marksman. When he commented on this, the Stafford corporal said: 'That's why we're drinking whiskey instead of beer, mate.'

'Aye mon, we're the boys for the job!' cried the ganch, spitting on his hands and slapping them together.

'What's the job?' asked Tommy.

The ganch started to reply, but the corporal caught him by the arm and said authoritatively: 'If the sergeant wants him to know he'll tell him soon enough.' The ganch winked conspiratorially.

When the sergeant returned again he had another man in tow, a Cameronian. Tommy looked at his sleeve ... crossed rifles. He waited until the three marksmen were engaged in a separate conversation and then broached the subject.

'What's the job?'

McKenna hesitated for a moment, pondering. Then he said:

'I was going to tell you. That's why I kept a lookout at the train. But then...'

Tommy sensed what he meant, though even now Amiens Street and the RTO hut seemed years behind him. Now was a clear circle in the fog that closed rapidly at his back and swirled impenetrably a yard in front of his face.

'I'm all right now,' he said.

'You're not, not near it,' growled the sergeant. 'But then who in the name of Christ is. I'll tell you, but under your hat, mind.'

He told Tommy, briefly, the nature of the job.

'How many?' asked Tommy.

'Thirty... three tens... one apiece,' sighed McKenna. 'And hard enough to scrape up when the huer-in-charge wants them all crossed rifle wallahs.'

'How many do you need still?'

'Three.'

'What about me? I'll do it for you.'

The sergeant doffed his cap and took something from the inside band. He laid it on the bar between them, a khaki patch embroidered with crossed rifles. 'There's not many of them in the Horse Guns, but the bastard'll never notice. Are you sure now?'

'I'm your man,' said Tommy, and pocketed the patch.

They visited two other pubs that night and Sergeant McKenna got rid of the last two patches from his cap band. He also had a needle and thread in the cap band, and in the packed lorry on the way to the billet he affixed the patches to the appropriate sleeves by the light of a carbide lamp. Tommy stood and looked out over the cab of the lorry as they ran in under a lighted archway to the billet. He saw a name carved in the stone above the archway but couldn't make it out in the dark.

Almost the next thing he remembered was a hand on his

shoulder and McKenna's voice saying: 'Stand to. Up you get, oul son.'

It was still dark. In the dim gaslight, only two small mantles at either end of the long barrack hut, hungover men struggled into cold-stiff uniforms. On the bed next to Tommy's the Cullybackey ganch spewed noisily into an enamel bucket. Sergeant McKenna and two corporals roved around like sheep-dogs, snapping at the heels of each man until he was ready and on his way to the square outside. At the door each was handed a rifle from a rack of thirty.

In the square they formed up and dressed off in a single line. After being inspected by the 'huer-in-charge', a young captain, they formed twos and then wheeled into six lines of fives. The paired lines were designated squads one, two and three; Tommy was in number two, rear rank. By this time one side of the sky was beginning to lighten.

'Number one squad, stand fast! Number two and three squads, dismiss!'

The corporals shepherded the dismissed men to a hut in the corner of the square in which there was a tea urn and a tray of wads. Tommy drew himself a mug of tea, but didn't feel hungry. He noticed that very few touched the wads. From the hut window he watched number one squad being inspected again by the captain; a rifle was found wanting and another fetched; the bamboo cane flicked a piece of maladjusted web-bing and Sergeant McKenna adjusted it; the encroaching light erased the last weak stars from the patch of sky bounded by the high roofs of the prison blocks. The sergeant's commands to move out were subdued. The squad marched off and disap-peared around the corner of the main block.

'Any minute now. They don't keep you waiting,' whispered a man beside Tommy. It was so quiet inside and out that Tommy could hear the first chirruping of sparrows. The two corporals stood on either side of the hut door, facing inwards, scanning the company and drawing nervously on cupped fags. It was full daylight now.

The crash of the volley cannoned wildly in the square, sending hordes of sparrows hurling skywards from the high eaves. Tommy saw the fag drop from a corporal's hand as he crossed himself. From down the hut came the thud and rattle of a body, rifle and tea mug hitting the earthen floor: the ganch had fainted.

There was a lot of noise after that. The corporals pounced on the prostrate ganch and hauled him onto a bench. Everyone crowded around and everyone seemed to be shouting. The Catholic corporal kept slapping the ganch's face and screaming, 'Wake up, you thick bastard!' Then Sergeant McKenna was amongst them, pushing, using his fists, bellowing. The men fell back and shut up – all except the corporal, who still screeched and lashed at the horizontal ganch. McKenna signalled to the other corporal and they took an arm apiece and ran him out of the hut. Some of the men managed to get the ganch sitting upright and poured tea down his throat. He awoke choking and immediately went into a bout of violent sobbing. When McKenna and the corporal returned, McKenna lifted the ganch's rifle off the floor, handed it to the corporal and shouted: 'Number two squad – fall in.'

'Just my bloody luck,' growled the corporal, opening the breech to check the barrel for dust.

The sergeant stood at the door of the hut and patted each man on the shoulder as he passed. Tommy looked at him as the hand fell, but it was as if the sergeant didn't see him, his lips forming the word 'seven'.

The captain was tall, thin and droop-moustached; a young Kitchener. He was the first officer Tommy had seen wearing a sword. Everything was to his liking until he came to the corporal, who had taken the ganch's place beside Tommy in the rear rank. He tapped the corporal's right sleeve with his cane and said: 'This man is not a marksman, sergeant.'

'Sah. We had a bit –'

'Report to me at stand down, sergeant. Carry on.'

'Squad . . . left turn. By the left, quick march.'

They rounded the corner of the main block and entered a narrow tunnel, the crash of hobnails deafening. Emerging into daylight, they were halted almost at once, the front two men close to a high wall.

'Left turn. Order arms.'

Tommy could see that they were drawn up at one end of a narrow yard, cramped between high walls, but not much else because of the tall fellow in front.

'Front rank – one pace forward. Front rank – kneel.'

He saw, at twenty paces, a sandbagged wall and a black-painted post. Just then the captain emerged from a door on the left of the yard, followed by two sergeant majors with silver-knobbed canes clamped under their oxters, marching on either side of a small man in dark trousers and a white shirt.

'Rear rank – port arms.'

When the little procession reached the black post, one of the SMs pulled the man's arms around the back of it and the other knelt in front. Tommy saw that there were straps on the post, one to circle his body, the other his legs. As they were doing this the captain stood facing the man and appeared to be reading something to him from a piece of paper. Their job done, the SMs marched back through the door. The captain finished his reading and fell back to take up position beside the squad.

Tommy could see the man clearly now. He had long grey hair that fell down over his ears. His eyes were closed and his lips were moving. Tommy could hear the drone of his voice in the drum of the killing alley, but indistinctly, as though very far away...

The captain's sword slid from its scabbard. He gave the orders now.

'Squad – load.'

Working the rifle bolt, Tommy kept his eyes on the man. His lips were still moving and his eyes were open now.

'Squad – present.'

It was the heaviest weapon he had ever hefted. His left arm started to tremble and he had difficulty centring on the white shirt...steady the Buffs...what the hell was keeping him? Tommy raised his eye from the sighting line to the man's face. He was still talking.

'Fire!'

Most of the white shirt vanished; the head slumped, grey hair spilling forward. The corporal beside Tommy dropped his rifle and clasped his ears, face twisted in agony. Tommy didn't hear it fall because he was stone deaf: the noise in the enclosed space had been shattering. McKenna moved to the front of the squad and made gestures as he shouted the commands to retire. The return march through the tunnel was a shambles. As he left the yard, out of the corner of his eye Tommy saw the captain remove plugs from his ears before moving towards the post, unholstering his pistol as he went. And he wondered if the talking man had known that the captain's ears were plugged.

For the twenty minutes or so it took number three squad to do its work, Tommy sat in the back of a lorry with the nine members of number two squad. Number one squad was sealed in a lorry alongside, another awaited number three. Their kits had already been loaded; all were for the boat, whether they wanted to or not. Curiously, no one talked or even smoked until the muffled crash of the third volley; then matches flared and voices were raised in obscene complaint about being shipped out without as much as a by-your-leave, and without as much as a decent breakfast. Presently number three squad marched out and the convoy set off for Kingstown, Sergeant McKenna riding with number two squad.

At Kingstown the sergeant stood at the bottom of the gangplank and counted off the men as they embarked. When his hand fell on Tommy's shoulder, Tommy paused and turned to face him.

'What was that fella talking about, sergeant?' he asked.

'Damn all of interest to the likes of you or me,' McKenna replied testily. 'An' for Christ's sake remember to take that patch off your sleeve before you report to depot. Damn few of them in the Horse Guns.'

But Tommy never did remember; and nobody noticed until one blacked-out evening twenty-eight years later, when a jeep-load of drunk Yanks mounted the pavement alongside the one-and-ninepennies at the Ritz.

BEATRICE

SHANE CONNAUGHTON

The demesne wall, crumbling under an age of ivy, snaked for miles round a vast estate of land, orchards, trees and lakes.

The wall was a green snake with an endless belly. Where the stonework bulged to bursting that was the serpent's undigested food.

In the heart of the demesne lived Lady Sarah Butler-Coote, an octogenarian spinster and the last of her line.

They were on the way to see her.

His father had shaved before coming out and stood in front of the mirror brushing the grey out of his hair with boot polish.

'Darling I am growing old, silver threads amongst the gold...' sang his mother, and his father flashed her a sharp look from the corner of the glass. He smiled.

'I'll knock on your door tonight, hah?' On the hill behind the barracks a dog barked.

'Not till that animal shites leather.'

'In that case,' replied his father, 'I'll leave out an old boot for its supper.' His mother laughed.

Preening and whistling, his father admired himself then, bunching his uniform buttons in a brass button-stick, began shining them with a Brasso-stained rag.

'What are you looking at? Go and get the bikes ready.'

Outside he heard the struggling and his mother protesting
– 'Later, later.'

As they rode through the main gates to the demesne he
wondered what it was his father wanted from her. Why was
there always such stern mystery in his face?

The massive gates were hung on stone pillars, each with a
sculpted acorn on top.

From the gatehouse a man waved to them. He stood in the
open door, a birdcage hanging above his head. He had a few
days' growth of beard, his belly bulged from his dirty shirt and
his simpleton grin as he waved frightened the boy.

'Poor Mickey. Less brains than a bucket. And isn't he the
happy man?'

'How, Daddy, if he's no brains?'

'Watch where you're steering or you'll wreck that bike
entirely!'

They were on the way to ask Lady Sarah for some firewood.
Trees tossed by the wind or trees in danger of falling were sold
off to the people. Bits of wood no bigger than a man's arm were
given free. His father called this ancient right estovers. His
father knew the law inside out and backwards. He sometimes
practised on him.

'What's pannage?'

'The right to let your pigs root in the forest for nuts, yes?'

'Good boy.'

'But we haven't got pigs, Daddy.'

'What's that got to do with the price of onions?'

He liked the woods with its deep pools of damp light lying
beneath the trees but he didn't like riding his bicycle along
the drive leading to Coote House. Certain stretches, in an attempt to render the endless potholes harmless, were strewn with
rough gravel inches thick so that riding over it was as great a
struggle as trying to run through deep water.

Mudguards rattling the bike juddered and jarred him from the saddle. For relief he steered onto the grassy verge but, the soft ground giving way, he skidded down into a clump of rhododendrons. Tangled in a sea of greenery, a bloom and blush of flowers danced wildly above his head. Spiders ran pell-mell along his legs. A frog peeped at him from a bed of wet leaves.

'I won't touch you if you don't touch me.'

The frog leapt towards him, its slimy body landing on his ankle. With a startled shriek he struggled from the bushes and hauled his bike back onto the drive.

The seat of his pants was damp from the wet earth. Clammy on his skin it reminded him of the frog.

His father, ploughing on ahead, had reached the smooth part of the drive round by the lake. He was looking back, waiting.

He grabbed the handlebars and instead of mounting ran alongside his bike until he too reached the smooth.

His father's eyes could bend bottles.

'What the hell are you playing at?'

'This is my horse and I'm a Red Indian.'

He felt foolish always having to follow his father every-where. Like a foal after a stallion.

His father sat on his motionless bicycle, one foot on a pedal, the other on the ground. He searched the boy's pale face as if looking for a clue. His eyes made you feel like a criminal. They were gripping bright like the silver sugar tongs his mother kept in the parlour.

Then he noticed his father wasn't looking at him at all. His eyes had glazed over, like the sugar tongs when you breathed on them.

A silence could last an hour. Sometimes when his mother was involved it could last all day. And the next day as well.

In a silence his father's face was a pile of stones.

'You're some Cherokee all right,' he muttered at last and they rode onwards.

The drive was lined with ancient trees. Great oaks, massive chestnut, raggedy elm and magnificent copper beeches.

Out on the lake the silver evening lay still as a stopped clock.

His father shouted back to him. 'You're a good boy.'

'And you're a good daddy, Daddy.'

His father's shoulders still shook with laughter as they turned into the straight leading up to Coote House.

Through a dim perspective of trees they could glimpse it half a mile away.

Crumbling Georgian. Twisted chimneys. Sagging lintels. Weeds and clods in the guttering like the edge of a turf bank.

'And she's got twenty-two cats!'

Though it was muttered to the world the boy knew he had to supply particular comment. Words were like pennies – they had to be picked up and handed back.

'How about kittens, Daddy?'

'I'm including them.'

'When does a kitten become a cat, Daddy?'

'Shut up!'

Stopping, they looked up to the left at a scraggy hill of wind-tattered pine and silver birch.

A lone ash leant back off the hill, the roots barely holding it in the boggy ground. It looked like a wispy old man unable to walk another step.

Round about them in the plushy trees pigeons cooed and shot up the sky with a prayer-book snap of wings. A sparrowhawk swirled lazily, then hovered, wings fluttering rapidly like a moth at a window.

'That'll be the beggar all right. As sure as there's cotton in Cork.'

'The hawk, Daddy?'

'No. The ash. That ash.'

They came out of the wood into a broad expanse of rich pasture, the drive flanked on either side by iron railings.

A huge horse chestnut stood in the middle of a field, its massive trunk ringed by a wooden bench. Lady Sarah was sometimes seen sitting there, painting at an easel.

The house loomed closer. His father to give himself courage began to mutter and heap contempt on the Butler-Cootes, going back for inspiration to the days of King James, when they were first planted in the county.

'All forest this one time. From here to Enniskillen in trees. Chopped. Chopped. To get at the rebels. The timber sent to London for their ships and palaces. The people sent to hell or Connaught. And we have to come bowing and scraping still, for a bit of firewood. Bet your bottom dollar she gives us that oul ash back there!'

Spittle flying, he looked furiously about, searching for something to give him offence.

'Damn the lot of them but we'll get even with them yet!'

He was really angry with himself. And that's when he was at his most dangerous. The boy knew when they met Lady Sarah or her steward his face would glow with sweetness and light. His father was only a sergeant. He had to be polite to his betters.

'What do you think?'

The boy hated being dragged into this conspiracy against the world. And the question was loaded. Wrong answers led to verbal abuse and threats. He hadn't been beaten yet but he feared the moment wasn't far away. If not now, later, if not tomorrow, soon. Every boy in the village got beaten. His turn was bound to come.

'Do you know what I'd do with them, Daddy? I'd stick them to a tree with six-inch nails and set them alight!'

He had learnt that going one better usually brought his father back to reality. Being a policeman, he was afraid of extremism in others.

'Oh! Oh! Big words in a small mouth. A poor old lady, never did harm to anyone, nailed to a tree?'

'But you said, Daddy, that . . .'

'Never mind what I said!'

To avoid arriving in a useless, self-defeating lather of passion, his father slowed down and stopped. The boy went past him, hit a pothole and came to a dead stop. For a moment he balanced in space, then as he began to keel over, pedalled hard to right himself. Losing direction, he careered wildly into the iron railings, the carrier over his back wheel flying backwards and clattering to the ground.

'Now you've done it!'

Picking the carrier up, his father tried to wedge it back into position. The required nuts and flange missing, he attempted to replace them with brute strength and fury. His every finger was a raw red angry thumb.

'There's a screw missing, Daddy.'

'There is indeed. And a screw loose as well.'

How was it he always had a cutting reply? Where did he find the words?

'Come on, you'll have to carry it. A fine sight you'll make for her ladyship. A carrier being carried.'

The lawns around Coote House were barbered neat, clean and crew-cut short. A green velvet sea sweeping between bobbing islands of Chinese lanterns, hollyhocks and rich red English roses, they were part of Lady Sarah's pride and joy. Time could ravish her house and life but her lawns, flowers, cats and trees she would defend until her last breath.

At the side of the house the lawn was given over to the

game of croquet, a game so alien to the locals they could neither understand it nor pronounce it.

As the boy and his father approached they saw a group of people standing about in sloping angles of inspection, lost from each other in a world of long-handled mallets, wooden balls and hoops stuck like toy railway bridges into the grass.

Men wore straw hats, shirts, flannel trousers and very white shoes.

The boy knew only Protestants wore white shoes.

Women were in thick brogues, thick stockings, tweed skirts, blouses and summer hats.

Lady Sarah, her arthritic back bent, was measuring distances and possibilities.

Straddling the wooden balls, the mallet back between her legs, she suddenly flicked it forward with ferocious decision. With a cluck and click the balls spurted away, then slowed down by the thick pile on the carpet of grass, rolled lazily to a halt.

The men laughed and one of them burped. Near the gable end of the house stood a small white table with a cloth, jugs and glasses.

'What are they doing, Daddy?'

'Crokee. It's supposed to be a game. You'd better go over and let them know we're here.'

The command with its cunning air of good advice annoyed the boy. He knew his father hadn't the courage or grace to break easily into Lady Sarah's dream-like world.

Still holding the carrier, like a drowning man clutching a straw, he stepped onto the lawn and made for the man nearest to him.

The grass springy under his feet, he had the sensation of swimming out into the lake, the waters getting deeper and more mysterious beneath him.

The strange faces were clean and fresh, the voices English. None of them had noticed his approach.

'Lady Sarah . . . Daddy wants you, please.' No one heard him.

He felt ashamed holding the carrier and wanted to throw it away so he wouldn't be seen with it.

After what seemed an age, the burping man turned and looked at him. At first regarding him blankly, then with an exaggerated shifting of eyebrows, popping of eyes and twitching of large moustache, he boomed in jovial surprise, 'I say, Sarah, we've got a little visitor.'

The entire party turned and viewed him. Confronted by such dazzling whiteness, he shyly lowered his head. There were holes in his gansey and his short pants, reduced from an old pair of his father's uniform trousers, were mud-stained.

Lady Sarah playfully raised his chin with her finger and he peered up into her eyes, which were grotesquely distorted by the thick lenses of her spectacles. There was a myth she was on name terms with every child in the village but the boy knew she had no idea who he was.

'Who IS the little poppet?' one of the guests asked.

He pointed to his father, standing stiffly by his bicycle, in the driveway.

'Ah,' Lady Sarah cried, 'the sergeant.'

Retreating from the pool of smiles and following her, he noticed her feet were nearly as big as his father's. The great brogues printed themselves in the lick of lawn dew all the way over to where she was greeted like a dear friend.

'Oh, Lady Sarah, what a charming evening!'

He winced at his father's modulated voice and the affected way he pronounced 'charming'. It sounded like 'chumming'.

Lady Sarah liked his father. In his dark blue uniform and with his chiselled features he was undeniably handsome. Despite her riches no man had ever married her. It was said that those not put off by her ugliness were soon sent packing by her intelligence.

'How "chumming" to see you,' said his father, 'and it's fresh and well you're looking.'

Lady Sarah giggled and resting her hand on the sleeve of his tunic, enquired about his health, his wife and the state of the country. Presently he took off his cap. A red line ran along his forehead and his hair was matted in sweat. The effort of keeping up the fawning accent was proving too great a strain. He mopped his brow with a big white handkerchief.

'Yes, it is rather humid, would you care for some barley water?'

Declining, he came straight to the point and asked for a tree.

'Winter will be upon us before we know.'

Lady Sarah, squinting up at him, stroked the thick black hair on her upper lip and, tapping the croquet mallet on the ground for inspiration, remembered there was a tree in danger of falling round by the lake. It was halfway up a hill surrounded by silver birch.

'Andy I call it,' she said, 'it's an ash.'

She would get her steward to mark it so it could be easily identified.

His father's face was a mask of interest and gratitude but behind the glazed eyes the boy knew the turmoil of rage, sarcasm and malice shunting round his head.

'Thank you, Lady Sarah, thank you so very much.'

Getting on their bikes, they rode homeward and as soon as they were out of earshot his father started.

'Well the oul vixen! The world wouldn't believe it! But she's got a Christian name for every single tree! Andy! I told you, didn't I? I knew that was the one she'd fob off on us! Well feck her! And her seed, breed and generation into the bargain! And their bloody oul crokee as well. Andy!'

When they reached the hill they stopped and looked up at the ash which to the boy looked even more withered and forlorn than before. Andy wasn't a particularly attractive name at the best of times and it seemed to him to be peculiarly suited to the lonely weakling tree.

'Well God blast you, but there's only about two months burning in you if that, which means we'll have to come back and start the whole business all over again!'

'Andy Ash,' said the boy, quietly.

'It's no joke! And it wasn't a joke either seeing them crokee players sniggering at you, standing there with your carrier in front of you like a squirrel holding a nut!'

Seeing the black rage in his father's face, he knew a syllable uttered in his defence could end with a raw red slap on the ear, a fist maybe in the face, a kick even. He'd seen it happening to his friends.

On the rest of the journey home he stayed well clear and that night went early to bed, saying his prayers extra loud so his father could hear him in the kitchen and think him far too pious for a beating.

Next morning he was told he had to stay at home to help cut down the tree.

'He's too young to help,' protested his mother, 'and anyway why can't you do it on Saturday when he doesn't have to miss school?'

'I'm doing it today and that's all!'

'Are you up to something?' enquired his mother crossly.

'No,' replied his father.

'Then why the rush to cut it down today?'

His father smiled but didn't reply. They watched as he sliced into a boiled egg, the top of which he gave to the boy.

After breakfast he wheeled out his father's bicycle then went back into the shed to get the implements needed for tree-felling.

The shed was a long narrow dark affair and so cluttered with gardening tools, wheelbarrows, bicycle wheels, pots and pans, tilley lamps, primus stoves, ropes, galvanised sheets and buckets, the boy was the only one able to negotiate the tangled chaos.

His mother had dubbed it the 'American Collection', because one day when his father had attempted to bring order to it, he kicked over a pile of empty paint cans and shouted angrily, 'I wish to God I'd gone to America years ago!'

The boy groped about in the dark searching for a hessian sack and knew he had found the right one when he heard the dull clink of heavy wedges. He humped, hopped and dragged them towards the light and his father's waiting hand.

'Get down that crosscut now.'

He reached to where the saw rested upside down on two nails. As if having life of its own it leapt from his grasp, whanging against a stack of oil drums, tumbling them over with a doomy clatter.

'Easy, easy!'

Round the front of the barracks his mother watched as they loaded the gear onto his father's bicycle. The wedges sat on the carrier and secured to the crossbar was an axe, a sledgehammer and a slash-hook. The boy had the crosscut and round his neck carried a rope. His mother put a bottle of tea into his father's pocket and they set off for the demesne entrance.

Soon they were deep in the lullaby silence of the wood.

He liked carrying the crosscut. It had two shiny hardwood handles and in the middle a smooth brassy solder, brazed there after being snapped by a falling tree. As he walked it bounced against his thigh and he imagined it was a bow with himself the arrow poised and ready for flight.

A beam of sunlight eased down through a tattered curtain of low cloud. It shone through the trees and brazed a small patch of open ground a bright golden colour just like the soldered spot on the crosscut.

'Look what's coming,' muttered his father, as Mickey the gatehouse simpleton came towards them, a bundle of twigs on his back.

'Grand day, grand day, grand day now,' he shouted to them, a huge grin bandaged on his lardy face.

'Lady Sarah gone to town?' enquired his father.

'Oh aye, oh aye, oh aye. Every Thursday.' He winked at the boy and stuck his tongue out; a poor fool compelled to confirm his idiocy at every encounter.

Going round by the lake, they disturbed a heron which rose in panic before them, desperately flapping its spindly body into the air.

'Greedy blaggards, the same herons.'

'Why, Daddy?'

'They gulp the fish in one end and to stop it coming straight out the other, they sit their bums on a stone.'

His father didn't have the imagination to invent fantastic tales. The truth in his mouth was lurid enough.

'Tell us how you won the medal for bravery, Daddy, ah go on.'

'You've heard it often enough. When we've the tree down and chopped up I might tell you.'

They came to the ash. Lady Sarah's steward had already marked it with a whitewashed circle. In contemptuous silence his father stared up at it. He still held on to his bicycle and, when the boy went to remove the wedges from the carrier, in surly anger rounded on him.

'What are you doing? That's not the one!'

'Yes it is, Daddy. Andy.'

'No it's not. Our one is further along.'

'No it's not. This is the one.'

'I tell you it's not!'

His eyes were glazed, his face cranky as the crosscut teeth. He looked at the boy, challenging him to contradict. In the silence the flies buzzed round the peak of his cap.

'But I thought, Daddy, that...' He could hear his heart beating as panic furred his tongue. His father was in the grip of some mad, mysterious plot. Looking up once more towards the ash, he knew it was the one. The white circle marked it out even more from the surrounding healthy trees. A scald-crow landed on it and with a melancholy screech proclaimed the truth for all the world to hear.

'It is the one, Daddy. I know it is!'

'Now you don't know everything. Come on.' He puffed his lips, winked and smiled, trying to soften the boy, lull him, make him an accomplice. They walked on, pausing occasionally to look up at the majestic trees flanking the drive. As he stared into the huge branches, his father had one side of his lower lip gripped in his teeth.

They came to a great elm, big as a circus tent. His father looked at it, stroking his chin, pondering, biting his lip. The boy with horror in his heart began to realise what it was they were about to do. His father, furtively looking up and down the drive, circled the tree, grunted at it, touched it with his fingers, then walked on. The boy was relieved.

'Oh yes, they chopped the woods to get at the rebels! It's time the rebels chopped back.'

Sick with worry he knew his father was going to cut down the wrong tree. On purpose. It had nothing to do with rebels. It was out of pure greed and a wild hope that Lady Sarah wouldn't notice. But the boy knew and everyone in the village knew, Lady Sarah would miss a leaf, never mind one of the great trees along the drive to Coote House.

How could his father dare? If discovered, how could he brazen it out? They stopped beside a magnificent copper beech. His father immediately growled approval as if looking at a thoroughbred animal.

'This is the one all right. We'll knock her back into that clearing there. Perfect.'

'It's not this one, Daddy. Honest. It's not.'

Throwing the bag of wedges to the ground, his father shouted angrily, 'Get me that axe, you pup you, and don't be annoying me. If I say it's the one, that's enough. It is the one! A beech. I know rightly this is the one. And you know it too!'

The meaning hidden in the last few words hung heavily on the dull air. If they were found out he would be blamed. He was powerless. And his mother at home, probably peeling potatoes into the aluminium basin and happily humming to herself.

'What if Lady Sarah comes along?'

'So? She gave it to us didn't she?'

'No she didn't!'

'Anyway she always goes to town on Thursdays. We'll have her felled, trimmed, sawn and chopped before she's back.'

So that's why it had to be today. He had it planned. Poor Mickey the simpleton had confirmed her absence.

He tried to circle the trunk with his arms but couldn't. And the topmost branches seemed to be sticking into the clouds.

'It's too big, Daddy. We'll never do it.'

But his father was no longer listening. Giving the trunk a whack with the axe he lifted the crosscut to the gash. Slowly the teeth tore into the tree. The boy did no more than steady his end as his father, on one knee, back and neck bent sideways, drove the saw over and back with a powerful urgent rhythm. Sawdust pumped out into the ground in bloody arcs.

Already the boy's wrists ached. His father had a cold passion which could burn at a task for hours nonstop. His iron will and ruthless strength, which grew more brutish as the minutes passed, would destroy the soul of a saint. Each time the saw stuck he grunted angrily and squealed as if the tree and the crosscut were ganging up on him. Already the boy's nerves were fraying.

His father loved working in the open air. He loved felling trees. He knew heavyweight boxers did it when training for title fights. His favourite song was Phil Harris singing 'Woodman Spare that Tree'. The only poem he knew began with the line, 'I think that I shall never see a poem as lovely as a tree'. He loved trees. He couldn't help chopping them down. He was beyond understanding.

Withdrawing the saw, his father got the axe and above the cut began to chop out the fall-hole. This huge bite taken out of the trunk would eventually force the tree to fall in a certain direction. With each axe blow a thick curl of wood flew out until the ground seemed scattered with pale lumps of pink flesh.

A copper leaf fell gently to the ground.

This time they would carry on cutting until the tree toppled down. It had stood for over a hundred years. Lady Sarah loved it. Only a short time before when interviewed in the *Anglo-Celt* she said that apart from oak her favourite species was the copper beech.

The boy felt they were committing murder. The swoosh and rip of the crosscut silenced all the birds. The sun came out and shone on them like a flashlamp on two thieves in the night.

Every move his father made had a crouched urgency. The job had to be done before Lady Sarah got back from town. He wasn't afraid of being caught by her steward. Her steward was an Englishman cashiered from the army for homosexuality. There was a file on him in the barracks. And he wasn't afraid of the workmen. They were Catholics.

Kneeling on the sack, to stop the damp penetrating his knees, and in a lather of sweat he cursed the flies that buzzed his face, the braces which kept slipping from one shoulder and the boy who was almost fainting with fatigue.

'I must have a rest, Daddy.'

'No, damn you! Not till she's down!'

The crosscut tore slowly into the belly of the tree. It made a deep swishing sound. The sound his mother's nails made when she scratched his back.

'Who the hell . . . ?'

A tall man approached along the drive. He wore knicker-bockers and on his head a deerstalker hat.

'It's one of Lady Sarah's visitors.'

The man nodded, smiled, and in a plummy accent said, 'Hot work, eh?'

His father had to stop to acknowledge him. The boy's head sunk to his chest in relief. He rubbed his wrists and stood up to stretch his back. His wrists were as thin as the legs of the heron dangling over the lake.

'Enjoying your holiday?'

'Oh yes, always do.'

'That's the stuff.'

The crosscut sagged in the tree, the golden solder sunk in the ever-deepening cut.

The man, unable to hold the unfriendly stare, walked on.

'I've seen some quare hawks in me time but that one takes the biscuit.'

The boy laughed, hoping to delay his father starting again.

'They wouldn't go round in England dressed up like that. But as soon as they set foot here out comes the Sherlock

Holmes attire and begod they think they're Lord and Lady Muck!'

The boy laughed again, but couldn't further delay the inevitable moment.

'Get hold.'

'I want to pee, Daddy.'

'No. Get hold.'

The sawdust pumped out again and the noise swished and sighed through the deep sweet wood.

'Blast.' The saw was stuck.

They tapped a small wedge into the slit, easing the weight of the tree from the saw. They cut further in and, as the pressure increased, drove in bigger wedges. The soldered repair was the problem. Though smooth it wasn't flush, catching easily, usually when it was the boy's turn to pull. He hated that golden mark now. Why couldn't his father buy a new crosscut? Why not a chain saw? Even a second-hand one. No. Heavyweight boxers were never photographed with chain saws. Besides they cost a fortune and his father was so mean he'd resist for ages having to buy a new battery for his bicycle lamp. He'd heat and reheat the old one in the oven to prolong its lingering life.

At last they passed the halfway mark and the weight of the tree began to tilt towards the fall-hole. The pressure eased, his father drove the saw to and fro at a frantic pace. His will whetted his strength and gave him furious power.

'Come on! Come on! Topple you beggar!'

A wedge fell out. The tree was beginning to go. The boy glanced up at it. He was worried. What if it fell on them?

'Run back that way when I tell you to!'

The tree was quivering. Nervous ripples ran through it. Like when a horse shivers its flesh against hornets.

His father looked up into the branches with a calculating eye. 'Just another bit now. Good boy.'

The tree creaked, groaned but still held. His father got the sledgehammer and drove the big wedge further in.

'Look out in case she kicks back at us.'

The boy was terrified. His father looked worried. The tree was immense. Their movements were slower now, tense; gently letting the saw nibble ever deeper, tapping the wedge in after it.

The sweat poured down their faces and hung at the end of their noses. Their clothes stuck like damp poultice to their skins. His father smiled at him. It was a smile of encouragement. He was proud of his father. Only a great man could dare knock down so great a tree. And he had helped. He loved his father.

They stopped sawing and listened to the tree. Starting again, his father murmured gently to it, calming it. Like a butcher with a sheep.

'That's the girl. Easy, easy.'

Suddenly a terrifying, tearing, bone-snapping crack rang out like a gunshot.

'She's going.'

Branches quaking, the huge tree tilted, twisted and, fighting to stay upright, grabbed at a neighbouring tree but, bowing to its fate, keeled over and with a creaking goodbye-sigh rushed to the earth with a thunderous hurricane crash. The boy felt the shock waves in his feet and saw the light flood in to the space where the tree had stood. Overhead the sky was bigger.

His father grinned.

'It's massive, Daddy. It's bigger than a ship.'

'It'll see us through the winter, thank God.'

As the boy skipped round the tree the enormity of what they'd done struck home. The shield and tangle of bough, branch and leaf looked impenetrable. It had taken them over two hours to knock it; it would take them the rest of the day at least to trim, lop, saw and chop it. Certainly they would not

be done by the time Lady Sarah returned. And even if they
were she could not possibly miss the pile of timber awaiting
collection.

'How will we get it home?'

'Barney Smith's tractor and trailer. Tomorrow evening.'

Tomorrow? Evening? It was mad. Ridiculous. Lady Sarah
was bound to find out.

Tired out, he sat on the tree stump beside his father and had
alternate swigs at the bottle of cold tea.

Hearing a noise he turned his head and instantly his body and
blood went cold. Approaching along the drive at the wheel of
her Wolseley car was Lady Sarah.

Time stopped dead. His father gave a strangled groan and
his face iced over in hatred. They were caught like rats in
a trap.

The car crunched to a halt. He was terrified in case his father
did something desperate and was all the more amazed when he
saw him smiling and in high good nature waving to Lady
Sarah as she, horror-stricken, stepped onto the drive. Wearing
a peculiar 1920s hat and a flapping plastic mac, she dismissed his
father's greeting and staggered towards the tree.

'What have you done, Sergeant, what have you done?' she
wailed. 'You have killed one of my beauties!' Grabbing and
clutching the stricken branches she buried herself in the copper
leaves. The boy could hear her sobs but couldn't see where
she was.

'Oh Beatrice, Beatrice my beauty, how has this occurred?'

His father winked.

'What's wrong, Lady Sarah, what seems to be the problem?'

'The problem,' she replied, stepping from the tree, 'is you
have murdered the wrong tree.' Behind the thick lenses of her
spectacles her eyes were tiny red dots of dismay.

'Oh no, we haven't, have we?' howled his father, his face a

dancing mask of pantomime surprise. 'Good Lord, I can't believe it. Are you sure Lady Sarah?'

'Oh yes I'm sure all right. I gave you a weakling ash, not this!'

Suddenly he turned to the boy and made as if to strike him.

'Didn't I tell you it wasn't this one? I told you all along!'

The boy hung his head in shame and didn't dare look at Lady Sarah because he knew she knew his father lied.

'I'll do anything I can by way of reparation, anything. I remember you saying the name, Andy. I think that's what confused me. That and the boy. Beech is no good to me anyway. It's a poor burner. A weakling ash is exactly what I wanted, Lady Sarah.'

He stalked over and back, feeling his brow, looking at the sky, at the ground, almost on the point of tears, imploring her to allow him make amends.

'One thing you cannot do is put it back up where it was this morning.'

There was a hint of hoping for miracles in her voice.

Once more he blamed the boy and made a run at him as if to hit him. Darting out of his way, he went close to Lady Sarah and looked into her eyes. She knew.

Turning away she faced the dead Beatrice and with her frail hand plucked a copper leaf. Resting on her fingers like a clot of blood, she held it to her mouth and nose and sighed as if kissing goodbye to a loved one. 'Beatrice, Beatrice, you were my father's favourite,' she whispered.

Tears welled in the boy's eyes. Lady Sarah looked very old, very sad and a little frightened. She owned the great demesne, employed many people, was kowtowed to in every town and village along the border but up against his father was just a lonely spinster, powerless to command. He was the sergeant.

She needed him to protect her property. The law was hers but it was on his word it was carried out.

His father stopped moving about, stopped cringing and with a steady gaze looked down at her.

The sweat dripping on his face, his chest heaving in his open shirt, his big thumbs twitching at his braces, his great booted feet straddling the driveway, the cold appealing look in his pale blue eyes were all too much for gentle hearts to cope with.

Getting into her car she spoke softly, her pride hurt, her spirit shocked. 'You may as well finish what you so cruelly started.'

'Well that's the only damn thing we can do now, Lady Sarah.'

Hours later, as they rode home past Andy, though his body ached, his soul raged rampant at the conquering smirk on his father's face.

THE CRY

JOHN MONTAGUE

Finally he rose to go to bed. His father had shuffled off a few minutes before and his mother was busy preparing a hot-water bottle, moving, frail as a ghost, through the tiny kitchen. Seeing her white hair, the mother-of-pearl rosary beads dangling from her apron pocket, the bunny rabbit slippers, he felt guilt at keeping her up so late. But he came home so seldom now that he was out of the rhythm of the household and tried to do only what pleased them. And sitting with their big Coronation mugs of cocoa, they had drunk in his presence so greedily that he felt compelled to talk and talk. Mostly of things they had never seen: of travelling in Europe, of what it was like to work on a big newspaper, of the great freedom of living in London. This last had troubled his father very much, centuries of republicanism stirring in his blood.

'What do you mean, son, freedom?'

'I mean, Father, nobody interferes with you. What you do is your own business, provided you cause no trouble.'

Seeing the perplexity in his father's face, he tried to explain in local terms. 'Nobody on the *Tocsin*, for instance, would dream of asking if you were Catholic or Protestant – at least not the way they do here. If they did ask, it would be because they were genuinely interested.'

'Then can you explain, son, why England has the reputation

she has abroad? Didn't she interfere with freedom everywhere she went, from Africa to the North here?'

'That's not the real England, Father; that's the government and the ruling class. The real Englishman is not like that at all, he stands for individual liberty, live and let live. You should hear them in Hyde Park!'

'I must never have met a real Englishman then,' said his father, obstinately. His face had gone brick-red and his nostrils twitched, showing spikes of white hair. With his bald round head and bright eyes he looked like Chad, in the wartime cartoon, peering over a wall, but it was anger, not humorous resignation, he registered.

'Maybe,' said his mother timidly, 'they're all right when they're at home.'

And there the matter rested. His father had always been violently anti-English: he remembered him saying that he would be glad to live on bread and water for the rest of his life if he could see England brought to her knees. And the struggle there had been when he had first announced his intention of trying to break into newspaper work in London! Dublin would have been all right, or America where his father had spent ten years as a cook in a big hotel, before coming home to marry and settle in the little newsagency business. But England! Religious and political prejudice fused to create his father's image of it as the ultimate evil. And something in his father's harshness called out to him: during his adolescence, he had contacted the local branch of the IRA and tried to join. They (rather he, a lean melancholy egg-packer called Sheridan who had the reputation of being a machine-gunner in the force) had told him to report for a meeting, but when the time came, he had funked it, saying that he had to go away.

And so, Peter changed the conversation. He spoke of shows he had seen, the big American musicals, the Bolshoi and Royal

Ballets. But his father still seemed restless: once he saw him glance mournfully across at his mother and wondered what he had said wrong. Her eyes glinted with pleasure as he described a Charity (tactfully amended from Command) Performance, with all the stars arriving in their glittering gowns.

'Oh, that must have been lovely,' she said, with placid yearning.

It was only when he was climbing the stairs that he realised what his father's glance had meant. 'Good-night, now, son, and don't forget to say your prayers,' his mother called after him. That was it; because of his visit, they had not said the regular family rosary, waiting for him to remember and suggest it. How could he explain that he had never seen anyone in England say the rosary, except two Irish lads in his first digs in Camden Town, who had embarrassed everyone by kneeling down at their bedside and saying it aloud in Irish. English Catholics did not believe in loading themselves down with inessentials. But if he had begun to explain all that, they would have jumped to the conclusion that he had lost his faith completely. Religion and politics he should try to leave alone for the short time he was home.

The room was on the top floor, that front bedroom in which he had always slept. The top sheet was turned down, with the same inviting neatness, the blue eiderdown was the same, even the yellow chamber pot beneath the bed. Over the fireplace was the familiar picture of Our Lady of Perpetual Succour, an angular Madonna cradling a solemn-faced Child, a slipper dangling from his chubby foot. Opposite it, on the wall over the bed, was a Victorian sampler, worked by his grandmother as a young girl: THERE IS NO FUN LIKE WORK.

It was all so unchanged that it was almost terrifying, like being confronted with the ghost of his younger self. He heard his father moving in the next room, shifting and sighing. Taking off his clothes, Peter knelt down in his pyjamas for a few moments at the bedside; he hoped the old man would hear the murmur and guess what it was. Then he wandered round the room for something to read.

Spurning the *Wolfe Tone Annual* and *With God on the Amazon* on the dressing table, he discovered a soot-stained copy of the *Ulster Nationalist* which had obviously been taken from the grate to make room for the electric fire; this he carried triumphantly to bed.

The editorial spoke with dignified bitterness of the continued discrimination against Catholics in the north of Ireland in jobs and housing. Facts were given and in spite of the tedious familiarity of the subject Peter felt his anger rise at such pointless injustice. He turned the page quickly to the Court Proceedings:

UNITED NATIONS FOR MOORHILL?

Moorhill Court was taken up on Wednesday with a lengthy hearing of a civil summons for alleged abusive language and assault.

Giving evidence, James MacKennie, Craigavon Terrace, said that Miss Phyllis Murphy had thrown a bucket of water over him as he was passing on his bicycle. Cross-examined witness admitted that he had spoken sharply to Miss Murphy but he had not threatened, as she said, 'to do her'. He admitted borrowing five shillings from Miss Murphy 'to cure a headache'. His solicitor, Mr John Kennedy, said that his client was a veteran of the First World War and had a disability pension. It was true he had been in jail several times, but he was very well thought of in the community.

The defendant, Miss Phyllis Murphy, said that James MacKennie was a well-known pest, and besides 'he had been coming over dirty talk'. She denied throwing water over him and said he had been making so many 'old faces' that he had

driven over the bucket of water. She denied saying she hoped
'that would make him laugh the other side of his Orange face'.

In giving his decision, the RM said it was a difficult case to
disentangle but he felt both parties were to blame and he therefore bound them over to keep the peace for a year. It was a pity,
now that people were trying to outlaw war, to find neighbours
disagreeing; maybe he should ask the United Nations to come
to Moorhill . . . (laughter in court).

Peter Douglas read on with delighted horror. For the first time
since he had returned, he felt at ease; he threw the paper on
the floor, and turned contentedly over to sleep. Somewhere
downstairs, the cuckoo clock he had brought his mother
was sounding.

II

Some time later, he came suddenly awake to a sound of
shouting. He listened carefully, but it could not have come from
the next room. Perhaps it was his mother; no, it was too strong,
a man's voice. It came from down in the street, but not directly
underneath; he sat bolt upright in bed and turned his head
towards the window. Yes, there it was again, clearer, and he
sounded as if he were in pain.

'Oh Jesus, sir, oh Jesus, it hurts.'

Maybe somebody had been taken ill suddenly and they were
carrying him to the ambulance? Or a fire: he remembered the
night, years ago, when old Carolan had been carried out of his
house by the firemen, screaming like a stuck pig, rags of cloth
still smouldering upon his legs. But who was the man in the
street talking to, whom was he calling sir?

'Oh Jesus, sir, don't touch me again.'

All across the town lights were beginning to come on;
the shadowy figure of a woman, wrapped in a dressing gown,
appeared at the window directly opposite; only something
unusual could sanction such loose behaviour in Moorhill.
Maybe it was a fight? Then, with a cold rush of certainty, Peter
Douglas knew what it was: it was someone being beaten up
by the police.

'Oh God, sir, don't hit me again.'

The voice was high and pleading. Then there was a scuffle
of feet and the sound of a blow, a sharp crack, like a stone on
wood. Throwing back the bedclothes, Peter ran to the window
and craned out his head. At the bottom of the street, he saw a
knot of people. One of them was kneeling on the ground, his
shape circled by the light of a torch held by one of the bulky
cape-clad figures surrounding him. In the windows above,
shadows moved, silent, watching.

'Come on to the barracks now and quit your shouting,' said
an impatient voice.

'Oh no, sir, I can't, I'm nearly killed. Somebody help me, for
God's sake, please.'

Again the voice was abject, but at a muttered order the torch
was extinguished and the four figures closed in on the kneeling
man. Was no one going to protest, none of those darkly
brooding presences? Peter Douglas opened his mouth to shout,
but he was forestalled. A door opened behind the men, letting
out a shaft of light. He heard a sharp, educated voice:

'What in blazes do you thugs think you are doing? Leave
the man alone.'

One of the four policemen turned, switching his torch
directly into the face of the speaker.

'Keep your bloody nose out of it, will ye? Do you want
to get a touch too?'

He heard further muttering and then a door slammed angrily.

The four figures seized their victim, who now hung like a sack between them, and half-walked, half-ran him down the street towards the barracks. There were no further cries, only the drag of boots on the pavement, an occasional groan and (as the barrack door opened and shut behind them) a gathering silence. One by one the lights went out over the town. Peter Douglas was one of the last to leave, his eyes sore (he had left his glasses on the bedside table) from straining after any further movement. As he climbed into bed again, he heard the cuckoo clock: Cuckoo, Cuckoo, Cuckoo.

III

When he came down to breakfast next morning, after a short and troubled sleep, he found his father waiting impatiently for him. Generally, he was in the shop by this time, but it was his mother's voice he heard, dealing with an early customer: 'Yes, Mrs Wilson, nice weather indeed, for the time of year...' And it was his father who prepared the meal, cornflakes, tea and toast, bacon sizzling fragrantly in the pan. It was clear he had something on his mind; Peter felt as suspiciously certain as a prisoner who finds his warder suddenly affable.

'You're pretty lively this morning, aren't you?' he said, digging into the cornflakes.

His father did not reply, fussing around the stove with plates and cloths until, triumphantly, he placed a full plate of bacon, eggs and sausages before his son.

'The old man can do it yet,' he said. Then he sat at the end of the table and watched his son eat, slowly, picking at his food.

'They don't seem to have much appetite in England, anyway,' he said, 'whatever else they have.' And then, without further preamble: 'Did you hear what happened last night?'

'I did,' said his son, briefly. 'Did you?'

'I only heard the tail end of it, but I heard them all talking this morning.'

'What did they say?'

'They said the B Specials beat up a young man called Ferguson, whom they accused of being in the IRA.'

'Was he?'

'Sure how would I know? Most people say not, a harmless lad that was courting his girl on the bridge, without minding anyone.'

'Then why did they attack him?'

'Why do you think? You know bloody well those boys don't need a reason for beating up one of our sort.'

'Maybe he had papers on him, or an explosive. After all, there's been a lot of trouble lately.'

In the preceding months, the IRA campaign against the North had been revived. It was the same sad old story, barracks, customs huts blown up, and police patrols ambushed. Several men had been killed on both sides, and the police force had been augmented, even in relatively quiet areas like Moorhill, which, though predominantly Catholic, was too far from the border for a raiding party to risk. A hut at the end of the town had gone on fire one night, but it turned out to be some children playing a prank.

'Damn the explosive he had with him, except,' his father smiled thinly, 'you count the girl. But those bloody B Specials are so anxious to prove their importance, strutting around the town with their wee guns. Besides, they're shitting their britches with fear and mad to get their own back.'

'I see.' Peter forbore from pointing out that some of these motives were mutually exclusive, recognising his father's mood only too well. He poured a last cup of tea.

'Well, what are you going to do about it?' said his father fiercely.

'What do you mean, what am I going to do?'

'You were talking last night about Englishmen and freedom. Well there's an example of your English freedom, and a fine sight it is. What are you going to do about it?'

'What do you want me to do? Look for a gun?' he said sardonically.

'You could do worse. But your sort would faint at the sight of one.'

Peter flared. 'Would we, indeed? Well, maybe we've seen too many, handled by the wrong people.'

'What the hell are you going to fight them with, then?' his father snorted. 'A pen nib? A typewriter? A fat lot of use that would be against a Sten gun.'

'It might be of more use than you think. Moral protest is always best, as Gandhi showed. But they did not teach you that in Ballykinler internment camp.'

'Moral protest, me granny. How are you going to bring moral protest to bear on bucks like that? Force only recognises greater force.'

Peter Douglas rose and, placing his back against the rail of the stove, looked down at his father. The dark blue pouches under his eyes, gorged with blood, the right arm raised as though to thump the table in affirmation: he could have been cast in bronze as The Patriot. His own limp ease, the horn-rimmed glasses, the scarf tucked in neatly at the throat of his sports shirt, the pointed black Italian shoes – everything represented a reaction against this old fire-eater who had dominated his childhood like a thundercloud. But now he felt no fear of him, only a calm certainty of his own position.

'You know well, Father, in your heart of hearts, that violence is the wrong way. Now you ask me what I can do. Well, in this specific case, I can do more than you or a whole regiment of the IRA. I can write an article in the *Tocsin* which will expose the whole thing. Good, decent – yes, English – people will read it and be ashamed of what is being done in their name. Questions will be asked, maybe in Parliament, if not this time, then the next. And gradually, if they are shown the enormity of what they are doing, the ruling classes of Ulster will come to their senses. One cannot hope to survive in the twentieth century on the strength of a few outdated shibboleths: prejudice always breeds violence.'

His father was silent, whether impressed or not, Peter could not say. Then, rising to clear away the breakfast things, he said:

'You'll do that then. You'll write the article.'

'I will.'

His father smiled, cunningly. 'Well, at least I got you to do something. You haven't completely lost your Ulster spirit yet.'

Peter's first task was to collect the information. He began to move around the town, listening to conversations in shop and pub. At first he drew a blank; seeing him enter with his pale look, his city air, the men at the bar went silent or whispered among themselves. When they had established his identity ('Oh you're James Douglas's boy', a double recognition of family and religion flooding across the face) they spoke again, angrily.

'Oh, the black boys gave him a good going over, like,' said one man with a knowing wink and nod. 'You don't get off lightly when you're in their hands.'

'Is he badly hurt?' asked Peter.

'Now I couldn't tell you that exactly, but the doctor was with him this morning. They say he has a broken arm, anyway.'

'I heerd he had two broken ribs and stetches in his head forby.'

'Oh, they gave him the stick all right.'

'You'll get no fair deal from the likes of them.'

'They're black as can be.'

But when Peter asked what was going to be done by way of protest, they looked at him bleakly, shaking their heads.

'Sure you know it's no bloody use,' said one, hopelessly.

'You'd be a marked man from that day out,' said another.

'Sure you know the black boys have it all sewn up,' said a third, joining the litany of defeat.

Their passivity only heightened Peter's resolution, the only thing troubling him being the lack of specific detail. Very few people seemed even to know the boy, who lived far out, in the Black Mountain district. And those who did, did not always approve of him; they said he was very 'close' and used to hang around the jukebox in Higgins's Café. Yet they were all agreed on the wanton brutality of the beating, though the majority confessed to having been too far away to see much.

The source for the earlier part of the story was the girl, but she had run away when the struggle started and her father had forbidden her to leave the house. Since the man whom Peter had seen rebuking the police was the schoolmaster, he would not be home until evening and the nearest to an eyewitness he could find was the owner of the Dew Drop Inn. He and his wife slept in a room overlooking the street, exactly where the worst of the struggle had taken place. Yes they had struck him a lot, he told Peter, but he had heard one of them say 'to be sure and hit him round the body, it leaves less mark'.

'There should be a boycott against them bucks,' concluded the publican, grimly.

In the Mountain Rest, however, Peter found the town clerk calmly drinking a large whiskey. Tall, with a drooping sandy moustache, he had served in an artillery regiment during the Normandy campaign and the boyish vigour with which he propounded atheism in a community highly given to religious hypocrisy had always amused Peter. The clerk thought that what had happened the previous night was a storm in a teacup.

The boy had been looking for trouble and the only mistake was that the police had not acted promptly enough. 'The only thing to do with a gulderer like that is to hit him on the head with a mallet: that puts a stop to the squealing!'

No one spoke. Gulping down his lager, Peter left: it was time to start his article.

> *It is depressing to encounter violence again, its familiar pattern of fear and impotence. The first time I met it was in New York: a huddle of boys under a streetlamp and then the single figure staggering backwards, hands to his side, while the others fled. My first impulse was to help but a firm hand held me back. By the time the ambulance arrived, the boy was dead.*
>
> *That is the classic scene of urban violence; the spectator is absolved in the sheer remoteness of the action. It is not quite so scenic when it happens among people one knows. Recently I returned to the small town in the north of Ireland . . .*

Well, it was a beginning at least; a little academic in its irony, and the 'philosophical' lead-in would probably have to be scrapped; but still, a beginning. It would improve when he got down to the actual incident: should he begin with a description of the town to give the background, or should he just plunge in? And there would have to be interviews with the police especially – not used to being taken up, they would probably condemn themselves out of their own mouths.

As Peter hesitated, he heard someone enter the bedroom where he was sitting, his portable propped on a suitcase in front of him. It was his mother; she had a brightly fringed shawl around her shoulders and she was carrying a hot-water bottle. This she inserted into the bed, with great ostentation.

'I thought I'd put it in early this evening, and have the bed warm for you. It was pretty sharp last night.'

Peter waited impatiently for her to leave, but as she delayed, rearranging the sheet several times, it became obvious that the hot-water bottle was only an excuse.

'I see you're writing,' she said at last.

'Yes.'

'Is it about last night?'

'More or less.'

'I suppose it was him put you up to it.' She always referred to his father in this semi-abstract way, as if he were not so much her husband as someone who had been wished on her years ago, a regrettable but unchanging feature of the household.

'More or less. But I would probably have done it myself in any case.'

'Do you think it's a sensible thing to do?'

'How do you mean, sensible? One can't let things like that pass without protest.'

She looked at him in silence for a few moments and then, placing her hands on her hips, said: 'You're much better out of it. You'll only make trouble for all of us.'

'That's not what Father thinks.'

'I don't care what he thinks. I've lived with that man, God knows, for over thirty years and I still don't understand him. I think he never grew up.' She offered the last sentence with a grimace of half-amused resignation.

'But I agree with him in this case.'

'Oh, it's easy for you. You don't live here all year round. That thing you're writing will create bad blood. I've seen too much fighting between neighbours in this town already.'

'But Mother, you used to be a great rebel!' His father had often told, with great amusement, how she had been arrested for singing 'The Soldier's Song' on the beach at Warrenpoint; she had picked off the policeman's hat with her parasol and thrown it into the bathing pool. This incident was known in the family as Susie's fight for Irish freedom.

'I've seen too much of it,' she said, flatly. 'My brothers fought for Irish independence and where did it get them? They're both in Australia now, couldn't get jobs in their own country. Look at you: when you want a job you have to go to England.'

'But I'm only writing an article, Mother, not taking up a gun.'

'It's all the same tune. Sour grapes and bad blood. It's me and him will have to live here if that thing appears, not you. Come down to your tea and leave that contraption alone.' She gestured towards the typewriter as if it were accursed.

Peter rose reluctantly. Despite her frail body, her china-pale complexion, her great doll's eyes, she had the will of a dragon. During the next few days, mysterious references to this article would crop up again and again in her conversation, references designed to make his father and himself feel uneasy, like guilty schoolboys.

'But surely you don't approve of what they did?' he said.

'Approve of them, of course I don't. They're a bad lot.' Muttering she disappeared into the kitchen, to reappear with an egg whisk and a bowl of eggs. 'But we have to live with them,' she announced, driving the egg whisk into the eggs like an electric drill. 'Why else did God put them there?'

IV

One must distinguish between the Royal Ulster Constabulary and the familiar English 'bobby'. The Ulster police are the only ordinary police, in these islands, to carry revolvers; during times of emergency, they are armed with Sten guns. Add to that 12,000 B Specials and you have all the elements of a police state – not in Spain or South Africa, but in the British Isles. Such measures are not, as is argued, preventive, but the symptoms of political disease.

Police! Peter Douglas never knew a moment when he had not feared and detested them. It was partly his father's example:

walking with him through the town, as a child, or on the way out to the chapel, he would feel him stiffen when a black uniform came in sight. If a constable, new to the place, dared salute him, he would gaze through him with a contemptuous eye. It was also the uniform; the stifling black of the heavy serge, the great belt, above all the dark bulk of the holster riding the hip: the archetypal insignia of brutality and repression. There was one, in particular, who was known as 'the storm-trooper': a massive ex-commando, he strode around the town with a black police dog padding at his heels. He had long left the district, but for Peter Douglas, he had become the symbol of all the bitterness of his native province, patrolling for ever the lanes of Ulster, as dark and predatory as the beast at his side.

And then there were the Special police, young locals, issued with rifles and Sten guns, and handsomely paid for night duty. The first time Peter had seen them he was about ten years old, cycling home one warm summer evening from his uncle's house in Altamuskin. There were about thirty, drilling before a tin-roofed Orange lodge. Although he knew most of them, local Protestants whom he had met in shop or street, or in whose farmhouses he had been, they ignored him, gazing bleakly forward. Three nights later, they had stopped him and his father at a street corner and, pretending not to recognise them, held them up for nearly half an hour.

Darkly unjust these memories might be, Peter Douglas reflected as he walked down the street, but the events of the previous night seemed to bear them out. From Higgins's Café came a gush of light and music, the harsh sound of a pop record. Under the circle of a streetlight stood the diminutive figure of Joe Doom, the village idiot, eating from one of his tin cans. A group of children surrounded him, but they shrank back into the dark as Peter passed.

Outside the barracks itself, on a hillock at the end of the

town, there appeared to be an unusual amount of activity. There was a Land Rover, containing several police, drawn up in front, together with a long black car, the wireless antennae and the dark glittering body of which unmistakably proclaimed a squad car. The barracks was a large building, painted in panels of white outlined with black; without the blue police sign over the door, it might have been a doctor's or a company director's house in some comfortable English suburb. But, surrounded on every side by great rolls of barbed wire and with a sandbag blockhouse, from the slit of which protruded a machine gun, it looked like a fortress, the headquarters of the Gauleiter in an occupied town. As he came up the path, he saw a flash of movement in the blockhouse; he was being kept under cover.

'Is the sergeant in?' Peter asked. And then, irritably: 'For God's sake, put that thing down. I live up the street.'

'What do ye want with him?' A young constable emerged, the Sten gun dangling on his arm, insubstantial in its menace as a Meccano toy.

'I'd like to interview him. I'm a journalist and I work for a paper in England. I'd like to discuss the incident last night with him.'

'You're a journalist,' said the constable, with an intonation of flat incredulity. 'In England?'

'Yes, and I'd like to see the sergeant, please.'

There was a moment's silence, while the policeman looked at him, his eyes pale blue and vacant in a dead-white face, emphasised by the black peak of the cap. Then he turned and motioned Peter to follow him into the day-room.

There were five men in the room, two local policemen whom he vaguely recognised, two rather sulky-looking B Specials and a fifth, who, by his bearing, tailored uniform with Sam Browne belt and polished leggings, seemed to be a superior officer. They looked surprised to see Peter.

'There's a man here, Sergeant,' said the constable, addressing one of the local policemen, 'says he's a journalist. He works for some paper, in England.'

The sergeant came forward, slowly. 'You're Mr Douglas's son, aren't you?' he asked, with a mixture of civility and doubt.

'Yes, Sergeant, I am. I work for a paper in England and I'm home on a short holiday. I'd like to get a few facts from you about the incident last night.'

'Last night?' The sergeant looked in half-desperation towards the well-dressed officer.

'Which paper do you work for?' said the latter in a crisp voice. As he spoke, he came forward to face Peter as if by his presence hoping to subdue the intruder. It was the unmistakable voice of authority, British and chilling, as level in tone as a BBC announcer's.

Peter explained, politely.

'Yes, I see,' said the officer, noncommittally. 'I think I know the paper.' Then, to the sergeant: 'Don't you think we should bring Mr Douglas into another room, Knowles?'

As Peter followed Sergeant Knowles into a large room at the back of the barracks, a thought struck him.

'That's the County Inspector, isn't it?'

'It is indeed,' said the sergeant. He looked as if he wanted to say more but thought better of it, poking the fire for an instant in an aimless way, before leaving the room. So that was it: they were definitely troubled about the incident last night and the County Inspector had come down in person to investigate. He was on the right track after all.

The inspector entered the room briskly a few moments later. Planting himself luxuriously in front of the fire, he turned to Peter with a bright energetic smile. Thin hair brushed back above his ears, a long oval face with neatly divided moustache, lean-bridge nose and almost slanted eyes, he was decidedly handsome, a man born and used to command.

'Well, now, Mr Douglas, it's not often we get one of you chaps knocking around this part of the country. Sorry I can't offer you a drink, but I doubt if the facilities of the barracks are supposed to rise to that.' He laughed briefly. 'You're a local man, I take it.'

'Yes,' said Peter. The bright offensiveness of the man's tone angered, but also cowed, him, so that, almost against his will, he found himself volunteering further information. 'But I went to school in Laganbridge.'

'Oh,' said the inspector with interest, sensing common ground. 'Went to school there myself. The Kings, I suppose.'

'No,' said Peter shortly. Then – incredulity merging into satisfaction at the unexpected trap into which the inspector had fallen, deceived by the British sound of Douglas and the fact that the *Tocsin* was a London paper – he added, 'St Kieran's.'

It was like confessing, Peter thought with a smile, to an un-reconstructed Southerner that though one looked quite normal, one really was a Negro. The Kings was one of the most famous Protestant schools in the north of Ireland, a Georgian nursery for cricketers, colonial administrators, gaitered bishops and even (as though to demonstrate its all-round ability) a distinguished literary critic. On the hill opposite, sheltering under the great bulk of the post-emancipation cathedral, was the diocesan seminary of St Kieran's where the sons of strong Catholic farmers, publicans and merchants studied, mainly for the priesthood.

'Oh.' The inspector paused. Then, with a gallant return to self-possession: 'Used to know your bishop a bit. Nice old chap. Don't fancy his taste in sherry much, though.'

'His sherry?' echoed Peter in amazement.

'Myas.' The way he pronounced it, with a prefatory hum and

a hissing follow-through, it could have been anything from 'my ears' to 'my arse'. 'Gets his shipped direct from Spain; our boys see it through the customs for him. Bit dry. Prefer Bristol Cream myself.'

If such a man thought about nationalists at all, it was probably as some obscure form of troublemaking minority; he did not mind contact with them providing it took place on the highest level, a maharajah or a bishop, or some complaisant, highly placed native official. And why should he change? Convinced of his tolerance, assured of his position within the framework of queen and country, he would probably end his days in honourable retirement with a minor decoration in the Honours List.

'I never met the bishop,' Peter said curtly.

He might have saved his breath, the irony of his remark falling like a paper dart from that unruffled brow. The inspector had already moved on.

'Well,' he said, 'about that little matter you mentioned. Don't think there's much in it for a fellow like you. Pretty small beer after all. Some young thug cheeked our boys and they took him in for a few hours to cool off. Released him in the morning. Routine affair.'

'After beating him up on the way,' Peter said stubbornly.

'Oh, I wouldn't say that,' said the inspector, judiciously. 'He did resist arrest after all, so they had to help him along a bit. May have got a few scratches, but that would be the height of it.'

'Enough to put him in a hospital bed.'

'Oh, you heard that, did you?' the inspector said with interest. 'Well, well, it's wonderful how rumours get round, though I'm afraid you won't find much substance in that one. Chap kept complaining so we called the doctor. He couldn't find much wrong with him but just to be on the safe side he sent him down to the County for an X-ray. Released in a few hours, right as rain. Mother came to bring him home.'

'So you mean it was all nothing?' asked Peter, incredulously.

'Pretty well.'

'But the noise woke up the whole town.'

The inspector laughed dryly. 'Yes, that was rather a nuisance. Chap was a bit of an exhibitionist. Roared like a bull, boys said, every time they laid a finger on him. Pretty cute trick when you come to think of it.'

'Trick?' Peter stared at the bland face opposite him. But he found neither deception nor doubt in the inspector's level gaze.

'Yes, a trick. Can't be up to some of these fellows. Bit of a teddy boy by all accounts, likes to show he's not afraid of the police. But I think he realises he went a bit too far last night, made a fool of himself.' The inspector rubbed his hands together in a gesture of satisfied dismissal. 'Well, there you are, there's the whole little story. Sorry I can't provide something more juicy for you. I know what you Johnnies like. Perhaps next time.'

Stunned, Peter followed him along the corridor and out through the door. He was halfway up Main Street before he realised that the IRA had not even been mentioned.

'So that's what he said to you,' said the schoolmaster admiringly. Peter had called on him on his way home and they had crossed the street to the nearest pub, the Dew Drop Inn.

'Yes, I'm afraid I was so taken aback I couldn't think of anything to say. I mean, it all sounded so plausible; maybe the man was telling the truth.'

'Still, that doesn't explain why he called upon me.'

'Oh, did he, indeed?' breathed Peter.

'Yes, when I drove in from school, there was His Nibs waiting in the parlour. Said he often heard my brother who works in the County Health Office speak of me and thought he should drop by. Then, cool as you please, mentioned the business last night and said I would be glad to hear it had all been a misunderstanding. They had given the boy a good talking to and sent him home. There was no further reason for me to be troubled *in any way*. Special Constable Robson was sorry for what he had said to me, but it was all in the heat of the moment and meant nothing.'

'So they *were* troubled . . . And what did you say?'

'What could I say? I just smiled back and said I accepted Robson's apologies and was glad to hear the boy was all right. I work here you know and so – as he delicately pointed out – does my brother. Besides' – he blinked nervously and hunched his narrow raincoated shoulders forward – 'I've been thinking the matter over and it seems to me we're not on very safe ground.'

'What do you mean? Surely a civilised man cannot let some-one be beaten up under his eyes without protesting.'

'In an ordinary case, no. But the boy doesn't seem to have been badly hurt and we wouldn't be able to prove anything definite. We'd only be playing into their hands by showing ourselves as troublemakers.'

Peter was silent for a moment, sipping his lager. 'That's more or less what my mother says,' he said eventually, 'but not my father.'

'Your father, if you don't mind me saying so, is nearly as thick as an Orangeman in his own way. His kind of talk may be fair enough in Dáil Éireann, but as you know yourself, it cuts very little ice here. After all, even if we did get a united Ireland we would still have to live with them so we'd better start now. And you must admit the police in the North have had a pretty rough time lately. If this was the twenties, there'd be a lot of dead Taigs around.'

'So you think I should drop the article I'm doing?'

'Oh, I don't know, that depends. Why don't you go and see the boy before deciding? After all, he was the one who was beaten up.'

The owner of the Dew Drop Inn peered hurriedly round the door. 'Come on, gentlemen, please,' he said. 'It's half an hour after the time already.' As they passed through the kitchen on their way out, a group of men were on their way in. They were the B Specials Peter had seen at the barracks. 'Good-night now, Mr Concannon, good-night, Mr Douglas,' the owner said as he shepherded them through the door. Then he turned to greet his new customers.

V

'That must be it,' said James Douglas, craning across the shoulder of the hackney cab driver. For ten minutes or so, ever since they had left the main road, they had been bumping along a narrow country lane. At first there were signs of habitation, but as they wound their way up the mountainside, first the houses and then the trees began to fall away, long stretches of melancholy bog opening up on either side. At last, just as the gravel surface of the lane began to merge into the muddy ruts of a cart track, they caught sight of a small cottage. White-washed, with a greening thatched roof, it stood on a mound, without any shelter or protection from the wind except a rough fence, hammered out of old tar barrels. Against the wall, its front wheel almost blocking the half-door, was a battered racing bicycle, painted a bright red.

'That's it, right enough,' said the driver. 'Any bids?'

'It looks bleak all right,' said Peter.

'Hungry's the word,' said the driver cheerfully, as he applied the handbrake.

'Do you want me to come with you?' his father asked, looking at Peter doubtfully. All the way to Black Mountain he had
been humming to himself, in evident satisfaction, but the sight
of the cottage seemed to have unnerved him.

'No,' said Peter shortly. 'I'll go myself.'

The swaying progress of the car up the lane had already at-
tracted attention: a brown and white mongrel dog came racing
down to greet it, and the startled face of a woman flashed briefly
at one of the two small windows. As Peter descended from the
car, his thin shoes sinking in the mud of the yard, the dog
plunged towards him.

'Down, Flo, down.' A woman of about fifty, wearing a
shapeless red jumper and a pair of thongless man's boots,
appeared in the doorway. She stood, drying her hands in the
corner of her discoloured apron, and waiting for Peter to speak.

'Does Michael Ferguson live here?'

A look of dismay, animal, uncomprehending, passed over
her face. 'God protect us,' she muttered, 'more trouble.' Then,
turning towards the door: 'He's in there, if you want him.'

After the light of the mountainside, the interior of the cottage
seemed dim as a cave. A crumbling turf fire threw a fitful smoky
light over the hunched-up figure of an old man who looked up
as the intruder entered and then, with a noisy scraping of his
stool, turned away. Beside the kettle in the ashes lay a sick
chicken, its scrawny red head projecting from a cocoon of
flannel. The other side of the room was taken by a cupboard and
a bed upon which a young man was lying. There was a bandage
around his forehead.

'Can't you rise, at laste, when someone comes to see you?'
said the woman, gruffly.

The young man raised himself stiffly from the bed. He was
about twenty, tall and rather well-built with broad shoulders.
He wore an imitation leather jacket, heavy with metal buckles

and clasps. It rode high above his waist, exposing a torn khaki shirt. This was stuffed loosely into a pair of threadbare jeans, supported by a studded leather belt with a horseshoe buckle. The outfit was completed by bright blue- and red-ribbed socks above the black heaviness of farm boots.

'Are you police?' His eyes, close-set in a face heavily blotched with acne, avoided Peter's; he could have been speaking to the dog, which by now whined and twined around his legs.

Peter explained as best he could. In his nervousness, he found himself using words that, by the puzzled expression in their faces, he knew they could not understand, so he repeated his story several times. 'I want to help, you see,' he ended.

'I don't think I can do much for you, mister,' the boy said, at last.

'What do you mean, you can't do much for me? That's not the point at all. I want to do something for you. I want to write an article that will expose the way you have been treated by the police. You don't mean to say you haven't been beaten up?'

From the hearth behind came an unexpected sound as the old man swivelled on his stool. His eyes, small and red-rimmed as a turkey cock's, were bright with venom, and as he spoke a streak of spittle ran down the front of his collarless shirt.

'If he'd stayed home with his mother the way a dacent-rared boy should, not a hate would have happened him. But nothing for it nowadays but running off to the pictures and the music boxes. He deserved all he got, and not half good enough for him, hell slap it up him!'

The boy's face flushed, but he remained silent. Instead, his mother spoke for him.

'To tell the truth, sir, we'd as lief the matter was forgotten. It would be better for all of us, like.'

'That's right, sir. The way it is, I wouldn't make too much of it, sir.'

So there it was, plain as a pikestaff. The police had spoken not merely to the boy, but also to the mother. They were quite prepared for the boy's sake and the sake of his parents that the matter should be overlooked; in their magnanimity, they had probably provided transport, an impossible expense, otherwise, for people in their position. Whatever redress Peter could offer, whatever hope or help, would mean nothing compared to their unspecified but real threats. He would never know the truth of the incident, now: whether the boy had connections with the IRA, whether he had provoked the police; whether even, his – Peter's – interpretation of their silence was correct. Between their helplessness and his freedom lay an unbridgeable gulf and, with a despairing gesture, he turned to leave. The boy and his mother accompanied him; the former, despite half-hearted attempts to conceal it, had a distinct limp.

'I'm sorry I can't help you now, sir,' he said. His voice, though flat in tone, sounded almost kindly. As he bent his head under the door, Peter noticed that, above the bandage, his hair was plastered back in two oily swathes, like the wings of a duck.

As the Austin Ten lurched down the mountainside, Peter and his father were both silent. A storm cloud was gathering over the valley, dark as a shawl. Only the driver seemed in a jaunty mood, as he expanded on the history of the Fergusons for their benefit.

'He's not a bad lad that, you know,' he said reflectively, 'rough and all as he is. The two other boys, cute enough, sloped off to England. He was in Barnsley too, but he came back when the old man had the operation. There's many wouldn't do it.'

It was only when they had reached home that James Douglas spoke, climbing laboriously through the door his son was holding for him, onto the kerb.

'Are you still going to write that article?' he asked apprehensively, peering into Peter's face.

Peter looked at him for a moment, as though in calculation. 'I don't really know,' he said.

. . . There is a way of dealing with such incidents of course, familiar to every colonial officer from Ulster to Rhodesia. The charge is dropped or minimised, the too zealous police or soldiers reprimanded, any public fuss avoided. Perhaps as the authorities claim, it is the best way in the end. But one is left wondering in how many small Ulster towns such things are happening, at this moment, in your name!

After his return, Peter had gone straight to his bedroom to continue the article, with little success. He could not even decide, staring blankly at the paragraph he had just written, whether to give it up or not: he could get a beginning and an end, but the whole thing did not cohere into the cry, logical but passionate, for which he had been hoping. He rose to pace the room; finally, he found himself at the window, vacantly looking out down Main Street, as he had done on that first night.

It had been raining heavily for an hour or so, but now it was clearing. On the rim of the sky, just to the west of the town, a watery sun was breaking through grey clouds. Soft, almost a dawn light, it shone on the town, making the long line of the main street, from the old tower to the war memorial and beyond to the railway station, seem washed and clear.

There it was, his home town, laid out before him, bright in every detail. He knew every corner of it, had gone to school in that low concrete building, run his sleigh down that hill, had even, later, brought his first girl down the darkness of that entry. He knew every house and nearly everybody in them. One did not like or dislike this place: such emotions were irrelevant, it was a part of one's life, and therefore inescapable. Yet all through his final year at school his only thought had been to escape; the narrowness of the life, the hidden bitterness of political feeling had suddenly seemed like the regime of a prison. The Irish were supposed to be a gay race, but there was something in Ulster people, a harsh urge to reduce the human situation to its barest essentials, which frightened him. It was years before he had felt able to come back, sufficiently secure in his own beliefs to be able to survive the hostility their ways seemed to radiate.

But did that strength now give him the right to sit in judgement, particularly where an incident like this was concerned? Already, only two days afterwards, indignation had died down in the town. Was it fear or an effort to foster that good will which people like his mother thought was the only solution? Or mere passivity, the product of a commercial spirit which saw everyone as a potential customer? Whatever destiny lay in these grey walls, they might surely be left to work out on their own, two peoples linked and locked for eternity.

As he looked over the town, sober with self-judgement, suddenly from out of a laneway, as though propelled, shot a dwarf-like figure. His clothes were of various colours, and he wore a tattered cap pulled squarely over his ears. One foot was bare, the other encased in an elderly boot. Around his waist hung a bandoleer of tin cans. Peter recognised him almost at once: it was Joe Doom, the village idiot. He lived in a tiny house on his own, at the end of the town, begging pennies from passers-by, stewing scraps in his tin cans. The people teased him, fed him, tolerated him, with a charity older than state institutions, and in return, his antics, the gargles and lapses of logic which were his sole method of speech, amused them. Now he looked wildly around, at the sky, at the watery sun, at the light shining on the fronts of the houses. Then, as though focusing, he saw Peter at the window above him. Their eyes met for a moment and something like triumph entered Joe Doom's. He fumbled frantically behind his back, the line of cans shaking, and produced a piece of white cardboard. With a quick glance behind him towards the entry, as though for confirmation, he held it high above his head, so that Peter – and anyone else in the street who was watching – could read. In large crude letters, like slashes of charcoal, it spelled

Nosy ParKer
Go home

PIGEONS

MICHAEL McLAVERTY

Our Johnny kept pigeons, three white ones and a brown one that could tumble in the air like a leaf. They were nice pigeons, but they dirtied the slates and cooed so early in the morning that my daddy said that some day he would wring their bloody necks. That is a long while ago now, for we still have the pigeons, but Johnny is dead; he died for Ireland.

Whenever I think of our Johnny I always think of Saturday. Nearly every Saturday night he had something for me, maybe sweets, a toy train, a whistle, or glass marbles with rainbows inside them. I would be in bed when he'd come home; I always tried to keep awake, but my eyes wouldn't let me – they always closed tight when I wasn't thinking. We both slept together in the wee back room, and when Johnny came up to bed he always lit the gas, the gas that had no mantle. If he had something for me he would shake me and say: 'Frankie, Frankie, are you asleep?' My eyes would be very gluey and I would rub them with my fists until they would open in the gaslight. For a long while I would see gold needles sticking out of the flame, then they would melt away and the gas become like a pansy leaf with a blue heart. Johnny would be standing beside the bed and I would smile all blinky at him. Maybe he'd stick a sweet in my mouth, but if I hadn't said my prayers he'd lift me out onto the cold, cold floor. When I would be jumping in again in my shirt-

tails, he would play whack at me and laugh if he got me. Soon
he would climb into bed and tell me about the ice-cream shops,
and the bird shop that had funny pigeons and rabbits and mice
in the window. Some day he was going to bring me down the
town and buy me a black and white mouse, and a custard
bun full of ice cream. But he'll never do it now because he died
for Ireland.

On Saturdays, too, I watched for him at the back door when
he was coming from work. He always came over the waste
ground, because it was the shortest. His dungarees would be all
shiny, but they hadn't a nice smell. I would pull them off him,
and he would lift me onto his shoulder, and swing me round
and round until my head got light and the things in the kitchen
went up and down. My mammie said he had me spoilt. He
always gave me pennies on Saturday, two pennies, and I bought
a liquorice pipe with one penny and kept the other for Sunday.
Then he would go into the cold scullery to wash his black hands
and face; he would stand at the sink, scrubbing and scrubbing
and singing 'The Old Rusty Bridge by the Mill', but if you went
near him he'd squirt soap in your eye. After he had washed
himself, we would get our Saturday dinner, the dinner with the
sausages because it was payday. Johnny used to give me a bit of
his sausages, but if my mammie saw me she'd slap me for taking
the bite out of his mouth. It was a long, long wait before we
went out to the yard to the pigeons.

The pigeon shed was on the slates above the closet. There
was a ladder up to it, but Johnny wouldn't let me climb for fear
I'd break my neck. But I used to climb up when he wasn't looking. There was a great flutter and flapping of wings when
Johnny would open the trap door to let them out. They would
fly out in a line, brownie first and the white ones last. We would
lie on the waste ground at the back of our street watching them
fly. They would fly round and round, rising higher and higher

each time. Then they would fly so high we would blink our eyes and lose them in the blue sky. But Johnny always found them first. 'I can see them, Frankie,' he would say. 'Yonder they are. Look! Above the brickyard chimney.' He would put his arm around my neck, pointing with his outstretched hand. I would strain my eyes, and at last I would see them, their wings flashing in the sun as they turned towards home. They were great flyers. But brownie would get tired and he would tumble head over heels like you'd think he was going to fall. The white ones always flew down to him, and Johnny would go wild. 'He's a good tumbler, but he won't let the others fly high. I think I'll sell him.' He would look at me, plucking at the grass, afraid to look up. 'Ah, Frankie,' he would say, 'I won't sell him. Sure I'm only codding.' All day we would sit if the weather was good, watching our pigeons flying, and brownie doing somersaults. When they were tired they would light on the blue slates, and Johnny would throw corn up to them. Saturday was a great day for us and for our pigeons, but it was on Saturday that Johnny died for Ireland.

We were lying, as usual, at the back, while the pigeons were let out for a fly round. It was a lovely sunny day. Every house had clothes out on the lines, and the clothes were fluttering in the breeze. Some of the neighbours were sitting at their back doors, nursing babies or darning socks. They weren't nice neighbours for they told the rent man about the shed on the slates, and he made us pay a penny a week for it. But we didn't talk much to them, for we loved our pigeons, and on that lovely day we were splitting our sides laughing at the way brownie was tumbling, when a strange man in a black hat and Burberry coat came near us. Johnny jumped up and went to meet him. I saw them talking, with their heads bent towards the ground, and then the strange man went away. Johnny looked very sad and he didn't laugh at brownie any more. He gave me the things

out of his pockets, a penknife, a key and a little blue notebook
with its edges all curled. 'Don't say anything to Mammie. Look
after the pigeons, Frankie, until I come back. I won't be long.'
He gave my hand a tight squeeze, then he walked away without
turning round to wave at me.

All that day I lay out watching the pigeons, and when I got
tired I opened the notebook. It had a smell of fags and there was
fag dust inside it. I could read what he had written down:

Corn	2s. 6d.
Club	6d.
3 Pkts. Woodbine	6d.
Frankie	2d.

He had the same thing written down on a whole lot of pages;
if he had been at school he would have got slapped for wasting
the good paper. I put the notebook in my pocket when my
mammie called me for my tea. She asked me about Johnny and
I told her he wouldn't be long until he was back. Then it got
late. The pigeons flew off the slates and into the shed, and still
Johnny didn't come back.

It came on night. My sisters were sent out to look for him.
My daddy came home from work. We were all in now, my two
sisters and Mammie and Daddy, everyone except Johnny.
Daddy took out his pipe with the tin lid but he didn't light it.
We were all quiet, but my mother's hands would move from
her lap to her chin, and she was sighing. The kettle began humming and shuffling the lid about, and my daddy lifted it off the
fire and placed it on the warm hob. The clock on the
mantelpiece chimed eleven and my sisters blessed themselves –
it got a soul out of purgatory when you did that. They forgot
all about my bedtime and I was let stay up though my eyes felt
full of sand. The rain was falling. We could hear it slapping in
the yard and trindling down the grate. It was a blowy night for

someone's back door was banging, making the dogs bark. The newspapers that lay on the scullery floor to keep it clean began to crackle up and down with the wind till you'd have thought there was a mouse under them. A bicycle bell rang in the street outside our kitchen window and it made Mammie jump. Then a motor rattled down, shaking the house and the vases on the shelf. My daddy opened the scullery door and went into the yard. The gas blinked and a coughing smell of a chimney burning came into the kitchen. I'm sure it was Mrs Ryan's. She always burnt hers on a wet night. If the peelers caught her she'd be locked in jail, for you weren't allowed to burn your own chimney.

I wished Daddy would burn ours. It was nice to see him putting the bunch of lighted papers on the yard brush and sticking them up the wide chimney. The chimney would roar, and if you went outside you'd see lines of sparks like hot wires coming out and the smoke bubbling over like lemonade in a bottle. But he wouldn't burn it tonight, because we were waiting on Johnny.

'Is there any sign of him?' said Mammie, when Daddy came in again.

'None yet; but he'll be all right; he'll be all right. We'll say the prayers, and he'll be in before we're finished.'

We were just ready to kneel when a knock came to the back door. It was a very dim knock and we all sat still, listening. 'That's him now,' said Daddy, and I saw my mother's face brightening. Daddy went into the yard and I heard the stiff bar on the door opening and feet shuffling. 'Easy now: easy now,' said someone. Then Daddy came in, his face as white as a sheet. He said something to Mammie. 'Mother of God it isn't true – it isn't!' she said. Daddy turned and sent me up to bed.

Up in the wee room I could see down into the yard. The light from the kitchen shone into it and I saw men with black hats and the rain falling on them like little needles, but I

· couldn't see Johnny. I looked up at the shed on the slates, the
rain was melting down its sides, and the wet felt was shining like
new boots. When I looked into the yard again, Daddy was
bending over something. I got frightened and went into my
sisters' room. They were crying and I cried too, while I sat
shivering in my shirt and my teeth chattering. 'What's wrong?'
I asked. But they only cried and said: 'Nothing, son. Nothing.
Go to sleep, Frankie, like a good little boy.' My big sister put
me into her bed, and put the clothes around me and stroked my
head. Then she lay on the top of the bed beside me, and I could
feel her breathing heavily on my back. Outside it was still blowy
for the wind was kicking an empty salmon tin which rattled
along the street. For a long time I listened to the noises the wind
made, and then I slept.

In the morning when I opened my eyes I wondered at finding myself in my sisters' room. It was very still: the blinds were
down and the room was full of yellow light. I listened for the
sound of plates, a brush scrubbing, or my big sister singing. But
I heard nothing, neither inside the house nor outside it. I remembered about last night, my sisters crying because our
Johnny didn't come home. I sat up in bed; I felt afraid because
the house was strange, and I got out and went into the wee
back room.

The door was open and there was yellow light in it, too, and
the back of the bed had white cloth and I couldn't see over it.
Then I saw my mammie in the room, sitting on a chair. She
stretched out her arms and I ran across and knelt beside her,
burying my face in her lap. She had on a smooth, black dress,
and I could smell the camphor balls off it, the smell that kills the
moths, the funny things with no blood and no bones that eat
holes in your jersey. There were no holes in Mammie's dress.
She rubbed my head with her hands and said: 'You're the only
boy I have now.' I could hear her heart thumping very hard,

and then she cried, and I cried and cried, with my head down on her lap. 'What's wrong, Mammie?' I asked, looking up at her wet eyes. 'Nothing, darling: nothing, pet. He died for Ireland.' I turned my head and looked at the bed. Johnny was lying on the white bed in a brown dress. His hands were pale and they were joined around his rosary beads, and a big crucifix between them. There was a big lump of wadding at the side of his head and wee pieces up his nose. I cried more and more, and then my mammie made me put on my clothes, and go downstairs for my breakfast.

All that day my mammie stayed in the room to talk to the people that came to see our Johnny. And all the women shook hands with Mammie and they all said the same thing: 'I'm sorry for your trouble, but he died for his country.' They knelt beside the white bed and prayed, and then sat for a while looking at Johnny, and speaking in low whispers. My sisters brought them wine and biscuits, and some of them cried when they were taking it, dabbing their eyes with their handkerchiefs or the tails of their shawls. Mrs McCann came and she got wine, too, though she had told the rent man about the shed on the slates and we had to pay a penny a week. I was in the wee room when she came, and I saw her looking at the lighted candles and the flowers on the table, and up at the gas that had no mantle. But she couldn't see it because my big sister had put white paper over it, and she had done the same with the four brass knobs on the bed. She began to sniff and sniff and my mammie opened the window without saying anything. The blind began to snuffle in and out, the lighted candles to waggle, and the flowers to smell. We could hear the pigeons cooing and flapping on the shed, and I could see at the back of my eyes their necks fattening and their feathers bristling like a dog going to fight. It's well Daddy didn't hear them or he might have wrung their necks.

At night the kitchen was crammed with men and women,

and many had to sit in the cold scullery. Mrs Ryan, next door, lent us her chairs for the people to sit on. There was lemonade and biscuits and tea and porter. Some of the men, who drank black porter, gave me pennies, and they smoked and talked all night. The kitchen was full of smoke and it made your eyes sting. One man told my daddy he should be a proud man, because Johnny had died for the Republic. My daddy blinked his eyes when he heard this, and he got up and went into the yard for a long time.

The next day was the funeral. Black shiny horses with their mouths all suds, and silver buckles on their straps, came trotting into the street. All the wee lads were looking at themselves in the glossy backs of the cabs where you could see yourself all fat and funny like a dwarf. I didn't play, because Johnny was dead and I had on a new, dark suit. Jack Byrne was out playing and he told me that we had only two cabs and that there were three cabs at his daddy's funeral. There were crowds of peelers in the street, some of them talking to tall, red-faced men with over-coats and walking sticks.

Three men along with my daddy carried the yellow coffin down the stairs. There was a green, white and gold flag over it. But a thin policeman, with a black walking stick and black legg-ings, pulled the flag off the coffin when it went into the street. Then a girl snatched the flag out of the peeler's hands and he turned all pale. At the end of our street there were more peelers and every one wore a harp with a crown on his cap. Brother Gabriel used to fairly wallop us in school if we drew harps with crowns on them. One day we told him the peelers wore them on their caps. 'Huh!' he said. 'The police! the police! They don't love their country. They serve England. England, my boys! The England that chased our people to live in the damp bogs! The England that starved our ancestors till they had to eat grass and nettles by the roadside. And our poor priests had to say Mass out on the cold mountains! No, my dear boys, never draw a harp with a crown on it!' And then he got us to write in our books:

> Next to God I love thee
> Dear Ireland, my native land!

'It's a glorious thing,' he said, 'to die for Ireland, to die for Ireland!' His voice got very shaky when he said this and he turned his back and looked into the press. But Brother Gabriel is not in the school now; if he was he'd be good to me, because our Johnny died for Ireland.

The road to the cemetery was lined with people. Little boys that were at my school lifted a fringe of hair when the coffin passed. The trams were stopped in a big, long line – it was nice to see so many at one look. Outside the gates of the graveyard there was an armoured car with no one peeping his head out. Inside it was very still and warm with the sun shining. With my daddy I walked behind the carried coffin and it smelt like the new seats in the chapel. The crowds of people were quiet. You could hear the cinders on the path squanching as we walked over them, and now and again the horses snorting.

I began to cry when I saw the deep hole in the ground and the big castles of red clay at the side of it. A priest, with a purple sash round his neck, shovelled a taste of clay on the coffin and it made a hard rattle that made me cry sore. Daddy had his head bowed and there were tears in his eyes, but they didn't run down his cheeks like mine did. The priest began to pray, and I knew I'd never see Johnny again, never, never, until I'd die and go to heaven if I kept good and didn't say bad words and obeyed my mammie and my daddy. But I wouldn't like Daddy to tell me to give away the pigeons. When the prayers were over a tall man with no hat and a wee moustache stood beside

the grave and began to talk. He talked about our Johnny being
a soldier of the Republic, and, now and then, he pointed with
his finger at the grave. As soon as he stopped talking we said the
rosary and all the people went away. I got a ride back in a black
cab with my daddy and Uncle Pat and Uncle Joe. We stopped
at the Bee Hive and they bought lemonade for me and porter
for the cab driver. And then we went home.

I still have the pigeons and big Tom Duffy helps me to clean
the shed and let them out to fly. Near night I give them plenty
of corn so that they'll sleep long and not waken Daddy in the
morning. When I see them fattening their necks and cooing I
clod them off the slates.

Yesterday I was lying on the waste ground watching the
pigeons and Daddy came walking towards me smoking his pipe
with the tin lid. I tried to show him the pigeons flying through
the clouds. He only looked at them for a minute and turned
away without speaking, and now I'm hoping he won't wring
their necks.

THE MASTER AND THE BOMBS

MARY BECKETT

'No news of Matthew?'

'Any word of the Master?'

They're all asking me, every man and woman in the place, and they look queerly at me when I just say, 'No. No news, no word.' It's not that they expect me to have heard anything but to have done something, either by myself or with their advice or help. They tell me about the fine man he is and the great teacher and the shame it would be if he got into trouble he didn't deserve. Then they make vague offers. 'If there's anything at all we can do, now, let us know,' and I promise.

But why must it all depend on me? Why must I decide? I'm a woman. I'm supposed to be passive. I've got three small children, I'm expecting another. At the moment I'm dull and stupid and slow and my feet swell. I am not going to rush round from PP to MP to get Matthew out. I could do it, I suppose, for the whole thing is ridiculous. He was never out of the house long enough to belong to any illegal organisation. Still, he decided to walk out on us so I'm going to pretend to respect his decision – I'm leaving it to him. He's the man, let him act like one. Or there's nothing to prevent the men he's been brought up with acting for him. He has a brother down the street with a pub, another a bit out of town with a farm. They're all his people, strangers to me. It's not their fault, they seem kind enough, but I never know what they will do or why they do it, the way I would with people from Belfast. I hear in their talk a cold curiosity, a gathering of gossip, a lack of warmth. But then I have a great lack in myself. If my marriage with Matthew had been happier I might have warmed to his neighbours more; or if I had been among my own people I might have warmed to Matthew more. But there it is.

The school should open on Monday. It will be a bit of a puzzle to everybody if he's not there to open it, but it will be a great relief to Matthew. I don't know is he as bad at his job as he thinks he is. The people now say he's grand but some parents and priests have been difficult to deal with and inspectors have criticised him and every time it happens he gets into a state. If he had got the pub or the farm instead of the education, he'd be a far happier man and easier to live with, I suppose. And still, it was because he was a teacher that I talked to him that first time I met him at a dance in Belfast. I have always thought it must be very exciting to be a teacher, to show children how many ways there are of using their minds. Of course people tell me it isn't like that at all, that I don't know what I'm talking about, but I've had teachers myself who were enthusiastic. Anyway, when Matthew told me he was a teacher I asked him all kinds of questions about it and he thought I had taken a fancy to him and he left me home.

Now when he comes in after a bad day at school and he has a beaten look in those big liquid brown eyes of his, appealing to me for comfort and sympathy, as he has every right to, I'm useless. I feel nothing but revulsion – I have to get away from him, out to a different room, not to breathe the same air that he sighs out of him. All I can do is wait until he has himself in hand again and then tell him to change his job, to take any other work under the sun that wouldn't torment him, even for far less money. We could manage. But he says he can't because of the children. What about the children now? Where is next month's pay to come from? He had no children before he married me; there was nothing to stop him changing then.

That's why I welcomed the holidays even though there were days I was sure the top of my head must be blown straight off with temper and bits of me stain the ceiling like out of the pressure cooker. He'd just sit there reading the newspaper in front of the fire, letting the fire go out, never giving me any offer of help. Only he'd tut-tut if Margaret and John were fighting or if Margaret put her dirty wee fingers on his trouser leg, so that in the middle of all my washing or baking or the baby's feed I'd have to whirl John and his tricycle out to the front path and Margaret through the back door to her sandpit. Then I'd try to remind myself that men need peace or that his suits had to last him a long time now so that he has to be careful. He'd continue reading the paper but I'd say he wasn't reading it; there never was enough in any paper to give such long reading. He must have been sitting there hating me – much more than I hated him because I was busy and I had the baby. It's impossible for me to bath the baby, to play with her or indeed to take her on my knee at all and not feel all my irritation melt away. I'd find myself saying, 'Look, Matthew. Look at her.' Only he never did look in time to catch whatever little unimportant thing she'd done that delighted me. I cannot easily forgive him for ignoring the children, especially now when he has withdrawn every support. 'You can take me away, Officer. I am entirely responsible.' That's what he said to those two astonished policemen that called last Wednesday. 'Officer'! Like in a silly detective story. And away he went off with them without even turning back into the house to tell me. He didn't know what to say to me of course, since I knew it was all nonsense. The policemen had found bombs or grenades or something like that in the school coal shed. They wanted to know had Matthew seen anyone in particular going in or out. It was a perfectly reasonable question. We live next door to the school and even though it's been shut all summer Matthew has the keys and goes over now and again to do records and to get peace from the children and me. He wouldn't go near the coal shed – it hasn't been used since Easter and won't again until the children have been thoroughly frozen for a few weeks in late autumn. I was waiting to hear what long-drawn-out account he would give of every passing cyclist that used the school lavatory – it's a thing annoys him. 'You can take me away, Officer. I am entirely responsible.' That's what I heard. And he just drops all his own real responsibilities off him – wife, children, work. He escapes from them all to a nice peaceful cell where nobody will expect anything from him and if he's brought to court he'll refuse to recognise the court and so he won't have to say anything. It's all so easy. That's what makes me mad. There are times I think I won't let him, that I'll go and tell the authorities that he suffers from delusions or brainstorms and really cannot be blamed for what he says. Everybody knows he had no hand, act or part in putting those things there to be a danger to all the children once the school would open. But he wouldn't like to be let home because he's a kind of an idiot. I couldn't do it to him. I don't wish him anything but good. I owe him a lot, poor Matthew, for he's done a lot more for me than ever I do for him.

Looking back I suppose I should never have married him, but it's easy to forget how unsettled I was then, how empty. And I wanted peace. Well, I got peace. Then, I would have never believed it possible that there could come such a dearth of desire so soon. That old mahogany bed he bought in an auction has always sagged down under his weight at his side and I spend all the warm nights clinging on to my edge so as not to roll down against him. If there was one flicker of love between us that would be a cause for laughing, but there never has been. He never loved me nor did he pretend to, either before or after we married. I had neither love nor respect for him and I never pretended to myself these things would grow. We were both lonely but we didn't help each other's loneliness; we didn't alter it at all.

We had started writing letters to each other but his mannered sentences annoyed me and I had stopped. Then one Saturday morning I was down town and I had that feeling of empty misery I used to have so often. It put black blinkers at the side of my eyes. It wasn't the kind of full sadness you can cry with and get relief; just a feeling of being useless and unwanted and of dwindling instead of growing. I was doing simple uninteresting work in a dull office, I read bits of silly plays in a playreading group, I went to an odd dance. My mother had died when we were small, my two brothers had left home, one as a radio officer on a boat, the other to Kenya. I was alone with my father but he didn't like my interfering with the housekeeping. He had had to do it so long himself he thought his was the only way. He had done his best for us. He had worried that we should be warmly clothed and well-fed and into jobs but all the affection went out of the house when my mother died. It was crowded down town that Saturday and a policewoman was at the pedestrian crossing. I stood among the crowd waiting to cross and it suddenly came to me that it was a very unimportant thing that I was unhappy. I had to put back my head and take breath because the thought came with such force. And when we were let cross I got an excitement out of the pushing two-way jostle of people and I felt it mattered only to be alive and to use every bit of one's life and that the only way I could do that was to have children. Matthew would do better than waiting around till I was past use because happiness was only the froth on the drink and a flat drink would quench thirst just as well as a fizzy one.

And of course I've had odd puffs of happiness – what else makes me lie with a great beaming silly smile on my face just after my babies are born? I'm good at having babies; I practise breathing beforehand, I go to the hospital at the right time, I make no fuss. If I lost control of myself like a few women I've heard in the labour ward and made that awful animal roaring or even if I whinged and complained, I should be ashamed. I should feel, I suppose, as Matthew does about his teaching. But I have found through him that one thing I can do with satisfaction. Another thing; though I'm lonely still – God knows I was never lonelier – I have a shield for my loneliness. Nobody need know and pity me. Matthew has found no addition to himself in his life with me.

I satisfy his appetites, nothing more, and I'm not even going to do that much longer. This is the last baby I'm having. Four is enough for us if I'm to rear them properly and be warm and sweet and loving as I remember my mother, not always tired and crabbed as I am. Anyway, we haven't really enough money for more even if Matthew doesn't lose his job. So we'll have to talk it over together after this baby is born and come to some arrangement to take care. It's a funny thing; these four were conceived without any love or friendship between us but we won't be able to stop having babies unless we manage to talk to each other with understanding. Once I get myself screwed up to it I know Matthew will agree in practice, but he might sulk. I've never allowed myself to long for affection between us, but now and again I have seen warmth and kindness in a man's face greeting his wife and her smile welcoming him and I imagine how beautiful it would be if Matthew would say then, 'My poor Helen, you've had it hard. You need a rest.' I don't think he could manage endearments but he could manage that. He won't though – but maybe I could to him when he comes home if I didn't sound too much of a hypocrite: 'My poor

Matthew, you've had a hard time. Come on and we'll be friends. Don't be out with me any longer.' Oh, I'd need to practise being a nice wife to him the way I've practised to give birth. But the way I am now I have no energy for anything extra – I've been married five years and this is my fourth child.

You see, I should sympathise with Matthew running away to prison. I've been doing it all along since my first pregnancy. It was a different world I discovered. I was placid, I was contented. Nothing penetrated me. I stopped aching for the people who were poor or lost or cold. I read books and couldn't remember a word of them. I sat in company with my hands in my lap not offering a word to the conversation. At Christmas I was so besotted that instead of talking to Christ in the stable I talked to Him as if He were the child moving in my own womb. I would have shared all this with Matthew, but he didn't seem to want to hear, nor to feel the child kicking nor to be seen out with me. So I didn't tell him about my discomforts either, although he saw me limping with the sciatica I have had with each of them. When my legs cramped at night I got up and came downstairs. When the doctor told me I must rest I didn't bother him. He never had the slightest worry passed on to him because he couldn't share my joy which was so much greater than all the pains I've ever known. Each time, though, when the baby was three or four months old the numbness began to wear off and the old pins and needles started pestering me again. I don't know what this inner restlessness is I suffer from. I used to think when I'd get married it would go but it's nothing to do with marriage. I don't understand it. I don't know how to cope with it so I dive back into pregnancy again. Only each time the weariness and worries are greater and now this time I have to search deep to find any joy.

I suppose I'd better go and see Matthew. The thought of all the effort it needs is what has kept me at home – that and the blessed peace we've all enjoyed in the house this week. I'll have to give the children their dinner, clean them up and park them with somebody and listen to the baby screaming – because that's the stage she's at – when I leave to catch the afternoon bus. I don't know what time of day or day of the week visiting is allowed. Maybe I should go down to Tom and ask him instead could he leave the pub for an afternoon and go and see Matthew for me. James would be too busy in the fields at this time. He might be able to find out better than I would from Matthew what he would like done. Not that Matthew seems intimate with either of them. I keep up visits and invitations to them and their families because they're fine, steady, cheerful people and I think their company good for the children. 'Uncles are joky men,' Margaret says and it's well she should see plenty of joky men. Matthew is ill at ease with them, mutters and mumbles so that they don't know what he's saying. It's peculiar that they who left school at fourteen should seem richer in themselves, more complete than Matthew who was at school, university and training college. We have queer ideas about education in this country; instead of looking on it as a furnishing of our minds so that we can use every room in them, we make it a ladder up the outside wall where we teeter round in every cold wind that blows.

Still, it's one of the few things in the world I'd be prepared to drop bombs about – the freedom to bring up my children with my attitude to God and people and work and money. I'd rather see them blown to bits or wasting with these diseases we hear about than systematically deprived of heaven. It would be big bombs I'd need though if that danger ever arose, not coal-shed hand grenades just big enough to kill or disfigure a few of the neighbours' children while they'd be playing.

I must go round the people I know in this town and impress on them that Matthew had nothing to do with endangering their children. They know he hadn't, but they might have doubts and I have none. He wouldn't even let a broken milk bottle lie in the yard a minute longer than he could help. I have kindly feelings for Matthew when I'm lying comfortably in the middle of a cool bed, but in the daytime when I meet people I find it difficult to do more than answer their civil enquiries. I must though, for once that's settled I've been thinking it might help Matthew to stay for a while in jail – provided we can get something to live on.

There's an aura about people here who have been in on political charges. I was told a few years ago by a shopkeeper, 'All the brave men in Ireland are in Crumlin Road jail.' He meant it too. It's dishonesty of course. It's stealing from men who are all old now but Matthew needs something and maybe this is the only way he can get it, although it seems shameful to me. Maybe while he's in his reputation will increase, if only in his own mind, so that he will imagine another side to his empty life as a revolutionary in a trench coat. A starving man is allowed to steal and he has shown that his real life is unbearable. It might give him a lift to come back and find himself even a little bit of a hero.

A BELFAST WOMAN

MARY BECKETT

I mind well the day the threatening letter came. It was a bright morning, and warm, and I remember thinking while I was dressing myself that it would be nice if the Troubles were over so that a body could just enjoy the feel of a good day. When I came down the stairs the hall was dark but I could see the letter lying face down. I lifted it and just my name was on the envelope, 'Mrs Harrison' in red felt pen. I knew what it was. There was a page of an exercise book inside with 'Get out or we'll burn you out' all in red with bad printing and smeared. I just went in and sat at the kitchen table with the note in front of me. I never made myself a cup of tea even. It was a shock, though God knows I shouldn't have been surprised.

One of the first things I remember in my life was wakening up with my mother screaming downstairs when we were burnt out in 1921. I ran down in my nightgown and my mother was standing in the middle of the kitchen with her hands up to her face screaming and screaming and the curtains were on fire and my father was pulling them down and stamping on them with the flames catching the oilcloth on the floor. Then he shouted: 'Sadie, the children', and she stopped screaming and said: 'Oh God, Michael, the children', and she ran upstairs and came down with the baby in one arm and Joey under the other, and my father took Joey in his arms and me by the hand and we ran out along the street. It was a warm summer night and the fires were crackling all over the place and the street was covered with broken glass. It wasn't until we got into my grandmother's house that anybody noticed that I had nothing on but my nightie and nothing on my feet and they were cut. It was all burnt, everything they had. My mother used to say she didn't save as much as a needle and thread. I wasn't able to sleep for weeks, afraid I'd be wakened by that screaming.

We stayed in my grandmother's house until 1935 and my grandmother was dead by that time and my father too, for he got TB like many another then. He used to say, 'When you have no house and no job sure what use are you?' and then he'd get fits of coughing. In 1935 when we got the letter threatening to burn us out I said to my mother, 'We'll gather our things and we'll go.' So we did and like all the rest of them in our street we went up to Glenard to the new houses. When we showed our 'Get out or we'll burn you out' note they gave us a house and we'd enough out to get things fixed up. We got new jobs in another mill, my mother and Patsy and me. Only my mother never liked it there. She always said the air was too strong for her. It was cold right enough, up close to the mountains. But when I was getting married to William, and his aunt who was a Protestant gave him the key of her house in this street, my mother was in a terrible state – 'Don't go into that Protestant street, Mary, or you'll be a sorry girl,' and she said we could live with her. But I didn't want William to pine like my poor father, so here we came and not a day's trouble until the note came.

Mind you, the second night we were here there was trouble in the Catholic streets across the road. We heard shots first and then the kind of rumbling, roaring noises of all the people out on the streets. I wanted to get up and run out and see what was wrong but William held on to me in bed and he said: 'They don't run out on the street here. They stay in.' And it was true. They did. I was scared lying listening to the noise the way I never was when I was out with my neighbours. It turned out some poor young lad had stayed at home when he should have gone back to the British Army and they sent the police for him. He got out of the back window and ran down the entry and the police ran after him and shot him dead. They said their gun went off by accident but the people said they beat him up. When I went over the next day I saw him laid out in the wee room off the kitchen and his face had all big yellowy-greenish blotches on it. I never mentioned it to my new neighbours and they never mentioned it to me.

I couldn't complain about them. They were good decent people. They didn't come into the house for a chat or a loan of tea or milk or sugar like the neighbours in Glenard or North Queen Street but they were ready to help at any time. I didn't know the men much because they had work so they didn't stand around the corners the way I was used to. But when Liam was born they all helped and said what a fine baby he was. He was too. Nine pounds with black hair and so strong he could lift his head and look round at a week old. They were always remarking on his mottled skin – purply kind of measles when he'd be up out of the pram – and said it was the sign of a very strong baby. At that time I had never seen a baby with any other colour of skin – I suppose Catholic babies had to be strong to get by. But when Eileen was born a year and ten months later she was different. She had beautiful creamy skin. She was plump and perfect and I loved her more than Liam, God forgive me, and more than William and more than anybody in the world and I wanted everything to be right for her. I thought to myself if I was a Protestant now we'd have just the two and no more and I'd be able to look after them and do well for them. So I didn't act fair with William at all.

Then I started having trouble. I looked as if I was expecting again and my stomach was hard and round but I had bleeding and I could feel no life so I was afraid. I went to the doctor and he said, 'No, Mrs Harrison, you're not pregnant. There is something here we shall have to look into.' And I said, 'Is it serious, doctor?' and he said, 'I can't tell you that, can I, until you go into hospital and have it investigated' and I said, 'Do you mean an operation?' and he said, 'I do, Mrs Harrison.' I came home saying to myself it's cancer and who will rear my Eileen and Liam. I remembered hearing it said that once they put the knife into you, you were dead in six months so I made up my mind I'd have no operation and I'd last out as long as I could. Every year I was able to look after them would be a year gained and the bigger they were the better they'd be able to do without me. But oh dear it was terrible hard on everybody. I told William and my mother and Patsy there was nothing at all the matter with me but they knew to look at me it wasn't true. I was a real blay colour and I was so tired I was ready to drop. I'd sit down by the fire at night when the children were in bed and my eyes would close and if I opened them I'd see William staring at me with such a tortured look on his face I'd have to close them again so that I wouldn't go and lean my head against him and tell him the whole thing. I knew if I did that he'd make me go back to the doctor and I'd be done for. At times I'd see against my closed eyes the white long roots of the cancer growing all over my inside and I'd remember the first time William brought me to see his father in the country.

He had a fine labourer's cottage for he was a Protestant and was head ploughman to some rich farmer down there. He was a good man. William's mother was a Catholic and she died when William was a wee boy but they brought him up a Catholic because it had been promised. He was cross-looking though, and I was a bit nervous of him. He had his garden all planted in rows and squares and he was digging clods in one corner and breaking them up fine and I could see all the long white roots and threads he was shaking the mud out of and he turned to us and he said: 'Sitfast and scutch! Sitfast and scutch! They're the plague of my life. No matter how much I weed there's more in the morning.' I told him about my grandfather and the big elderberry tree that grew behind the wee house he'd got in the country when he was burnt out in Lisburn. It wasn't there when he went into the house and when he noticed it first it was only a wee bit of a bush but it grew so quickly it blocked out all the light from his back window. Then one summer it was covered with black slimy kind of flies so he cut it down to the stump, but it started growing again straight away. One day when my father took Patsy and Joey and me down to visit him he had dug all around the stump and he was trying to pull it out with a rope. He told my father to pull with him. My father tried but then he leant against the wall with his face pale and covered with sweat. My grandfather said. 'Are you finished, Michael?' and my father said, 'I'm clean done', and my grandfather said, 'God help us all' and brought us into the house and gave us lemonade. It was just after that my father went into the sanatorium and my mother was all the time bringing him bottles of lemonade. At the funeral I asked my grandfather if he got the stump out and he didn't know for a minute what I was talking about. Then he said, 'No, no. Indeed the rope's still lying out there. I must bring it in or it'll rot.' I never saw him again, never saw the wee house either. My mother never was one for the country.

She wasn't old herself when she died – not that much over fifty, but she looked an old woman. She wore a shawl at times and not many did that any more. She was always fussing about my health and me going to the doctor but I managed fine without. I didn't look much. I had this swollen stomach and I got into the way of hiding it with my arms. But every year I got through I'd say to myself, wasn't I right to stick it out. When the war finished and the free health came, everybody thought I'd get myself seen to, and my mother was at me she'd mind Liam and Eileen. Of course there were no more children but I kept those two lovely. There was no Protestant child better fed or better dressed than those two, and I always warned them to fight with nobody, never to get into trouble. If any of the children started to shout at them about being Catholics or Fenians or Taigs they were just to walk away, not to run mind you, but just walk home. And Liam was the best boy ever. He wasn't great at his lessons but the masters said how pleasant and good he was. Eileen was inclined to be a bit bold and that was the cause of the only terrible thing I ever did. I can't believe even now how I came to do it. It was the week after my mother had died.

I blamed myself for what happened to my mother. I should have seen in time that she wasn't well and made her mind herself and she'd have lasted better. She came into my house one day with her shawl on and I was going to say I wished she'd wear a coat and not have my neighbours passing remarks, but she hung the shawl up on the back of the door and she looked poorly. She said she'd had a terrible pain in her chest and she had been to the doctor and he'd told her it was her heart. She was to rest and take tablets. She had other wee tablets to put under her tongue if she got a pain and she was not to go up hills. She looked so bad I put her to bed in the wee room off the kitchen. She never got up again. She had tense crushing pains and the tablets did no good. Sometimes the sip of Lourdes water helped her. The doctor said he could do nothing for her unless she went into hospital and she wouldn't hear of that. 'Ah, no, no. I'm just done, that's all.' Every now and again she'd say this would never have happened if she hadn't been burnt out of her home down near the docks and had to go half-roads up the mountains with all the hills and the air too strong for her. 'And

your father wouldn't ever have got consumption if he hadn't
had to move in with my mother and spend his days at the street
corner. You wouldn't remember it, Mary. You were too small,'
she'd say and I never contradicted her, 'but we hadn't left as
much as a needle and thread. The whole block went up.
Nothing left.' She was buried from our house even though she
kept saying she must go home. She had a horror of my
Protestant neighbours even though she liked well enough the
ones she met. But at her funeral, better, kinder, decenter neighbours you could not get. When it was over, all I could do was
shiver inside myself as if my shelter had been taken away.
William was good to me, always good to me, but I had to keep
a bit of myself to myself with him. My mother never looked for
anything from me. I'd tell her what I needed to tell her and
she'd listen but she never interfered. And she was as proud of
Liam and Eileen as I was. I'd see the way she looked at them.

The week after she died Eileen came home from school
crying. She was ten years of age and she didn't often cry. She
showed me the mark on her legs where the head-teacher had
hit her with a cane. A big red mark it was, right across the back
of her legs. And she had lovely skin on her legs, lovely creamy
skin. When I think of it I can still see that mark. I didn't ask
her what happened. I just lifted my mother's shawl from where
it was still hanging on the back of the kitchen door and I flung
it round me and ran down to the school. I knocked the door
and she opened it herself, the head-teacher, because the most
of the school had gone home. She took one look at me and ran
away back into a classroom. I went for her. She ran into another
room off it and banged the door. My arm stuck in through the
glass panel and I pulled it out with a big deep cut from my wrist
to my elbow. She didn't come out of the door and I never
spoke to her at all. There were a couple of other teachers over
a bit and a few children about but I couldn't say anything to

anybody and they just stood. To stop the blood pouring so much I held my arm up out of my mother's shawl as I went back up the street. There was a woman standing at her door near the top of the street. She was generally at her door knitting, that woman. She had very clever children and some of them did well. One got to be a teacher, another was in the Post Office, which is about as far as a clever poor Catholic can get. She asked me what happened but when I couldn't answer she said, 'You'd need to get to the hospital, missus. I'll get my coat and go with you.' I didn't want to go to any hospital. I just wanted to go home and wash off all the blood but my head was spinning so I let myself be helped on the bus. They stitched it up and wanted me to stay in for the night but I was terrified they'd operate on me just when I was managing so well. I insisted I couldn't because the children were on their own and Mrs O'Reilly came with me right to the end of my own street. 'If your neighbours ask what happened, just tell them you fell off the bus,' she told me. 'You don't want them knowing all about your business.' I've heard she was from the west of Ireland.

When I went into the kitchen I was ready to drop but Eileen started screaming and crying and saying how ashamed of me she was and that she'd never go back to school again. Liam made me a cup of tea and stood looking worried at me. When William came in from work he helped me to bed and was kind and good but I could see by the cut of his mouth that he was shocked and offended at me. It took a long time to heal and the scar will never leave me. The story went around the parish in different ways. Some said I hit the teacher. Some said she knifed me. I was too ashamed ever to explain.

Eileen never was touched in school after that, though, and when she left she learnt shorthand and typing and got an office job. She grew up lovely, and I used to think, watching her going out in the morning in the best of clothes with her hair shining, that she could have gone anywhere and done herself credit. She wasn't contented living where we did. At first I didn't understand what she wanted. I thought she wanted a better house in a better district. I didn't know how we could manage it but I made up my mind it would have to be done. I went for walks up round the avenues where there were de-tached houses with gardens and when I saw an empty house I'd peer in through the windows. Then one day a woman from the parish, who worked cleaning one of those houses, saw me and asked me in because the people of the house were out all day. Seeing it furnished with good solid shining furniture, I knew we'd never manage it. In the sitting room there was an old-fashioned copper canopy and when I looked into it I could see the whole room reflected smaller, like a fairy tale with flowers and books and pictures and plates on the wall. I knew it wasn't for us. How could I go in and out there? William and Liam wouldn't look right in their working clothes. Only Eileen would fit in. I was a bit sad but relieved because at no time could I see where the money would have come from. I told her that night when she came in but she looked at me all puzzled. 'But that wasn't what I meant, Mammy,' she said. 'I have to get away from everything here. There's no life for me here. I'm thinking of going to Canada.' That was before any trouble at all here. People now would say that was in the good times when you could get in a bus and go round the shops or into the pictures and nothing would have happened by the time you came home except that the slack would have burnt down a bit on the fire.

Off she went anyway and got a job and wrote now and again telling us how well off she was. In no time at all she was married and was sending photographs first of this lovely bungalow and then of her two wee girls with the paddling pool in her garden or at their swing when they were a bit bigger. I was glad she was doing so well. It was the kind of life I had reared her for and dreamt of for her only I wished she and her children were not so far away. I kept inviting her home for a visit but I knew it would cost far too much money. Only I thought if she was homesick it would help her to know we wanted to see her too. Once the Troubles came I stopped asking her.

Liam at that time was getting on well too. He was always such a nice pleasant big fellow that a plumber in the next street to ours asked him to join in his business at putting in fireplaces and hot-water pipes. He put in a lovely fireplace for me with a copper canopy like the one I'd seen years before and built me a bathroom and hot water and put in a sink unit for me till I was far better off than any of my neighbours even though a lot of them had their houses very nice too. They were able to get paint from the shipyard of course, and marble slabs and nice bits of mahogany. He got married to a nice wee girl from the Bone and they got a house up in one of the nice streets in Ardoyne – up the far end in what they call now a mixed area. It's all gone now, poor Liam's good way of living. When that street of houses up there was put on fire in 1972 his wife Gemma insisted on coming back to the Bone and squatting in an empty house. They did their best to fix it up but it's old and dark. Then when the murders got bad his partner asked him not to come back to work any more because he'd been threatened for working with a Catholic. I was raging when Liam told me, raging about what a coward the plumber was but then as Liam said, you can't blame a man for not wanting to be murdered. So there he is – no work and no house and a timid wife and a family of lovely wee children. He had plenty to put up with. But where else could I go when I got the note. I sat looking round my shining kitchen and the note said, 'Get out or we'll burn you out', and where could I go for help but to Liam.

Still I was glad William was dead before it happened. He

would have been so annoyed. He felt so ashamed when the Protestants did something nasty. I could swallow my own shame every time the IRA disgraced us. I lived with it the same as I lived with the memory of my own disgrace when I went for the teacher and ripped my arm. But William had always been such a good upright man, he could never understand wickedness. Even the way he died showed it. He was a carter all his days, always in steady work, but for a while before he died they were saying to him that nobody had horses any more and they were changing to a lorry. He could never drive a lorry. He was afraid he'd be on the dole. It wasn't the money he was worrying about for I kept telling him it would make little difference to us – just the two of us, what did it matter. It was his pride that was upset. For years there was a big notice up on a corner shop at the bottom of the Oldpark Road. It said: 'Drivers, dismount. Don't overload your horses going up the hill.' He used to remark on it. It irked him if he didn't obey it. So one day in March when there was an east wind he collapsed on the hill and died the next day in hospital with the same disease as my mother.

There was a young doctor in the hospital asked me did I need a tranquilliser or a sleeping tablet or something to get over the shock. I told him no, that I never took any tablets, that I had had cancer when I was in my twenties and that I was still alive in my fifties with never a day in bed. He was curious and he asked me questions and then he said, 'Mrs Harrison, of course I can't be absolutely sure, but I'd say it was most unlikely you had cancer. Maybe you needed a job done on your womb. Maybe you even needed your womb removed but I would be very, very surprised if you had cancer. You wouldn't be here now if you had.' So I went in and knelt down at William's side. He still had that strained, worried look, even then. All I could think was: 'Poor William. Poor William. Poor, poor, poor William.'

It wasn't that I was lonely without him for I'd kept him at a distance for a long time, but the days had no shape to them. I could have my breakfast, dinner and tea whatever time I liked or I needn't have them at all. For a while I didn't bother cooking for myself, just ate tea and bread. Then Liam's wife, Gemma, said the butcher told her that I hadn't darkened his door since William died and that if I wouldn't cook for myself I'd have to come and have my dinner with them. So I thought to myself I wasn't being sensible and I'd only be a nuisance to them if I got sick so I fixed everything to the clock as if there was no such thing as eternity. Until that morning the note came and then I just sat, I didn't look at the clock. I didn't make a cup of tea. I didn't know how long I stayed. I felt heavy, not able to move. Then I thought maybe Liam could get somebody with a van to take out my furniture and I could think later where to go. I took my rosary beads from under my pillow and my handbag with my money and my pension book and Eileen's letters and the photographs of her children and I shut the door behind me. There wasn't a soul in the street but there was nothing odd about that. You'll always know you're in a Protestant street if it's deserted. When I went across the road to get to Liam's house there were children playing and men at the corner and women standing at the doors in the sun and a squad of nervous-looking soldiers down at the other end.

Liam wasn't in but Gemma and the children were. The breakfast table wasn't cleared and Gemma was feeding the youngest. When he finished she stood him up on her lap and he reached over her shoulder trying to reach the shiny new handle Liam had put on the door. He was sturdy and happy and he had a warm smell of milk and baby powder. I wanted to hold him but I was afraid of putting her out of her routine. Sometimes I wonder if she has a routine – compared to the way I reared mine. Nothing was allowed to interrupt their feeding times and sleeping times. Maybe I was wrong and I'll never know what way Eileen managed hers. I would have liked to do the dishes too but I was afraid it might look like criticising. After a wee while chatting Gemma got up to put the child in his pram and make us a cup of tea. 'You don't look great, Granny,' she said. 'Are you minding yourself at all?' I opened my bag and showed her the note.

She screamed and put her hands up to her face and the baby was startled and cried and bounced up and down in his pram with his arms up to be lifted. I said, 'Don't scream, Gemma. Don't ever scream, do you hear me', and I unstrapped the baby and hugged him. She stared at me, surprised, and it stopped her. 'You'll have to come and stay here,' she said. 'We'll fit you in.' She gave a kind of a look around and I could see her thinking where on earth she could fit me in. Still, where could I go? 'All I wanted was for Liam to get a van and take out my stuff,' I explained. 'Maybe my sister Patsy would have more room than you.' She took the baby and gave me my cup of tea. 'You'll come here,' she said. 'You'll count this your home and we'll be glad to have you.' She was a good kind girl, Gemma, and when Liam came in he was the same; only anxious to make me welcome and he went off to get the van.

After a while Gemma said, 'Write to Eileen straight away. She's the one you should be living with anyway – not all alone over yonder. All her money and her grand house. She's the one should have you.' I laughed but it hurt me a bit to hear it said. 'What would I do in Eileen's grand house in Canada? How would I fit in?' And Gemma said: 'You could keep her house all shining. She'd use you for that. Where would you see the like of your own house for polish! You'd do great for Eileen.' I looked round her own few bits and pieces – no look on anything, and a pile of children's clothes on the floor waiting to be washed and the children running in and out and knocking things over. Mary, my wee godchild, came and stood leaning against my knees, sucking her thumb. She was wearing one of the dresses I make for them. In the spring when I was fitting it on her I was noticing how beautiful her skin was with little pin-prick freckles on the pink and white and I was thinking when she's so lovely what must Eileen's children be like. Then she turned her head and looked at me and her eyes were full of love – for me! I couldn't get over it. Since then sometimes she'd just hold my hand. When Liam came back I said, 'Liam, I'm going home. I'm sorry about the bother. I just got frightened but you can cancel the van. I'm going home and I'm staying home. I've a Protestant house to the right of me and a Protestant house to the left of me. They'll not burn me out.' They argued with me and they were a bit upset but I knew they were relieved and I stuck to it.

Liam insisted on going back to the house with me although since the murders started I had never let him come down my side of the road. There was a Land Rover with soldiers in it not far from my door and no flames, no smoke. But when I opened the door, such a mess. There was water spouting out of a broken pipe in the wall where they had pulled out my sink. The Sacred Heart statue and the wee red lamp were broken on the floor. My copper canopy was all dinged. The table had big hatchet marks on it. The cover on the couch was ripped and the stuffing pulled out. And filth. For months I thought I could get the smell of that filth. I wouldn't let Liam turn off the water until I had it washed away. We cleaned up a bit but Liam said he'd have to get help before he could do much and not to touch the electric because the water had got into it. He had been very quiet so I jumped when he shouted at the soldiers once he went out the door. They drove up very slowly and he was shouting and waving his arms and calling them names. One of them looked into the house and started to laugh. Liam yelled at him about me being a widow woman living alone and that they were here to protect me but one of them said, 'You've got it wrong. We're here to wipe out the IRA.'

'Oh, Liam,' I said, 'go home. Go home before harm befalls you', and he shook his fist at the soldiers and shouted, 'I'm going now but I'll be back and I won't be on my own then. Just look out. I'm warning you.' He turned and ran off down the street and the soldier turned and looked after him and I thought he was lifting up his gun and I grabbed at his arm and the gun went off into the air and I begged, 'Don't shoot at him. Oh don't shoot him.' He said, 'Missus, I have no intention . . .' and then I fell against the wall and when I came to they were making me drink whiskey out of a bottle. It made me cough and splutter but it brought me round. They weren't bad to me I must admit. When I was on my feet they corked up the bottle and put it back in the Land Rover and drove off. Not one of my neighbours came out and all evening when I worked at tidying up and all night when I sat up to keep watch, not one of them knocked at my door.

Next day Liam brought back two other lads and they fixed up the electricity and the water. It took a while to get everything decent again but they were in and out every day, sometimes three or four of them and it never cost me a penny. Then a queer thing happened. My neighbours began moving out. The woman next door told me out of the side of her mouth that they had all been threatened. I didn't understand how a whole Protestant area could be threatened but out they all went. Of course I know they can always get newer, better houses when they ask for them and indeed there was a lot of shooting and wrecking on the front of the road, but still I often wondered what was the truth of it. Maybe I'm better off not knowing. As they left, Catholics from across the road moved in – mostly older people and I have good friends among them although it took us a while to get used to each other. I didn't take easy to people expecting to open my door and walk in at any hour of the day. They thought I was a bit stiff. I have no time for long chats and I never liked gossip. But Mrs Mulvenna, next door now, has a son in Australia – farther away than my Eileen and I think sons are even worse at writing home. I listen to her and I feel for her and I show her my photographs. I didn't tell her when Eileen wrote about how ashamed she was of us all and how she didn't like to let on she was Irish. I see talk like that in the papers too. It's not right to put the blame on poor powerless people. The most of us never did anything but stay quiet and put up with things the way they were. And we never taught our children to hate the others nor filled their heads with their wrongs the way it's said we did. When all the young people thought they could fix everything with marches and meetings I said it wouldn't work and they laughed at me. 'All you old ones are awful bitter,' they said and they jeered when Hannah in the shop and I were warning them, 'It'll all lead to shooting and burning and murder.'

Still, last November a man came round here trying to sell venetian blinds. Some of the houses have them but I said no, I liked to see out. I pointed to the sunset behind Divis – bits of red and yellow in the sky and a sort of mist all down the mountain that made it nearly see-through. The man looked at it for a minute and then he said, 'Do you know Belfast has the most beautiful sunsets in the whole world?' I said I didn't because I'd never been any place else to look at sunsets and he said, 'They tell me Belfast has the best and do you know why? It's because of all the smoke and dirt and dust and pollution. And it seems to me,' he said, 'it seems to me that if the dirt and dust and smoke and pollution of Belfast just with the help of the sun can make a sky like that, then there's hope for all of us.' He nodded and winked and touched his hat and went off and

I went in and sat down at the table. And thinking of it I started to laugh, for it's true. There is hope for all of us. Well, anyway, if you don't die you live through it, day in, day out.

FATHER AND SON

BERNARD Mac LAVERTY

ecause I do not sleep well I hear my father rising to go to work. I know that in a few minutes he will come in to look at me sleeping. He will want to check that I came home last night. He will stand in his bare feet, his shoes and socks in his hand, looking at me. I will sleep for him. Downstairs I hear the snap of the switch on the kettle. I hear him not eating anything, going about the kitchen with a stomach full of wind. He will come again to look at me before he goes out to his work. He will want a conversation. He climbs the stairs and stands breathing through his nose with an empty lunch box in the crook of his arm, looking at me.

This is my son who let me down. I love him so much it hurts but he won't talk to me. He tells me nothing. I hear him groan and see his eyes flicker open. When he sees me he turns away, a heave of bedclothes in his wake.

'Wake up, son. I'm away to my work. Where are you going today?'
  'What's it to you?'
  'If I know what you're doing I don't worry as much.'
  'Shit.'

I do not sleep. My father does not sleep. The sound of

ambulances crisscrosses the dark. I sleep with the daylight. It is
safe. At night I hear his bare feet click as he lifts them, walking
the lino. The front door shudders as he leaves.

My son is breaking my heart. It is already broken. Is it my fault
there is no woman in the house? Is it my fault a good woman
should die? His face was never softer than when after I had
shaved. A baby pressed to my shaved cheek. Now his chin is
sandpaper. He is a man. When he was a boy I took him fishing.
I taught him how to tie a blood-knot, how to cast a fly, how
to strike so the fish would not escape. How to play a fish. The
green bus to quiet days in Toome. Him pestering me with
questions. If I leave him alone he will break my heart anyway.
I must speak to him. Tonight at tea. If he is in.

'You should be in your bed. A man of your age. It's past one.'
　'Let me make you some tea.'
　The boy shrugs and sits down. He takes up the paper bet-
ween him and his father.
　'What do you be doing out to this time?'
　'Not again.'
　'Answer me.'
　'Talking.'
　'Who with?'
　'Friends. Just go to bed, Da, will you?'
　'What do you talk about?'
　'Nothing much.'
　'Talk to me, son.'
　'What about?'

My son, he looks confused. I want you to talk to me the way
I hear you talk to people at the door. I want to hear you laugh
with me like you used to. I want to know what you think.

I want to know why you do not eat more. No more than pick-ings for four weeks. Your face is thin. Your fingers, orange with nicotine. I pulled you away from death once and now you will not talk to me. I want to know if you are in danger again.

'About . . .'
  'You haven't shaved yet.'
  'I'm just going to. The water in the kettle is hot.'
  'Why do you shave at night?'
  'Because in the morning my hand shakes.'

Your hand shakes in the morning, Da, because you're a coward. You think the world is waiting round the corner to blow your head off. A breakfast of two Valium and the rest of them rattling in your pocket, walking down the street to your work. Won't answer the door without looking out the bedroom window first. He's scared of his own shadow.

Son, you are living on borrowed time. Your hand shook when you got home. I have given you the life you now have. I fed you soup from a spoon when your own hand would have spilt it. Let me put my arm around your shoulders and let me listen to what is making you thin. At the weekend I will talk to him.

It is hard to tell if his bed has been slept in. It is always rumpled. I have not seen my son for two days. Then, on the radio, I hear he is dead. They give out his description. I drink milk. I cry.
  But he comes in for his tea.

'Why don't you tell me where you are?'
  'Because I never know where I am.'

My mother is dead but I have another one in her place. He is

an old woman. He has been crying. I know he prays for me all
the time. He used to dig the garden, grow vegetables and
flowers for half the street. He used to fish. To take me fishing.
Now he just waits. He sits and waits for me and the weeds have
taken over. I would like to slap his face and make a man out
of him.

'I let you go once – and look what happened.'
   'Not this again.'
The boy curls his lip as if snagged on a fish-hook.

For two years I never heard a scrape from you. I read of London
in the papers. Watched scenes from London on the news, looking over the reporter's shoulder at people walking in the street.
I know you, son, you are easily led. Then a doctor phoned for
me at work. The poshest man I ever spoke to.
   'I had to go and collect you. Like a dog.'
The boy had taken up a paper. He turns the pages noisily,
crackling like fire.
   'A new rig-out from Littlewoods.'
Socks, drawers, shirt, the lot. In a carrier bag. The doctor said
he had to burn what was on you. I made you have your girl's
hair cut. It was Belfast before we spoke. You had the taint of
England in your voice.
   'Today I thought you were dead.'

Every day you think I am dead. You live in fear. Of your
own death. Peeping behind curtains, the radio always loud
enough to drown any noise that might frighten you, double-
locking doors. When you think I am not looking you hold
your stomach. You undress in the dark for fear of your
shadow falling on the window-blind. At night you lie with the
pillow over your head. By your bed a hatchet which you

pretend to have forgotten to tidy away. Mice have more courage.

'Well I'm not dead.'

'Why don't you tell me where you go?'

'Look, Da, I have not touched the stuff since I came back. Right?"

'Why don't you have a girl like everybody else?'

'Oh fuck."

He bundles the paper and hurls it in the corner and stamps up the stairs to his room. The old man shouts at the closed door.

'Go and wash your mouth out.'

He cries again, staring at the ceiling so that the tears run down to his ears.

My son, he is full of hatred. For me, for everything. He spits when he speaks. When he shouts his voice breaks high and he is like a woman. He grinds his teeth and his skin goes white about his mouth. His hands shake. All because I ask him where he goes. Perhaps I need to show him more love. Care for him more than I do.

I mount the stairs quietly to apologise. My son, I am sorry. I do it because I love you. Let me put my arm around you and talk like we used to on the bus from Toome. Why do you fight away from me?

The door swings open and he pushes a handgun beneath the pillow. Seen long enough, black and squat, dull like a garden slug. He sits, my son, his hands idling empty, staring hatred.

'Why do you always spy on me, you nosy old bastard?' His voice breaks, his eyes bulge.

'What's that? Under your pillow?'

'It's none of your fucking business.'

He kicks the door closed in my face with his bare foot.

I am in the dark of the landing. I must pray for him. On my
bended knees I will pray for him to be safe. Perhaps I did not
see what I saw. Maybe I am mistaken. My son rides pillion on
a motorbike. Tonight I will not sleep. I do not think I will
sleep again.

It is ten o'clock. The news begins. Like a woman I stand drying
a plate, watching the headlines. There is a ring at the door. The
boy answers it, his shirt-tail out. Voices in the hallway.

My son with friends. Talking. What he does not do with me.

There is a bang. A dishcloth drops from my hand and I run to
the kitchen door. Not believing, I look into the hallway. There
is a strange smell. My son is lying on the floor, his head on the
bottom stair, his feet on the threshold. The news has come to
my door. The house is open to the night. There is no one else.
I go to him with damp hands.
  'Are you hurt?'
  Blood is spilling from his nose.
  They have punched you and you are not badly hurt. Your
nose is bleeding. Something cold at the back of your neck.
  I take my son's limp head in my hands and see a hole in his
nose that should not be there. At the base of his nostril.
  My son, let me put my arms around you.

THE DAILY WOMAN

BERNARD MAC LAVERTY

She woke like a coiled spring, her head pressed onto the mattress, the knot of muscle at the side of her jaw taut, holding her teeth together. The texture of her cheeks felt tight and shiny from the tears she had cried as she had determined herself to sleep the night before. She lay for a moment trying to sense whether he was behind her or not, but knowing he wasn't. The baby was still asleep. She could tell by the slight squeaking movement of the pram springs from the foot of the bed whether it was asleep or not. The house was silent. She was a good baby. When she woke in the mornings she kicked her legs for hours. Only once in a while she cried.

Liz got up and went to the bathroom. In the mirror she saw where he had snapped the shoulder strap of her slip. It looked like a cheap off-the-shoulder evening dress. She examined her face, touching it with her fingertips. It had not bruised. He must be losing his touch. Her mouth still tasted of blood and she tested the looseness of her teeth with her index finger and thumb.

When she heard Paul thumping the sides of his cot she quickly finished her washing and went in to him. She tested if he was dry.

'Good for you,' she said. He was coming three and a half but she couldn't trust him a single night without a nappy. She gave him his handful of Ricicles on the pillow and he lay down beside

them with a smile, looking at them, picking them up with
concentration and eating them one by one like sweets. She
went back to the kitchen and began heating the baby's bottle.
The cold of the lino made her walk on tiptoe and she stood on
the small mat, holding her bare elbows and shivering while the
water came to the boil. She hated waiting – especially for a short
time. Waiting a long time, you could be lazy or do something
if you felt like it. She saw last night's dishes congealed in the
sink, the fag ends, but had no time or desire to do anything
about it. In short waits she was aware of the rubbish of her life.

After the milk heated and while the bottle was cooling in a
pot of cold water, she looked into the front room. Light came
through the gap in the curtains. Eamonn lay on his back on the
sofa, his shoes kicked off, breathing heavily through his slack
open mouth. When she came back after feeding and changing
the baby, he was still in the same position. She whacked the
curtains open loudly. His eyes cringed and wavered and he
turned his face into the sofa. He closed and opened his mouth
and from where she stood she could hear the tacky dryness of it.

'Fuck you,' he said.

He lay there as she tidied around him. On the cream tiled
hearth a complete cigarette had become a worm of white ash
on brown sweat.

In the kitchen she began to wash up and make a cup of tea.
They had run out of bread except for a heel of pan. She opened
a packet of biscuits.

'Liz,' Eamonn called her. 'Liz.'

But she didn't feel like answering. She went and picked Paul
out of his cot and let him run into the front room to annoy his
daddy. When she was sitting at her tea Eamonn came in, his shirt-
tail out, and drank several cups of water. He looked wretched.

'There's a sliding brick in my head,' he said. 'Every time I
move it wallops.'

Still she said nothing. He shuffled towards her and she looked out of the window at the corrugated-iron coal house and the other prefabs stretching up the hill.

'Let me see,' he said and turned her face with the back of his hand. 'You're all right.'

'No thanks to you,' she said. The ridiculous thing was that *she* felt sorry for *him*. How could anyone do that to her? How could anyone knock her to the floor and kick her, then take off his shoes and fall asleep? Why did she feel pity for him and not for herself? He sat down on a stool and held on to his head.

'I suppose you don't remember anything,' she said.

'Enough.'

'I'll not stand much more of it, Eamonn.'

'Don't talk shit.' He wasn't angry. It was just his way. Sober she could handle him. The next day he never apologised – not once, and she had learnt not to expect it. Last night he had got it into his head that the baby wasn't his. This was new and she had been frightened that in drink he might do something to it, so she had let him work out his anger on her.

Only she knew it was a possibility. Those nights had been long, sitting on her own minding her child, bored to tears with television, so that when Barney started to call – she had known him since her days in primary school – it had been a gradual and easy fall. He worked in a garage and was a folk singer of sorts. He made her feel relaxed in his company and she laughed, which was unusual for her. Even while they were at it behind the snibbed door of their small bathroom he could make her laugh – his head almost touching one wall while he got move-ment on her by levering his sock soles off the other.

Then he just stopped calling, saying that he was getting more and more engagements for his folk group. But that was nearly two years ago and she was disturbed that she should start being hit for it now. She wondered who had put it into his mind. Was it a rumour in that Provos club where he spent the most of his time drinking? God knows what else he got up to there. Once he had brought home an armful of something wrapped in sacking and hid it in the roof space. When she pestered him as to what it was he refused to tell her.

'It's only for a couple of nights', was all he would say. Those two days she fretted herself sick waiting for an army pig to pull up at the door.

Liz threw her tea down the sink.

'I suppose there's no money left,' she said, looking out the window. He made a kind of snort laugh. 'What am I going to use for the messages?'

'Henderson pays you today, doesn't he?'

'Jesus, you drink your dole money and I work to pay the messages. That's lovely. Smashin'.'

Paul had wandered in from the other room, shredding the cork tip of a cigarette butt, and Eamonn began to talk to him, ignoring her.

'Mucky pup,' he said taking it from between the child's fingers and roughly brushing them clean with his own hand.

'That's right, just throw it on the floor at your arse. I'm here to clean it up,' shouted Liz. She began thumpingly to wash the dishes. Eamonn went to the bathroom.

The hill to Ardview House was so steep that the pram handle pressed against the chest muscles just beneath her small breasts. Liz angled herself, pushing with her chest rather than her arms. It was a hot day and the lack of wind made her feel breathless. Halfway up she stopped and put the brake on with her foot.

'Paul,' she said, panting, 'get off, son, before I have a coronary.'

The child girned that he didn't want to but she was firm with him, lifting him under the armpits and setting him on the ground.

'You can hold on to the handle.'

In the pram, sheltered by its black hood, the baby was a pink knitted bonnet, its face almost obscured by a bobbing dummy. She continued up the hill.

She seemed to be doing this journey all the time, day in day out, up and down this hill. She knew where the puddles were in the worn tarmac of the footpath and could avoid them even though she was unsighted by the pram. A police car bounced over the crest of the hill, its lights flashing and its siren scream-ing. It passed her with a whumph of speed and gradually faded into the distance, spreading ripples of nervousness as far as the ear could hear.

When she turned off the road into the gravelled driveway she noticed that there was jam or marmalade on the black pram hood. She wiped it with a tissue, but the smear still glistened. She wet her finger and rubbed it, but only succeeded in making her fingers tacky. The pram was impossible to push on the gravel and she pulled it the rest of the way to the house. Paul was running ahead, hurrying to get to the playroom. The Henderson children had left a legacy of broken but expensive toys and usually Paul disappeared and gave her little trouble until she had her work finished.

She wondered if Mr Henderson would be in. She was nervous of him, not just because he was her boss, but be-cause of the way he looked at her. Of late he seemed to wait around in the mornings until she came. And then there was the money business.

Henderson was a bigwig who had made his money in paints, and on rare occasions when there were more than six guests his wife would invite Liz to dress up a bit and come and help serve dinner. Although a Unionist through and through, Henderson liked to be able to say that he employed Catholics.

'It's the only way forward. We must begin to build bridges. Isn't that right, Mrs O'Prey?' he'd say over his shoulder as she cleared the soup plates.

'Yes, sir,' said Liz.

In his house the other guests nodded.

'I make no secret of it. It's my ambition to become lord mayor of this town. Get others to put into practice what I preach.'

As she washed the dishes in her best dress she heard them laugh and guffaw in the other room.

The baby was sleeping, so Liz left her at the front door in the warm sunlight and went down to the pantry where she kept her cleaning things. She heard a door close upstairs and a moment later Mr Henderson came into the kitchen. He looked as if he had just had a shower and his hair, which was normally bushy, lay slick and black against the skin of his head. He wore a sage-green towelling dressing gown knotted at the waist. His legs were pallid and hairy and he wore a pair of backless clog slippers. Standing with his back to her his heels were raw red.

'Good morning, Mrs O'Prey.'

She nodded at his back, Vim in one hand, J Cloths in the other, and excused herself. But he put himself between her and the door.

'That's a pleasant morning,' he said. 'Hot, even.'

She agreed. He bent to the refrigerator, blocking her way. He poured himself a glass of orange juice and leant his back against the breakfast bar. He was tall and thin, in the region of fifty, but she found it hard to tell age. He wasn't ugly but she wouldn't have called him good-looking. His face had the grey colour of someone not long awake and his eyes behind dark-rimmed spectacles had the same look.

'How are things?'

'All right,' she said.

'Have you thought about my proposition?'

'Eh?'

'Did you think about my offer?'

'No,' she said and edged past him to the door to go upstairs. She began by cleaning the bathroom, hoping that Mr Henderson would leave for work before she would make the beds. She put his denture powder back in the cabinet and returned his toothbrush to the rack. She hosed round the shower with the sprinkler and with finger and thumb lifted a small scribbled clot of his black hairs which refused to go down the rose grating and dropped them into the toilet bowl. The noise of the flush must have camouflaged his footsteps on the stairs because Liz, squatting to clean some talc which had spilt down the outside of the bath, did not notice him standing in the doorway until he spoke.

'How remarkably thin you keep,' he said. She did not look round but was aware of a large gap between her jumper at the back and her jeans tight on her hips.

'It's hard work that does it.' She tried to tug her jumper down. He probably saw right into her pants. Let him. She turned round, her elbow resting on the lavatory seat. 'And not eating too much.'

'Oh, Mrs Henderson asked me to pay you this week.' He slippered off to his bedroom and came back a moment later with a wallet. He sat on the edge of the bath. If Liz was to sit the only place was the lavatory, so she stood while he drew clean notes from the wallet.

'She was in a rush this morning going out. How much is it?'

Liz told him and he counted out the twelve pounds. He set the money on the Vanitory unit, then went on taking out notes. Blue ones, slightly hinged from the bend of the wallet.

Five – ten – fifteen she saw him mouth. He stopped at seventy-five. A strand of his damp hair detached itself from the rest and hung like a black sickle in his eye. He looked at her.

'I can afford it,' he said. 'It's yours if you want it.'

She could see herself reflected from neck to knees in a rectangular mirror that ran the length of the bath. Would he never give up? This was a rise of twenty-five from the last time. She remembered once up an entry doing a pee standing up for thruppence and the boys had whooped and jeered as she splashed her good shoes and had run off and never paid her. Afterwards she had cried.

'I can afford better but I want you,' he said. 'It will be on the desk in my room.' His voice was hoarse and slightly trembling because she had not said no. He moved towards his room, saying over his shoulder, 'I'm not going in to the office this morning.'

Liz heard the one-stair-at-a-time stomp of Paul and went to the door to meet him.

'Muh,' he said.

'Yes, love.' She could feel the shake in her knees as she carried him down the stairs.

She began to scrape and put the accumulated dishes into the dishwasher. The bin yawned with bad breath when Paul pushed the foot pedal with his hand so she emptied it and cleaned it with bleach. At the sink the wing bones of her pelvis touched the stainless steel of the sink and she winced. She must have bruised. Eamonn would probably have gone back to bed now that he had it all to himself. He would get up about midday and go to either the pub or the bookies. Probably both. They were next door, the one feeding off the other. She had noticed a horseshoe of wear in the pavement from one door to the other. At night he would go to the Provos club. The drink was cheaper there because most of it was hijacked. He would not

be home until midnight at the earliest and there was no
guarantee they wouldn't have another boxing match. She
breathed out and heard it as a shuddering sigh.

'Muh,' Paul said.

'Yes, love, whatever you say.'

What could she do with that kind of money? Eamonn would
know immediately – he could smell pound notes – and want to
know how she got it. If she got a new rig-out it would be the
same. He would kill her. Before or after she had spent the
money didn't matter. Her mother had always harped on that Liz
had married beneath her.

She wiped down the white Formica and began to load the
washing machine from the laundry basket. Or toys or kids. She
could think of no way of spending where questions wouldn't
be asked. At eleven she made a coffee. She opened a window
and smoked a cigarette, sharpening its ash on a flowered saucer.

'Buh?' Paul asked, reaching her a pot lid.

'Thanks, son.' She took it off him and set it on the table.

When Liz reached three-quarters' way down her cigarette
she stubbed it out with determination, bending it almost
double. She got up and brought Paul with a biscuit and milk in
his baby cup into the playroom.

'There's a good boy,' she said. 'Mammy will be cross if you
come out.'

She had walloped him round the legs before for keeping her
back with her work, so he knew what was in store for him if
he wandered. She went outside and checked the baby in the
pram. She was still asleep, so she closed the front door quietly
and climbed the stairs.

In his room Mr Henderson sat at a small desk strewn with
papers. At her knock he raised his glasses to his hairline
and turned.

'Yes?'

'It's me.'

'Well?'

'All right,' she said. Her voice caught in her throat as if she had been crying for a long time. 'Just so long as you don't kiss me.'

'That will not be necessary.' His face broke into a frightened smile of disbelief. He was still in his dressing gown, a furry thigh sticking out. He came to her, his arm extended – fatherly almost.

'You're sure? I would get very angry if you were to change your mind once we had started.'

She nodded. 'What do you want me to do?'

'I want you to lie down.' That was a favourite song of Barney's – 'Croppies Lie Down' – but now in her tension she couldn't remember the words.

'In fact I want you to do nothing. That's the way I like it.'

'Could I have the money?'

'Yes, yes.' He was impatient now and fumbled with the wallet, then saw the money on the desk. The roll of notes made a comfortable bulge in the hip pocket of her jeans. He locked the door as she lay on the bed. It was like being asked to lie on a doctor's couch. Mr Henderson knelt and patted and prodded her to his liking. No sooner was she settled than he said, 'Perhaps you'd better take your clothes off.'

She had to get up again. There was a hole in her pants stretched to an egg shape just below her navel. She turned her back on him then, when undressed, lay down, her body all knuckles.

His eyes widened and went heavy. He couldn't decide whether to take off his glasses or leave them on. He began to talk baby talk, to speak to her as if she wasn't there. He told her how he had ached after her slim undernourished body for months, how he had watched her from between the banisters, how he loved to see her on her hands and knees and the triangle of light that he could always see between her thighs when she wore her jeans. He was fascinated by her bruises and kissed each one of them lightly. Spoke to her bruises. She was sweating a nervous sweat from her armpits. Praised her thinness, her each rib, the tent bones of her hips and her tuft of hair between. He smelt all over her as she had seen dogs do, but by now she had closed her eyes and could only feel the touch of his breath, his nosing. It went on for ages. Her fists were clenched. She tried to remember her shopping list. A pan loaf, maybe some small bread – sodas. Sugar – she needed sugar and potatoes and tea bags and mince and cornflakes. Mr Henderson climbed onto the bed, having opened her legs, but succeeded only in delivering himself somewhere in the coverlet with a groan. She looked down at him. His hair was still damp and moistening her belly. His face was hidden from her. The back of his neck was red and crisscrossed with wrinkles. Beneath the window she could hear her baby crying and farther away the sound of a blackbird.

When he got his breath back he went to the bathroom. Liz dressed in a hurry and went downstairs, trying to master the shudders that went through her like nausea. She inserted the dummy in the baby's mouth, grabbed Paul from the playroom and fled the house, drawing the pram after her against the gravel.

The kiosk outside the Co-op smelt of piss, would have smelt worse if it had not been for the ventilation of the broken panes. A taxi arrived within minutes and she coaxed the driver to collapse the pram and put it in the boot.

'In the name of God, missus, how does this thing operate?'

In a traffic jam – there must have been a bomb scare somewhere – she fed the baby milk from a cold bottle.

Her mother lived at the other side of town and was surprised to see her drawing up in such style. Liz told the driver to wait and hurried her mother into accepting the story that a friend's husband had run off with another woman and the girl was in a terrible state and she, Liz, was going to spend the night with her, and Mammy would you mind the kids? Her mother was old but not yet helpless and had raised six of her own. At twenty-two Liz was the last and felt she could call on her for special favours. She gave her a fiver to get herself some wee thing. A tenner, she thought, would have brought questions in its wake.

'You're a pet,' she called to her, rushing from the door.

Coming from Marks and Spencer's, she walked past the Methodist church in Donegall Place. An old man was changing the black notice board which kept up with the death toll of the Troubles. She hesitated and watched him. He had removed a 5 from 1875 and was fumbling and clacking with the wooden squares which slotted in like a hymn board. He was exasperatingly slow and she walked on but could not resist looking back over her shoulder.

Going through security, the woman stirred her jeans and jumper tentatively at the bottom of her carrier bag. The hotel lobby was crowded with newsmen with bandoleers of cameras, talking in groups. She asked the price of bed and breakfast and found that she had more than enough. Would she be having dinner? Liz leant forward to the clerk.

'How much?'

The clerk smiled and said anything from five to fifty pounds. Liz thought a moment and said yes. She wanted to pay there and then but the clerk insisted that she could settle her bill in the morning.

'Elizabeth O'Prey' she signed on the register card, taking great care to make it neat. At school she had never been much good but everybody praised her handwriting; teachers said she had a gift for it. She had been Elizabeth Wilson and one of the few advantages of her marriage, she thought, had been the opportunity of a flourishing Y at the end of O'Prey. As she had signed for her family allowance and sickness benefit she had perfected it.

She tried not to stare at the magnificence of the place, the plush maroon carpet, the glittering lights, the immaculately uniformed staff. She felt nervous about doing or saying the wrong thing. She didn't have a posh accent like those around her and rather than put it on she said as few words as possible. She was conscious of people looking at her and was glad that she had changed in the shop. As the desk clerk answered the phone she saw herself in a mirrored alcove, new shoes, hair done, new peach-coloured summer dress, and was happily surprised. For a second she didn't look like herself. Her Marks and Spencer's polythene bag was the only thing that jarred. She should have bought a real bag.

'Excuse me, madam,' said the clerk, clamping the earpiece against her shoulder, 'would you mind if security checked you out again?'

'They already searched me.'

'If you wouldn't mind.'

A woman in uniform came out and showed Liz to a small room. She was stout with blond curly hair bursting from beneath her peaked cap, chewing gum in a mouth heavy with lip gloss. Her body seemed pumped into the uniform. She searched Liz's carrier bag thoroughly.

'Why are you searching me twice?'

'You have a Belfast address, you have no luggage.' She came towards Liz, who raised her arms obediently. 'Why are you staying here?' Her heavy hands moved over Liz's small breasts, beneath her arms to her waist, down her buttocks and thighs. She had never been searched as thoroughly as this before – a series of light touches was all she'd had. This woman was groping her as if she expected to find something beneath her skin.

'My husband put me out,' said Liz. A forefinger scored up the track between her buttocks and she jumped.

'That's all right, love. We have to be sure.' She smiled, handing her back her carrier bag. 'I hope you and your man get it sorted out.'

A bellboy who was twice her age turned his back to her in the quiet of the lift before he showed her to her room. He made no attempt to carry her polythene bag.

When she closed and locked the door she felt for the first time in years that she was alone. She could not believe it. She stood with her back to the door, her hands behind her resting on the handle. The room took her breath away. Matching curtains and bedspread of tangerine flowers with one corner of the sheets folded back to show that they too matched. She walked around the room touching things lightly. From her window she could see a wedge of redbrick Belfast vibrating in the heat. This height above the street she could hear no sound. She lay on the bed, trying it for size and comfort, and to her disappointment it creaked slightly. The bathroom was done in rust shades with carpet going up the outside of the bath.

The first thing she had decided to do was to have a shower. Her new dress did nothing to remove the crawling sensation on her skin when she thought of Mr Henderson. Before undressing she turned on the test card on the television just for a bit of sound. She had never had a shower before and it took her ages to get it to work, then even longer to get the temperature right, but when she did get in she felt like a film star. Her instinct was to save the hot water but she remembered where she was and how much she was paying. She must have stayed in the shower for twenty minutes soaping and resoaping herself, watching the drapes of suds sliding down her body and away. The bruises remained.

She put on the new underwear and felt luxuriant to be padding about free in her bra and pants. Although the shower was good she decided that before she went to bed she would have a bath so hot the steam would mist the mirrors. She would buy some magazines and smoke and read, propped up by all those pillows. Watch television *from* bed, maybe.

In the bar she felt good, for the first time in years felt herself. She sat at a stool at the counter and sipped a vodka and orange. The bar was loud with groups of people talking. She caught herself staring in the bar mirror as she looked around. A man came in and sat next to her on a free stool. She wondered if he was waiting for someone. He ordered a drink, asked her to pass the water jug for his whiskey. She smiled. He slowly tilted the jug until it was upright and obviously empty and then they both laughed. He asked the barmaid for water.

'Are you American?' Liz asked. He nodded. He looked a good deal older than her, in his mid-thirties or forty, she guessed, with a plain face and blond moustache. He had bad skin, pockmarked, but it gave him a rugged look. She imagined him on horseback.

'Yeah, and you?'

'Oh, I'm from here.'

'There's no need to apologise.' He laughed and poured water into his whiskey slowly. She watched it mix in wreaths with the spirit. He tasted the drink and seemed satisfied. She became alone again as she bought herself cigarettes and matches. They drank separately in the noise. She crumpled the silver paper, dropped it in the ashtray and offered him one. He refused with a spread hand. He asked the barmaid for a menu, which he studied.

'Are you gonna eat?' he asked. She nodded, with her mouth

full of vodka and orange. 'It's quite good here. I can recommend their *coq au vin.*'

'Are you staying here?' He nodded. She asked him if he was on holiday and he said that he was working, a journalist of sorts.

'Oh, how interesting.' When she had said it she could have bitten her tongue out, it sounded so phoney. She heard Eamonn mimicking and repeating her tones, but this man did not seem to notice. She asked, 'What paper?'

The piece he would do would be syndicated. She nodded and took another sip of her drink. There was a pause as he studied the menu.

'Excuse my iggerence,' said Liz, 'but what does that mean – sin . . . sin . . . ?'

'Sorry. It just means that the same story goes in lots of papers – and I get more money.'

Liz tap-tapped her cigarette with her index finger over the ashtray but it was not smoked enough for any of it to fall.

'You say you're from here,' he said. 'If you don't mind me asking, which side are you on?'

'I'm sort of in the middle.'

'That can't help.'

'Well I was born nothing – but a Protestant nothing and I married a Catholic nothing and so I'm now a mixture of nothing. I hate the whole thing. I couldn't give a damn.'

'One of the silent minority.' He smiled. 'Boy, have you got problems.' Liz thought he was talking about her.

'Me?'

'Not you – the country.'

They talked for a while and went separately in to dinner. When he saw that she too was eating at a table on her own he came over and suggested that they eat together. She agreed, grateful for someone to help her with choosing from the menu. Rather than attempt to say the dishes, she pointed and he ordered. The array of knives and forks frightened her but she did what he did, American style, cutting up and eating with the fork alone. He told her that he had been a Catholic priest and that he had left when he had had a crisis of conscience, Vietnam, contraception, the nature of authority all contributing. As a priest he had written a weekly column for a Catholic paper in Boston, and when he left the church to continue working in journalism was natural. He admitted to being married shortly after being laicised. She said she too was married.

He made her feel good, relaxed. In his company she felt she could say anything. After telling of himself he asked her questions about her life. The questions he asked no one had ever asked her before and she had to think hard to answer them. In her replies she got mixed up, found she was contradicting herself, but got out of it by laughing.

'This is like an interview on the TV,' she said and he apologised but went on asking her questions, about her life, about the way she felt and thought. His eyes were blue and gentle, widening at some of the things she said. Except for his pitted skin she found him attractive. He listened with the slightest inclination of the head, looking up at her almost. Being from America he probably didn't know about her accent. Maybe she looked high-class in her peach rig-out. Liz spoke until she realised she was speaking, then she became self-conscious.

'I hope you're not taking all this down,' she said laughing.

'No, but it sure helps to talk to someone like you – a nothing as you so nicely put it. It helps the balance.'

Hesitatingly she told him something of her relationship, or lack of it, with Eamonn. 'You have your troubles,' was all he would say.

When they had finished eating he suggested that they go through to the bar to have a liqueur. He was behind her, easing her seat away from the table before she realised it and he was

equally attentive and concerned holding the bar door open
for her.

'You're a gentleman,' she said.

'My old man used to say that a gentleman was someone who
made a woman feel like a lady.'

He introduced her to Bailey's Irish Cream.

'It's gorgeous,' she said, 'like sweets. You could drink that
all night.'

'You could not,' he said, smiling.

Liz settled back in the seat and lit a cigarette. She slapped her
stomach lightly.

'God, I'm full,' she said, 'and I feel great. I haven't felt
like this for ages.'

They had another Bailey's Irish Cream, which she insisted on
buying. Then when he had finished it he said, slapping his
knees, 'I must go. I have some work to finish for tomorrow.
Will you excuse me?'

'Sure.' She tried to make it sound as if she was not disappointed at all but was conscious that some of his accent was
invading her speech. She detained him a little longer, asking
him to wait till she finished another cigarette but eventually he
said he must go up to his room.

'I don't want to sit here on my owney-o,' said Liz. 'I think
I'll just go up too.'

In the lift there was a silence between them. Liz felt she
had to talk.

'What floor are you on?'

'I pressed number four and you're on six.'

'That's right.'

She told him her room number and then thought it too
forward. She hadn't meant to tell him but the silence of the
humming lift forced her to say it.

Getting out of the lift, he touched her arm with his hand,
then shook hands.

'It's been a real pleasure meeting you,' he said. The lift doors nipped her view of his smile as he waved goodbye.

In her room the aloneness changed from what she had felt earlier. Now it seemed enforced. She wanted to go on talking. In the mirror she shrugged, made a face and laughed at herself. The only thing to read was a Bible on the bedside table and she was annoyed that she had forgotten to buy some magazines. She had the hot bath she had promised herself, but afterwards was too warm so she opened a window on to the distant sound of the street.

She prodded the buttons on the television set and for want of anything better settled on *Call My Bluff* with that nice man with the pink bow tie and the moustache. In her new under-wear she sat propped up on tangerine pillows, smoking – view-ing in style. Where did they get the words from? Clinchpoop? Liz guessed it was the thing the man said about the plague but it turned out to be somebody who didn't know what to do – like eating peas with your knife or backslapping at a funeral. That was her, she thought. She never knew what to do at the time. Later on she knew what she should and could have done. And it was not just with manners. She had no control over the direction of her life. She was far too bloody soft. From now on she should lock Eamonn out and begin to fight her own corner – for the children's sake at least.

She jumped out of bed and pressed the channel buttons. After the ads it was part three of something so she switched off. The room was very quiet. She got back into bed again, hearing its annoying creak and the crispness of its sheets.

She should have told that Henderson to get knotted. It was the end of her job – there was no way she could go back there again. He would hang about like a dog every morning from now on pointing at her with his trousers. Resignation. That was all that was left to her. But then Eamonn would want to know why she had quit. Tell him Henderson had made a pass at her – which was true. Maybe he'd want to know where she'd spent the night. She had run to her mother's before because of a fight. If he noticed she'd been away at all. The peach dress she would have to leave in the wardrobe. Or she could leave it at her mother's until she found an excuse to bring it home. Why hadn't she thought of it before? She could pass it off as good jumble sale stuff.

Pleased with herself, she lay down among the pillows and spread her feet warm and wide. With the lamp out, car head-lights swung yellow wedges across the ceiling. The net curtains ballooned slowly and fell back again. She thought of her baby sleeping in the spare bed at her mother's, walled in by pillows, and Paul, open-mouthed in sleep, snuggling in to his gran. 'That child has knees on him like knuckles,' the old woman had once complained. Liz spread her opened fingers across the sheets, try-ing to take up as much room as possible in the bed. She smelt the strange perfumed hotel soap off her own body, felt the sum-mer night warmth on her face and tried, as she drifted off to sleep, to forget the fact that Eamonn, for the loss of her weekly wage, would kill her when he got her home – if not before.

WALKING THE DOG

BERNARD Mac LAVERTY

As he left the house he heard the music for the start of the nine o'clock news. At the top of the cul-de-sac was a paved path which sloped steeply and could be dangerous in icy weather like this. The snow had melted a little during the day but frozen over again at night. It had done this for several days now – snowing a bit, melting a bit, freezing a bit. The walked-over ice crackled as he put his weight on it and he knew he wouldn't go far. He was exercising the dog – not himself.

The animal's breath was visible on the cold air as it panted up the short slope onto the main road, straining against the leash. The dog stopped and lifted his leg against the cement post.

'Here boy, come on.'

He let him off the leash and wrapped the leather round his hand. The dog galloped away then stopped and turned, not used with the icy surface. He came back wagging his tail, his big paws slithering.

'Daft bugger.'

It was a country road lined by hedges and ditches. Beyond the housing estate were green fields as far as Lisburn. The city had grown out to here within the last couple of years. As yet there was no footpath. Which meant he had to be extra careful in keeping the dog under control. Car headlights bobbed over the hill and approached.

'C'mere!'

He patted his thigh and the dog stood close. Face the oncoming traffic. As the car passed, the undipped headlights turned the dog's eyes swimming-pool green. Dark filled in again between the hedges. The noise of the car took a long time to disappear completely. The dog was now snuffling and sniffing at everything in the undergrowth – being the hunter.

The man's eyes were dazzled as another car came over the hill.

'C'mere you.' The dog came to him and he rumpled and patted the loose folds of skin around its neck. He stepped into the ditch and held the dog close by its collar. This time the car indicated and slowed and stopped just in front of him. The passenger door opened and a man got out and swung the back door wide so that nobody could pass on the inside. One end of a red scarf hung down the guy's chest, the other had been flicked up around his mouth and nose.

'Get in,' the guy said.

'What?'

'Get in the fuckin car.' He was beckoning with one hand and the other was pointing. Not pointing but aiming a gun at him. Was this a joke? Maybe a starting pistol.

'Move or I'll blow your fuckin head off.' The dog saw the open door and leapt up into the back seat of the car. A voice shouted from inside, 'Get that hound outa here.'

'Come on. Get in,' said the guy with the gun. 'Nice and slow or I'll blow your fuckin head off.'

Car headlights were coming from the opposite direction. The driver shouted to hurry up. The guy with the gun grabbed him by the back of the neck and pushed – pushed his head down and shoved him into the car. And he was in the back seat beside his dog with the gunman crowding in beside him.

'Get your head down.' He felt a hand at the back of his neck forcing his head down to his knees. The headlights of the approaching car lit the interior for a moment – enough to see that the upholstery in front of him was blue – then everything went dark as the car passed. He could hear his dog panting. He felt a distinct metal hardness – a point – cold in the nape hair of his neck.

'If you so much as move a muscle I'll kill you. I will,' said the gunman. His voice sounded as if it was shaking with nerves. 'Righto, driver.'

'What about the dog?' said the driver.

'What about it? It'd run home. Start yapping, maybe. People'd start looking.'

'Aye, mebby.'

'On you go.'

'There's something not right about it. Bringing a dog.'

'On you fuckin go.'

The car took off, changed gear and cruised – there seemed to be no hurry about it.

'We're from the IRA,' said the gunman. 'Who are you?'

There was a silence. He was incapable of answering.

'What's your name?'

He cleared his throat and made a noise. Then said, 'John.'

'John who?'

'John Shields.'

'What sort of a name is that?'

It was hard to shrug in the position he was in. He had one foot on either side of the ridge covering the main drive shaft. They were now in an area of street lighting and he saw a Juicy Fruit chewing-gum paper under the driver's seat. What was he playing the detective for? The car would be stolen anyway. His hands could touch the floor but were around his knees. He still had the dog's lead wrapped round his fist.

'Any other names?'

'What like?'

'A middle name.'

The dog had settled and curled up on the seat beside him. There was an occasional bumping sound as his tail wagged. The gunman wore Doc Martens and stone-washed denims.

'I said, any other names?'

'No.'

'You're lying in your teeth. Not even a confirmation name?'

'No.'

'What school did you go to?'

There was a long pause.

'It's none of your business.' There was a sudden staggering pain in the back of his head and he thought he'd been shot. 'Aww – for fuck's sake.' The words had come from him so he couldn't be dead. The bastard must have hit him with the butt of the gun.

'No cheek,' said the gunman. 'This is serious.'

'For fuck's sake, mate – take it easy.' He was shouting and groaning and rubbing the back of his head. The anger in his voice raised the dog and it began to growl. His fingers were slippery. The blow must have broken the skin.

'Let me make myself clear,' said the gunman. 'I'll come to it in one. Are you a Protestant or a Roman Catholic?'

There was a long pause. John pretended to concentrate on the back of his neck.

'That really fuckin hurt,' he said.

'I'll ask you again. Are you a Protestant or a Roman Catholic?'

'I'm ... I don't believe in any of that crap. I suppose I'm nothing.'

'You're a fuckin wanker – if you ask me.'

John protected his neck with his hands thinking he was going to be hit again. But nothing happened.

'What was your parents?'

'The same. In our house nobody believed in anything.'

The car slowed and went down the gears. The driver indicated and John heard the rhythmic clinking as it flashed. This must be the Lisburn Road. A main road. This was happening on a main road in Belfast. They'd be heading for the Falls. Some republican safe house. The driver spoke over his shoulder.

'Let's hear you saying the alphabet.'

'Are you serious?'

'Yeah – say your abc's for us,' said the gunman.

'This is so fuckin ridiculous,' said John. He steeled himself for another blow.

'Say it – or I'll kill you.' The gunman's voice was very matter-of-fact now. John knew the myth that Protestants and Roman Catholics, because of separate schooling, pronounced the eighth letter of the alphabet differently. But he couldn't remember who said which.

'Eh... bee... cee, dee, ee... eff.' He said it very slowly, hoping the right pronunciation would come to him. He stopped.

'Keep going.'

'Gee...' John dropped his voice, '...aitch, haitch... aye jay kay.'

'We have a real smart alec here,' said the gunman. The driver spoke again.

'Stop fuckin about and ask him if he knows anybody in the IRA who can vouch for him.'

'Well?' said the gunman. 'Do you?'

There was another long pause. The muzzle of the gun touched his neck. Pressure was applied to the top bone of his vertebrae.

'Do you?'

'I'm thinking.'

'It's not fuckin *Mastermind*. Do you know anybody in the
Provos? Answer me now or I'll blow the fuckin head off you.'

'No,' John shouted. 'There's a couple of guys in work who
are Roman Catholics – but there's no way they're Provos.'

'Where do you work?'

'The Gas Board.'

'A meter man?'

'No, I'm an EO.'

'Did you hear that?' said the gunman to the driver.

'Aye.'

'There's not too many Fenians in the Gas Board.'

'Naw,' said the driver. 'If there are any they're not EO class.
I think this is a dud.'

'John Shields,' said the gunman. 'Tell us this. What do you
think of us?'

'What do you mean?'

'What do you think of the IRA? The Provos?'

'Catch yourselves on. You have a gun stuck in my neck
and you want me to . . .'

'Naw – it'd be interesting. Nothing'll happen – no matter
what you say. Tell us what you think.'

There was silence as the car slowed down and came to a stop.
The reflections from the chrome inside the car became red.
Traffic lights. John heard the beeping of a 'cross now' signal. For
the benefit of the blind. Like the pimples on the pavement. To
let them know where they were.

'Can you say the Hail Mary? To save your bacon?'

'No – I told you I'm not interested in that kind of thing.'

The driver said, 'I think he's OK.'

'Sure,' said the gunman. 'But he still hasn't told us what he
thinks of us.'

John cleared his throat – his voice was trembling.

'I hate the Provos. I hate everything you stand for.' There

was a pause. 'And I hate you for doing this to me.'

'Spoken like a man.'

The driver said, 'He's no more a Fenian than I am.'

'Another one of our persuasion.' The gunman sighed with a kind of irritation. The lights changed from orange to green. The car began to move. John heard the indicator clinking again and the driver turned off the main road into darkness. The car stopped and the handbrake was racked on. The gunman said, 'Listen to me. Careful. It's like in the fairy tale. If you look at us you're dead.'

'You never met us,' said the driver.

'And if you look at the car we'll come back and kill you – no matter what side you're from. Is that clear? Get out.'

John heard the door opening at the gunman's side. The gunman's legs disappeared.

'Come on. Keep the head down.' John looked at his feet and edged his way across the back seat. He bent his head to get out and kept it at that angle. The gunman put his hands on John's shoulders and turned him away from the car. There was a tree in front of him.

'Assume the position,' said the gunman. John placed his hands on the tree and spread his feet. His knees were shaking so much now that he was afraid of collapsing. 'And keep your head down.' The tarmac pavement was uneven where it had been ruptured by the tree's roots. John found a place for his feet.

The dog's claws scrabbled on the metal sill of the car as it followed him out. It nudged against his leg and he saw the big eyes looking up at him.

The gunman said, 'Sorry about this, mate.' John saw the gunman's hand reach down and scratch the dog's head. 'Sorry about the thump. But we're not playing games. She's a nice dog.'

'It's not a she.'

'OK, OK. Whatever you say.'

The car door closed and the car began reversing – crackling away over the refrozen slush. In the headlights his shadow was very black and sharp against the tree. There was a double shadow, one from each headlight. From the high-pitched whine of its engine he knew the car was still reversing. It occurred to him that they would not shoot him from that distance. For what seemed a long time he watched his shadow moving on the tree even though he kept as still as possible. It was a game he'd played as a child, hiding his eyes and counting to a hundred. Here I come, away or not. The headlights swung to the trees lining the other side of the road. His dog was whimpering a bit, wanting to get on. John risked a glance – moving just his eyes – and saw the red glow of the car's taillights disappearing onto the main road. He recognised where he was. It was the Malone Road. He leant his head against the back of his hands. Even his arms were trembling now. He took deep breaths and put his head back to look up into the branches of the tree.

'Fuck me,' he said out loud. The sleeve of his anorak had slipped to reveal his watch. It was ten past nine. He began to unwind the leash from his hand. It left white scars where it had bitten into his skin. He put his hand to the back of his head. His · hair was sticky with drying blood.

'Come on boy.' He began to walk towards the lights of the main road where he knew there was a phone box. But what was the point? He wouldn't even have been missed yet.

The street was so quiet he could hear the clinking of the dog's identity disk as it padded along beside him.

THE DARK HOLE DAYS

UNA WOODS

Wednesday night or Thursday morning 12.15

Madge heard them saying in the taxi going down the road that it's all about to blow up again. She's not the only one either. People are fed up with initiatives. They don't know what they are. I heard a woman saying why don't they do something real. Most people don't know what.

Went out with Matt tonight. To the pictures. It wasn't much good. I can't even remember the name. I'd rather be somewhere having a chat, but where is there? We walked home and that was good though we were a bit nervous. Mam says when they were going out they used to walk across to the east. It's a bad time. We might move, Dad says, but where would you go?

Brought Matt in but it was mad, with the eight of our ones milling around. You can't get those kids to bed. They want to see everything. Dad was out but came home early. Mam says she doesn't rest till the door's closed and we're all safe.

Our kids have rings round their eyes.

Chuck was in with Dad tonight. He's got all the solutions. He says take the politicians away and let the people get on with sorting it out. Our Pete said sure the people don't agree because they listen to the politicians on television telling them they don't agree. Television should be done away with, Chuck says. Television and politicians.

1.00 in the morning

They're still down there. Our kids have finally fallen asleep, and I can hear them talking although Dad doesn't say much. He told me the other day there's too much talking, there are hardly any quiet people around these days. Where's the dignity of the past, he asked me. I couldn't tell him. The only person he really likes listening to is Mam. You wouldn't think she was from Belfast at all, Aunt Sadie used to say. Aunt Sadie's dead.

Thursday 0130 hours

Out with Gerry and Sam getting some information for protection purposes. Learning how not to be selfish. Have learnt a lot since I met Gerry and Sam in the dole. There aren't enough people who care, Sam said. I was one. I was just messing around, playing billiards. I let others get on with it. Like politicians. Can politicians protect us, Sam asked me. I said no. We have to protect ourselves, Gerry said. Even the security forces can't. They're not inside. But we are.

Was at a meeting earlier. Can't say much about it. Even to myself. But I'm a part of something now. I have friends and important thoughts about history and the country. I hated history at school. Now I'm in it.

Sam said we might be in action soon. For our protection. He and Gerry and a few others are getting us ready.

I can't say anything about it.

Thursday morning 10.30

Our four away to school. Pete still in bed, Denny at work, Sadie teaching in the nursery school, Madge down in the café. Dad gone for the paper and a pint after. I did the usual, helping to get the wee ones out and then a bit of tidying up. Dad was paid off last year, before I kept a diary. I thought of it to fill in time till I get a job. Dad says with six O levels and two A's it's only a matter of time. I'm young. He's not the same since. He liked work, though I'd get bored in a factory. He said it was worth it for the weekends. Now it's all the same, each day, nothing to look forward to. But he doesn't complain much. He likes a visit to the pub in the morning. He has some good friends.

I think of other places. I could go to England. Why would young people stay here? It's dead. It's only for people who can't get out. Yet some come back. They can't stand to be away. Like the Munroes round the corner. Imagine coming back from Australia to that. It's hard to understand it. Matt and me talked about going to America when (if) we get married but there's the possibility that I would wither away amongst strangers. So that's my question answered – why people come back.

I'm looking down on the estate now. It's a weird sort of wilderness, yet in every house there's a story. I think about the stories. Sometimes they are sad and then there's a white flash. It might be a wedding or a christening and white laughing teeth. I think of blacks and whites. If I wrote stories, some would be black and some white.

Thursday 1300 hours

Just had breakfast. Ma said Gerry left word to meet him at Coal Bunker. That's code. Ma doesn't like it. She says I've no sense, that God knows who I'll get mixed up with. But she doesn't know anything really. She thinks it's just a game, like gangs when you're a kid. And she likes Sam. He always treats her well. One day he gave her a box of chocolates. It's the first time I saw her blushing. It's the others she doesn't know that she's worried about. I tell her I'm playing billiards most of the time. She's turned against billiards. I said at least I don't drink or take drugs. I don't even smoke. She said that was true.

It doesn't seem so bad not having a job now. I used to lie in bed most of the day.

Off to meet Gerry.

Thursday evening 7.15

Paul broke off with our Madge. Madge ate no tea. She'll be hanging around all night with a face like the longest day. She's only known him three weeks, but that's our Madge. I might try to get her interested in a game of draughts. On the other hand she may call for Laura Munroe. Laura who talks with an Australian accent even though she was only there for two years. She has a guy there, she says, who's waiting to marry her. I asked her why she didn't stay and she said her mum said good people are needed here, it wouldn't be right to desert it. I asked her what she was doing except working in the café with Madge, and she turned up her nose and said spreading sanity around. I hope she's right. Dad laughed when I imitated her to him but he said, Oh they're all right, the Munroes. Harmless people. Maybe that's all we need.

I've tried on three jumpers and I don't know what to wear with these green trousers. Not that it matters. Me and Matt'll probably just have a wee walk up the road.

Thursday 2005 hours

Down by the embankment. Autumn colours made me think of Da's funeral. It was blowing hard and leaves were swirling in our faces. I remember Uncle George's big heavy coat. It was the fashion then with a thick belt and big lapels. He asked me to come under it, for my face was blue. I refused. Ma had on a

black coat she borrowed from Mimi Roberts. It was too long.
Why didn't she wear her own? Dark blue would have been all
right. You can't talk to Ma.

Friday 0100 hours

God you want to have seen them all tonight. I can't believe it's
real. I think I'm dreaming or maybe watching a film, but then
I realise it's me there with all the lads. Got a glimpse of the boss
but he had a mask. Sam said he can't afford to take chances, even
in front of us. There's always traitors and it might be who you
least expect. It could even be you, he said to me. It gave me
an eerie feeling but then he burst out laughing and I laughed
too. We're all together.

Friday 2.35 in the morning

Beat our Madge at draughts, two to one, but then our Sadie beat
me two to nil. So what does that prove? I'm better than Madge
but Sadie's better than me. I strolled up the road a bit with Matt.
He seems depressed, what with no work, and this place. He
might go to England to his brother. He's a carpenter. Matt
could work for him. He says what's keeping me here, but I
don't know. I'd have to think about it. Sometimes I think even
though I love Matt, I should take some time to myself. If I went
with him now I'd be giving myself over, wouldn't I? But then
what do I want to do? I wouldn't mind writing some of these
stories I think about. Achieve something on my own. Maybe
even earn some decent money. Now that wouldn't be bad. I
was looking at a suit the other day. It was made up of lovely
autumny shades. I could see me strolling in the country in that
suit. I showed it to Teresa but she apparently found it amusing.
Who do you think you are? she said. It's not exactly the moon

I'm asking for but surely all my dreams don't end here: me in a duffle coat signing on the dole and walking in the debris of Belfast. Then again I look at Mam, so at home with herself, and I think, why should I want more. Or different. She impresses me. She's part of ongoing life, or something like that.

It's a predicament.

Saturday 1900 hours

In town all afternoon. So much going on you wouldn't believe it. I'm sure it's like every other city. Except me and Gerry and Sam walking through Smithfield knew we had a secret. Gerry bought tapes, the Police and others. Says he might have a party and would I like to come. Would I not! Sam disappeared for half an hour. Me and Gerry dandered round. I looked at some fishing tackle. Might take it up with Uncle George. But not now. Later, when there's time. When it's all over. It will be all over, Sam and Gerry say. They know things that I don't know – yet. But once you're in, Sam says. I looked at myself in a shop window and liked a new kind of serious look in my eyes. I always thought I would be something. Maybe an actor. Sometimes it feels like that. Sam brought back fish and chips. We ate them beside Kavanagh's. There was too much vinegar. Still it was good. You know that wintery feeling. Gerry saw a girl he fancies but Sam said there'll be plenty of time for all that. Anyway Gerry said he wouldn't go after her with the smell of fish and chips.

The shops were lighting up when we walked home.

Saturday evening 8.30

Missed last night but not much happened. Mam and Dad went to the club together. We persuaded them because they don't go out together enough. Eddie Stewart left them home and Chuck called in to hear the gossip. We managed to get all the wee ones into bed to give them peace. Mam likes the men around – but don't take that up the wrong way. Pete came home about twelve. Dad's worried about his drinking. Madge and Laura spent the night looking through catalogues. The things they're sending away for! You'd look daft in them around these parts. Laura says they're for wearing back to the outback and Madge is talking about going with her. Our Sadie was out with John. When she came in she made us all tea. Then she sat and read. Sadie's the quiet one, the discreet one. Dad calls her the thinker. What's our Sadie thinking about us now, he says. She smiles, like a lady. Our Madge is jealous.

Went down the town this afternoon. I like Saturdays in the town. I went an hour before I was to meet Matt so as to walk about a bit myself. The suit was gone but maybe there are more inside. Walked around by North Street and through Smithfield. The music coming from the record shops somehow gave me a feeling of freedom and made me imagine I was going to do things – interesting and adventurous. I think really I must leave Belfast at some stage. The more I think of it the more it seems I could not justify spending my life in this corner. But it's all very vague. Like trying to make a decision when the alternatives aren't yours to begin with. Are there possibilities? When I look back I'll say, at nineteen you must have had possibilities. From here they're in a mist. Trying to find your way in a fog. When the fog lifts it was all so clear after all.

The other evening Denny had a ladybird on his arm. One of the kids went to swat it but Denny said, Hey you, that ladybird's life is as important as yours. He went to put it outside but he dropped it. Ah, it's gone, he said, groping round the floor. Oh well, he said, and sat down again. Our kids all roared laughing. I mentioned that because it struck me, although I'm not sure why. I'll read it later and maybe something will click.

Met Matt in White's café. Had a cup of tea and a doughnut, and Matt had coffee. He looked well. Nicely dressed and in good form. His brother says Birmingham's great. You can do what you want in your own flat and at night you don't have to worry about anything. How would you like a weekend in Birmingham, Matt asked me. I might, I said.

And I might.

Sunday 0200 hours if the clock's right

Shattered, but in a satisfied way. Sam's very happy with my progress. You're doing well kid, he said to me. After practice I was in the flat of a friend of his. Vera. Something going on there, though she looks no chicken to me. Still, not bad in the figure. I'd say Sam would have no problem there. She made us coffee. I felt a bit out of it when they left me with a pile of Jim Reeves LPs. I'd never heard of the guy and have no wish to again. Heard noises from the other room which made me wish I had a girl beside me there on the couch. Never really had a girl, well, not serious. At that point I wouldn't have said no to Vera and her Jim Reeves LPs.

Sam cheered me up when we were walking home. What I like about you kid, he said, is that you're the dedicated sort. It's true. I always was.

Sunday afternoon 5.20

Sunday dreary Sunday. When, if, I get some control the first thing I'll do is change Sunday. It deserves a good shaking at the least. Is it different in other places or do people everywhere sit around in their good clothes waiting for nothing to happen? Some thoughts. Are we dressed up for God's entertainment or are we clinging to tradition? Do we need to be freed from it all or should we find an alternative first? Was any of it ever good or did it only distract us?

After dinner, which takes up most of the day anyhow, we spend the rest of the time bumping into each other. Madge and Sadie have resorted to the draughts, but only in a half-interested way. I'm glad to sneak away to this. Roll on Monday.

Sunday 1900 hours

Sam and Gerry not available on Sundays. That's a rule. I usually sleep late. Ma gets the dinner which we eat silently or Ma might say, Now just content yourself around the house for today. Sometimes I walk through the park and meet up with some of the old mates although I haven't much time for idle chat these days. There's no meaning. Today I went out alone. I had a sense of power and even superiority. Ma tried to talk to me at tea. Things about Mimi Roberts's husband and holidays and Mimi's bad leg that she has to lift onto the bus. I said, Aye it's terrible right enough. I suppose she used to tell Da. Then she asked me did I notice the new heels on my brown boots. I lied that I did. What do you want for your birthday next week, she said. I've just thought of a shirt. I'll go down and tell her a blue shirt, or she might end up getting me another white one.

Monday evening 6.30

We've been worried about wee Dan. He hasn't been himself and the doctor's sending him to the hospital for tests. I can hardly look at him for fear it's something serious. I feel it's a threat and everything could change for us overnight. Maybe I'm just a pessimist. Mam and Sadie are sensibly controlling their feelings. I'm thinking to myself, life will be difficult if I fall apart so readily. After all he's only going for tests, I'd better catch myself on.

Still I'm looking forward to seeing Matt tonight. The people closest to you are the ones who matter. It's a question of developing, keeping those relationships. Why look beyond that? Or is that selfish or narrow? I don't know.

I can hear Sadie singing to Dan. Why is she singing to Dan? She's singing to Dan because she knows he likes it. She's not wrapping herself up in her own anxiety. I'm going to try.

Monday 1915 hours

Gerry seemed concerned, as if he was miles away. And he asked me a strange thing. What do you think you'd have done if you'd lived in a different time? I said how do I know and anyway I like it now. Then he said, or if you'd been rich, up the Malone Road, or something? Did you ever think of that, he said. I said no, can't say I ever did. I do, he said. I don't believe him. Gerry's not the sort to think. You know what we'll end up doing, Gerry, I told him. Protecting the people up the Malone Road. That's what I told him. Will we, he asked me. He looked at me, sensing the importance of my words. We will, I said and he shook his head. He was amazed. Sometimes I can't believe the things I come out with these days. I've got a future.

Tuesday 12.50 in the morning

Had a close night with Matt. We went up the road for a walk and called in for one drink. You wouldn't believe the drinking that goes on. Tables and glasses and waiters falling over themselves and the sad ones at the bar. I wonder who's at home waiting for them night after night. When I was a child I used to walk in the middle of the road passing a pub. One day in

Royal Avenue I heard the awful thud of a drunk man's head on the pavement. People around said the drink'll save him. He won't feel it the same as if he was sober.

I was relieved when we came into the air and when we were walking down I had this feeling again, that what I have is as good as anybody could hope for. But I'm guilty and embarrassed about that feeling. As if that's a thought for old age. Not now. I haven't earned it.

Madge is complaining about the light. She's raging because she hasn't been able to sneak a look at this. I told her it's only a diary and she said, I hope there's nothing about me in there. I said don't be daft, I only write about important things – which she did not appreciate. Our Sadie is sleeping. Good-night Madge. Madge is a bit of a problem. But then, what does she think of me? What does anyone think of me?

Tuesday 0120 hours

Can't say anything about tonight. The lads, you know. But it's under control. Ma waited up. Says I'm prowling about like a foreigner and to take that look off my face. The radio was on when I came in. Old dance music and she was dressed up, that blue dress she used to wear when she and Da went dancing. Now what's she up to? I've been dancing, son, she said with a peculiar smile and she tried to twirl me in the kitchen. Give us a break, I said and came up the stairs. It's not long since you used to have a wee dance with me, she shouted up from the bottom of the stairs. It seems a long time to me. And you used to shine your daddy's black shoes, do you remember that? Aye, I said, but I don't think she heard me. I might have a word with Mimi Roberts about her tomorrow if I've time. Right enough she's always polishing at them few cups my da and her won. Hope she's all right but I can't let it get in the way of the bigger good.

As Sam says, we're only insects but some are more important insects than others.

Wednesday afternoon 4.15

Watching the evening light, the sunset, from my window. I used to wish I was from the country. I couldn't get over the stillness across the fields and the slow talk of country people. I thought my appreciation could make it mine. I sat on a bridge one day and thought, this is part of me. But you can't start from what you're not. I'm a city person. A suburban girl. That's what I am.

Great news about Dan. The specialist found nothing and he's picked up already. A big weight is lifted off us. Dad has him down in the park. He was bouncing up and down on Dad's shoulders delighted with the fuss that's being made of him.

I have just finished a very good book. It made me think there's a fair chance I'll settle to write sometime. I'd like to capture a quality of ordinary life or something. That book did it.

Mam took a turn down the town on her own. She used to go with Aunt Sadie. Aunt Sadie made a big issue of it, with her fur coat and brown felt hat with a feather on it. Mam used to say somehow she was out of place on the bus, kicking away the rubbish under her seat and poking in her purse for the fare. Soon after the start of the Troubles they stopped the routine. Aunt Sadie said things will never be the same again. Dad used to call her a wee china doll. So straight and uppity without anything to be uppity about, and her little bulgy cheeks all powdered and rouged and her poppy eyes. But, as Chuck says, it's the outlook that counts. It was a shock when she died upright in her floral-covered chair. She had the *Irish Times* on her knee. It just shows you, Chuck said. You never know what secrets people have. Chuck took it badly. It was rumoured that he'd been saving for years to ask her to marry him. She would never have married Chuck. Not when he wears dungarees and drinks out of a black mug.

There's our Sadie calling me for tea and the sun's gone down.

Wednesday 2348 hours

Rock on, what's the latest. I can't tell me. Sam and Gerry had other business. Suggested I stay in house till I got word to come. Ma got the wrong impression and got the ludo out at which point I reminded her I'm not a child any more. That hurt her. You know ludo's not like snakes and ladders, she said. I played one game to please her. She kept getting sixes and fives and I got ones and twos. I didn't even get my last man out. She laughed and said, You remember I used to give you chances when you were young? You're too old for chances now. If Sam and Gerry saw me they'd die.

Sam sent his kid brother at ten. Ma said she was just making me chips and a tin of red salmon, a big tin. Bring all your friends round, we'll have a bit of a night, she said. I told her, It's a man's world, Ma. To please her I said maybe we'll go to Butlin's next year and asked her to brush the back of my jacket.

Sam's kid tried to get some info from me but I had no trouble dealing with that. Lay off kid, I said. Me and Sam's got business to attend to. That's what I said. Lay off kid.

Met Sam in Hanky-Panky Alley (code). Sam was walking up and down. He put his arm round my shoulder. Talked. That's all I'm prepared to say. Gerry arrived. Gerry's got a worried look. Maybe Gerry's not up to it. But, as Sam says, once you're in. When we parted, as Gerry and Sam were walking up the other way, I watched after them. Sam was talking into Gerry's face and I heard Gerry saying, OK, I've got it. Got it. Sam's a born leader. He could talk you into anything.

The salmon was OK but the chips were cold and Ma was asleep in the chair.

Wednesday night or Thursday morning 12.50

Matt's serious. About us going to Birmingham for the weekend. We'd get the ferry and train. Pool our doles. What would Mam and Dad think about that? I will have to put it to them tomorrow. Matt wants to do it soon. Can't deny I'm getting excited in more ways than one. The thought of branching out, just lifting up, almost like flying, even for a couple of days. But then, how can you be free within those limits? If you know you're coming back. Will the coming back ruin it from the start? Chuck says freedom does not exist or it does. If it does you could be in prison and it will still be yours. If it doesn't you could be sailing round the world and be a prisoner. Chuck sets us thinking. He should have been something. He gets the odd job polishing for people but, as he says, it's more fashionable now not to have your wood polished. Nobody's interested in specialists these days. It's a ram-stam world. That's another of Chuck's opinions. Dad says he should have a book published – 'Chuck's Views in Alphabetical Order'. It would be a best seller, he says. Dad's the opposite. He keeps it all to himself.

Sadie and Mam are talking downstairs. I've a feeling Sadie will marry John next year after he finishes university. Everything will be proper and smooth. Sadie has already thought of the answer before you ask her a question. She looks in as though from a height. She'll leave Belfast with John or they will live around the university and shop in Botanic Avenue. Sadie will dress well and everyone who knows her will taste the better side of life.

Now our Madge. I can hear her banging things away in the kitchen. Looking for notice. Maybe she'll pull out of it. She's a year younger than me. Sadie is two years older. Madge does weird things like wearing big woollen socks with a long skirt. She says she's different, and she's always listening to the radio and humming to herself. She criticises Mam and Dad and says there's no fire in them. I don't know what she expects after nine children. She sits on the kitchen table swinging her legs and eating jam doughnuts which she sends the young ones for. She's plump and no wonder. It doesn't help matters. She started doing exercises but she said they made her hungry and it was necessary to send for more jam doughnuts. She's not the most refined of people. Our Pete says he'd prefer to be served in a café by the Incredible Hulk any day.

Eddie Stewart called with the news that our Barney's been mitching school. It's not easy for a fourteen-year-old lad. The teachers don't understand. They just see you as a pupil, not a person who has another life behind. Sometimes they clash, especially today. Barney says he can't concentrate and he's punished for not doing his homework. But I saw him trying. It's not easy with so many in the house. Our Barney is a nice kid but he's getting moody. Here's Madge. I'd better hide this.

Friday 1350 hours

Signed on. The faces in that dole queue. You'd think they were lining up for the Last Judgment and not too sure about where they'd be put. Some people have nothing to look forward to. Their eyes show it, just staring at the next man's back and not even seeing it. It used to get me down when I was one of them. And then the odd Cheerful Charlie who tries to liven them up. But it's all out of place – like shouting in the church. And there's me and Sam and Gerry who have something to do. Even the girl behind the desk knows I'm not just like the man in front. She respects me. One day she almost said something to

me, the way she opened her mouth. But she couldn't, with the
queue and everything, and then she wouldn't be sure if I would
have time. Isn't it funny how the way you feel changes the way
you look. She can see my dignity. I might pass her a note sometime telling her I'll take her out. I like that spotted blouse, the
tight one, and the way her hair just touches her breast. She's not
like some of the others who treat men like dirt. She's nice. I
could see us down at the embankment or even on Vera's couch.
I would tell Sam she's OK.

She's OK but if she was my girl I'd get her out of that place.
I'd show her there's more to life than lines of men in donkey
jackets queuing to write their names.

Met Sam. Only a word. Not good to be seen too much together during the day, Sam said. Will call me later. Had a chat
with Gerry in the street. Did you hear the latest, Gerry asked
me. What latest, I said. On the political side, he said. No, I said,
never listen to those guys these days. Some joke, Gerry said and
went on. I came in and asked Ma. She likes the news. Och, she
said, another one of them what-do-you-call-thems. What, I
said. Och you know, she said, it begins with 'in'. After a while
I guessed – initiatives. Aye, them things, Ma said and went on
cleaning the cups. Is that all, I said, and came up here. As Sam
says, they haven't a clue.

There's a cold wind. Hope the stars are out tonight. We'll be
on the hill looking down on the lights of the city. There it is,
the boss said, that's what we're defending. Ma will be sitting up
at the fire, which reminds me I must fill the coal bucket. Don't
forget the hero's always good to women, so long as they don't
get in the way of his work.

Friday afternoon 2.45 or thereabouts
Laura Munroe's mother bought thirty tins of baked beans this

morning. They're for the siege, she said. She was fuming when somebody accused her of buying up everything and leaving nothing for others. How dare you, she said. My house will be an open door when the time comes. Maggie Denver thought it was a great joke. We'll be all right now, she shrieked, as long as there's beans at Munroes'. But what I want to know, she added, is who's going to provide the toast?

Chuck and Dad came in together. Chuck issued immediate advice that we were not to listen to the gossipmongers. The gossipmongers and the press are panickers, he said. If we listened to all they had to say, we might as well not get out of our beds in the morning. Dad and he and Mam set about discussing it. How they create a dangerous climate and make life more difficult for the rest of us. Mam said, Well let us deal in fact, which is hard enough to take, God knows, and leave fiction for those who need it. Madge left the kitchen at this point, saying was it any use her having *The Archers* on if she couldn't hear a damned word they were saying. Dad got up to go after her for her lack of manners but Chuck said who could blame the child for trying to escape into a world of petty happenings. She still has dreams, he said. Sometimes this house is nuts. The next thing they were all singing 'Beautiful Dreamer'. When they had finished I thought it might be the moment to discuss my dreams of a weekend in Birmingham. I purposely raised it in front of Chuck, hoping for his support. But Chuck can be unpredictable. Birmingham's a dump, he said. He then launched an attack on anyone who hadn't appreciated the fact that he'd worked his guts out in the slums of Birmingham and other such places for the British economy. What thanks did he get, he asked us. None, I said, knowing by his tone that this was the case. I worked my way up to the scrap heap, he said, and his head sank on his chest at a melancholy angle. I left the room, as this was not the reaction I had hoped for.

Nothing will stop me going to Birmingham. Too many people are living with regrets. The best course you can take, I've decided, is to do what you think you should do when you think you should do it. Then at least, whatever happens, you'll have the satisfaction of knowing you did it.

Keeping a diary is good. I can react to my own thoughts.

Saturday 0330 hours

A bit muddled. Try a drink, Sam said, but I didn't really get through it. Maybe not, Sam said, on second thoughts. It was in Vera's. Remember Vera is a friend, Sam said. If you're ever in trouble, come here. Vera was standing in her dressing gown when I arrived. It was slung round and tied. Royal blue. I'd nipped home to tell Ma not to worry, I was back. Sam said nip round to Vera's after if you like. Ma wanted to know how come I'm away again if I'm back. I'm just finishing off a game, you go on to bed, I told her. When I was going down the hall she said, Son, you're all I've got. I'll definitely have to see Mimi Roberts about her.

Vera thought I'd need a coffee so Sam left on an errand. Does Gerry ever come here, I asked Vera. Son, they all come here, she said, even you. She started sort of rolling over to me on the couch. I told her I liked her dressing gown. I was nervous the way she was doing it and all. She's a grown woman. I moved away. Sam should be back any minute, I said and stood up. But she was up like a shot and not allowing me an inch against the wall. I look after Sam, don't worry, she sort of murmured. It's funny, I said, Sam strikes me as the sort who can look after himself. You know what I mean, cheeky, she said. She pulled my ears and I had no choice but to get back on the couch. I was terrified out of my mind when she flapped open the dressing gown. I'm waiting for the girl from the dole, I shouted. This got to her because she pulled herself together. Finish your coffee, she said. She put on a Jim Reeves LP and was singing away in the kitchen when Sam came back. Sam looked at me. I was glad I hadn't stolen his woman. Vera came out and leant against the kitchen door. She winked at Sam. Sam laughed. I laughed.

But I'm not sure about it all. I think it was a test and I don't know if I passed or failed. Maybe they're too smart for me. But then why would they waste their time on me?

By the way, my birthday.

Saturday afternoon 1.15

It's decided. Next weekend. Dad was doubtful but was persuaded a weekend out of this place could only be good. Sadie said I could borrow some of her clothes and Madge said I'll have a rotten time. Pete told me to look out for a job for him. I'll do anything, he said. Tell them that.

Barney was sent home for fighting yesterday. Dad says it's hopeless. He's quite depressed about it. How can you correct somebody without offering them hope? What can he tell our Barney? He's going up to see the principal anyway, to talk. Barney's out hanging about somewhere.

Chuck says somebody has to do something. When Pete sighed and said, We've heard that before, Chuck was on his feet. No, he said, I mean really. Really, something completely new. When are they going to realise there's no hope in any of this? What do you suggest, Dad asked him. At this point everyone was looking as though nothing had any point to it. Everyone except Chuck, that is. Do you know what I've been thinking, he said. Divide the people. A new partition, but not of places, of people. Because, the way I see it, until everybody realises you can't change people's minds we'll get nowhere. Pete went to interrupt but Chuck was in one of his excitements. Nowhere, he repeated. So here's what we do. We let those who want to belong to Britain be ruled by the British government, and those who choose to be ruled by the Republic of Ireland be governed by the Southern government. Pete said that's rubbish, and I asked how it could be worked. How do you expect me to know, Chuck said. It's not up to me to work out the details. Dad said anything new is worth a try at this stage, but there are those who will accept nothing. And yet, Mam said, if they had a decent job there's many who'd leave it at that.

All the people's thoughts. Ideas floating and clashing and breaking and falling and out of the dust another spark, another thought.

Another man was shot today.

Saturday 1829 hours

My birthday. Got the shirt. Blue with white stripes and a card from Ma to her loving son. Mimi Roberts got me a tie to match. I'll wear them tomorrow, I promised Ma, and we'll visit Uncle George and Aunt Jo-Jo. Ma's fussing around flapping her wings like a big hen. Makes me feel I've just hatched out of an egg. I'm the ugly duckling, all awkward and out of place, only Ma doesn't notice. She baked me a cake and put candles on it and her and Mimi sang 'Happy Birthday'. Ma cried and said not to mind her, she'd cried every year since I was born. Then she twiddled the radio knobs until she found dance music and her and Mimi waltzed. They tried to get me up but I said I'd probably end up walking on Mimi's bad leg or something. Don't worry, Ma laughed, we'll have the great nights when he brings a nice wee girl home. I'd love to see their faces if I strolled in with Vera. What a laugh. They're prancing about down there still. Some pair.

Never mentioned it to Sam and Gerry. What's a birthday?

They didn't show up in town. Must have had important business. Smithfield seemed empty without them but I bought chips and listened to music and thought about the times we're having.

They'll send for me tonight.

2350 hours

Strange. Got a message to go to Starker's Strip (code). When I got there there were a few hanging about, but not Sam. Someone's coming to talk to us, they said. Must be important. A weird feeling. Everybody was afraid to say anything to everybody else, not being sure who we were, in case you said the wrong thing. Nobody arrived to talk to us and about eleven we started to drift out. We're being watched, Gerry said. That's it, another guy agreed. And a bloke said, you see that's the whole point of it.

Haven't seen Sam all day, and tomorrow's Sunday. When I came in early Ma said, I'm glad you made a special effort on your birthday. Wasn't it a great party?

Sure was Ma. A party and a half. Pity Mimi's leg played up, she said after me up the stairs. Pity indeed.

Saturday night or Sunday morning 12.40

Matt and I talked about our plans. He got the tickets today. We'll go on the ferry on Friday night to Heysham. It can be a bit rough with drunks and seasickness and that, Matt says, but we'll try to find a wee corner. We walked up the road and talked. Matt's so earnest about everything. We kept each other warm against the night and I had a feeling that together we can reach the centre of something. How can I explain? Well, instead of reaching upwards or outwards, maybe the search should be inwards. I'm not sure, but it's all there already. It's just yourself. The other day I was looking at a simple scene, just the blue sky and white clouds puffing by, and birds drifting easily across. But it gave me a lovely surge of contentment.

Why should I let Matt go? He understands me. Can there be many who understand me? It's just that sometimes in my mind I see myself alone, striding in an unknown place and being in control. Me, of this time. Sitting in a café looking out through the window, fashionably dressed but deep. Take note, you people passing by. Remember this moment. Matt wouldn't fit in there. No, he would lessen my presence.

Dad was out for an hour with Chuck and Eddie Stewart. They brought Pete back. Dad was depressed. If you'd seen him up there, Sarah, he said. Sitting at the counter staring at the bottles. You wouldn't have thought there was one belonging to him. God, does that mean our Pete's one of the sad ones?

Chuck said don't worry, we'll nurse him through this bad patch. He's just lost his dignity for a while. Dad's worried in case he did the wrong thing keeping our Pete in at night and that. It was only to keep him out of trouble, he told Chuck. But now he hasn't really any friends. Chuck said, it's only that you've a family of individuals around you. They'll find their way.

Met Teresa in town today. She envies me getting away for the weekend. She says I won't want to come back. People from all over the world live in Birmingham but it's nothing like London. London is the world. Teresa's cousin lives in London. When she comes home on holiday she's always talking about the bloke upstairs and the bloke downstairs. You should see her clothes, Teresa says. She's a secretary. She has to wear something different every day. According to Teresa.

Belfast would fit into a corner of London. Not that it would fit in.

Sunday 1910 hours

When I walked into that there saloon, gee, ya wanna seen them. Afraida turn their heads, their hands ashakin' before ma mighty presence. A slid ma glass down that there counter an' ya never seen anything like the way that there barman jumped. An' when ah left know what ah heard them say? He never even told us his name.

Spent the afternoon in Aunt Jo-Jo's. Me and Uncle George talked a bit about life. Think he feels responsible for me since I've no da. He said to me, son, you know one day all this will be over and you and I will be left, we hope. I know what my life consists of, but yours, what's yours going to be? I said, What exactly do you mean Uncle George, I'm no different to the fellows anywhere else. Maybe not, son, he said, maybe not. I looked into his face and saw his innocence. And you know, I felt sorry for him. We went for a stroll just as dusk was falling, through the streets and down to the river. We looked into the water and talked about the reflections and he told me my da and him spent many's the hour racing along the banks and playing cowboys. In our bare feet and braces, son. His face looked old in the grey light and I felt sorry for him again. I wanted to tell him I was working for him but I couldn't. As we walked back I thought it's all the more noble not to boast.

When we got back to the house Ma and Aunt Jo-Jo had the table set. They stood back and Aunt Jo-Jo said how she just could not get over how well I looked. We had our tea and I offered to feed the cat.

Ma and me came home in the bus. Uncle George stood at the stop waving after us. Ma said it was a lovely day. When we got off the bus I raced on down to the house in case there was a message for me. There wasn't.

I didn't expect one on a Sunday.

Sunday evening 7.30

Sunday again. I spent most of this Sunday wondering what next
Sunday will be like. Can't imagine it – Sunday out of Belfast.
I made lists today of what to take. Eddie Stewart's leaving us to
the boat. Our wee ones are asking me to bring them something
back. I don't know how I'll manage that, although Dad says he
has a few pounds by and he'll give me something. Hope you're
not eloping, he said to Matt. Because we want to be there when
the day comes. It made me feel a bit uncomfortable. I'm so im-
mersed. I'd like to please them but sometimes it's as though I
can't see properly from in here. Maybe next weekend will make
things clearer.

Might get my hair cut this week, though not short. What way
would you like it, I asked Matt. The way it is, he said. Mam said
my fringe would be better shorter. Maybe a bit.

Our Denny finished a chest of drawers today. He's very
handy. Always working on something. Pete says, So what, anybody could hammer a few nails into a lump of wood. Denny
said that's not the point – anybody didn't do it – I did it.

Pete and Madge are alike. In a way they feel they've nothing
to offer. They have just the same as me, the same as Sadie. Only
they can't see it. Sadie's always had confidence in herself. And
me? I knew there were possibilities. With writing this I feel they
may be opening up. And if I never do anything, at least I'll have
this. It's an extra me. I've created an extension. Sometimes I
think I love it so I can escape into its meaning. But in another
way I'm ashamed of it, like I'm ashamed to cry or I'd be humil-
iated if somebody walked into my room and I had nothing on.
How can I describe it? The rawness or something. You know
what I mean?

I told Matt we shouldn't see each other on Sundays but I
could give him no reason that made sense. He says he needs to
see me especially on Sunday, it's such a lonely day. I hear him

downstairs. We'll have a wee walk, I suppose, and come back and share some of Sadie's cheese on toast. Or he might want me to go over to his house. Sometimes we get a room to ourselves.

Monday 1815 hours

Gerry called this afternoon. Thought we should go out and have a chat. We went to a club he belongs to. He drank beer. I said a couple of shandies will do me no harm, but I must be sure to keep my wits about me. What do you think of this place, Gerry asked me. It's a fine place, Gerry, I said. A fine place, now what's the problem? No problem, Gerry answered, only, what do you think of Sam? What do I think of Sam, I said. It was a bit of a surprise, him coming out with that. He was taking a chance, I would have thought. But I had no trouble with my answer. I think Sam's a genius, a leader of men, I said. Gerry appeared thoughtful, rubbing his beard and sipping away slowly. I see, he said, a leader of men. Then he turned to me. What about women, he asked me. Out of the blue like that. Women? I said. Yes women, you know, and he made a shape in the air. I know what they are, I said. What about them? He said nothing more but kept staring at me. As far as I know, I continued, Sam is a one-woman man. A one-woman man, he repeated. Are you by any chance referring to Vera? Yes, I said. Vera, that's right, Vera. I was drinking away casually at my shandy, thinking to myself how careless Gerry was, talking like this in a public place, when it came to my notice that his cheeks were bulging and he was trying not to laugh. I stood up at this point, feeling my presence was no longer useful. If it's all right with you, I'll leave now, I said. Sure, Gerry answered, that's all right.

Gerry's a peculiar type, though I wouldn't mention it, not even to Sam.

When I came in Ma met me in the hall. I was just going out

to the door to watch for you, she says. Why, I asked her. I walked past and into the kitchen. You know what Mimi Roberts was telling me? she said. Mimi says she wouldn't trust the ones that's playing billiards these days. I was rinsing my hands under the tap. Where's the towel, I asked her. Behind the door where it always is, she says. There's none there, I said. What? She didn't believe me until she looked for herself. My God, she said and scurried off to the hot press. Mimi Roberts doesn't know everything, I shouted after her. Between puffing back down the stairs she said, Nobody knows everything, but some people know a lot, and Mimi Roberts has contacts. Contacts? I took the towel from her. It was nice and warm. Now, she said, all pleased with herself, don't you be so sure of yourself in future. What are you talking about, Ma, I said, but she had her head in the oven getting my dinner out.

When I was eating away at it she stood over me. She nearly always does that, in case I need the salt passed or something. Your oul' ma hasn't her head in the sand, she said. Just remember that.

There's no good me talking to Mimi Roberts about her if that's the sort of talk Mimi Roberts is coming out with. I'll just carry on regardless. It's my quiet importance they don't understand. My rise from nothing.

Anyway I'd better get ready. I've got somewhere to go.

Monday night 11.52

A word before midnight. Laura Munroe has disappeared. She hasn't been seen since yesterday. The police and everybody are looking for her. They're working on the theory that she has run away. Still, it's dangerous these days. Madge is wandering about as if she's the star of a show or something because she was the last one to see Laura. They went down to Ken's chippy last night. Madge has told the story a hundred times but it's not really much of a clue. She was fed up, Madge says. She told me she was fed up. She misses that guy from Australia. We got a bit of a shock when Mrs Munroe said there is no guy from Australia. It's all in Laura's mind, she said. That's what's wrong with our Laura. She's a dreamer. She imagines things that aren't there at all. Mrs Munroe is in an awful state. We all promised if Laura's found we'll not pretend we know about the guy. But I wouldn't depend on our Madge, she gives the impression she's gloating. There was a photo of Laura in tonight's *Telegraph*. Laura's dad hired a car and he and Dad drove around most of the day looking for her. Our Madge went with them. It's getting very worrying, going into a second night. Madge says she's going down to the local radio station to make an appeal for her friend to return.

Tuesday morning 11.15

Laura was picked up on the airport road. It was an awful night and she was sitting on a bank along the road, soaked and shivering. She hardly seemed to remember who she was or where she'd been. The man who picked her up said she just kept saying, I've got to get out of here. He took her to the police station. Mrs Munroe was over here a while ago. She says Laura's in bed resting, and at the moment they can't say much about it. The doctor gave her a sedative. Madge is down in the dumps, as if she almost had importance but it faded before she could grasp it. And, after all, it's Laura who's the centre of attention and Madge is away down to Ken's café to serve teas as usual.

I can see Laura bogged down. She tasted a bigger possibility and then she was led back here when she was too young to decide. For a while, I suppose, it was a novelty but now what are her options? Something will have to be done for Laura.

Something will have to be done for Madge. Something will have to be done for Pete. Something will have to be done for Barney. Barney's the luckiest. For the others it may be too late.

Mam and I are taking a turn in the town when Dad comes in. I'll pick up a few bits and pieces for Birmingham. I can't imagine life now without the prospect of Birmingham. My little bored brain is churning out all sorts of ideas. It will have the responsibility if things go wrong. I'll never forgive it. I'll beat it back to its limits if it takes me beyond the physical possibilities. Does that mean anything? I wonder.

Tuesday 1335 hours

Not long up. Didn't report last night. Well I did, but not to me. Had a game of billiards in the hall. Some of the old mates but, although I'm for them, I'm beyond them in a way. It's difficult. Only my nobility carries me through at such times. It's a question of quality. I mean, it would be easy to be a bully, but this is different. I feel a better person than them but I wouldn't treat them roughly. Some of us are chosen to stand out, and when I watched them last night talking to each other about nothing, I could hardly understand or remember what their lives are about. I nearly despised them but then I recognised my duty to win something back for them.

There's the difference. When I came in, Ma said Sam had called. Did he leave a message? I asked her to which she replied that she wasn't sure he wanted me at all. He accepted a cup of tea and a buttered soda farl, she said, and we had a great chat altogether about the olden times. Sam's not old, I said to her. He may not be, she says, but he has the wit to know what's in a woman's soul. Not like most these days who couldn't string two words together that make sense at all, let alone get to the core of the matter. I asked her again what did he say and finally she admitted – well he did say one thing. What was that, I asked her. She was straightening the covers on the couch and taking her time about answering me. She likes to play it cool some-times, especially when she thinks she has a secret. Well? I asked her. Oh, yes, she said. Wait till I get it right now, and if she didn't sit down on the couch and stare across at the window as if her memory was floating somewhere there, or on out in the yard. Now what was it? Yes, it was – The waters may separate man from his destiny for a time, but undefeated his spirit will return to raise those who waited in hope. Is Sam going away? I asked her. She shook her head and when she went past me into the kitchen she tapped me on the cheek. In ways you're still a child, she said. She was getting my goat up now. Well, what does it mean then, I said after her, you tell me. Well, she said, it wasn't so much the words. It was the way he said them. In the name of God, Ma, I said, did he tell you to tell me that or what. I was afraid it might be somewhere I was to go. Son, she said, I can't remember that he mentioned your name. Then she went off humming one of those old-time songs.

It's just that you don't understand Sam's cleverness, I said. And what's more, I know exactly what he meant. I wonder what she thought of that. As for me, there was no need to act on such unreliable information. Sam found I wasn't at home and he decided to humour Ma. Still, I'm sorry I missed him. It mightn't look good. I'll take a walk around later and see if I can run into him. Anyway, I'm thinking of waiting outside for the girl at the dole. I feel I could approach her today.

Tuesday evening 7.40

I liked Mam's plaid coat. We had tea in White's café. It's easy to feel she'll always be there. It doesn't change. Not that she should be, but that you know she would. And yet in another way, I wanted to be detached. To have been doing just that, but from a stronger position of my own. Sitting opposite her with my own statement.

The town was normal enough. We peeked into Ken's chippy. Mam said, for God's sake don't let her see us. There she was, hanging over the counter gazing into some bloke's jaw. I'm sure all he wanted was a plate of chips. Madge says you could deep-fry chips off some of the faces you see in there. His did not appear to be one of them. He was good-looking and Madge was making no bones about it. We hurried on.

We had a table near the window in White's. We watched the world and I snapped it as one of those moments. Aunt Sadie liked near the window, Mam said. She watched the fashion and imagined she played a full part in the life of the city. Then she did, I said. We talked a bit about the sickness now, under the outer layer of normality. The feeling that some of the men passing by might not be just men passing by. The niggling fear that made you glance to make sure that anyone who took a parcel in, took it out with them. I had a feeling of being one of the people of this place, of this time, maimed by it all and not able to do anything about it.

Yet there was some sort of tiny mood edging in. A small uplift, that we two were lucky because of a certain amount of control, because of the strength of our family, maybe a refinement. Something that's difficult to describe. But you know, I came out of White's feeling overall secure and optimistic.

I dropped some coins into a tramp's hat. He reinforced my mood. He didn't threaten me and he was like an old building – a necessary part of the city. He suggested permanency and I admired him for having survived the turmoil of the last few years. When I looked into his weak, distant eyes I thought, maybe he hasn't noticed any difference. What are a few bangs, a photo in the paper, and some extra rubble in the life of a man

who has no one to mourn and whose bed is the grey brick
of a doorway?

Big thoughts.

We did some shopping in the British Home Stores. Under-
wear for me, slippers for Dad.

She doesn't show her emotions easily. Neither do I. But I
think we both knew. I had that feeling coming back in the taxi.
You know, easy.

Wednesday 0050 hours

I'm in about a half an hour. Mimi Roberts was at the door and
she called me over. Do you know how much your mother worries about you? she asked me. I'm worried about her, I said.
Have you noticed how often she cleans those cups? Never mind
the cups, Mimi said. Do you know the sort that's in the city
these days? She's worried you're mixed up in something. The
last thing I am, I said to Mimi, is mixed up. I had to keep it light.
But she went on, She's worried sick. Why don't you stay in at
night? Just until this is all over. You're all she's got, you know.
I'm all right, I said, don't you worry about me. It's only a game.
What's a game, she asked me. Billiards, I said. I declare to God,
she said, and shut the door. I stood a minute looking at the dark
green door and I could see old Mimi limping back into the
kitchen. But what could I say to her? What can you say to
Mimi Roberts?

Anyway, Ma wasn't bad when I came in. She still had a big
fire and music on the radio. Mimi was at the door, I told her,
for something to say. I had a word with her. She was looking
at the stars. A fat lot of stars she can see between them roofs,
Ma said. I boiled the kettle and she took a drink of tea. She
started telling me again about the time the three of us stayed in
Newcastle for our holidays and they took me down to the

beach at night to see the moon on the sea. It was like a picture, she said. There wasn't a breath, and to top it all we heard music in the distance.

I came on up here. About earlier on – I hung around outside the dole till some of the office workers came out. I watched from across the street. Then she came, but she was with another girl. They were laughing. She was wearing a blue trench coat with a belt. I followed them down the street. The other girl was chattering away, but she was listening mostly. She has class, and the odd time she shook her hair back over her shoulders. They parted at the corner. I stood and watched her walking on up towards the city centre. Just watched her and thought of her standing in the shadow of her room, near the window with the curtains open, quietly taking off her clothes and letting them drop on the carpet. I couldn't have interrupted that. Not then.

Gerry called tonight with Sam's orders to go and meet some people in the Nutcracker's Suite. Gerry remarked to me that Sam's keeping a low profile these days. The more important you get, I said. A couple of big names talked to us about the future, the way it's going to go, how much we are needed. This type of thing. We're getting closer, Gerry said on the way home.

Wednesday afternoon 12.30

Chuck says, how can you compare a life with an idea. You can't kill one person to achieve something, not even one. You haven't the right, it just isn't yours. Pete argued about extreme frustration, but Chuck said, even that. There are more effective ways anyway, ways that would unite people. Killing only divides them more. Because killing is the ultimate fear.

Dad is sporting his new slippers and he came up with a good idea. What about a dartboard, Sarah, he said. To keep the boys going. And myself and Chuck might even join in. We might even make it into a club if it's successful. Mam smiled at him as if he was a child and he sat down at the fire with his folded paper on his knee, looking into the flames and seeing his dart-board and all the lads around it. And maybe something from his past. I know he's thinking about our Barney as well because the principal says he needs careful watching. He feels he has a grievance and he could be perfect bait. They've agreed to let up on the homework to try to take the pressure off. It's only right. School should be a haven for children these days. To keep them from escaping into the arms of something worse.

School should be happy. A place for unworry. Because boys and girls aren't sure. Tasting, touching, sampling, waiting. And letting it be.

Matt and I walked and talked last night. And planned. We went through it all again so there won't be any hitches. Sailing out and away. Away from what? All this, all of it crowding behind and us separating away, drifting out in a dark water cloud. Swaying on top of it like the waves we used to draw on the page in school. The squiggly waves with the ship sailing above. Always across the horizon. Never coming back. Never really.

Wednesday 2350 hours

Just back from Vera's. Went to check Sam's whereabouts. She was on her own. I'm waiting for him too, she said. Sam's an elusive hawk, she said. The royal blue dressing gown was belted. I said I didn't mean to interrupt, I'd head on if Sam's not here. After all, he could be at my house. Come in, she said, the coffee's on. If there's one thing about this house, she said when she was going into the kitchen, it's that the coffee's always on. And the dressing gown, I thought.

I couldn't imagine Vera with relatives, or a job or anything. She's just Vera.

Where did you meet Sam, I asked her, when we were sitting drinking our coffee. The record-player was on low, the man's voice was scraping. It was thin, sort of like an echo I heard one time in a cave. Matt Monro's great, she had said when she was dusting the record with the sleeve of her dressing gown. Great, I said. I always agree when it's not worth disagreeing. I was beginning to think that on Vera's turntable everybody sounded the same. Reduced to the same small squeak. Maybe Sam would buy her a new one some day.

It wasn't a case of meeting Sam, she said. He just sort of arrived, or maybe he was always here. I seem to forget, she laughed. She was sitting on the couch with her legs up under her. One bare knee was sticking out. There were goose pimples on it, or maybe it was her age. But it had a mystery I would have liked to explore. Sam knew it. Even it was Sam looking out at me.

To get off the subject of Sam, in case it got to him that I was making enquiries, I told her I had met a nice girl. Oh really, she said and leant towards me. Now you tell me, 'cause I'd really like to know, what's a nice girl? It embarrassed me. Well, it's not something you can describe. You just know.

It was getting late and the cup was empty.

I'll tell Sam you called, Vera said. It was just in case I was needed, I said. Of course, Vera said.

Women like Vera are to be taken with a pinch of salt. She makes you feel like Matt Monro sounds on her record-player. But who is she, anyway? Who is Vera?

Ma's still padding about the room. What does she be doing? Drawers opening, scrawling closed, things thudding on the floor. Sometimes I think it's her, but I hear the noises again and her breath. She breathes heavy these days. I wait for the click of the light switch and the springs of the bed. Then silence.

Thursday evening 7.40

Another day to go. Most of my stuff is packed. Me and Sadie went through it all. You've enough there for two weeks, Sadie said. It's hard to judge, I told her. She's lending me her good coat with the felt collar.

Our Pete's looking at me like a sorry pet dog I'm leaving behind. I never thought of it that way but maybe with me and him not working, he thought we were, well, the same. He's watching me from a corner, a dark corner with the light shining away from it. You know the feeling on a sunny day when the sun suddenly vanishes and dullness takes over. I feel like that when I look at him. He's making me feel guilty. He's making me sink. At least our Madge moans openly, never leaves you in any doubt about how she's feeling. She spits it all out before it gets near the depths. Our Pete's a sad soaker, a sad soaker without an outlet. Like a black hole in the sand when the tide comes in and gradually it fills up. It's bound to overflow.

Our Pete is the black hole.

Dad came into the room a minute ago. He gave me twenty pounds. I told him about the diary. He said that's good, that's very good. I thought he was going to say something else but he didn't seem to think of anything. When he left I wondered did he feel out of place now with us all growing up and him not coming in on a Friday with his pay or anything. He always shaves and dresses well. At first he used to say, in case somebody calls from the dole. To show I'm ready for a job. But nobody ever called and he just kept up the habit. Dad believes in an even life. Keep on the smooth surface, no matter who around is rising or falling.

Private thoughts for England. To keep me company. To remind me and maybe deepen the experience or detach me from it. If I want that.

Friday 1420 hours if the clock's right

I wish I had a longer name. She smiled. Warmer than for the man in front. I drank her perfume and it tingled through my body. I can still smell it. Maybe it passed onto my clothes. My hand nearly touched hers when she reached to take the card. It nearly did, and we looked straight into each other's eyes so that we were telling each other. I swear we were. Hers are round and almost green. In a dark entry they would shine and melt in sorrow. It would be like a close-up in a film. I would make her cry just to watch her tears and to protect her. And then she would sleep with her hair falling all over the white pillow and she would know that I was there, so that a silent peace would rest on her lips. I love her. She knows my name.

Time out in Birmingham

It began when they were met at the station. She stepped inside the person who was waiting on the platform.

Matthew's brother was also waiting with a broad smile and a look of possession on his face. He could have been standing at the entrance to a large country house. He could have been saying, 'I bought this with my own money. Welcome.' He did say 'Welcome'. Colette smiled shyly and gratefully.

'This is Colette,' Matthew said.

Colette peeled herself from the memory of the crossing

and held her hand out to the stranger grinning self-assuredly before her.

'This is Christopher,' Matthew said.

'Christopher,' she repeated, 'good to see you.'

'And a pleasure to meet you.' Christopher bowed slightly towards her.

Matthew looked from one to the other. Proudly. 'Right,' he said, 'are we right?'

Colette walked between them out of the station. She was distantly present, relieved at the refinement of the people around. They were having polite conversations, in twos and in groups and weren't spitting and swearing and sliding in pools of Guinness.

'How was the crossing?' Christopher asked.

'Dreadful,' Matthew said.

'They always are,' Christopher commented. 'On account of the peasants.' He laughed.

Colette stepped into the car. She sat in the back behind the two brothers and looked from side to side as they drove through the streets of Birmingham. In order not to miss anything, not to miss Birmingham. To encapsulate it, store it.

'Lin will have a nice lunch prepared.' Christopher inclined his head towards her. 'Chinese style. I hope you'll like it.'

'We've eaten Chinese food,' Matthew said casually.

Christopher laughed. 'In the restaurants you mean? Oh please, don't say that to Lin. Oh no, that wouldn't do.'

Matthew looked at his brother in slight confusion.

'I'm sure we'll love it,' Colette said, demurely.

She was relieved that she hadn't been the one to mention the Chinese restaurants. Exercising caution often paid off. Maintaining silence could be interpreted in many ways, ignorance being only one of them, but making an outright blunder – well, that was unambiguous to say the least.

Christopher pointed out various places of interest along the way. Colette listened but asked no questions.

There were people from various parts of the world here. Apart from the coloured soldiers who moved in sunlight and shadows close to garden walls, and of course (dare she mention it even to herself?) the men and women who served in the Chinese restaurants, and their attractive children, all the people she had ever known wore the same pinky, whity skin, with slight variations of red and even purple. But nothing like this. She was surprised that she had to admit to a feeling almost approaching fear, or was it simply strangeness?

She was struck by the volume of traffic and the scale of the movement of people. There appeared to be more hurry than in Belfast. She remembered the unemployment situation but considered that, nevertheless, the people she saw through the window had somewhere to go. She also had somewhere to go. She and Matthew had travelled across the Irish Sea. They had chosen to do so and here they were being driven through the streets of Birmingham. It was movement. It was choice and, more than these, it was like a flower of possibility opening up its petals.

'Of course we'll have a closer look at the centre of Birmingham,' Christopher was saying. 'Maybe this afternoon if you're up to it. A weekend isn't very long but we have a few things lined up.'

'We might never go back.' Matthew smiled round at Colette. She looked confidently happy in the shadow of the back seat.

'Anything's possible,' she said. But then, not to give the wrong impression, not to worry Christopher with the thought that, secretly, they might be planning to plant themselves on him, she added, 'If only we had no commitments.'

'Indeed, commitments,' Matthew agreed.

'Well, let's forget about those for the weekend,' Christopher said.

'This is Smethwick now,' he told them as they drove down a road with no special features. He looked at his watch. 'We're fairly well on time. Lin likes punctuality.'

This extension to the previously uncomplicated portrait of Lin, the Chinese girl, caused Colette's thoughts to jolt. It was definite and demanding, to like punctuality. She considered what it implied and wondered what could be said of her – 'Colette likes – ?'

'Yes, I'm pretty keen on being on time myself,' Matthew said. He was straightening his tie. 'Isn't that right, Colette?'

The houses and people moved back in a bleary way, out of her gaze. She continued staring through the side window but somehow Lin stood there. Waiting. An uneasy thought buzzed in her mind. What was it Matthew was saying about punctuality? But Christopher saved her from having to respond. He turned to his brother.

'What, you?' he said derisively. 'That's something new if you do.'

'What do you mean?' Matthew accosted him.

'I seem to remember that you held the school record for late marks,' Christopher answered.

'What's that got to do with it?' Matthew said. He laughed and his brother joined in. Colette laughed. She noted how similar the backs of their heads were, and tried to picture them running, school bags slung into the school yard. She heard children's voices of abandon in the past.

The car stopped. They were outside a three-storeyed terraced house in a long street of three-storeyed terraced houses.

'This is it,' Christopher announced.

There was nothing to say. No need to comment on the fact that this was it. Matthew stretched, yawned and, as his brother got out of the car and went to the boot, he turned and looked at Colette.

'Are you all right?' he asked, reaching his hand in and touching hers.

'Yes, I'm really fine,' she answered. She smiled.

'You've been strange since we met Christopher,' he said.

'How?' she asked and inclined her head a little to the side.

'I don't know,' he hesitated. 'Just strange.'

'I'm not used to meeting people,' she said unconvincingly.

But she was pleased because it meant that Matthew had noticed she was different.

'Come on, you two, I'm not carrying all this myself,' Christopher shouted in at them.

'Coming,' Matthew said.

'He has a slight Birmingham accent,' Colette said when they were climbing from the car. Christopher was at the front door.

'Well, here goes,' Colette whispered.

'Hi, darling.' Lin smiled over Christopher's shoulder, out of his embrace, regarding the newcomers from the security of her world. Colette was struck by a mysterious beauty in her face. It was mysterious yet open. Both these qualities merged and Colette found herself having to reconsider. Start again. Because this was Lin. That was the point.

Colette stood apart from Matthew. She could not have smiled out of his embrace. Not publicly. But it wasn't only that. The smile she returned, though genuine, was not out of a world. It was out of uncertainty. It was on the edge of a background that at this moment shimmered and shook and threatened to crumble and fall away.

'You're welcome,' Lin said. She came forward and took each of their hands in turn. 'We will try to make your stay enjoyable.'

Her English was impeccable and attractively spoken.

'Thank you,' Colette said.

Everything here is wonderful, Colette thought. She accepted a second glass of wine and said aloud, 'Everything here is wonderful.' Was it giving too much away? In other words, if everything here was so wonderful, what was she used to? So far all she had done was have a Chinese lunch, delicious though it was, and one glass of wine. But they were all smiling and she had spoken out confidently. Matthew was puffing on a large cigar and, in the slight haze which had developed, it appeared to Colette that nothing suited Matthew better than to puff on a large cigar. Another way of looking at it was that the cigar was in control and was commanding clouds of smoke to emanate from Matthew's mouth at irregular intervals.

It was relaxing. Christopher insisted on showing his brother the many cupboards, units, drawers and wooden things with no names which he had made to adorn the flat. Matthew asked questions about how they were assembled.

Colette watched Lin's face discreetly and saw the Oriental darkness of her past and the bright fulfilment of her present. She helped her to clear the lunch things away but she felt clumsy in the kitchen and a little light. She made the excuse that she was tired after the journey and came back to the room to finish her glass of wine. She smiled broadly and thought the afternoon would wave comfortably in front of her. And that she would talk presently.

Lin curled up on the couch. She had her shoes off and her head was resting on Christopher's shoulder. It upset Colette who thought, we don't do things like that in Belfast. Not in front of people. Besides, it's difficult to converse with people who are stuck together. Whose brains are interwoven.

'I'd like to unpack please,' Colette said. She glanced towards

Matthew who smiled as though to say, go ahead.

Lin sprang up. 'Of course,' she said. 'I shall take you to your room.'

Your room. In the plural. She sat on the bed and thought about that. It was so natural. Like 'our room'. This is our room. But it was so stupid the way she had blushed and looked confused. Because there was no answer to that. Yet it was pleasant. It was wavering in front of her like she had expected.

She began unpacking. There was a chest of drawers each. How does one achieve this, she thought. She sat on the bed and laughed at the idea of it all. She laughed at the two chests of drawers, tidied out and prepared, with clean brown paper lining each drawer. She laughed at the dressing table with its white lace mats. At the empty wardrobe with hangers waiting. At the fresh pink bedspread and the clean white pillows.

She laughed and became serious in anticipation of the stranger who would enter the room. They were all strangers down there. All together and strangers, and across the blue depths, the sinking, moving, gathering waters of separation there was the family. She had been peeled off. Was it too much to ask, that she could act separately, whole? She got up and stood at the window. Looking across the stark, still roof tops and, all the way, the buildings pushed into the skyline, all the way, with the many people of a city huddled underneath. Was it any different? But it was, because of the Oriental girl downstairs and Matthew's brother who had made all the cupboards, and their lives together. And the fact that she was up here alone looking out at unfamiliarity.

It was the thin shaft of light that woke her, that caused her thoughts to climb and wander through amazement and doubt and shivery secret knowledge. He was there, sleeping intimately. They hadn't discussed it but she had been preoccupied for the rest of the day. As though she had made a statement about herself. To him. To them. And yet what had she done other than to accept the room?

It was being taken for what she maybe wasn't. Publicly.

Privately, his whole skin was surprisingly babyish. They fitted in warm shapes and she had the same doubts and joys about their intimacies. The intimacies of those who aren't quite ready. It was no different, sleeping together, except the long closeness. Matthew hinted at a sophistication but was calmed and ultimately satisfied. Enough to grunt and snuggle into her silence. It was all right, but the yellow line of light persisted and unsettled her and in the end it was the knowledge of the couple lying in the next room, enwrapped in complacency, which disturbed her rest.

So that Matthew awoke to find her sitting at the bottom of the bed, fiddling with her nightdress ribbons.

'Colette?'

She moved to the window and parted the curtains slightly. A weak morning light sprinkled across the bedclothes. She closed the curtains and moved over to the wardrobe.

'I'm getting up,' she said.

Matthew poked for his watch. 'It's only a quarter past seven,' he mumbled.

'Is it?'

'Come on back to bed.'

What was there to do at a quarter past seven? In the house of strangers in an unfamiliar city? What was there to do that they would notice, become aware of?

'I'm too quiet,' she said. She was lying staring upward and Matthew was on his side watching her. He laughed affectionately and moved closer.

'How do you make that out?' He kissed the side of her face.

'No,' she said. She wriggled further to the edge of the bed.
'I mean I'm too quiet. I am.'

They walked amongst busy market stalls and foreign coloured
fabrics. Rising, chattering, singing accents, broken and un-
broken, speckled the confused air, the crowded picture sucking
them forward, spurting them backwards. Colette wandered in
the force. On her own she could have wandered tastefully, still
with the taunting vision, alone, experiencing. But Lin's pace
scorned hesitation, darting playfully, she knew where she was
going, what she wanted. And even if she didn't, there was
knowledge in that. It was her manner. Lifting materials grace-
fully and expertly, her deft handling unaffected by scrutiny.
'What do you think of this, Colette? For the bathroom window.' 'Very nice. It would do well.' Rejected, dropped into the
shocking pile, swallowed back by the heaving patchwork cloth
monster. It was horrible in the first place. But she had been
asked and she wanted to be right. It was stupid, she had been
unprepared, unthinking. She trailed and she was being denied
the experience.

The brothers were in a nearby bar, together, where she
would have liked to have been, sharing, talking. Why had he
assumed she would wish to shop. A woman likes to shop even
if she's buying nothing. Women together, he would expect
them to come back with a developed togetherness. He would
see her alienation, her slumped quietness. He would see Lin's
radiant satisfaction, her plastic bag of success, the fresh fish, her
bargaining power written all over the loose vegetables, the
specialist spices. The ingredients of a well-planned meal. An
ordered half of a solid relationship, a carved corner protected by
sureness. He would see her empty arms beside, her sullen attitude, because she felt it. And it wasn't that she wanted to be
like Lin. It was that she didn't know.

★ ★ ★

'I'm tied up,' she said. 'I've a feeling I might never get free.'

'Free from what?' Matthew asked her, but he didn't want a long discussion. He was tired of discussions about freedom and oppression and downtrodden people. He was enjoying this, immediately enjoying it and planning in his brain that it would be his. And hers. He wanted her to snap out of it.

'You seemed so confident on the way here in the car.'

'I was.'

'Are you worried about them at home?'

'Who?'

'Your family.'

'I don't think so. Not worried.'

'Then what?'

'I might have to go off on my own.'

'Why?'

'Because I might not be capable of it. I might not.'

'They seem very happy, don't they?' He nodded towards the other room.

'Seem. But it's superficial.' She had to say that. And she had to say, 'If you want that with me you'll never have it. It's neat. You know what I mean, neat. Neat and nothing.'

Matthew spent some time over his preparations.

'We never do things like this at home,' he said. He was combing his hair above her, into the dressing-table mirror, perfecting its shape, parting the smooth thickness and finally leaving it to rest like a carefully placed cap.

Colette glanced up. She had a smudge of beige foundation liquid unspread on her cheek.

'You've a fine head of hair,' she said.

'Do you like it?' He patted it, pleased.

'It's healthy,' she said.

They would look good together. It was good to look good

together. She was at ease when they stepped into the car. Eating
out represented equality. Eating together, drinking wine, and
talking. It was an even, undemanding thing to do.

She suggested a lot. A lot behind, before, after. And mysterious pauses. Lin did not understand, clearly could not fathom
the loops and folds, the profundities. Matthew supported,
denied, stated that it was all dreadful, strangling, but could be
sorted out or left. He would leave it, they would leave it.

'I have left it,' Christopher said. He turned his soul to Lin
who spread herself into a smile and cut them out momentarily
with a kiss.

'Just right, and I will too,' Matthew said. 'We will, won't we,
Colette? It's her large family, coming from a large family.'

'Oh, yes, I would love a large family,' Lin said. 'In fact I shall
have a large family.'

'It's to be with, yet alone,' Colette said, leaning forward as
though that were it, the final word. She raised her wine glass
and smiled at Matthew who sat back relaxed, and sipping.

'It's been good but it's nearly over,' Matthew said.

'I spoke to a coloured man,' Colette said. She was drinking
tea and kneeling flipping over Christopher's LPs.

'It's a bit much, all the same, them taking off like that at this
time of the evening. I mean with us here as guests and all.'

'It's been a tiring weekend for them. They need a rest.' She
examined the cover of one of the records, accentuating her
detachment.

'Some rest,' Matthew sulked.

She got up and came towards him, with the record swinging
teasingly in her hand. 'I tell you what,' she said, 'we'll go up
ourselves for half an hour.'

A bright suspicion flickered in Matthew's eyes.

'Go on, you go on up, I'll follow you when I rinse these

cups.' She nudged him encouragingly and affected an innocent cuteness by lowering her head and widening her eyes.

Matthew went to rise, then changed his mind. 'You're having me on,' he said.

'Am I? Oh, all right then, we'll forget it. Forget I ever said it.' She got up and went towards the kitchen.

'No, listen, I'm away up. I'll expect you.' Matthew touched her shoulder, gave her a long look, then left the room.

Colette sat on the floor and listened to the music, the words, the experienced meaning of Paul Simon. It was new to her, new yet old. She wondered had Matthew fallen asleep or was he seething.

Finally the voice irritated her, the message, line after line, the air to make it attractive, the message or the meaning, the song after song, and the threat that there was another side. It was an interference after all.

She went upstairs. Matthew was pulling on a jacket. He scarcely glanced when she closed the door behind her.

'Are you going somewhere?' she asked.

'I'm going to the pub. I'll be back for dinner.' He opened the door.

'No, wait,' she said, 'I might as well...'

'Might as well what?'

'Go too,' she said.

'I'll see you,' he said.

'I'm going out,' she shouted after him. 'I'm going out. I'm not sitting here for the next hour and a half.' But he was gone. And they probably heard her, through one wall they were bound to, and it would sound awful to hear her shouting that, that she couldn't spend the next hour and a half sitting here. It was ungrateful to say the least. She would be embarrassed at dinner and maybe that was what mattered, that she would be embarrassed.

★ ★ ★

They were furrowing in a huge blob of rippling ink. The drone of the boat sliced through the dark blue desert, cutting it and leaving it intact. Behind, it sprayed and settled, met and bobbed, and the increasing mass of rolling liquid shimmered permanently.

'We're nowhere,' Colette said.

'You're never nowhere,' Matthew said. They were looking into it, across it. Colette had her collar up against the cold and her hair blew wildly. He was holding on to her, as if afraid she might be sucked into the black force of air and water.

'It's the nearest thing to nowhere,' she said. If you thought of nowhere you thought of darkness, a sort of falling black. Like death. Was it because when you closed your eyes you saw black, or because the night brought darkness. Those who believed in an afterlife thought of light, light glowing radiantly, everywhere. Those who didn't believe saw themselves sinking into dark permanent nothingness. Some could cope with that.

'Oh God, I forgot to ask for Pete,' she said.

'Ask what for Pete?' When he spoke he was receiving comfort from her nearness. She felt that and it sparked a thin flame of regret that she hadn't made more of it, that they had had all that time together and, in a way, she had been foraging into its possibilities, irritably shutting off little openings, nipping buds. Standing between herself.

'For a job. I told Pete.'

'It's freezing up here,' he said. 'Come on down, we'll have a cup of tea.'

They sat opposite each other. She warmed her hands on the cup and felt the coldness drain from her face.

'There's nobody to ask,' he said.

'What?' She was smoothing her hair down now and thinking she wanted to lie in the warm shape. Now that she couldn't.

Nobody would take away what they had known, yet they could lose it themselves.

'There's nobody to ask for Pete,' he said.

'I wish I could say I tried,' she said. 'At least that would be something.'

Bangor for the day

Fragmented thoughts of her. There was a lot he didn't understand – the people who stood in the four corners of his mind. His mother, Sam, Vera, and her. They were in his mind, so he possessed them, their experience of him. He told of it in the diary and of his growing importance, the swaying reality of his fringe involvement.

When he was a boy they used to take to the mountain occasionally. They always seemed to be looking for the path. Everybody uses it, they would say, it must be here somewhere. Maybe it's overgrown, they said. When they found a path they climbed ecstatically, only to find often that it led nowhere, but faded into the general growth. His mother would say, 'I couldn't have gone any further anyway. It's time to rest.' And she would plant herself on a stone and point out to him the city below. He would drink water from the big lemonade bottle. It was as if they had reached the summit.

You were always working on hints. It was a question of interpretation, acting on a look, a word that to someone else could appear meaningless. It was to be on the uptake, to accept messages. He knew. It was why they needed him.

Sam had called and was gone, but the point was not that he was gone, but that he had called. There were instructions, passed on by his mother who thought they were all to do with the game of billiards. Or in letter form. Places mentioned, meetings taking place, doors opening on to other doors which sometimes seemed to shut just as he reached them, whereupon he reinterpreted the original message or accepted the test patiently.

Protection was a word he understood. It referred to people, to territory, to ideas. To be the protector, not the aggressor, was to be on the side of right. He accepted his role. It had been given to him, but in a sense it had always been his. There were examples from his school days, so that it would be said later it was always obvious he would stand out. Leaders had a certain look too, a look that suggested their experience of the deeper aspects of life, a look that was lacking on the face of any businessman he had seen in the newspaper. Or any politician, for that matter. He had that look. He could see it in the mirror. It was there all right.

It was some vague thought or maybe a dream in the early morning, that hazy floating period when the eyes refuse to recognise the return of the conscious state, and thoughts and dreams overlap, that set the plan in motion. When he got up it became clearer and stronger, it became a message. It was to go to Bangor, to wander around Bangor because that's where he would take her on their first date. Out of the city and down to Bangor. In the train. Bangor had class and it had anonymity. He wondered had Vera ever been to Bangor. Had she ever been out of her flat, when it came to it, not that it mattered. Not that it mattered what Vera did, except in so far as she was a part of Sam's world.

'I'm going on a bit of a trip today,' he told his mother. He was eating the juicy buttered baps she had set before him, the fresh buttered baps she ran out to get every morning for his breakfast. Behind him the morning fire blazed. He never came down to a cold grate. She was slithering between the table and the fire, tending to both, but when she heard his threat she stood before him, rubbing her hands on the front of her apron.

'A trip?' she repeated.

'Down to Bangor,' he said, ignoring her alarm and continuing to stuff the fresh dough into his mouth, following each mouthful with a gulp of tea.

'I'm going to Bangor for the day. It's a treat. I'm treating myself to a day in Bangor.'

She was concerned to establish that he was going alone, and when she was reassured that he was friendless, she sat down at the corner of the fire.

'Mimi's calling on her way from the shops,' she said.

When he was setting off down the hall she called after him to mind the water.

Along the street he met Mimi, straining to one side to balance the black, bulging shopping bag which burdened her other arm.

'I'm going to Bangor for the day,' he told her. He walked on before she had time to react.

There was destiny in the reflection in the train window. Beyond and through it fields and trees fled. It was amazing what could be accomplished; he saw the flame that never went out. It burnt there, constantly threatened, often almost extinguished, but it came back before it had gone. It never went. Damn, he'd forgotten to leave a message for Sam. What if today was to be a big day? You would never know until it arrived. What if he missed it? Gone to Bangor for the day. How would that sound? He felt an itchy heat rising inside his clothes, causing him to shift about in his seat. He knew he was blushing and that the woman opposite would notice him. She had failed to be impressed by his equanimity. In fact she had not raised her eyes from the book she was reading. But she would become aware of him now. He was willing her to look, despite himself.

He rose suddenly and let down the window, offering his face to the disturbed air, letting it cool and bathe him rapidly. And then it occurred to him. He would ring Vera, leaving a message for Sam, gauging from her reaction whether he was needed. Because she mightn't say anything direct. He wouldn't expect her to say anything direct.

He closed the window and resumed his seat. Taking his comb from his top pocket, he rearranged his hair and turned to look into himself in the window again. The woman shuddered slightly, feeling the sharpness of the cold air, and sent a disapproving glance his way. Then she went back to her fictitious world.

'Vera? Have you seen Sam today?'

'Sam? No, not today.'

'How are things, Vera?'

'Things? All right. Everything's all right.'

'In the city – I mean is everything – em, under control?'

'What are you talking about?'

'Nothing, Vera, nothing, I'm probably just a bit – homesick.'

'Homesick? Look, where are you?'

'Me? In Bangor.'

'Bangor?' Vera's scornful laugh rang in his ear but he managed to convey his message in an even, controlled voice.

'If Sam rings, tell him I checked in. Goodbye, Vera.'

He put the receiver down and left the phone box. As he walked down the main street he considered the fact that Vera could be a spanner in the works. With a woman like Vera you were never quite sure. She could know everything or she could know nothing.

When he reached the bottom of the hill he turned and began to walk back up again, this time with his head raised and his eyes alert. For interesting places to bring her.

A couple of elderly people sat in the shelter, huddling against the sea wind. The old woman had a tartan blanket over her knees. They stared beyond, drawing separate lines with their eyes, out to the chopping white frills which adorned the expansive waste of flouncing green silk. They could have been seeing the hacked wasteland of their lives, or their gaze might have been one of resignation, that after all it had come to this. Slow days of watching and waiting, knowing there was nothing more to do but watch the endless, changing motion of the sea. Accepting the reassurance of its moving beauty. Their look could have been one of peace. They may have turned and smiled serenely at one another when he passed.

He did not know what they were doing there. Maybe they were out of a home and were put down there every day for the good of their health. Maybe they were waiting to be brought back, thinking of a warm fire and their dinner. Perhaps they complained bitterly every day, old people did complain a lot, but could do nothing about it. And it wasn't the warmest day to be sitting in an open shelter with the sea air blasting in at you. The old man's nose was blue.

He turned across the hard, wet sand, pressing the soggy, grey-brown wrinkles with his shoes. It was as if he was going to meet her at the edge.

And there she was, a distant figure but it was clearly her. At first, as he approached her, she grew no closer. He was tramping along the meeting place of land and water so that the shallow, spreading water squelched under his feet. He could feel it seeping through a hole in the sole of his shoe, sending a cool dampness into his sock, gradually moistening the skin on his foot. He tried walking on the side of his foot to lessen the discomfort but that was worse, so he decided to pretend it wasn't there.

At first she didn't see him coming. She was facing outward, paddling in water up to her ankles, hoisting up her skirt, even though there was no need to. She was holding her face towards the salty freshness. It suited her so much more than the background of office walls and piled files, and here he was, a lone, dark, walking figure with a fixed, serious gaze. He had stepped from the queue of names as she knew he must. She turned towards him, shyly at first, and then ran, spraying water from each foot in turn, and they were laughing and holding each other in a wilderness where only they mattered.

He saw the figures of the old people labouring towards the steps and then, looking around, he realised he had the whole beach to himself. He wished they hadn't left because he felt an intense loneliness now. He remembered a similar feeling before. It was on a sunny day during the school holidays when he ran out onto the street, full of expectancy, and there was no one there.

On the way home in the train he thought he might call in to see Vera. But there was something about the way Vera treated you. He was afraid he might break down and tell her that underneath it all he was alone, that he would cry into the deep crevice between her big, soft breasts. And that she would rock him and maybe after a while take him in to her bed.

If it hadn't been for Sam he might have done that.

'There's a lot of old people in Bangor,' he told his mother. She was fussing over him, especially after he'd mentioned the hole in his shoe. He had his bare foot up at the fire and she had the shoes out in the hall to remind her to bring them to the mender's the next morning.

'They go down to the seaside to end their days,' she said. 'But I don't know. I'd rather die near me own.'

'They spend the day looking at the sea,' he said. 'There were two doing it today. Just staring out there.'

'Mimi Roberts is coming over to hear all about it,' his mother said.

Gerry expressed dissatisfaction. He was impatient with the setup. The initial excitement of involvement was over and it seemed to be dragging on, with nothing happening.

'We're not doing anything,' he said. 'If you ask me, we're being left out.'

'We're preparing,' Joe told him. 'You can't just walk in at the top. Everybody has to be sure of you.'

'I'm beginning to think there is no top to this,' Gerry persisted. He had his forlorn face resting on the palm of his hand, his elbow on the table.

'Wise up,' Joe said. Gerry's dismal expression irritated him. 'Where do you think Sam is? If there's no top?'

'I don't know. You tell me.' Gerry livened up, took his arm down and looked angrily at Joe, as if this was the point he was trying to make.

'If you ask me, he's giving us the shove,' he said.

'Important people can't be around,' Joe said.

'Important people,' Gerry echoed. 'What proof have we that Sam's important? You give me one example –'

Joe rose from his seat. 'Shut up, Gerry,' he said, trying hard to control his voice. 'You'd better watch what you say. You're annoying me now, and you're saying too much.'

As he turned to go he said, 'You know you're ruining your chances of getting anywhere. Don't say I didn't warn you.'

Sam had left a message. He felt like racing back and showing Gerry the proof. 'Meet at Cronies Cove. Tomorrow night 10.30.' Just that.

'Did Sam leave it himself?' he asked his mother. He was

looking at the words again and feeling a surge of importance and excitement.

'Didn't I tell you he did?' she said. She was craning her head round his shoulder, trying to read it. 'What does it say?' she asked.

'Say? An important message – a game,' he said. 'I'm in the finals.'

'Wouldn't you know yourself if you were in the finals?'

He was taken aback by her apparent comprehensive knowledge of the game.

'Well, no, not exactly,' he said. 'They had to toss for it in the end.'

'What did you pick?'

'Heads.'

He was away running up the stairs, crazy to get drinking in the words again because, although he hadn't admitted it at the time, Gerry's mood had disturbed his confidence. But it was Gerry who was the unfortunate one because his problem was that he'd no faith.

As soon as he had gathered himself he came down for his supper.

'Is there no music on?' he asked his mother.

'Do you want some?' She hurried over to the radio and began journeying through the stations.

'Now, is that all right?'

It sounded like jazz to him but it wasn't bad at all.

'Aye, that's OK,' he said. 'Here, Ma, would you give us a bit of a haircut in a minute?'

She got up straight away.

'My God, you don't have to jump up as if the house was on fire,' he said as she passed him like a bolt into the scullery.

'I want to find them sharp scissors,' she said. He heard her rummaging in the drawer and then she came in, smoothing the bright silver on her skirt. 'I always keep them in that drawer,' she said.

'Then you didn't have to find them,' he said. He turned in his chair and faced her.

'What do you mean?' She sat at the fire, continuously rubbing the silver on the check fabric of her skirt, and giving him a cautious stare.

'If you knew where they were.'

'You're in a funny mood,' she said, with a hint of a smile.

A shade had settled over the estate now. Colours were dulled by thoughts of away. Looking down from her bedroom, the drab houses squatted in lowering lines, making descending patterns into the city. The alien noises of children, their commonness, their accents and loudness grated on her ears. She resented their infringement, and even her family crowded her privacy, leaving little outlet for indulgence in memory. They were all so close, buzzing in and out of rooms, forever talking. What had been hinted to her before was now blasting in her ears, the constant presence, the lack of respect. It was all the same – herself, Sadie, Madge, Pete, the rest, even her mother and father. No one stood out. And from house to house unimportant people lived unimportant lives, and around the city unimportant people were killing equally unimportant people. Did they not realise it was all so trivial? It was all so insular and self-defeating? There was no growth, no outward, magnanimous gesture of living. They were like little sparrows chirping around and picking at each other to get a few paltry crumbs, unable to see the open sky above them.

They weren't flying to where the reward was worth the

effort. It seemed to her that she had flapped her wings and had sensed that there were pastures where the grass was not swamped. It was anywhere, but it was not here. Not here where it was swamped with tears over country, territory, crown, religion, flags. She thought of the little voices twittering each other down on the television every night and that they didn't realise it had nothing to do with her. Nothing at all.

'Did you see that?' Her father eased his darts from the board and looked around the company proudly.

'One hundred and twenty. I'm getting better every day,' he said.

The younger children sat on the table at the back of the room and clapped, while the men stood about.

Madge and Colette watched from armchairs. Madge was flinging herself up and down with elation. Colette thought she looked silly, daft to get so excited about a game of darts.

They were all in a tunnel, a tunnel which made them appear small and distant. Like looking through the wrong end of binoculars. And they were dull. She was ashamed to admit it, but they were dull. Even Chuck's wisecracks thudded weightily so that she could only smile falsely.

Pete aimed clumsily but it was obvious from the outset that his darts would never reach the board. One hit the television and he stumbled to retrieve it.

The children laughed but there was a nervous hollowness in their laughter. Their mother, having heard the front door close, came in from the kitchen and ushered them out, saying it was well past their bedtime.

Madge sat back boldly because Madge liked a scene, at anyone's expense.

Colette watched her father's face, his controlled frustration, and Chuck had already approached Pete and was saying something like, 'Come on son, you and me'll take a wee walk.' But

Pete pushed him out of the way and pointed a shaking finger towards his father.

'He's the perfect one,' he accused. 'Never did anything wrong in his life. Except bringing us into this bloody awful world of course.'

Colette was jolted out of her daydream and the scene before her was large and real, the draining colour in her father's face and the bustling figure of Chuck, his colour rising, actively trying to restrain Pete. 'Come on now, lad, don't say anything you'll regret. Catch yourself on now, lad.'

Her father, a man of few words, spoke slowly, in an emotional voice. 'You know, Peter,' he said, 'we're all the same in this, all in the same boat. There's none of us has any privileges. It's up to each of us to make the best of it.'

'Boat,' Pete repeated, coming close to his father and swaying in front of him. 'Some of us should never have been in the boat in the first place.'

'You've said it,' Denny said. He had been standing back but was now over facing his brother, looking at him with disgust. 'The ones who can't cope with it should never have been in it. Now get out and leave us in peace. We're having a game of darts, in case you didn't notice. And if you can't even throw a dart straight you shouldn't be here.'

'Here, here! Man overboard!' Madge shouted. She was standing in the middle of the men now, looking from one to the other in anticipation.

Pete went to lunge at Denny but was restrained by his father and Chuck.

'Colette, would you make Peter a cup of strong coffee?' Her father turned to her without releasing his grasp on his son's arm. He had never struck her as a physical man but he was tall and well built and at this moment she saw a strength in him that she admired.

From the kitchen she heard further voices, her mother's amongst them now; and Pete's sounded more anguished than angry and then she heard what sounded like crying. Madge came dashing into the kitchen.

'Oh God, that's the limit,' she said. 'A man crying.'

Saturday afternoon 4.00

Pete's remorseful. And then he does it again. He's on a course and I don't know what will stop him.

I've applied to the Civil Service, for a job somewhere in England or Scotland. Any place will do for a start. It's the only way to find out certain things, or simply to be on my own. I know at some time I will have to be on my own. Matt is going to Birmingham. He wants me to go but understands I can't. This could be my biggest mistake. I can always come back here, but Matt...

He tried to get it down in the diary but he couldn't. Not yet. It was too confusing and his hands were shaking, shaking so hard he couldn't get his coat off. But then again, did he want his coat off?

There was once a boy. Or he didn't know, how could he know. His Uncle George would vouch for him. Or her, she would tell them of their plans for love. Or the two old people on the beach at Bangor, they with their long experience of life, they with their distant eyes, they would provide the alibi. He was the only figure between them and their sea. But that was the wrong day. Another day altogether.

If he could get to Vera's house. He would go down the stairs,

quietly and without anyone knowing, he would be away to
Vera's house. He fumbled to tighten the zip on his anorak but
it was already tightened, right up to his throat. He loosened it
a little and went towards his bedroom door. When he opened
it he heard sounds from the kitchen, so familiar, the strains of
dance music. He marvelled how she always managed to find it
on some station. It was always on. And shuffling, like feet, feet
dancing. Now who was she dancing with? A step on her own,
perhaps, or the ghost of his father, a gaunt shadow in step.
Imagine losing your dance partner and nobody ever fitting in
again. No one ever did but the music kept on. Had he told
Mimi Roberts about her? About his worry? It was such a relief
to know Mimi would look after her.

He was halfway down the dark staircase, hesitating because of
the sounds in the kitchen and because he noticed that some of
the paint on the wall was peeling and he had to pick it with his
finger. It would have been easy to have put a coat of paint on
the walls. So easy and soothing, and she would have brought
him mugs of tea. He sat on the stairs picking the yellow paint
from his nail and rubbing his finger on the wall to get rid of it.

He could have been picking blood.

He shuddered and rubbed both his hands hard on the frayed
stair carpet. Frayed? It was in ribbons and it was a cold place to
be sitting with the draught blowing in under that front door. It
would have been easy to have put a flap down there along the
bottom of the door. Most houses had a flap. Mimi Roberts
certainly had a flap. Had Vera a flap? Flap, trap. The reason for
not going to Vera's.

He huddled into himself there until it appeared that he was
warm. Warm except for his face which felt not so much cold
as empty. An empty face like the man's, the man who looked
into his eyes with a grey fear that was more awesome than
death itself.

It was death.

He was probably dead now.

But he didn't kill him. He had nothing to do with it. He stood up on the stairs, elated. He was innocent. He was also noble and could face his mother.

It was no ghost. He slunk in under the stair rail with a new panic in his throat for if that was not Sam's voice it was . . .

The music started up again and the sliding on the kitchen lino so that the fading flowers could be nothing more than vague pink smudges. They wouldn't stand up to Sam's scraping boots. He tried to get clear in his mind what it was he was trying to get clear. Then there was a high-pitched sound in his head and he was crawling up the stairs and back into his room. He went under the bed.

Sam was waiting for him. He had betrayed Sam.

He was a cold, hollow frame, stiff and silent under the bed, crouching in the grey, fluffy dust.

He came out from under the bed and considered the fact that he was acting like a lunatic, that no one in his right senses hid under a bed. No one would want to harm you if you acted honourably. There was always the police, the law. In the final analysis there was always the law to protect you.

He had walked away from a murder. He had walked away. No, he had run away. He had run away and he had seen them, seen them and been one of them. They had seen him, had pointed a gun at him. His lay on the ground, emptied into the dirt.

At least the man knew. The dead man knew. He wouldn't do it.

It was who to tell. When he'd worked out who to tell, it was so plausible, his position, so right. He was right. Whoever he told would sort out the details of his freedom. His freedom from fear or guilt. If he should be thought to be guilty, which was impossible since he'd done nothing wrong.

What about the maxim 'once you're in'?

If you stayed in your bedroom for the rest of your life, or under the floorboards. That was a real possibility, yes, he remembered a report in the paper about a man who had hid under the floorboards for years. It mightn't be too bad. You could build yourself a real wee nest. You could have everything you wanted down there – compared with facing the barrel of a gun. If the man had had that choice now, would he not have delighted in every moment of every dark day? Tucked away in his self-contained haven with the reassurance of his family's life going on above him.

He thought of the man's face, his fine features rigid with terror, his hands shaking and fidgeting. He could have imagined him lighting a cigarette, steadily, comfortably, or pouring a Guinness into the side of his glass, smiling upward out of the corner of his eye at his friend. It was a black and white snapshot of someone who was dead.

He would live with the face under the floorboards. They would live together.

But he hadn't done it. He had run away. That was why he had to go under the floorboards.

Protector. Preparing. Idealism sparkling the night air. A murky corner, with a man leaving a pub with his friend. A sober man, all the worse. He probably only had a couple. Let him get this straight, the point of the operation was to take the lone man, bundle the ordinary man. In a frantic scuffle to detach him from his friend who protested vehemently then feebly when he saw the guns. Reduced to pleading nonsensically, 'Come on now, lads, give him a break, not him, he's one of the best, what's it for, for Christ's sake, boys, we can sort this all out together, he's not in anything you know.' He was left standing and the only reason it wasn't him was that he was further from the kerb. It was the only reason.

When he was manhandled into the car the man said back in a thin, dull voice, 'Look after them, will you, Chuck?'

Gerry was right, there was no top to this, only a bottom.

Only his mother could bring the food, lift the floorboards and hand it down. He felt a warm tingle of excitement gathering in his gut, dispelling the horror, so that he blushed and was impatient to get down the stairs to make the plans because it had to be done this night.

Already he saw her face looking down at him, into his dark world. She would be like an angel with the light all around her. And she wouldn't have to worry where he was. He would be there all the time. That would be her big consolation.

Her biggest problem might be keeping it from Mimi Roberts.

All sorts of wee treats would be devised, like when he was a boy and was confined to bed with an illness. His every whim would be indulged because he was living under the floor. He might even order the odd pack of Guinness from the off-licence down the street, to help pass the long hours, pouring it slowly, sipping in its froth in long slow sucks, thinking, growing old. And then the diary. Of course, there was the diary. What new significance would the diary have now? On second thoughts, the Guinness would be a problem on account of the suspicion it would arouse. He would have to forget about the Guinness but it wasn't a major sacrifice, since he'd never drunk Guinness anyway.

Joe has gone to England for a job.

Thursday afternoon 3.40

There was a drizzle in the graveyard. It never let up and I could not find one break in the clouds. We all looked miserable, not

at all brave and upstanding. If the sun had been out we could
have held our heads up at least. But maybe we wouldn't. Mam
was so grateful to get his body back, to bury him properly. I
think she feels he's resting now.

I could write some bitter things and God knows bitter things
have been said by some of us. But where's the point in record-
ing it? And all the usual statements have been issued, but what's
the use in that? People have been so kind, and that is the only
flicker of hope for here. But it's not really for here, it's only for
people wherever they are.

Chuck and Pete are the worst. Pete is burying himself and
Chuck keeps saying he should have offered to be taken instead,
because of having no wife or children. Maybe he's right.

We're stamped as victims now. We'll always be the victims
of the Troubles, and I thought I was before. But it was the
knowledge that I could be.

We want to say things to each other about him, about how
he was, but we can't. We only look and choke on thoughts and
our own personal regrets. Pete won't sit in the same room as
any of us. Madge had to stay in the Munroes'. She couldn't go
to the funeral, she was in such a state. Her eyes are all puffed
out with bawling. Most of us are sedated to deaden the hell of it.

But really I think the shock has not yet reached the centre.
They say it's after, when the fuss has died down, the attention,
when things are as they were before except that they no longer
are and never will be.

Matt put off going for a couple of weeks. He's been great but
I think his relief will be even bigger now, getting away, getting
out of the pit. The pit of mourning.

                                           Saturday 2230 hours
We managed. I'm in here now. It will all be told, how we did

it, her reaction. She couldn't take it in at first. I gave her as few
details as possible, not to burden her with secrets. Made it seem
I just happened to be somewhere at the wrong time and,
because I saw something I shouldn't, my life is in danger. She
wanted me to go to the police but I persuaded her the only way
in this situation is to lie low. You don't know the sort that's
around these days, I told her. Isn't that what I've been telling
you all along, she said. I didn't involve anyone else, Sam
or anybody.

I can't work it all out myself, what I was really in, and that
it all amounted to taking a man because of where he lived,
because of the club he was coming out of.

I saw the details in the paper. There was a photo but I didn't
need a photo.

She's not sure of me. She doesn't know what to believe, and
sometimes at night I can imagine her thoughts, up there on her
own at the fire, putting pieces together. She tries to put Mimi
Roberts off coming over. Mimi thinks she's fretting because I'm
away but she can't talk to Mimi now. How can she, with me
down here?

It's basic at the moment, only a torch for light, and it's pretty
cramped, but we'll improve it in time. The main thing is I'm
safe. We've had a few hairy moments. The first time a knock
came to the door she was handing me something down. We
both froze and she got all agitated, rubbing her face and muttering, Oh my God, this is it, this is it. I managed to calm her
down. I told her no one could possibly notice anything and I
got her to repeat after me, Joe has gone to England for a job.

Tell Joe his friends will be looking forward to seeing him,
when he comes for his holidays like, they said after she had told
them. That set her off for a while, talking to herself and asking
herself what was going to become of us. I had to tell her if she
didn't catch herself on and practise self-control, the whole thing

would be ruined. Do you want me to be caught, I said. No, she said. Then put on some music and act the way you used to, I said. Put on a cup of tea or sit at the fire.

It's not too bad. I can come up at night when the curtains are closed and sit in the kitchen, although it can be awkward when she answers me sharply, cuts me off. Then there's no point to it, I maybe read a bit and come on down again. Down to my hole, like a giant rat.

Wednesday 1435 hours

Life goes on, one dark hole day after another. Things that worry me. 1, No money now and she's finding it very tough on her pension. 2, When she races out for my fresh baps in the morning or to do any shopping, for that matter – what if she's knocked down, if she just doesn't come back and I don't know what's happened to her – what do I do? 3, If she gets ill in the house. 4, If I get ill. It can't be healthy down here and never getting fresh air. 5, No hope of a girl.

Think a lot about the girl from the dole. It gives me a pain that I didn't let her know how I felt. Sometimes I think of it now, of sending her a letter, getting Ma to take it round, letting her know. My lover under the floor. My dreams and imagination tell me there is a future for her and me. I wake up with her beside me and go through all our meetings. It's a message. I hate that she thinks I'm in England, that I went away without saying anything. Ma had to go round and tell them. If she loves me I could trust her, I could take a chance if I could find a way of letting her know. Something to be worked out.

Ma just handed me down tea and biscuits. She hadn't much of a smile on her face. If I could get her to believe I'm right, I'm only in here because of the state of this place, not because I did anything wrong. The police would have been here, I said, if I'd done anything wrong, or the army. And maybe they will too, she said. Couldn't it take them years to get round to it. Then she added with a sly look on her face, What about that final? Did you win it? No, I said, I lost.

Thursday 1000 hours

I was woken this morning by an awful nightmare. I was walking to meet the man, we were walking towards each other, keeping walking yet never getting any closer. He had a queer smile on his face and his face was white with the light of the moon. It was a country road with miles of fields on either side. I was terrified, not of the man, but of who might be hiding behind the hedges. Then, coming out of the shadows behind him, I saw men with vicious scowls on their faces. He didn't see them but just kept walking on. I shouted to warn him but he didn't hear me. He never took the smile off his face, his moon smile. I looked behind me and there were men there too, coming after me with weapons, though it wasn't clear what the weapons were. I started to run and I heard their feet running behind me. I was shouting, Help me, to him and I didn't know which way to run but it didn't matter because when I started to run I wasn't going anywhere. I couldn't move and they were coming nearer. And then he wasn't there at all. It was Sam – I woke up and my whole body was soaked with sweat.

I waited for her to come to the board, to open it up and let me see her, and the light from the kitchen. When I heard her feet on the floor I said up, Ma will you open this? She rolled back the mat and lifted the lino where we slit it. She had her coat wrapped round her and all. For God's sake Ma, never mind the baps, I said. Just a cup of strong tea. Sure doesn't he keep them over for me under the counter, she said. She was rummaging in the drawer for her purse. Anyway they'd wonder if I never showed up for them.

Doesn't he know I'm away? I asked her.

I'm not beyond liking a bap myself, she said. I'm away on.

She banged the kitchen door when I was just saying don't be long, and I heard her slippers trailing down the hall. I remembered the two sounds and then the final bang of the front door. Me lying upstairs in my bed and Da down in the kitchen, when she went over to Mimi Roberts of a night. I thought I would lie awake to hear her coming back, but I was always asleep.

The baps were lovely. It was worth it.

Friday 2100 hours

We've been doing a bit of cleaning down here and laying some mats. I think she's coming round. Last night we had a game of ludo. She was giving me chances and hoping I wouldn't notice, like not taking two goes when she got a six, or not taking another man out. She's also gone back to the music but the most important clue was when I was closing in for the night. I suppose it's not your fault son, she said. Jesus, the door.

I'm still shaking. That was Vera. She managed to get Ma to bring her in. I've something very important to talk to you about, she said. What about, Ma said. Your son, she said. They came into the kitchen and were above me, talking. It was eerie. All Ma kept repeating was, Joe has gone to England for a job. No forwarding address yet. No, I haven't heard from him. Look, I want to help, said Vera.

What do you mean, Ma asked, all innocence.

He might think he's in trouble, Vera says.

Trouble? Ma said.

Look, he has nothing to worry about, Vera said. Absolutely nothing.

If he gets a job, Ma said.

That's another thing, Vera said. But he's à free man, he has nobody to fear.

Free man? Nobody to fear? Ma had scorn in her voice. In this place? He's gone to England for a job.

Get him to write to me, Vera said. Her voice was genuine and I could hardly breathe for not knowing what to think.

Aye, I might, Ma said.

He's got the address, Vera said and then it was obvious she was leaving for I heard the door handle.

Has he indeed, Ma said.

When they were going down the hall Vera was saying, I'm a friend you know, and God knows in this place you need friends. As the front door was opening she said, He's an honest boy.

He was brought up to be, Ma said and closed the door.

The first thing I wanted to know was what was Vera wearing. I had this picture of her up there in her blue dressing gown. Ma couldn't remember the colour of her coat but said she had white high heels on with the toes worn.

I had to explain away knowing Vera. Ma kept saying, I don't like the look of that one. I couldn't argue with that but I had to explain knowing her. She's the secretary of the billiards, I said.

I'm sure I don't know, Ma said. She was poking the fire and I looked on this as a bit of a setback. Anything that made me more complicated or mysterious. It had to be all simple to win her favour back.

Look at it this way, I said to her. She knows I'm honest. She knows I did nothing wrong.

One like that one would be better off not knowing anything about you, she said.

I've been tormenting myself. Maybe Vera was my one

chance. Should I have come up, but then, how can you be sure with a woman like Vera?

He'll get no job in England, Mimi Roberts said. No chance. Sure they can't give work to their own.

He's out of this place, Ma said.

Mimi was still smarting from not having been warned that I was going away. I never dreamt, she said. If you'd told me, I could have given him a wee something to help him on his way. Going off like that into the night.

He just upped and went, Ma said. It got him down.

Mimi cheered up. Sure look at it this way, she said, maybe he'll bring home a nice wee girl.

Aye, Ma said and I heard her chair creaking. I'll make the tea, she sighed.

Mimi started humming, some old Irish air or something, and Ma was shuffling about in the kitchen. I crouched completely still in my black dugout and heard the dull sounds of cups on saucers, the teapot dumped back on the stove, the heavy top of the bread bin clanking. It was away inside me, happening, and out of my reach on the outside. It was like in the dentist's chair, under the gas, and somewhere above the depths were real sounds and voices. They were there but you couldn't get to them. Not yet. You were sinking in your own darkness. Until there was a floppy haze and you were in it. I hit the nurse on the face one time.

I'm like somebody who's just become blind. Sounds make all the pictures. I knew when the cup left the saucer and pictured it at Ma's mouth and the red roses on the side.

There were murmurs and drolls of sentences without much connection. It went on for ages.

He's as well out of it, Mimi said.

Ma's chair creaked and after a slither on the lino there was a click and then voices and music sliced through as she searched the stations.

You couldn't have got in that door for people, she said, when she settled for a band playing something old-time.

Aye, Mimi said and I knew the looks they had in their eyes. Like the old people staring across the sea at Bangor.

                                                    Saturday 1900 hours

Fish and chips with plenty of vinegar, making greasy blobs on the outside of the brown paper. Da used to bring them in and if she hadn't the bread and butter and tea out ready on the table, he sat at the fire and started eating them out of the paper, with the steam and smell travelling across the kitchen. The thing about chips, he said, is that they must melt the butter on your piece. If they're not hot enough for that you might as well eat them out of the paper. Forget about the bread.

What keeps me going? That I didn't kill the man, that it will all be over some day. I will walk out free. The police won't want me for whatever I was in, whoever was in it won't want me for opting out. And that girl from the dole loves me. She loves me.

All thoughts stop with Sam.

THE DEATH OF MEN

LINDA ANDERSON

I was eating Christmas pudding when the news broke. The first sign was my brother's alarmed voice in the hallway. He was on the phone. 'You're joking. Naw. You're kidding. But... you're joking. Oh Jesus. Yes. I'm sure my mother will go round and see Laura.'

'Samuel's gone and died in his sleep!' Jimmy announced, returning to the dining room. My mother's hands flew to her face. 'On Christmas morning,' Jimmy said. 'Imagine.'

I considered for a moment. 'Well, why not? There is no amnesty.' I didn't know what to do next. I resumed eating. Dark bittersweet pudding. Dollops of brandy butter.

'They would like to see you, Mum,' Jimmy said sheepishly.

'I'll go with you,' I volunteered. 'But later. Not yet.'

We took hours to get ready. We knew we had to go. We had to comfort the bereaved.

'But you won't have to attend the funeral,' I said.

'Their church is just round the corner. They'll expect me to go.'

'No one will expect it.'

'Should you wear that red scarf?'

'Yes.'

I had been wearing a red scarf every day for months. Except for the occasion of my father's funeral when I swapped it for a black one. Red and black. Anger and death.

We stepped outside. The evening was beautiful, cold and starry. 'Oh, Christmas night!' I exulted for a moment. We linked arms. I wished that Samuel's home were farther away, that we could walk and walk.

'I never liked him,' I said. A natty little man, florid complexion, stentorian voice.

'Yes, he always sounded as if he was quarrelling with you,' my mother said. 'He wasn't bad, though.' It was her habit to echo my furies and then let gentleness and justice reclaim her.

We were nearly there. The bungalow of mourning was in sight.

'Will the body still be inside?' I asked. 'Do undertakers work on Christmas Day?'

'He got off lightly,' my mother said with sudden bitterness. 'No suffering. No awareness. Just fell asleep.'

I had a vision of my father in his coffin. A diminutive waxwork with golden skin. A shrunken lookalike.

'We won't stay long,' I assured her.

'Oh, Patricia, there you are!' shouted the widow. Laura. My father's cousin. She wept, waving her crumpled handkerchief.

The poky room was overheated and packed with people. Daughters of the deceased, their husbands, their children. Everyone looked huge, giants in a Wendy house. Samuel's daughters gawped at me.

'You've put on weight,' Brenda said eagerly.

'The poor girl's lost her daddy and now we've lost ours.' Sally spoke almost reproachfully, as if I had instigated some distressing trend.

The much-married Marlene ignored me. Brenda, Sally, and Marlene. I had not met them for twenty years. A trio of platinum blondes with discreetly ample figures encased in good suits and frilly blouses. They all looked impeccable and yet strangely vulgar, like strict barmaids.

'We're in the same boat, Patricia,' the new widow declared.

I registered my mother's imperceptible wince. No, you're not, I thought. My mother is on a raft. A raft for one.

'Aye. Dear dear . . . To think it was only six weeks ago that we put your Robert in the ground. And now my Samuel will be laid beside him. Aye. Friends in life they were, and now . . .'

I remembered my mother in the bedroom trying to choose the clothes for my father's body. His good dark suit. There was a masonic pin in the lapel. A dazzling white shirt. I touched each garment.

I had rarely touched my father. Now I could take liberties with his clothes.

'A tie?' said Moira. 'What about a tie?'

We stared at the fat tangled maypole of his ties hanging in the wardrobe. My mother removed a wide striped one.

'That's unfashionable,' I protested, snatching out the green silk one instead.

'Shoes,' said Moira. 'Will he need shoes?'

My mother began to weep. Moira was standing behind her. She placed a hand on her right shoulder. And I put my hand on Moira's shoulder as if to transmit more strength. We stood there like that, in a line, like Pharaoh's wives.

Your husband is an also-ran, lady, I thought.

'God moves in mysterious ways,' said Florrie, Laura's sister.

'Yes . . . I just thank God that my Sam didn't suffer. For the Lord knows he didn't deserve to. No, and I couldn't have borne to watch him . . . Such a good soul . . . Oh, not that anyone deserves to suffer, of course.'

'That's right,' I said, making my voice as chilly as possible.

'Isn't she just like her father?' Laura responded. 'They live on, they live on . . .'

Just like her father. That sentence had followed me since

childhood. A chip off the old tower block. The old iceberg. I
did not want to resemble my father. A joyless and forbidding
man. Until cancer stripped away his flesh and with it all signs
of his cruelty and remoteness. It reduced him to a tenderness I
had longed for but could not stand. Too much, too late.

The widow launched into an inventory of her husband's final
day. He made the breakfast. He polished his shoes. He went to
the shops. He peeled the potatoes. He looked after his grand-
daughter, Amanda Jayne. He drove Laura over to her sister's
and fetched her home later. That night he kneeled by his bed
and prayed, listing everyone in his family by name. He prayed
then for some trawlermen lost off the Antrim coast.

Did he pray aloud? I wanted to ask but managed to stop the
impulse. I had a sense of trespass. I hate the way the most private
things about the dead become instant public property. But I was
intrigued by this new image of Samuel. The jaunty splenetic
Samuel transformed into a kind vulnerable old man in pyjamas.
After a day crammed with chores, favours, and piety, he drew
a neat line under himself and unobtrusively stopped breathing.

Laura's monologue moved on to other recent deaths in
the district. The reaper had been busy. There was Arnold
Mulholland who paid all his bills one day, ironed all his shirts,
went to bed quietly and never rose again. And then there was
Stanley who made his wife a cup of tea before sinking unfussily
into his armchair... Such orderly demises. I began to hear an
implicit criticism of my father, his noisy toilsome death, the
wild incontinence of it.

Laura turned to my mother: 'How did you get your
Christmas in, Patricia? Did you have a dinner? Of course, none
of us can eat a thing. Whole place coming down with turkey
and mince pies and we can't manage a bite.'

'You're going to have to eat some of that turkey after all the
trouble I've had with it,' Brenda said sullenly.

'Aye, our Brenda has had a hell of a time with her turkey this year,' Laura confided.

'It was a bloody fiasco!' Brenda said.

'She was done,' said Sally. 'Well and truly done.'

'What happened?'

'I went to that butcher, you know the one, McMullen's. Couldn't have a better reputation. Well, I asked him for a fresh turkey. I warned him: "None of your frozen!" It was last minute on Christmas Eve and I needed a fresh turkey. He gives me a bird. "Madam dear, here's one that's as fresh as your face." But here, when I tried to cook it, it just would not cook. And gallons of water pouring out of it. After hours and hours it was still pale as a snail drowning in a pond. So it was a frozen bird that he had partly thawed and passed off as a fresh one.'

A chorus of advice chimed out: 'She should have stuck it in the microwave...' 'She should have held it under the hot tap...' 'She should have hurled it through the butcher's window...'

'I'm going to see that man as soon as his shop opens up again. I'll put him out of business. I'll sue the arse off him!'

'You're just right, Brenda. Imagine doing the like of that to someone on Christmas Eve.'

'Man's inhumanity to man,' I muttered to myself.

A debate ensued on the comparative merits of frozen versus fresh poultry.

'You can always tell frozen. I don't care what anyone says.'

'No, you can not. If you were blindfolded and had to taste a range of samples...'

'Now, don't you contradict me, Sally.'

An exchange of recipes followed. 'I'll tell you something that makes a good meal for a Saturday night – economical, too.'

Samuel probably died of boredom, I decided. I intervened by telling them my turkey anecdote. A true story. My sister Moira prepared and cooked her turkey a couple of weeks before Christmas: it was stuffed, basted, roasted, glazed, cooled, and wrapped in a freezer bag. All sacraments completed, Moira placed the bag on the floor and instructed her husband to put it in the freezer outside in the garage. On Christmas Eve she retrieved the bag, opened it and found – rubbish! Litter, a stiff collage of discarded food, old tea bags... 'Kenneth!' she shrieked, realising in a flash what had happened. Freezer and pedal bin bags being indistinguishable, he had deposited the turkey in the bin, the rubbish in the freezer. Kenneth was a man living in a perpetual fog. His wife was always unconsciously devising 'Spot the Mistake' contests for him to fail. The hapless husband bought her a surrogate turkey.

'Ah well, no harm done, then,' I had suggested.

'But it just wasn't the same. It just couldn't be the same as my lovely, my *original* turkey that I slaved over. I suppose that in the context of Lockerbie and Armenia, it seems trivial but...'

I knew my sister and could imagine the celebratory dinner at her house. The superior beloved bird would be invoked at every penitential mouthful.

I told the story in my best 'comedienne' manner. I waited for laughter. A ring of scowling faces, a tribunal.

'That's not funny,' Brenda chided at last to a chorus of agreement.

'God, what a moron!'

'I'd have made him eat the rubbish.'

'What was he playing at?'

These women took their fowl seriously, I was beginning to understand. My story was not one of womanly overreaction but of husbandly transgression.

'She punched him in the face,' I said, despising myself for making the placatory offering. I had omitted this fact at first, regarding it as shameful.

'Just right!' Brenda was mollified.

I realised suddenly that Moira was just like these sisters, even in appearance. They were of the same tribe. Bright blond women, divas of the kitchen, each with a brace of dainty coddled children. Each with a defeated man in tow. Loud women with lulled men.

Oh Dad, why did you inflict these relatives on me? These smug saturnine Protestants?

I wished I could resemble them less. I wished I could be utterly different. I became aware of my body, the dense materiality of it, its overstatement. Why couldn't I be a willowy Catholic with a soulful face, a pilgrim to Croagh Patrick with stones lacerating my ascetic feet?

My Aunt Florrie came and lowered herself cautiously into the sofa beside me. Her eyes were alarmingly magnified behind the thick lenses. I stared at the faint hem of her moustache.

'How are you doing, darlin'?'

'Fine.'

'Miss your father?'

'Yes.'

'God's will, darlin'... Long time, no see.' She laughed. 'Do you remember the time you slammed the door in my face?'

'No.'

'Yes, you do. When I was collecting money to build an Orange arch at the entrance to the housing estate.' She smiled indulgently, sure that I must have long outgrown such youthful waywardness.

'To keep the Catholics in their place?'

'Your father was ashamed of you for turning me away. Mortified he was. He called you a Fenian-lover.'

'You got your revenge. At my wedding,' I reminded her. She looked baffled, no idea what I meant.

My wedding joined my best Catholic friends and my worst Protestant relatives under the same roof. I had to watch with horror while alcohol drew Florrie and her boss-eyed husband out of their usual semi-autistic slumber and into a high-decibel belligerence. She danced a jig around my friends, bellowing insults at the Pope. Seán, Sinéad, and Michael. My lifelong friends, all disappeared now. Ditto the till-death-do-us-part bridegroom. But I was still linked to this affable gorilla sprawling beside me on the sofa. Blood is thicker than glue.

'No sign of more wedding bells for you?' she asked coyly.

'Is that your Marlene's new husband over there?' I said, indicating a bashful little man perched on the side of an armchair across the room.

'Aye. *Numéro trois* – Husband number three,' she translated helpfully. 'Third time lucky, maybe.'

'Maybe,' I said. First a wife-beater, then an alcoholic, and now a dwarf, I thought charitably.

'Are you courting?' she persisted.

'I have no use for men,' I said, noticing the ambiguity of that. Was I subject or object? I have no use? I am of no use?

'Oh, I can't believe that. You were always a dark horse.'

Dark riderless horse, I rose, and gathering some used cups as pretext, I left the room. I went searching for the kitchen, afraid of the unknown geography of this house. What if a door were ajar and I might glimpse the corpse? We've forgotten him, I realised. Poor Samuel, upstaged by a turkey! The light was on in the kitchen and there was the lamented carcass of the half-raw bird on the table. Bald and yellowish, there was something both doleful and festive about it. I stared at its pitiable dark cavity. They'll have you tomorrow, I told it silently. They'll want to eat a piece of death. Bite back, so to speak.

'You look as if you're communing with that turkey.'

I jumped. It was the jarringly robust voice of one of the mute men who had followed me out.

'Only intelligent form of life round here, I suppose?' he added. He opened the back door, letting in the crisp night air. The sky was navy blue. Without thinking, I stepped outside.

'You can see the stars here,' I said. 'You can't in London.'

'Yeah. The cloudless skies of Northern Ireland . . . You live in London, then?'

'Yes.'

'Are you on drugs?'

'Drugs?'

'Cocaine and stuff?'

'Of course. I've got half of Peru up my nostrils.'

'What? Oh. Don't treat me like a country bumpkin!'

'Don't treat me like a big city debauchee!'

'Sorry . . . I'm ever so slightly . . . drunk.'

'Who are you?'

'Son-in-law of the late great.'

'I know. I mean, what's your name?'

'Jack. Jack of Brenda and Jack.'

'I see.'

'Yes, I know you see. I watched you in there, looking at everybody like a she-wolf. And who are you? Do you come here often?'

'I'm the daughter of –' I stopped. 'I'm Helen Forrest.'

We were silent for a moment.

'It's a bad thing to happen at Christmas,' I said awkwardly. 'Christmas will never be the same again.'

He snorted. 'Oh, that's too much to hope for. It'll be the same all right. Gloom and gluttony. Laura will have to eat for two.'

Silence again. Then he looked at me with sudden concern.

'It must be dreadful for you to have to come round here.

You're demoted! Overnight you've gone from chief mourner to mere bystander.'

'Oh well. Samuel was my father's best friend. He helped us when...'

'How did he help you?'

'He came round.'

'And?'

'You know. He extended his sympathy.'

'How extensive was it?'

Jack stared at me. There was something needling and coercive about him. He began to whistle through his teeth, a tuneless sibilant sound. Then he tapped his feet. I began to laugh. He was mimicking Samuel, the maddening whistler.

'Yes, yes, that's what he did. While my father was dying and after he was dead, Samuel just sat there and whistled.'

' "And flights of angels sing thee to thy rest!" So Sammy whistled your dad into the hereafter. It was his all-purpose response.'

I felt a sudden pity. 'Poor bastard. Whistling in the dark. Just six weeks later...'

'Yes. Togetherness has its drawbacks, eh?'

We giggled.

'Is the body here?' I asked, ashamed of something avid in my voice.

'Sure. Tomorrow's Boxing Day, isn't it?'

'That's a terrible joke.'

'Don't smile, then.'

'You didn't like him much, did you, Jack?'

'No. Although I'm already getting confused. I hate the way the dead change, don't you? Suddenly Sammy is this very good-natured guy. A tireless helper of mankind. By tomorrow morning he'll be a saint.'

'Oh yes. I couldn't believe what my sister said to the

mourners at my father's funeral. He was the handsomest man we ever saw, the kindest man we ever met. No one could surpass him in generosity. He was even developing a belated sense of humour! I thought we were burying the wrong man.'

Jack smiled at me. I could see the wet gleam of his teeth in the dark. 'You're a bit of a fervent disliker yourself. My partner in crime?'

I noticed the dark stubble on his jaw. I had a momentary impulse to stroke it.

'There must have been something you liked about your father?'

'He went out a lot. I liked that. I used to pray he would never come back.'

'Was he violent?'

'He made me afraid. He sank my spirit. There was something poisonous about him. A rage held back by a terrible blankness. I used to hate the way he would do all kinds of pointless stupid things with this solemn look on his face. Like he had this Swiss army knife that he was proud of and he used to sit whittling sticks with it, gathering up little shavings and chips of wood.'

'The rage? What was the rage about?'

I shrugged. It was too big to describe. 'One day he was staring out of the window and he looked so full of wrath. There were two dogs outside greeting and wagging their tails at each other. He said: "See dogs! First thing a dog does when it meets another dog is - it sniffs its behind." And he was scandalised! I guess that's what it was all about. He hated animals to be animals and he hated human beings to be animals too. He policed his body and his feelings all his life.'

'Poor man,' Jack said.

'I stole his knife.'

'Like some old schoolmarm confiscating a toy?'

'I needed it.'

'What for?'

'I used to cut myself.' I looked at him quickly. 'People think you have to be mad to do something like that.'

Jack said nothing but he seemed unflinching.

'I used to do it in the bathroom while I listened to him prowling about downstairs. I was calm when I did it, almost meditative. I made very neat incisions, in the thighs and arms mostly. It made me feel better. It was like drawing boundaries to keep him out. Does that make any sense?'

'Oh yes. Blood lines. The bloody old blood lines.'

'I had my rituals. I cleaned up afterwards. Lots of TCP and bandages.'

'When did you stop?' Jack's voice was near and very gentle.

'When I met a man.'

'Of course.'

I thought he was going to kiss me. That was the expected outcome, after all. Strangers in the night, impulsive confessions. The meeting of bruised minds, the mating of bitter lips . . .

'You don't have to cut him out of yourself,' Jack said. 'Just cut him down to size.'

'Like the cancer?' I spoke so venomously that he turned away. In that moment I started to guess something I could only fathom later. I hated the cancer for its vengeful revelation of my father's frailty. I was in love with his bogus power. He was the hollow colossus in my featureless landscape. I did not want him toppled.

'Want a smoke?' Jack offered a pack of cigarettes.

'No, I don't.'

'Oh, I'm sorry. I forgot. I'll wait.'

'His lungs were rotten. In the end. He had to keep the oxygen mask on almost all the time. The seals were dying all through the autumn. Every night on the news they would report how many seals died on the north coast, how many on the east coast. It was as if they were circling us. My father and the seals gasping to death. His whole life was a long slow suffocation. He took his own life.'

I felt Jack's hand soft on my hair. 'Take *your* life. Take your life and use it.'

'Helen!' My mother came into the kitchen. 'There you are! Do you think we could go now?'

The retrieval of coats, the gauntlet of goodbyes, the condolence routine again. Sorry sorry sorry for your trouble trouble trouble. At last we were outside. Our feet rang on the pavement. I began to do a sort of backwards laugh: 'Ah ah ah ah!'

'God, that was dreadful,' my mother said.

'And where do you stand, missus, on the controversial question of frozen versus fresh?' I asked.

'It hasn't hit them yet.'

'No.'

'I don't know what to do.' I knew she was talking about her whole future.

'Neither do I.'

Take your life and use it.

She started to laugh. 'We could always do the turkey trot!'

Suddenly we skipped and ran like girls getting out of a bad school.

LEAVING

ANNE-MARIE REILLY

Ever since I can remember my mother wanted to move house. 'Up the road' was what she called it. I wasn't sure where 'up the road' was, but even then I knew it would be somewhere wonderful. I think it must have been my mother who sowed the seeds of wanderlust and discontent in me, although [what she longed for was a far cry from what I eventually yearned after.] *different paths*

We lived in a small rented house in a street off the Falls Road. Gradually I learnt that 'down the Falls' was anywhere below the Falls Park and 'up the road', the longed-for paradise, was any-where further than the Falls Park. My aunt lived there, my mother's younger sister. She had 'married well'. Her husband *resentful but unwilling to change* drove a car. My father <u>disliked them intensely</u>. They had achieved material success, my father never would. I loved going there, so did my mother. They had a garden and a bathroom and a proper sitting room with a piano in it. My Uncle Peter played the piano and the banjo and was great fun. He was never crabby like my father, although my aunt was an absolute 'targe'. She didn't allow him to smoke his pipe indoors and always spoke sharply to him as though he were another child. As the years passed, his own children treated him the same way and I used to <u>wish he were my father</u> so that I could be good to him. He and my mother adored each other, and the other two were well met. They fought and argued and my aunt was the only one I knew who could get the better of my father. I often wished they could all swap over so that my mother was married to Uncle Peter.

Our street was <u>small</u> and <u>parochial</u> and very <u>clannish</u>. (Everyone) gossiped and borrowed and visited. My mother stayed apart from all this, she wouldn't be there for long, she hoped. When I was born she'd been there fifteen years already and still she wanted desperately to live somewhere else. My father, as usual, was the problem. He was frightened of the responsibility of buying a house. He might have to sacrifice his social life and he wasn't prepared to do that. That my mother was unhappy did not affect him in any way. He had all he wanted, he could not understand her need. She wanted to bring us up in a better area, she wanted to be part of a more socially acceptable environment. All that was beyond my father. As the years passed my mother grew more and more embittered. The chances of owning her own home faded with advancing age, but still she could not accept, nor ever become part of, the community we lived in. In some ways my sisters and I had stayed aloof also, always waiting for the day when we would move 'up the road'. My sisters married and bought houses with bathrooms and gardens. In some ways this compensated my mother but in others it made her resent my father even more. They had achieved in no time what she could not in a lifetime.

Life is nothing if not ironic. My mother finally got to move, and to exactly where, thirty years before, she would have chosen to go. Our street was one of the first to be burnt and my parents had to run from the house they had lived in for thirty-two years, clutching a very few personal belongings.

They were rehoused in a top floor maisonette 'up the road'. What my mother had hoped to escape from came with her 'Up the road' became the new Catholic ghetto, following the gutting of many streets in the Lower Falls. In the panic of

except them

leaving my mother lost a navy suit, bought for a wedding. *denial*
[She talked for weeks about that suit, never mentioning once *or*
the home she had lost] I can still feel the shock of finding my *twisted*
father in tears as he heard over the radio which homes had *pride*
been destroyed.

They have never settled in their new home. They won't buy
a fitted carpet, 'in case they move', or new furniture, 'in case
they move'. Yet I know my mother has long since given up
hope of that much-wanted house. Strangely, it's for my father's
sake that she keeps up the pretence. The consequence of my
mother's life is now surfacing in mine. I won't waste time longing for something better,[I'll go out and fight for it and that is
bringing its own heartache.] *generational change*

THE DISTANT PAST

WILLIAM TREVOR

In the town and beyond it they were regarded as harmlessly peculiar. Odd, people said, and in time this reference took on a burnish of affection.

They had always been thin, silent with one another, and similar in appearance: a brother and sister who shared a family face. It was a bony countenance, with pale blue eyes and a sharp, well-shaped nose and high cheekbones. Their father had had it too, but unlike them their father had been an irresponsible and careless man, with red flecks on his cheeks that they didn't have at all. The Middletons of Carraveagh the family had once been known as, but now the brother and sister were just the Middletons, for Carraveagh didn't count any more, except to them.

They owned four Herefords, a number of hens, and the house itself, three miles outside the town. It was a large house, built in the reign of George II, a monument that reflected in its glory and later decay the fortunes of a family. As the brother and sister aged, its roof increasingly ceased to afford protection, rust ate at its gutters, grass thrived in two thick channels all along its avenue. Their father had mortgaged his inherited estate, so local rumour claimed, in order to keep a Catholic Dublin woman in brandy and jewels. When he died, in 1924, his two children discovered that they possessed only a dozen acres. It was locally said also that this adversity hardened their will and that because of it they came to love the remains of Carraveagh more than they could ever have loved a husband or a wife. They blamed for their ill-fortune the Catholic Dublin woman whom they'd never met and they blamed as well the new national regime, contriving in their eccentric way to relate the two. In the days of the Union Jack such women would have known their place: wasn't it all part and parcel?

Twice a week, on Fridays and Sundays, the Middletons journeyed into the town, first of all in a trap and later in a Ford Anglia car. In the shops and elsewhere they made, quite gently, no secret of their continuing loyalty to the past. They attended on Sundays St Patrick's Protestant Church, a place that matched their mood, for prayers were still said there for the King whose sovereignty their country had denied. The revolutionary regime would not last, they quietly informed the Reverend Packham: what sense was there in green-painted pillar boxes and a language that nobody understood?

On Fridays, when they took seven or eight dozen eggs to the town, they dressed in pressed tweeds and were accompanied over the years by a series of red setters, the breed there had always been at Carraveagh. They sold the eggs in Keogh's grocery and then had a drink with Mrs Keogh in the part of her shop that was devoted to the consumption of refreshment. Mr Middleton had whiskey and his sister Tio Pepe. They enjoyed the occasion, for they liked Mrs Keogh and were liked by her in return. Afterwards they shopped, chatting to the shopkeepers about whatever news there was, and then they went to Healy's Hotel for a few more drinks before driving home.

Drink was their pleasure and it was through it that they built up, in spite of their loyalty to the past, such convivial relationships with the people of the town. Fat Driscoll, who kept the butcher's shop, used even to joke about the past when he stood with them in Healy's Hotel or stood behind his own counter cutting their slender chops or thinly slicing their liver. 'Will you ever forget it, Mr Middleton? I'd ha' run like a rabbit if you'd lifted a finger at me.' Fat Driscoll would laugh then, rocking back on his heels with a glass of stout in his hand or banging their meat onto his weighing scales. Mr Middleton would smile. 'There was alarm in your eyes, Mr Driscoll,' Miss Middleton would murmur, smiling also at the memory of the distant occasion.

Fat Driscoll, with a farmer called Maguire and another called Breen, had stood in the hall of Carraveagh, each of them in charge of a shotgun. The Middletons, children then, had been locked with their mother and father and an aunt into an upstairs room. Nothing else had happened: the expected British soldiers had not, after all, arrived and the men in the hall had eventually relaxed their vigil. 'A massacre they wanted,' the Middletons' father said after they'd gone. 'Damn bloody ruffians.'

The Second World War took place. Two Germans, a man and his wife called Winkelmann who ran a glove factory in the town, were suspected by the Middletons of being spies for the Third Reich. People laughed, for they knew the Winkelmanns well and could lend no credence to the Middletons' latest fantasy: typical of them, they explained to the Winkelmanns, who had been worried. Soon after the war the Reverend Packham died and was replaced by the Reverend Bradshaw, a younger man who laughed also and regarded the Middletons as an anachronism. They protested when prayers were no longer said for the royal family in St Patrick's, but the Reverend Bradshaw considered that their protests were as absurd as the prayers themselves had been. Why pray for the monarchy of a neighbouring island when their own island had its chosen president now? The Middletons didn't reply to that argument. In the Reverend Bradshaw's presence they rose to their feet when the BBC played 'God Save the King', and on the day of the coronation of Queen Elizabeth II they drove into the town with a small Union Jack propped up in the back window of their Ford Anglia. 'Bedad, you're a holy terror, Mr Middleton!' Fat Driscoll laughingly exclaimed, noticing the flag as he lifted a tray of pork steaks from his display shelf. The Middletons smiled. It was a great day for the Commonwealth of Nations, they replied, a remark which further amused Fat Driscoll and which he later repeated in Phelan's public house. 'Her Britannic Majesty,' guffawed his friend Mr Breen.

Situated in a valley that was noted for its beauty and with convenient access to rich rivers and bogs over which game birds flew, the town benefited from postwar tourism. Healy's Hotel changed its title and became, overnight, the New Ormonde. Shopkeepers had their shop fronts painted and Mr Healy organised an annual Salmon Festival. Even Canon Kelly, who had at first commented severely on the habits of the tourists, and in particular on the summertime dress of the women, was in the end obliged to confess that the morals of his flock remained unaffected. 'God and good sense,' he proclaimed, meaning God and his own teaching. In time he even derived pride from the fact that people with other values came briefly to the town and that the values esteemed by his parishioners were in no way diminished.

The town's grocers now stocked foreign cheeses, Brie and Camembert and Port-Salut, and wines were available to go with them. The plush Cocktail Room of the New Ormonde set a standard: the wife of a solicitor, a Mrs O'Brien, began to give six o'clock parties once or twice a year, obliging her husband to mix gin and Martini in glass jugs and herself handing round a selection of nuts and small Japanese crackers. Canon Kelly looked in as a rule and satisfied himself that all was above board. He rejected, though, the mixture in the jugs, retaining his taste for a glass of John Jameson.

From the windows of their convent the Loretto nuns observed the long, sleek cars with GB plates; English and American accents drifted on the breeze to them. Mothers cleaned up their children and sent them to the golf club to seek employment as caddies. Sweet shops sold holiday mementoes. The brown, soda and currant breads of Murphy-Flood's bakery were declared to be delicious. Mr Healy doubled the number of local girls who served as waitresses in his dining room, and in the winter of 1961 he had the builders in again, working on an extension for which the Munster and Leinster Bank had lent him twenty-two thousand pounds.

But as the town increased its prosperity Carraveagh continued its decline. The Middletons were in their middle-sixties now and were reconciled to a life that became more uncomfortable with every passing year. Together they roved the vast lofts of their house, placing old paint tins and flowerpot saucers beneath the drips from the roof. At night they sat over their thin chops in a dining room that had once been gracious and which in a way was gracious still, except for the faded appearance of furniture that was dry from lack of polish and of a wallpaper that time had rendered colourless. In the hall their father gazed down at them, framed in ebony and gilt, in the uniform of the Irish Guards. He had conversed with Queen Victoria, and even in their middle-sixties they could still hear him saying that God and Empire and Queen formed a trinity unique in any worthy soldier's heart. In the hall hung the family crest, and on ancient Irish linen the cross of Saint George.

The dog that accompanied the Middletons now was called Turloch, an animal whose death they dreaded for they felt they couldn't manage the antics of another pup. Turloch, being thirteen, moved slowly and was blind and a little deaf. He was a reminder to them of their own advancing years and of the effort it had become to tend the Herefords and collect the weekly eggs. More and more they looked forward to Fridays, to the warm companionship of Mrs Keogh and Mr Healy's chatter in the hotel. They stayed longer now with Mrs Keogh and in the hotel, and idled longer in the shops, and drove home more slowly. Dimly, but with no less loyalty, they still recalled the distant past and were listened to without ill-feeling when they spoke of it and of Carraveagh as it had been, and of the Queen whose company their careless father had known.

The visitors who came to the town heard about the Middletons and were impressed. It was a pleasant wonder, more than one of them remarked, that old wounds could heal so completely, that the Middletons continued in their loyalty to the past and that, in spite of it, they were respected in the town. When Miss Middleton had been ill with a form of pneumonia in 1958 Canon Kelly had driven out to Carraveagh twice a week with pullets and young ducks that his housekeeper had dressed. 'An upright couple', was the canon's public opinion of the Middletons, and he had been known to add that eccentric views would hurt you less than malice. 'We can disagree without guns in this town,' Mr Healy pronounced in his Cocktail Room, and his visitors usually replied that as far as they could see that was the result of living in a Christian country. That the Middletons bought their meat from a man who had once locked them into an upstairs room and had then waited to shoot soldiers in their hall was a fact that amazed the seasonal visitors. You lived and learnt, they remarked to Mr Healy.

The Middletons, privately, often considered that they led a strange life. Alone in their two beds at night they now and again wondered why they hadn't just sold Carraveagh forty-eight years ago when their father had died: why had the tie been so strong and why had they in perversity encouraged it? They didn't fully know, nor did they attempt to discuss the matter in any way. Instinctively they had remained at Carraveagh, instinctively feeling that it would have been cowardly to go. Yet often it seemed to them now to be no more than a game they played, this worship of the distant past. And at other times it seemed as real and as important as the remaining acres of land, and the house itself.

'Isn't that shocking?' Mr Healy said one day in 1969. 'Did you hear about that, Mr Middleton, blowing up them post offices in Belfast?'

Mr Healy, red-faced and short-haired, spoke casually in his Cocktail Room, making midday conversation. He had commented in much the same way at breakfast time, looking up from the *Irish Independent*. Everyone in the town had said it too: that the blowing up of sub-post offices in Belfast was a shocking matter.

'A bad business,' Fat Driscoll remarked, wrapping the Middletons' meat. 'We don't want that old stuff all over again.'

'We didn't want it in the first place,' Miss Middleton reminded him. He laughed, and she laughed, and so did her brother. Yes, it was a game, she thought: how could any of it be as real or as important as the afflictions and problems of the old butcher himself, his rheumatism and his reluctance to retire? Did her brother, she wondered, privately think so too?

'Come on, old Turloch,' he said, stroking the flank of the red setter with the point of his shoe, and she reflected that you could never tell what he was thinking. Certainly it wasn't the kind of thing you wanted to talk about.

'I've put him in a bit of mince,' Fat Driscoll said, which was something he often did these days, pretending the mince would otherwise be thrown away. There'd been a red setter about the place that night when he waited in the hall for the soldiers: Breen and Maguire had pushed it down into a cellar, frightened of it.

'There's a heart of gold in you, Mr Driscoll,' Miss Middleton

murmured, nodding and smiling at him. He was the same age
as she was, sixty-six: he should have shut up shop years ago. He
would have, he'd once told them, if there'd been a son to leave
the business to. As it was, he'd have to sell it and when it came
to the point he found it hard to make the necessary arrangements. 'Like us and Carraveagh,' she'd said, even though on the
face of it it didn't seem the same at all.

Every evening they sat in the big old kitchen, hearing the
news. It was only in Belfast and Derry, the wireless said; outside Belfast and Derry you wouldn't know anything was happening at all. On Fridays they listened to the talk in Mrs
Keogh's bar and in the hotel. 'Well, thank God it has nothing
to do with the South,' Mr Healy said often, usually repeating
the statement.

The first British soldiers landed in the north of Ireland, and
soon people didn't so often say that outside Belfast and Derry
you wouldn't know anything was happening. There were incidents in Fermanagh and Armagh, in border villages and towns.
One prime minister resigned and then another one. The troops
were unpopular, the newspapers said; internment became part
of the machinery of government. In the town, in St Patrick's
Protestant Church and in the Church of the Holy Assumption,
prayers for peace were offered, but no peace came.

'We're hit, Mr Middleton,' Mr Healy said one Friday morning. 'If there's a dozen visitors this summer it'll be God's own
stroke of luck for us.'

'Luck?'

'Sure, who wants to come to a country with all that malarkey
in it?'

'But it's only in the North.'

'Tell that to your tourists, Mr Middleton.'

The town's prosperity ebbed. The border was more than
sixty miles away, but over that distance had spread some wisps

of the fog of war. As anger rose in the town at the loss of fortune so there rose also the kind of talk there had been in the distant past. There was talk of atrocities and counter-atrocities, and of guns and gelignite and the rights of people. There was bitterness suddenly in Mrs Keogh's bar because of the lack of trade, and in the empty hotel there was bitterness also.

On Fridays, only sometimes at first, there was a silence when the Middletons appeared. It was as though, going back nearly twenty years, people remembered the Union Jack in the window of their car and saw it now in a different light. It wasn't something to laugh at any more, nor were certain words that the Middletons had gently spoken, nor were they themselves just an old, peculiar couple. Slowly the change crept about, all around them in the town, until Fat Driscoll didn't wish it to be remembered that he had ever given them mince for their dog. He had stood with a gun in the enemy's house, waiting for soldiers so that soldiers might be killed; it was better that people should remember that.

One day Canon Kelly looked the other way when he saw the Middletons' car coming and they noticed this movement of his head, although he hadn't wished them to. And on another day Mrs O'Brien, who had always been keen to talk to them in the hotel, didn't reply when they addressed her.

The Middletons naturally didn't discuss these rebuffs but they each of them privately knew that there was no conversation they could have at this time with the people of the town. The stand they had taken and kept to for so many years no longer seemed ridiculous in the town. Had they driven with a Union Jack now they would, astoundingly, have been shot.

'It will never cease.' He spoke disconsolately one night, standing by the dresser where the wireless was.

She washed the dishes they'd eaten from, and the cutlery. 'Not in our time,' she said.

'It is worse than before.'

'Yes, it is worse than before.'

They took from the walls of the hall the portrait of their father in the uniform of the Irish Guards because it seemed wrong to them that at this time it should hang there. They took down also the crest of their family and the cross of Saint George, and from a vase on the drawing-room mantelpiece they removed the small Union Jack that had been there since the coronation of Queen Elizabeth II. They did not remove these articles in fear but in mourning for the *modus vivendi* that had existed for so long between them and the people of the town. They had given their custom to a butcher who had planned to shoot down soldiers in their hall and he, in turn, had given them mince for their dog. For fifty years they had experienced, after suspicion had seeped away, a tolerance that never again in the years that were left to them would they know.

One November night their dog died and he said to her after he had buried it that they must not be depressed by all that was happening. They would die themselves and the house would become a ruin because there was no one to inherit it, and the distant past would be set to rest. But she disagreed: the *modus vivendi* had been easy for them, she pointed out, because they hadn't really minded the dwindling of their fortunes while the town prospered. It had given them a life, and a kind of dignity: you could take a pride out of living in peace.

He did not say anything and then, because of the emotion that both of them felt over the death of their dog, he said in a rushing way that they could no longer at their age hope to make a living out of the remains of Carraveagh. They must sell the hens and the four Herefords. As he spoke, he watched her nodding, agreeing with the sense of it. Now and again, he thought, he would drive slowly into the town, to buy groceries and meat with the money they had saved, and to face the silence that would sourly thicken as their own two deaths came closer and death increased in another part of their island. She felt him thinking that and she knew that he was right. Because of the distant past they would die friendless. It was worse than being murdered in their beds.

THE WALL-READER

FIONA BARR

'Shall only our rivers run free?' The question jumped out from the cobbled wall in huge white letters, as The People's taxi swung round the corner at Beechmount. Looks like paint is running freely enough down here, she thought to herself, as other slogans glided past in rapid succession. Reading Belfast's grim graffiti had become an entertaining hobby for her, and she often wondered, was it in the dead of night that groups of boys huddled round a paint tin daubing walls and gables with tired political slogans and clichés. Did anyone ever see them? (Was the guilty brush ever found?) The brush is mightier than the bomb, she declared inwardly, as she thought of how celebrated among journalists some lines had become. [Is there a life before death?] Well, no one had answered that one yet, at least, not in this city.

The shapes of Belfast crowded in on her as the taxi rattled over the ramps outside the fortressed police barracks. Dilapidated houses, bricked-up terraces. Rosy-cheeked soldiers, barely out of school, and quivering with high-pitched fear. She thought of the thick-lipped youth who came to hijack the car, making his point by showing his revolver under his anorak, and of the others, jigging and taunting every July, almost sexual in their arrogance and hatred. Meanwhile, passengers climbed in and out at various points along the road, manoeuvring between legs, bags of shopping and umbrellas. The taxi swerved blindly into the road. No Highway Code here. As the woman's stop approached, the taxi swung up to the pavement, and she stepped out.

She thought of how she read walls – like teacups, she smiled to herself. Pushing her baby in the pram to the supermarket, she had to pass under a motorway bridge that was peppered with lines, some in irregular lettering with the paint dribbling down the concrete, others written with felt-tip pen in minute secretive hand. A whole range of human emotions splayed itself with [persistent anarchy] on the walls. One could do worse than be a reader of walls, she thought, twisting Frost's words. Instead, though, the pram was pushed past the intriguing mural with much gusto. Respectable housewives don't read walls!

The Troubles, as they were euphemistically named, remained for this couple as a remote, vaguely irritating wart on their life. They were simply ordinary (she often groaned at the oppressive banality of the word), middle-class, and [hoping the baby would marry a doctor] thereby raising them in their autumn days to the select legions of the upper class. Each day their lives followed the same routine – no harm in that sordid little detail, she thought. It helps structure one's existence. He went to the office, she fed the baby, washed the rapidly growing mound of nappies, prepared the dinner and looked forward to the afternoon walk. She had convinced herself she was happy with her lot, and yet felt disappointed at the pangs of jealousy endured on hearing of a friend's glamorous job or another's academic and erudite husband. If only someone noticed her from time to time, or even wrote her name on a wall declaring her existence worth while; 'A fine mind' or 'I was once her lover'. That way, at least, she would have evidence she was [having impact on others.] As it was, she was perpetually bombarded with it. Marital successes, even marital failures, evoked a response from her. All one-way traffic.

That afternoon she dressed the baby and started out for her walk. 'Fantasy time' her husband called it. 'Wall-reading time' she knew it to be. On this occasion, however, she decided to avoid those concrete temptations and, instead, visit the park. Out along the main road she trundled, pushing the pram, pausing to gaze into the hardware store's window, hearing the whine of the Saracen as it thundered by, waking the baby and making her feel uneasy. A foot patrol of soldiers strolled past, their rifles, lethal even in the brittle sunlight of this March day, lounged lovingly and relaxed in the arms of their men. One soldier stood nonchalantly, almost impertinent, against a corrugated railing and stared at her. She always blushed on passing troops.

why'd she go there?

The park is ugly, stark and hostile. Even in summer, when courting couples seek out secluded spots like mating cats, they reject Musgrave. There are a few trees, clustered together, standing like skeletons, ashamed of their nakedness. The rest is grass, a green wasteland speckled with puddles of gulls squawking over a worm patch. The park is bordered by a hospital with a military wing which is guarded by an army billet. The beauty of the place, it has only this, is its silence.

The hill up to the park bench was not the precipice it seemed, but the baby and pram were heavy. Ante-natal self-indulgence had taken its toll – her midriff was now most definitely a bulge. With one final push, pram, baby and mother reached the green wooden seat, and came to rest. The baby slept soundly with the soother touching her velvet pink cheeks, hand on pillow, a picture of purity. The woman heard a coughing noise coming from the nearby gun turret, and managed to see the tip of a rifle and a face peering out from the darkness. Smells of cabbage and burnt potatoes wafted over from behind the slanting sheets of protective steel.

'Is that your baby?' an English voice called out. She could

barely see the face belonging to the voice. She replied yes, and smiled. The situation reminded her of the confessional. Dark and supposedly anonymous. 'Is that you, my child?' She knew the priest personally. Did he identify her sins with his 'Good morning, Mary', and think to himself, and I know what you were up to last night! She blushed at the secrets given away during the ceremony. Yes, she nervously answered again, it was her baby, a little girl. First-time mothers rarely resist the temptation to talk about their offspring. Forgetting her initial shyness, she told the voice of when the baby was born, the early problems of all-night crying, now teething, how she could crawl backwards and gurgle.

The voice responded. It too had a son, a few months older than her child, away in Germany at the army base at Münster. Factory pipes, chimney tops, church spires, domes, all listened impassively to the Englishman's declaration of paternal love. The scene was strange, for although Belfast's sterile geography slipped into classical forms with dusk and heavy rain clouds, the voice and the woman knew the folly of such innocent communication. They politely finished their conversation, said goodbye, and the woman pushed her pram homewards. The voice remained in the turret, watchful and anxious. Home she went, past vanloads of workers leering out at the pavement, past the uneasy presence of foot patrols, past the church. 'Let us give each other the sign of peace,' they said at Mass. The only sign Belfast knew was two fingers pointing towards heaven. Life was self-contained, the couple often declared, just like flats. No need to go outside.

She did go outside, however. Each week the voice and the woman learnt more of each other. No physical contact was needed, no face-to-face encounter to judge reaction, no touching to confirm amity, no threat of dangerous intimacy. It was a meeting of minds, as she explained later to her husband, a new opinion, a common bond, an opening of vistas. He disclosed his ambitions to become a pilot, to watching the land, fields and horizons spread out beneath him – a patchwork quilt of dappled colours and textures. She wanted to be remembered by writing on walls, about them that is, a world-shattering thesis on their psychological complexities, their essential truths, their witticisms and intellectual genius. [And all this time the city's skyline and distant buildings watched and listened.] *city is aware*

It was April now. More slogans had appeared, white and dripping, on the city walls. 'Brits out. Peace in.' A simple equation for the writer. 'Loose talk claims lives,' another shouted menacingly. The messages, the woman decided, had acquired a more ominous tone. The baby had grown and could sit up without support. New political solutions had been proposed and rejected, inter-paramilitary feuding had broken out and subsided, four soldiers and two policemen had been blown to smithereens in separate incidents, and a building a day had been bombed by the Provos. It had been a fairly normal month by Belfast's standards. The level of violence was no more or less acceptable than at other times.

One day – it was, perhaps, the last day in April – her husband returned home panting and trembling a little. He asked had she been to the park, and she replied she had. Taking her by the hand, he led her to the wall on the left of their driveway. She felt her heart sink and thud against her. She felt her face redden. Her mouth was suddenly dry. She could not speak. In huge angry letters the message spat itself out:

(TOUT) *got what she wanted*

The four-letter word covered the whole wall. It clanged in her brain, its venom rushed through her body. Suspicion was enough to condemn. The job itself was not well done, she had seen better. The letters were uneven, paint splattered down

from the cross T, the U looked a misshapen O. The workman-
ship was poor, the impact perfect.

Her husband led her back into the kitchen. The baby was
crying loudly in the living room but the woman did not seem
to hear. Like sleepwalkers, they sat down on the settee. The
woman began to sob. Her shoulders heaved in bursts as she
gasped hysterically. Her husband took her in his arms gently and
tried to make her sorrow his. Already he shared her fear.

'What did you talk about? Did you not realise how dangerous
it was? We must leave.' He spoke quickly, making plans. Selling
the house and car, finding a job in London or Dublin, far away
from Belfast, mortgages, removals, savings, the tawdry affairs of
normal living stunned her, making her more confused. 'I told
him nothing,' she sobbed, 'what could I tell? We talked about
life, everything, but not about here.' She trembled, trying to
control herself. 'We just chatted about reading walls, families,
anything at all. Oh Sean, it was as innocent as that. A meeting
of minds we called it, for it was little else.'

She looked into her husband's face and saw he did not fully
understand. There was a hint of jealousy, of resentment at not
being part of their communication. Her hands fell on her lap,
resting in resignation. What was the point of explanation? She
lifted her baby from the floor. Pressing the tiny face and body
to her breast, she felt all her hopes and desires for a better life
become one with the child's struggle for freedom. The child's
hands wandered over her face, their eyes met. At once that
moment of maternal and filial love eclipsed her fear, gave her
the impetus to escape.

For nine months she had been unable to accept the reality of
her condition. Absurd, for the massive bump daily shifted position and thumped against her. When her daughter was born, she
had been overwhelmed by love for her and amazed at her own
ability to give life. By nature she was a dreamy person, given to

moments of fancy. She wondered at her competence in ful-
filling the role of mother. Could it be measured? This time
she knew it could. She really did not care if they maimed her
or even murdered her. She did care about her daughter. She
was her touchstone, her anchor to virtue. Not for her child a
legacy of fear, revulsion or hatred. With the few hours' respite
the painters had left between judgment and sentence she
determined to leave Belfast's walls behind.

The next few nights were spent in troubled, restless sleep.
The message remained on the wall outside. The neighbours
pretended not to notice and refused to discuss the matter. She
and the baby remained indoors despite the refreshing May
breezes and blue skies. Her husband had given in his notice at
the office, for health reasons, he suggested to his colleagues. An
aunt had been contacted in Dublin. The couple did not answer
knocks at the door. They carefully examined the shape and
size of mail delivered and always paused when they answered
the telephone.

The mini-van was to call at eleven on Monday night, when it
would be dark enough to park, and pack their belongings and
themselves without too much suspicion being aroused. The
firm had been very understanding when the nature of their
work had been explained. They were Protestant so there was
no conflict of loyalties involved in the exercise. They agreed to
drive them to Dublin at extra cost, changing drivers at Newry
on the way down.

Monday finally arrived. The couple nervously laughed about
how smoothly everything had gone. Privately, they each expected something to go wrong. The baby was fed, and played with,
the radio listened to and the clock watched. They listened to the
news at nine. Huddled together in their anxiety, they kept vigil
in the darkening room. Rain had begun to pour from black

thunderclouds. Everywhere it was quiet and still. Hushed and cold they waited. Ten o'clock, and it was now dark. A blustery wind had risen, making the lattice separation next door bang and clatter. At ten to eleven, her husband went into the sitting room to watch for the mini-van. His footsteps clamped noisily on the floorboards as he paced back and forth. The baby slept.

A black shape glided slowly up the street and backed into the driveway. It was eleven. The van had arrived. Her husband asked to see their identification and then they began to load up the couple's belongings. Settee, chairs, television, washing machine – all were dumped hastily, it was no time to worry about breakages. She stood holding the sleeping baby in the living room as the men worked anxiously between van and house. The scene was so unreal, the circumstances absolutely incredible. She thought, what have I done? Recollections of her naïveté, her insensibility to historical fact and political climate were stupefying. She had seen women who had been tarred and feathered, heard of people who had been shot in the head, boys who had been kneecapped, all for suspected fraternising with troops. The catalogue of violence spilt out before her as she realised the gravity and possible repercussions of her alleged misdemeanour.

A voice called her, 'Mary, come on now. We have to go. Don't worry, we're all together.' Her husband led her to the locked and waiting van. Handing the baby to him, she climbed up beside the driver, took back the baby as her husband sat down beside her and waited for the engine to start. The van slowly manoeuvred out onto the street and down the main road. They felt more cheerful now, a little like refugees seeking safety and freedom not too far away. As they approached the motorway bridge, two figures with something clutched in their hands stood side by side in the darkness. She closed her eyes tightly, expecting bursts of gunfire. The van shot past. Relieved, she asked her husband what they were doing at this time of night. 'Writing slogans on the wall,' he replied.

The furtiveness of the painters seemed ludicrous and petty as she recalled the heroic and literary characteristics with which she had endowed them. [What did they matter?] The travellers *av impact* sat in silence as the van sped past the city suburbs, the glare of police and army barracks, on out and further out into the countryside. Past sleeping villages and silent fields, past white-washed farmhouses and barking dogs. On to Newry where they said goodbye to their driver as the new one stepped in. Far along the coast with Rostrevor's twinkling lights opposite the bay down to the border check and a drowsy soldier waving them through. Out of the North, safe, relieved and heading for Dublin.

Some days later in Belfast the neighbours discovered the house vacant, the people next door received a letter and a cheque from Dublin. Remarks about the peculiar couple were made over hedges and cups of coffee, the message on the wall was painted over by the couple who had bought the house when it went up for sale. They too were ordinary people, living a self-contained life, worrying over finance and babies, promotion and local gossip. He too had an office job, but his wife was merely a housekeeper for him. [She was sensible, down-to-earth, and not in the least inclined to wall-reading.]

A SOCIAL CALL

BRENDA MURPHY

I liked wee Bernie. She was what my mammy would call a
decent girl. She had just had her fourth child, another boy,
the fourth in four years. It had been a breech birth with a
difficult and prolonged labour. I went up to see her because
my sister said she had been a bit down and weepy and looked
very pale. It was no wonder she looked pale. She signed herself
out of hospital after only three days because her man said he
couldn't cope. So I thought I'd drop in and cheer her up. I'd
a wee present for the new baby and a half-bottle of Pernod
for her.

She welcomed me with open arms and the teapot was on
before I'd my coat off. 'Ah sure you're lookin' great, so you
are, Teresa. Shove them toys off that chair and sit yourself
down. I'm just getting the kids up to their beds,' she said.

I helped her get them washed and dressed for their beds. Passing flannel and basin of water between us, we washed faces,
bums and sticky hands, pulled on babygrows and pyjamas. We
had just got them into cots and beds and sat down, when her
husband came in. He had two other men with him. His eyes
took me in. His mouth said nothing.

Then he snapped at Bernie. 'You still sittin' on yer arse? Why
don't you tidy this place up a bit? There's kids' clothes and
toys everywhere.'

'I've just this minute sat down, Joe, just put the kids up to bed. I'll pick the clothes up in a minute. Sit down and I'll get you your tea,' said Bernie.

'Don't bother. I'm going straight out again in a minute. Make these fellas a cuppa tea, I'm going up to get changed,' he replied as he turned and walked out of the room.

Bernie got up. 'If you two come into the scullery,' she said, 'I'll make yous a sandwich and a cuppa tea.'

'Right, thanks missus,' said one of them, and they followed her out into the small kitchen.

I could hear her chatting away and bustling about in the scullery.

Then she came in to me. 'Teresa love, I'm going up to get my wages off Joe 'cos he'd walk out and forget all about it. They'll be gone in a couple of minutes and me and you'll get the house till ourselves,' she said.

I sat looking round the living room; the lino on the floor was shiny clean and had wee rugs scattered about it. The whole house was bright and fresh. There were the clothes we had just taken off the children sitting on a chair and half a bucket of children's building blocks spread on the floor. Hardly the pigsty he had implied. I folded the clothes and was starting to lift the blocks when I heard the thumps and muffled shouts from up-stairs. I tried to ignore them and finished picking up the blocks.

Then I heard the eldest child screaming, 'Daddy, Daddy, don't.'

I went to the foot of the stairs. The words were clear now.

'I'll do what I want, ye stupid bitch,' he was shouting, then another thump.

I ran up the stairs and was in the bedroom before I knew it. Bernie was lying on the floor, hands up over her face, knees drawn up close to her belly. He was standing over her, legs apart. He lifted his boot to kick her. I shoved him then – he went flying, falling heavily against the dressing table.

'You dirty bastard, leave her alone,' I screamed. 'She's just had a baby.'

I bent down to help Bernie up but he'd got back on his feet. He grabbed me by the sweater and flung me against the wall. He grabbed a handful of sweater again just below my neck, pulled me over to him, nose to nose. I could smell the drink on his breath.

'Now you listen, you interfering wee whore. This is my house, that is my wife. Keep your fucking nose out of my business or I'll break it for you,' he snarled, spraying me with his spittle.

He let me go, picked his jacket off the bed, pushed his son out of his way and went downstairs. I could hear him call for his two mates to come on. I went over to Bernie and helped her up onto the bed. Her nose was swollen-looking. Big fat droplets of blood plopped from it. She cupped her hands round it.

'Ah God, Teresa. I'm sorry, love,' she muttered.

'You're sorry? You've done nothing to be sorry for. Look, go on into the bathroom and clean yourself. I'll put the child into bed,' I said.

I lifted him and carried him back to bed. 'My daddy hit my mammy,' said the child, eyes wide and wet.

'Yes, son, but he didn't mean it,' I lied, and calmed him down. Then Bernie came into the room and added her lies to my own with a smoothness and ease that told me she'd done this before.

When he was quiet we went back downstairs. I poured her a drink and sat on the arm of her chair. She put her head on my thigh and sobbed – deep, soft sobs. I could feel her tears soak through my trousers. I stroked her hair and put my arm round her shoulder. I stayed like that a while, then she sat up, searched in her apron pocket for something to dry her eyes and nose with, pulled out a whack of toilet roll and blew her nose and wiped her eyes.

'God, look at me, smothering and girning all over ye,' she said.

'Bernie, did you get that face for asking for your wages?' I asked.

'Jesus Christ, my wages! I forgot about them. No, Teresa, I didn't even get round to that. When I went up he was unwrapping something that was in a cloth. He didn't hear me go up. It was a gun, Teresa, he put it down the waistband of his trousers. I asked him where he got it, had he hidden it in our house, where he was going with it. Then I said he was not leaving the house with it. I was going down to tell them two to take it out of the house with them. That's when he cracked, said I wouldn't make a fool out of him and he tore into me.'

I sat with her till about eleven o'clock, looking at her sad, pale face, now bruised and swollen. We talked of school days, and the Plaza dance hall and the Astor, and who we did and didn't 'touch' for. I walked home through the black shiny wet streets of Ballymurphy, sad and sickened. I went to bed and couldn't sleep for a long time wondering if he would come in and hit her again. She'd told me he wouldn't.

The next morning I was sitting with my first fag and cuppa tea of the day. I lifted the *Irish News*. My eyes fell on an article headed 'Punishment Shooting'. Beneath it I read how a sixteen-year-old had been dragged from his home by three men. Two held him down while a third shot him in both knees. The incident happened in Ballymurphy. The local paramilitary group, who claimed they were responsible, said they shot the boy for repeated anti-social behaviour.

GREEN ROADS

MAURICE LEITCH

The old man was sitting on the bus seat buried in the bank outside his cottage when the army Land Rover went past in the late afternoon. It churned up the steep slope in the direction of the bog where no wheeled traffic had ever been known to go before and, as it topped the incline, the old man saw a soldier with a black face staring out at him over the tailboard. The colour was natural, not camouflage, he could tell, even though it was his very first Negro. This darkie soldier held a rifle and looked straight through him as if he didn't exist. The old man sat pondering in the dying sunlight. Something, he didn't know what, held him back from going inside to tell his daughter what he had seen, yet seldom did anything like this ever happen to him. One day followed another in the same dream-like fashion, day after day after day spent here on this old summer seat. He stroked its warm, worn upholstery. His daughter kept saying his memory was going but it was more a case of not being able to make it do his bidding, for something remembered, but deeply submerged, about men in uniform passing this way once before refused stubbornly to surface. He would just have to wait until the memory, whatever it was, floated up of its own accord. It was just that you could never tell when; perhaps today, perhaps tomorrow, perhaps never.

The old man looked at a distant staining of smoke in the evening sky. Someone had started to burn whins on their land.

The others would follow suit now, he told himself; there always had to be one to start the first fire somewhere or other, for the rest to follow.

The driver of the Land Rover was a corporal named Jessop from Devizes in Wiltshire, unmarried, in his early thirties, with the reputation for keeping himself to himself. A self-contained character, some would even say dour, but then that may have been because of his background. Everyone else in the platoon seemed to be from an industrial northern city and took much pleasure in reminding him of that fact. Even Carlton, despite the colour of his skin, would chance his luck now and again, slyly joining in. Coming from Streatham put him on an equal footing with the others, as far as he was concerned.

At the corporal's side rode the young lieutenant who had the map spread on his knees. The Land Rover bucked and bounced and Carlton in the rear swore fluently but the corporal stared straight ahead. A perverse pleasure was making him aim for every bump and pothole in their path for he knew that they were lost and this track they were on led nowhere. The young lieutenant, however, would not admit to the fact. It was part of his class 'thing': something the other two recognised.

On either side stretched desolate moorland the colour of the vehicle they travelled in, without break or respite for the eye. They passed sheep with splashes of dye on their fleece but they kept their heads resolutely lowered. Carlton aimed his rifle, taking silent pot shots, but even he seemed to feel their chill disregard. Light rain began to fall and the rhythm of the windscreen wipers beat time with their thoughts, or it may have been the other way round, while a mood of gloom settled on the Land Rover and its three occupants. It was as if it had shrunk or been reduced in some way to the size of an insect crawling along under a vast and darkening sky.

There came a stretch when all heard the sump drag itself

over the long, stony ridge that now seemed to bisect the track. Jessop put his foot hard on the brake and sat looking out at the gathering dusk until the lieutenant said, 'Yes, let's stop here. Get our bearings, shall we?' He marched to the front and spread his map on the bonnet and began to pore over the brown and green contours.

Carlton sang softly, 'I was onlee twentee four hours from Tulsa', until Jessop told him to be quiet. Then the lieutenant was waving him over and together they studied the map.

'You can see we're roughly here,' said the lieutenant, his finger on a line of dots hugging the contours.

Jessop noted that there were quite a number of these fine lines curving and snaking across the terrain. 'Sheep paths, sir?'

'Definitely not. No question. Perfectly passable routes each and every one of them. If we stay with this one we're on, as you can see, we'll strike this secondary road here and then it's only a matter of time before we're on course for base. The map is perfectly clear about that.'

'When was it made, sir? The map, I mean.'

The lieutenant looked at him. 'No one has more up-to-date information than we have, Corporal, always remember that.'

They climbed back into the Land Rover and Carlton said, 'How far now?' but no one answered him. They drove on and for a time the track seemed to be improving. The lieutenant handed cigarettes around, even joked a little, and Carlton sang the whole of his song now without any trace of irony.

Then they began to descend, slowly at first but finally in a rush, scattering countless small stones loosened by the rain. These rattled off the metal beneath their feet with a noise like gunfire and the corporal went even faster, as though fleeing from an invisible attacker. That was how the young lieutenant saw it. An imaginative side to his nature still lingered even after all his training. But the reality was that Jessop had spotted a steep

incline ahead, one in ten at least to his eyes, despite the
visibility, and he wanted to tackle it at speed. But, as it turned
out, it was to be the dip at the base of both hills that was to
prove their undoing. With engine roaring the Land Rover
bounded downhill and raced across the flat stretch of track. At
first their route seemed smooth, almost finished in fact, but then
the corporal noticed that the wheels were slowing, as though
some exterior force was at work. He pressed the accelerator but
the engine only screamed on a higher, more maddened note. At
a point halfway along this valley floor the Land Rover finally
came to a halt, its rear wheels spinning in troughs of mud.

The lieutenant sat stiff and silent while Carlton in the back
swore and gave advice. Jessop, who was an experienced driver
and proud of his skills, went through every combination of gears
before finally switching off the engine.

The lieutenant said, 'Is there a problem, Corporal?' Carlton
laughed. 'We do have four-wheel drive, don't we?'

'Correct, sir.'

'So, why do we have a problem?'

Jessop sighed and got out. Kneeling down, he stared blankly
at a wheel, noting with no real interest that it was already buried
to the hub and appeared to be sinking. His own boots were, as
well, a strange sensation and, straightening up, he walked off a
few paces, leaving behind well-defined tracks. The ground had
a curious consistency, not quite solid. The corporal lifted a large
flat rock and pitched it several yards then watched it settle in the
hollow it had formed.

Standing there he was barely conscious of the fine rain on his
face, or anything else for that matter. The Land Rover and its
occupants and their plight meant nothing to him. He might
have been one of those sheep they had passed earlier. He didn't
feel angry, as might be expected. Instead, as he listened to the
silence he felt inert as stone.

Then the young lieutenant joined him, making a great play of kicking the tyres and stooping to peer underneath. The corporal stared at the back of his head, young and vulnerable under his beret, and he felt dizzy for a moment, sweating at the sudden and unexplained violence of his thoughts.

The lieutenant straightened up. 'Have we anything we can put down, an old blanket, tarpaulin, that sort of thing?'

'Not really, sir. We can't get purchase.'

'I can see that for myself, Corporal.' Carlton had joined them and both he and the lieutenant were looking expectantly at Jessop now.

Then the lieutenant said, 'Get me the machete, Private', and Carlton, suddenly energetic and grinning, brought it to him in its canvas sheath. 'We'll make a start by cutting some of this gorse. If it works in snow I don't see why it shouldn't do the trick in this muck as well.'

He slid out the greased blade – it had never been used – and held it out to neither of them in particular, but Jessop turned away almost fastidiously. Then Carlton seized it and began hacking at the tough stalks.

The lieutenant watched the growing pile. He was remembering with fondness one Boxing Night when his MG had got stuck not far from Dorking. While the other three had laughed and continued to drink in the car he had worked like a demon among the drifts, foraging and, finally, bedding the wheels with bracken, and although it had been a sudden impulse on his part it had done the trick. Much later he had found out, indirectly, that the girls in particular had been most impressed but it was his own private pleasure that meant more to him, despite having ruined a perfectly good dinner jacket.

With the mood of that snowy night still upon him he began furiously laying armfuls of the stuff around and under all four wheels. Then he stamped and pounded with his boots until the

Land Rover seemed to be resting on a thick, sodden, brown carpet. Carlton stood watching, as did Jessop, but when he tried to signal to the corporal his amusement at the sight of this odd war dance the other turned his face away.

The lieutenant shouted, 'Let's see if *that* will do the trick!' and Jessop went over to the Land Rover and climbed in. For a moment he sat there as though he had never seen a dashboard or steering wheel in his life before, then, shaking his head violently, he pressed the starter. All his old skills returned to him and with infinite patience he began coaxing the engine to its task.

For a long time he hung in the seat, oblivious to everything but the sounds of the motor and the straining of the transmission then, above the roar, he heard someone shouting his name and the lieutenant was at the open door. The corporal looked at him in surprise. His face and front were coated with mud, great gouts of it. Why was he shouting? the corporal asked himself. He was genuinely confused. The lieutenant reached in and switched off the engine, then began wiping his face with his coarse mesh scarf. He spat disgustedly. Carlton came into view, winking at Jessop. 'Your driving, Corp, blimey!'

The lieutenant said, 'What a God-awful, bloody country', then he looked at Jessop who still sat grasping the wheel. 'I really think you've done enough for one day, Corporal, don't you?' and his voice had taken on the leisurely drawl of his class, something the two men had never heard before.

'Looks as if we're bogged down then, sir,' said Carlton cheerfully. 'What we need is a tow.'

The lieutenant stared about him. 'Smoke over there.' He sniffed as if he could smell it. 'Now, if they have a tractor...'

Jessop had got out by now and, speaking quietly as if to the ground, said, 'No tractors. Not out here, not these people.'

The other two exchanged glances. Carlton was grinning

again but the lieutenant's face had set hard as stone. 'Yes, you *would* know all about that, wouldn't you, Jessop?'

Then he reached under the passenger seat, pulling out the handset of the radio. They listened to him talking to base, explaining their plight and position on the map, and at first his voice was patient and unhurried just as if he was speaking to one of them. But then there were angry blizzards of static from the other end and they could hear him protesting.

At one point he said, 'Some joker must have turned the signposts around, sir', and it registered with Jessop even in his dulled state that he had been right about the lieutenant all along. But there was no satisfaction in the knowledge. He was standing a little way off by himself with his head raised, as if he was picking up signals of his own from the air.

They were in a glen of sorts, ringed on all sides by moorland, the rim blue-black and clearly defined against the sky. The low murmur of running water could be heard nearby. Jessop felt something he could not put into words. It was as if he had stood like this in such a place once before in a dream. For a dizzy moment he seemed to be looking down onto the scene from a great height, the Land Rover the size of a matchbox toy, himself a figure tiny in scale a little way off. He felt, he felt – it seemed to him he was on the point of getting to the secret core of it when the moment passed and the lieutenant shouted for him to return to the Land Rover.

He was sitting in the front with a look on his face that said he would be doing everything strictly by the book from now on. 'No tow truck until 0900 hours, I'm afraid.'

The grin left Carlton's face. *'Tomorrow!'*

The lieutenant ignored him. 'So it looks like a night on the bare mountain for us all, chaps.' A wintry little smile at his private joke came and went.

'Jesus Christ, sir!' Carlton cried out. 'Not out *here*!' His grip

had tightened on his weapon while his eyes went darting
about him.

'Oh, relax, Private, you're not in bandit country now.
Certainly not around here. Believe me, I do know.' And he did,
for it was something he took pride in, the young lieutenant, his
'demography', as he liked to call it back in the mess.

'I don't care a toss what side they're on, you can 'ave 'em!
Bleedin' sheep-shaggers, the lot of them!'

The lieutenant laughed, looking at Jessop as he did so,
but the corporal had returned once more to his own private world.

'Come,' said the lieutenant, jumping out of the Land Rover,
'we must build a shelter before it gets too dark.'

Carlton grounded his rifle in disbelief. 'Shelter! Sir?'

The lieutenant held out the machete, but this time it was
clear that it was intended for Jessop. For a moment the corporal
weighed it in his hand, looking at it strangely, then he began
clearing a patch a little way off where the ground was firm. The
corporal worked, slightly bent at one knee, the blade cutting
low and close, and there was such economy and ease about the
operation that the other two watched in silence. Heaps of the
tawny gorse began to rise about the sides of a perfectly formed
rectangle. The revealed sward was pale and cropped and the
lieutenant stared at its perfection. An anger was growing in him,
for what he and the private were witnessing was nothing more,
it seemed to him, than yet another ploy intended to make him
look foolish.

'All right,' he managed to call out at last. 'All right, you've
made your point!' but Jessop continued to work on.

The lieutenant's face became redder. Rising, he strode across to the toiler, laying a hand on his shoulder. Instantly he
felt the heat of the man's body through the khaki wool and,
in the same moment, Jessop jerked as though stung. Then he

raised a face with such savagery in it that the lieutenant fell back. They both looked down at the blade in the corporal's hand, then the moment passed.

The lieutenant called out, 'We'll bed down here', striking a heel deep in the turf. Then he made off in the direction of the stream, tracking it by sound, for he felt certain there would be saplings growing there, and he was right, too. But before doing a thing he carefully wiped the haft of the machete and his own hands to remove all traces of the corporal's sweat.

Carlton said, 'Answer me one question, just one question', when the lieutenant disappeared from sight. 'Why can't we just kip in the 'Rover? I mean, did we join the boy scouts, or what?' He offered Jessop a smoke from his tin but the corporal declined.

'No?' said the other, then he leant close. 'Here, what you on, man? You're on something, ain't you, sly old sod.'

The corporal got up from the bumper and moved back to the space he had just cleared. He stood there at its heart while Carlton continued to eye him slyly.

'Give us a taste, man,' came that soft voice. ''Cause I know you're on something, that's for sure.'

Jessop turned his head away as if to hide the evidence, though the truth was that he had taken nothing, never had for that matter. Something deep-seated had always made him shy clear of such things, even now when the right pill could see him through this. For two weeks he hadn't slept. He wondered how long he would be able to keep going. A numbness and a trembling had begun in one of his legs and he knew his reactions were slowing, but he didn't want any help from anything or anyone. The word punishment entered his head for some reason. He supposed this must be his way of punishing himself, his body, for that night in the pub car park near Swindon. He closed his eyes, breathing

in deeply, willing himself to remember. The images began
to burn.

It had been the last night of his leave and it had been a pub
picked at random, not that he was a great one for pubs, never
had been, but before going back for another tour of duty
something made him walk into this place in the heart of the
country. He had imagined what it might be like inside, horse
brasses, oak settles, a real fire of logs even, and it was as he'd pictured it, something to remember over there, take the edge off
things when it all started getting you down. He ordered a pint
and sat in a corner out of the way, a habit, when he heard this
man at the bar. There were other people in the place as well,
regulars, but the man's accent, although it was soft, seemed to
go through him like a knife. He began to tremble, he didn't
know why, sitting there with his tankard in front of him, and
as the time passed and the stranger with the brogue began to talk
more and more loudly he found he couldn't rise to go up for
a refill. He just listened and shook with lowered eyes. Nothing
like this had ever happened to him before, such a terrible hatred
for a complete stranger. There seemed no answer to it. The man
was neither a bully nor loudmouth; he seemed genuinely liked
in the place. It was obvious, too, that he was country-bred, like
everyone else there, himself included, nothing could disguise it.
At one point he did cry out passionately, 'Don't call me *Pat*. I'm
not a *Pat*. I'm as British as the rest of you. Nobody knows our
history. *Our* history. Or cares', and they all laughed at him.
Then he laughed, too, and ordered a round for the house and
Jessop, in his corner, knew it was time to go for he felt he
mustn't allow his hate to be diluted, so he quickly rose and
walked out.

   In the car park in the dark he waited for almost an hour, it
seemed, before the man came out to relieve himself. He was

singing, something sad like all their songs, and even when Jessop felled him he still continued to sing a little. Then the kicking began in earnest, for the corporal had been trained to inflict the utmost damage as speedily and as effectively as possible and he had been taught well, yet the man curled up on the ground barely uttered a sound, a protest or cry, even, while it was happening to him. Almost as if he felt he deserved it in some strange way.

That was a fortnight ago and he had walked off into the night not knowing or caring if the heap on the ground was alive or dead. The following day he was back on patrol, over here, on the stranger's own terrain.

The corporal looked down now at the carefully mown patch of turf at his feet. Punishment. The word came into his head again. How long must he have to wait? Not long now, he told himself, almost soothingly, not long now, for it seemed to him, standing here in this place, that he had already prepared the ground for it.

Returning with his booty the young lieutenant saw the corporal standing there as though defending his newly acquired territory. The sight displeased him for some reason and he shouted out for him to come and give a hand, dropping his burden where it lay. At the stream, he had carefully trimmed, then pointed, the stakes and the look of them lying together now so healthy and still full of sap filled him with pride. Already he could smell the never-to-be-forgotten tang of his old tree hut in the garden at Weybridge.

He watched while Carlton and the corporal constructed a rough shelter using the materials at hand and when it met finally with his approval they all stood back to look at it. Darkness had crept up and with it a chill mist. Carlton shivered dramatically. 'How's about a nice little fire, then, sir?'

'No fire. No lights.' The lieutenant's face seemed to have lost its youthful outline in the little light remaining.

'But you said it was all right, sir. Out here, sir. No bandits, remember, sir?'

'I know I did. Another thing, no smoking, either. I'll take the first watch.'

He waited until they crawled inside the makeshift bothy before going over to lean against the side of the grounded Land Rover. First watch, he knew, was the soft one to draw but he didn't care, that was his prerogative. He was piqued, as well, if the truth were known because, too late, he'd realised that he would have to share his hut, when what he really wanted all along was to have it all to himself the way he remembered it from those long magical school holidays.

Carlton and the corporal lay in the close, itchy darkness, side by side, not talking, because they both knew the lieutenant was only a matter of yards away. A low moaning sound was the nearest Carlton could get to his greatest desire which was to complain loudly and at length. He tossed and turned on their bed of bracken while the corporal lay unmoving, staring up at a gap in the low roof. Presently a star could be seen framed there. It looked like an eye to the corporal but the thought didn't disturb him. Ever since they had arrived in this place he had felt he was being watched. All he could do now was wait, he told himself, for whatever was out there to catch up with him. It was only a matter of time.

At midnight by his watch the lieutenant put his head into the darkness of the shelter. Carlton was snoring steadily, the corporal lay alongside, silent as a log, and the lieutenant smiled to himself, for the past four hours on his own had, strangely enough, smoothed away all his earlier vexation. These were his men, he thought fondly to himself, see how they depended on him. The way they slept out here in this place so trustingly was the measure of that. He decided he was a lucky man after all, that he really had found his true vocation. He put out a searching hand to grasp Carlton's ankle, it really had to be done, when he felt another hand take his before it could close on the sleeper's foot. A voice from the darkness said quietly, 'I'll take the next watch, sir', and the corporal's body slid swiftly past and out into the night air before he had time to think or make any sort of reply.

A full moon had come out by this time and Jessop felt dwarfed by the glare. He hunkered down; his shadow contracted even more. Far off somewhere the cry of an animal in pain quickly came and went and he was left to his watch.

As he crouched there, everything about him seemed to imprint itself upon his brain with terrible clarity as if he could read the landscape like no one else before or since. Grasping a tussock of grass to anchor himself he saw how the encircling rim of hills ran with barely a dip in its outline even where the track entered and left it, and the track itself had a similar perfection of line. It brought to mind old Roman routes from his own part of the country yet he had read that no Roman had ever set foot here. Before, it had lain there barely visible to the eye but now, by this trick of the light, the path had come back into its own. He thought of all those other old forgotten tracks lying hidden on the lieutenant's map and only returning to life like this while people slept.

The lethargy had left him now; his brain felt clear and responsive. He looked at the Land Rover, then at the shelter where the others were sleeping, oblivious. The Land Rover looked as though it had sunk even further, was still sinking, in fact. As for the shelter, it seemed reclaimed already; nothing but a handful of sticks and dying grasses. The corporal knew with total certainty now that he would never leave this place. It was an irony, even though it barely registered, for it to happen to him out here, he thought, in such a setting, and not in some alleyway in the city he had left that morning, the way he'd always expected it to be. And so he waited almost calmly, for he knew he could take the last watch as well if it was to take that long.

But then something strange and most unusual happened. The corporal fell asleep out there in the open and when he awoke, stiff and damp, the moon had gone and in its place a ribbon of light was beginning to brighten the sky to the east. He rubbed his eyes and tried to get up from where he had fallen. Instinct made him reach out in a panic for his weapon but it was there by his side, wet to the touch. Then he looked up and, where the distant rim of the high moor was turning to pink, he saw a number of objects breaking its outline. They looked like fencing posts at first, but then he saw that they weren't spaced evenly and that they varied in height and bulk as well. He shielded his gaze with his hand, squinting into the growing light, and then at last he saw what they were. At least thirty motionless figures stood there looking down at him and even at that distance he could feel the terrible intensity of their gaze. There was great patience there as well, it seemed to him, as if, while he slept, they had waited without movement or complaint. He began to notice other things as well. Most of them held implements in their hands, a few scythes, but mainly pitchforks and long poles tipped with metal. Their clothes looked outlandish as well, old and worn out from the effect of weather and long drudgery in the open.

Jessop, the corporal from Wiltshire, stood there as though on trial but already knowing the verdict. He felt calm and curiously rested. The watchers on the horizon had made no move but by now he knew they never would. There was a great silence all around. It was time. The corporal knelt down and, taking off his beret, laid it on the ground by his side. He took up his rifle. Its metal was cold and damp to the touch from where it had lain on the grass and, as he brought the barrel up under his chin, the last thing to reach his senses was the pungent odour of gun oil.

Propped up in bed – it was the only way he could sleep now he found – the old man came sharply out of a fitful dream. He listened for the sound that had woken him to come a second time but it refused. A sharp crack like the snap of a dry twig but distant, very distant, that was all the impression he was left with. The window was brightening now: he watched the room take form. At this hour he had only his thoughts to occupy him, his daughter wouldn't stir until her alarm went off in the middle of the morning, so he allowed memories, fragments of the past, free play.

On the wall facing him was a posed photograph of his own father holding a Union Jack and a curved ornamental sword. He could barely remember him yet, strangely, everything about his grandfather would always fall into sharp focus. He had been thinking about him only last night in the kitchen and about the way he had of slowly lifting live coals out of the fire between finger and thumb to light his pipe, when it had come to him about the soldiers going up the bog road. It was a story from the old, almost forgotten days when every house had a pike buried in the thatch in readiness for the call. Then, after the big battle and the rout, a troop of Fencibles, that was the name his grandfather had called them, were supposed to have ridden past this way in pursuit of some rebels, another unusual name for people from these parts. But the English troopers had got caught in the bog, men and horses sinking, so the story went, deep in the moss, and after a time the men in brown coats, as they were known, came down from the high ground and piked all of them to death. No trace had ever been found, not a bone or a belt buckle. All that remained was an old story, for the bog never gave up any of its secrets.

The old man thought of the road; he hadn't been that way for twenty years. It used to be a beautiful, wild place even then. In time no one would even remember that a track had once run that way. It would all go back to its original state; soon he, himself, would be joining it. The old man wept a little, for no one likes to contemplate that sort of thing without some sadness.

KILLING A BRIT

DAVID PARK

'Kiernan Caffrey, this homework is a slovenly insult to your Maker. Stay in this afternoon and do it properly.'

Kiernan Caffrey did not lift his head but continued to stare blankly at his open jotter, determined not to let Father Brophy see his disappointment. He had known, however, that it was only a question of time before he received this sentence. He had managed to slip his homework into the bottom of the pile, but when they returned from lunch Father Brophy had set them a composition and settled himself comfortably behind his desk to mark them. From the start, he had known that his homework would not be acceptable, but he had scrawled a half-hearted attempt at the questions, only in order to avoid the cane. Now he felt it would have been better to have presented no homework and have taken the cane, than to sacrifice his afternoon. After all, unless he was angry, Father Brophy didn't really cane that hard. His lack of judgement began to rankle.

He returned again to his composition. They had been given three titles to choose from, and he had chosen 'Cruelty to Animals'. The other two were 'My Favourite Television Programmes' and 'Old Age'. No thoughts at all came into his mind on old age, and although he wanted to write about his favourite television programmes, he knew it would be a mistake. Brophy only set titles like that to glean information from them. So by a process of elimination, he had decided upon 'Cruelty to Animals'. This choice was also prompted by the fact that a week earlier they had listened to a tape on the subject. Much to his surprise, he remembered a good deal of it. He had written:

> Some sports are very cruel to animals. The sport of horse jump-ing has horses jumping very large fences. Sometimes the fence is so high that the horse can't jump it and has to pull up quickly or else it might crash into the fence. Also sometimes the horse hits the fence with its leg and this might damage the horses leg and the horse might have to be put down.
>
> Zoos are also very cruel to animals. Animals that are kept in the zoo are kept in very small cages and they can't move around like they do in the wild. Some animals don't mind being in cages but birds suffer the most because they can't fly very far. Large cats suffer to because they can't run very far in there cages.
>
> Whales are killed to make fancy womens perfume. Animals which have a furry skin are killed to make fur coats. The fur costs a lot of money and only rich people can buy them. Elephants are killed for there tusks to make necklases and ornaments.
>
> Lots of animals are killed in science experiments each year.

He had been going well, but when Brophy had told him to stay in after school, all the enthusiasm went out of his work. He looked at it without interest and, as a gesture of resentment towards Brophy, decided to end it. He wrote: 'And as you can see that man is very cruel to animals in many different ways and I think it is wrong as animals never do anything to hurt us.'

The essay was obviously too short, but it was a safe gesture. Brophy would be content to punish him for his homework and would turn a blind eye to its brevity.

His half-hour of detention was made worse by the fact that he had no company. The homework he had to repeat was a Maths one which consisted of working out percentages of given amounts. He found he could handle the percentages when they were whole numbers, but when fractions became involved, he floundered hopelessly. He knew he was still arriving at incorrect answers, but he tried to compensate for his lack of success by presenting the work as neatly as he could. More of his time was spent underlining in red and ensuring a pleasing layout. Father Brophy had often said he would never punish a boy for stupidity – dishonesty, laziness, maliciousness – these were punishable offences, but never stupidity. Kiernan did not entirely believe Father Brophy, but at this particular time it suited him to pretend he did.

Father Brophy sat at his desk reading a book, seemingly oblivious to his captive. Kiernan could see from its cover that the paperback was not a religious one. The classroom was disturbingly silent and each empty desk reminded him that its usual occupant was enjoying himself elsewhere. But sooner than he could have hoped for, the work was finished. He approached Father Brophy's desk slowly and stood silent and penitent before him. Father Brophy let him stand for about a minute, pretending he wasn't aware of his presence, then gave the homework a cursory inspection before wordlessly indicating that the boy could go.

Walking home through the housing estate, the boy slowly recovered a feeling of wellbeing. Perhaps the day could still be salvaged – after all it was Monday, and Monday was his favourite television evening. He made a mental list of his intended viewing. That evening, he knew the film was a Clint Eastwood western, and the prospect made him give a little shuffle of pleasure as he walked. On Mondays, too, his parents both went out to the club, and as his older brothers were usually out, he often had the house to himself. He liked Clint Eastwood a lot. There was never much talking and plenty of action in his films. He loved the way he always looked half-asleep until he had

to draw his gun. Father Brophy would not approve of Clint
Eastwood, but to Kiernan Caffrey there seemed little in the
world that the Father did approve of.

He walked on past the row of shops which formed the centre
of the estate. Most of their windows were boarded up and their
open doors gave no indication as to what was sold inside. Posters
and graffiti spewed over every inch of space, last year's names
and events overlaid with fresher additions, like so many layers
of skin. A dog sniffed round the wheels of a pram. A wire grille
swung loosely like a page in a book. A group of women
huddled outside the newsagent's, one still in her slippers and
clutching a bottle of milk. He saw two of his classmates come
out holding single cigarettes they had bought. He was glad he
had stopped smoking, and although he still had the odd one occasionally, he only did it to pass himself. His mind went back
to the tape he had heard in school about how scientists made
dogs inhale cigarette smoke to find out about lung cancer.

Remembering it was Monday, he walked a little quicker. His
mother liked to get the tea over early so that she could get ready
to go to the club. Thinking of this reminded him that he was
hungry. Tea on Monday was never anything much, but he con-
soled himself by thinking of the television programmes he was
going to enjoy. He cut down an entry. As he turned the corner
he almost tripped over a figure crouching in at the hedge of one
of the gardens. It was a Brit. They stared into each other's faces,
but nothing passed between them except the distancing of
caution. The boy saw about six others in similar positions ahead
of him. At the start it had been different. Some of them had
tried to be friendly and would speak, but too many things had
happened since then. But except when there was trouble on and
the word was out, only the very young children bothered to
stone them. Mostly they were just ignored. He adopted an
attitude of casual indifference to the soldiers' presence as he

walked by, pulling a twig out of a hedge and beginning
systematically to shed its leaves. Two of them carried guns for
firing plastic bullets as well as their rifles. All the soldiers he
passed stared closely at him, but no one said anything and no
one stopped him to look into his school bag. Then all but the
last man stood up and moved out. As he turned round and
watched them go, he saw the first soldier covering their exit and
observing the length of the entry. His sleeves were rolled up
and he had tattoos on both arms. He was chewing gum with
exaggerated movements of his mouth and just before he too
left, he winked in the boy's direction. The boy turned away and
continued to shed leaves.

As he was walking he saw a small green caterpillar on the cuff
of his pullover. He stopped and delicately removed it, then
rumbled in his pockets for a tin to put it in. Among the clutter
of debris produced was nothing suitable, but then he remembered his lunch box. Taking it out of his bag he placed the
caterpillar inside. He knew his mother would not be pleased,
but he could remove it as soon as he reached home. There was
a rifle shot. He wondered if it would be possible to keep it and
look after it until it grew into a butterfly. He had nearly been
successful the previous year with frogspawn, but something told
him that this would be more difficult. From the sound he knew
that it had come from an Armalite. He turned and walked back
up the entry. When he reached the top his lunch box was
almost knocked from his hand by a boy running. It was one of
his classmates charging in the direction of the shops.

'They've got a Brit! They've got a Brit!' he shouted breath-
lessly.

Kiernan sealed the lunch box and, carefully placing it in his
bag, followed the boy. A small crowd of youths had gathered
already on a little patch of green that faced the shops. There was
a soldier lying on the pavement outside the butcher's shop. His

helmet had been taken off and his flak jacket flung open. A soldier on his knees cradled the wounded man's head in his lap. Splatters of blood stippled the shop window and a rivulet of red seeped down the pavement towards the gutter. Near by on the pavement a bottle of milk lay broken. The expression on the face of the soldier who was crouched over the wounded man told that he was dying, and would be dead before medical help arrived. The other soldiers stood upright, their faces pale with fear, holding their rifles to their shoulders and moving them from side to side to cover potential vantage spots where the sniper might be hiding. But they knew, just as the crowd knew, that he would be long gone.

The boy watched as the blood reached the edge of the pavement and trickled into the gutter. An old woman stood motionless in a doorway fingering rosary beads. From the interior of the butcher's shop, faces peered through the meat hanging on skewers, but no one came out. The boy noticed that the shot soldier had tattoos on his arms. A priest came running from somewhere – it was Father Brophy. He started to administer the last rites. The soldiers looked at him with suspicion and listened to his words as if he was mouthing some final curse. The boy felt vindicated in his dislike of the priest.

The crowd had increased in numbers now. Some of them began to shout abuse. The boy was worried that Father Brophy would see him, and slowly he slipped through the crowd to its rear. The shouting grew, with people whistling and banging the ground with anything that came to hand. Then, deepening his voice to try to sound like a grown-up, he shouted at the group huddled in front of the shops, 'Go on, die, ya bastard!'

His voice blended with the others and then he turned away. Soon, more Brits would come and they would be angry. It would be better to be indoors when that happened. Besides, it was Monday, his favourite television night, and his mother always liked to get the dinner over early so that she had plenty of time to get ready for the club. As he broke into a run he reminded himself to remove the caterpillar from his lunch box before he left it in the kitchen. He wondered if it would turn into a butterfly.

ORANGES FROM SPAIN

DAVID PARK

It's not a fruit shop any more. Afterwards, his wife sold it
and someone opened up a fast-food business. You wouldn't
recognise it now – it's all flashing neon, girls in identical
uniforms and the type of food that has no taste. Even Gerry
Breen wouldn't recognise it now. Either consciously or unconsciously, I don't seem to pass that way very often, but when I
do I always stop and look at it. The neon brightness burns the
senses and sears the memories like a wound being cauterised;
but then it all comes back and out flows a flood of memory
that nothing can stem.

I was sixteen years old and very young when I went to work
for Mr Breen in his fruit shop. It was that summer when it seemed
to rain every day and a good day stood out like something special.
I got the job through patronage. My father and Gerry Breen went
back a long way – that always struck me as strange, because they
were so unalike as men. Apparently, they were both born in the
same street and grew up together, and even when my father's
career as a solicitor took him up-market, they still got together
occasionally. My father collected an order of fruit every Friday
night on his way home from work, and as children we always
talked about 'Gerry Breen's apples'. It's funny the things you
remember, and I can recall very clearly my mother and father
having an argument about it one day. She wanted to start getting fruit from the supermarket for some reason but my father

wouldn't hear of it. He got quite agitated about it and almost
ended up shouting, which was very unlike him. Maybe he acted
out of loyalty, or maybe he owed him some kind of favour, but
whatever the reason, the arrangement continued.

If his name is mentioned now they never do it in front of me.
It's almost as if he never existed. At first it angered me – it was
almost as if they thought I would disintegrate at its sound – but
gradually I came to be grateful for it. I didn't even go to the
funeral, and from that moment it was obvious my family sought
to draw a curtain over the whole event. My mother had taken
me away for a week's holiday. We stayed with one of her sisters
who lives in Donegal, and I've never had a more miserable
time. Inevitably, it rained every day and there was nothing to
do but mope around and remember, trapped in a house full of
women, where the only sounds were the clink of china cups
and the click of knitting needles. It was then the dreams started.
The intervening years have lessened their frequency but not
their horror. When I woke up screaming for about the tenth
time, they took me to a special doctor who reassured them with
all the usual platitudes – I'd grow out of it, time was a great
healer, and so on. In one sense I did grow out of it – I stopped
telling anyone about the nightmares and kept them strictly
private. They don't come very often now, but when they do
only my wife knows. Sometimes she cradles me in her arms like
a child until I fall asleep again.

I hadn't even really wanted a job in the first place. It was all
my father's idea. He remembered the long weeks of boredom
I had complained about the summer before and probably the
nuisance I had been as I lazed about the house. I walked right
into his trap. He knew I'd been working up to ask if I could
have a motorbike for my next birthday. The signs weren't good,
and my mother's instinctive caution would have been as difficult a barrier to surmount as the expense, so it came as a

surprise when my father casually enquired if I'd be interested in starting to save for one. I took the bait, and before I knew what was happening, I'd been fixed up with a summer job, working in Gerry Breen's fruit shop.

I didn't like the man much at first. He was rough and ready and he would've walked ten miles on his knees to save a penny. I don't think he liked me much either. The first day he saw me he looked me up and down with unconcealed disappointment, with the expression of someone who'd just bought a horse that wasn't strong enough to do the work he had envisaged for it. He stopped short of feeling my arm muscles, but passed some comment about me needing to fill out a bit. Although he wasn't tall himself, he was squat and had a kind of stocky strength that carried him through every physical situation. You knew that when he put his shoulder to the wheel, the chances were the wheel would spin. He wore this green coat as if it was some sort of uniform, and I never saw him in the shop without it. It was shiny at the elbows and collar, but it always looked clean. He had sandy-coloured hair that was slicked back and oiled down in a style that suggested he had once had an affinity with the teddy boys. The first time I met him I noticed his hands, which were flat and square, and his chisel-shaped fingers. He had this little red penknife, and at regular intervals he used it to clean them. The other habit he had was a continual hitching up of his trousers, even though there was no apparent prospect of them falling down. He was a man who seemed to be in perpetual motion. Even when he was standing talking to someone, there was always some part of him that was moving, whether it was transferring his pencil from one ear to the other, or hoisting up the trousers. It was as if there was a kind of mechanism inside him. Sometimes I saw him shuffle his feet through three hundred and sixty degrees like some kind of clockwork toy. For him sitting still would have been like wearing a straitjacket, and

I don't think any chair, no matter how comfortable, ever held him for more than a few minutes.

On my first morning, after his initial disappointment had worn off and he had obviously resolved to make the best of a bad job, he handed me a green coat, similar to his own but even older. It had a musty smell about it that suggested it had been hanging in a dark cupboard for some considerable time, and although I took it home that first weekend for my mother to wash, I don't think the smell ever left it. The sleeves were too long, so all summer I wore it with the cuffs turned up. My first job was chopping sticks. As well as fruit and vegetables, he sold various other things, including bundles of firewood. Out in the back yard was a mountain of wood, mostly old fruit boxes, and for the rest of that morning I chopped them into sticks and put them in polythene bags. At regular intervals he came out to supervise the work and caution me with monotonous regularity to be careful with the hatchet. It was obvious I wasn't doing it to his satisfaction; his dissatisfaction was communicated by a narrowing of his eyes and a snake-like hiss. As far as I was concerned, there weren't too many ways you could chop sticks, but I was wrong. Unable to restrain his frustration any longer, he took the hatchet and proceeded to instruct me in the correct technique. This involved gently inserting it into the end of the piece of wood and then tapping the other end lightly on the ground so that it split gently along the grain. When he was assured I had mastered the method, he watched critically over my first efforts.

'Too thick, son, too thick. Did your da never teach you how to chop sticks?'

It was only when I had produced a series of the thinnest slivers that he seemed content. I suppose it meant he got more bundles of firewood, but you wouldn't have got much of a fire out of them. It made me feel guilty somehow, like I was an accessory to his stinginess. 'Did your da never teach you how to?' was a phrase I heard repeatedly that summer, and it inevitably prefaced a period of instruction in the correct technique and subsequent supervision.

The rest of my time that first morning was divided between sweeping up and humping bags of spuds from the yard into the storeroom. No matter how often I brushed that shop floor, it always seemed to need to be done again. I must have filled a whole dump with cauliflower leaves, and I never stopped hating that smell. Perhaps, if I'm honest, I felt the job was a little beneath me. By the time the day was over, my back was aching and I was still trying to extract splinters from my hands. The prospect of a summer spent working like that filled me with despondency, and the attraction of a motorbike lost some of its appeal. I thought of telling my father I didn't want to go back, but was stopped by the knowledge that I would have to listen to eternal speeches about how soft young people were, and how they wanted everything on a plate. That I didn't need, and so I resolved to grit my teeth and stick it out.

The shop was situated at the bottom of the Antrim Road, and while it wasn't that big, every bit of space was used, either for display or storage. It started outside on the pavement where each morning, after carrying out wooden trestles and resting planks on them, we set out trays of fruit, carefully arranged and hand-picked, designed to attract and entice the passer-by. Above all this stretched a green canvas canopy which was supported by ancient iron stanchions, black with age. When it rained it would drip onto the front displays of fruit and so all that summer I had to carry them in and out of the shop. Inside was a long counter with old-fashioned scales and a till that rang as loudly as church bells. Under the counter were paper bags of every size, miles of string, metal hooks, bamboo canes, withered yellow rubber gloves, weights, elastic bands and a paraphernalia of utensils of unfathomable purpose. On the wall behind the counter was an assortment of glass-fronted shelving, sagging under the weight of fruit and vegetables. Above head height, the walls were covered in advertising posters that had obviously arrived free with consignments of fruit and looked like they had been there since the shop opened. On the customer side was more shelving and below it a clutter of wooden and cardboard boxes that seemed designed to ladder tights or catch the wheels of shopping trolleys. If there was any kind of logical system in the layout, I never managed to work it out. I got the impression it had evolved into a sprawling disorder and that so long as everything was close at hand, the owner saw no reason to change it.

In the back of the shop was a storeroom where among merchandise and debris stood a wooden table, two chairs, a gas cooker and a sink. The only other room was a small washroom. Beyond this was a small cobbled yard, enclosed by a brick wall topped with broken glass. Over everything hung the sweet, ripe smell of a fruit shop, but in Mr Breen's shop it was mixed with a mildewed mustiness, a strange hybrid that stayed in my senses long after I had left the scene.

I worked my butt off that first day and it was obvious he intended getting value for money out of me. Maybe my father had told him it was what I needed – I don't know. It was nearly time to close and the shop was empty. He was working out some calculations on the back of a brown paper bag and I was moving fruit into the storeroom, when he glanced up at me with a kind of puzzled look, as if he was trying to work out what I was thinking.

'Sure, son, it's money for old rope. Isn't that right?'

I gave a noncommittal nod of my head and kept on working. Then he told me I could go, and I could tell he was wondering whether he would see me the next day. Returning to his calculations again, he licked the stub of the pencil he was using and hitched up his trousers. I said goodbye and just as I was going out the door he called me back.

'Do you want to know something, son?'

I looked at him, unsure of what response he expected. Then, signalling me closer, he whispered loudly, 'My best friends are bananas.' I forced a smile at his joke, then walked out into the street and took a deep breath of fresh air.

The fruit shop did steady business. Most of the trade came from the housewives who lived in the neighbourhood, but there was also a regular source of custom from people who arrived outside the shop in cars, and by their appearance didn't live locally – the type who bought garlic. He knew them all by name and sometimes even had their order already made up, always making a fuss over them and getting me to carry it out to their car. They were obviously long-standing customers, and I suppose they must have stayed loyal to him because they were assured of good-quality fruit. He had a way with him – I had to admit that. He called every woman 'madam' for a start, even those who obviously weren't, but when he said it, it didn't sound like flattery, or like he was patronising them. It just sounded polite in an old-fashioned way. He had a great line in chat as well. If he didn't know them it was usually some remark about the weather, but if he did, he would ask about their families or make jokes, always cutting his cloth according to his audience. When a gaggle of local women were in, it was all 'Now, come on, ladies, get your grapes. Sweetest you can taste. Just the thing for putting passion into your marriage', or 'Best bananas – good enough to eat sideways'. They all loved it, and I'm sure it was good for business. Whatever their bills came to, he always gave them back the few odd pence, and I'm sure they thought he was very generous. As far as I was concerned, I thought he was one of the meanest men I'd ever met.

For a start, he never threw anything away – that was one of the things that was wrong with the shop. Whether it was a bit of string or a piece of wood, he stored it carefully, and if he saw me about to throw something away, he'd stop me with a 'Never know when it might come in useful, son'. Most of the produce he collected himself from the market early in the morning, but whenever deliveries were made, he inspected each consignment rigorously, with an energy that frequently exasperated the deliverer. If he found a damaged piece of fruit, he would hold it up for mutual observation and, wrestling up his trousers with the other hand, would say something like, 'Now come on, George, are you trying to put me out of business?' and he'd haggle anew over already arranged prices. Watching him sniffing out flawed produce would have made you think he'd an inbuilt radar system. And he was always looking for something for nothing. Sometimes it was embarrassing. If the Antrim Road had still had horses going up and down it, he'd have been out collecting the droppings and selling them for manure.

One day Father Hennessy came into the shop. Mr Breen's face dropped noticeably and about half a dozen parts of his body seemed to fidget all at once.

'Hello, Father. What can I do for you?'

'Hello, Gerry. How's business?'

'Slow, Father, very slow.'

The priest smiled and, lifting an apple, rubbed it on his sleeve, the red bright against the black.

'I'm popping over to the Mater to visit some parishioners. I thought a nice parcel of fruit would cheer them up. Help them to get better.'

He started to eat the apple and his eyes were smiling.

'Of course, Father. A very good idea.'

With well-disguised misery, he parcelled up a variety of fruit and handed it over the counter.

'God bless you, Gerry. Treasure in heaven, treasure in heaven.'

With the package tucked under his arm, and still eating the apple, the priest sauntered out to his car. If he had looked back, he would have seen Mr Breen slumped on the counter, his head resting on both hands.

'The church'll be the ruin of me. He does that about three times a month. Thinks my name's Mr Del Monte, not Gerry Breen. Treasure in heaven's no use to me when I go to pay the bills at the end of the month.'

The frustration poured out of him and I listened in silence, knowing he wasn't really talking to me.

'Does he go up to Michael Devlin in the bank and ask him for some money because he's going to visit the poor? Since when did it become part of my purpose in life to subsidise the National Health system? I pay my taxes like anyone else.'

I think he'd have gone on indefinitely in a similar vein, but for the arrival of a customer, and then it was all smiles and jokes about the rain.

'Do you know, Mrs Caskey, what I and my assistant are building out in the yard?'

Mrs Caskey didn't know but her aroused curiosity was impatient for an answer.

'We're building an ark! And whenever it's finished we're going to load up two of every type of fruit and float away up the road.'

'Get away with you, Gerry. You're a desperate man.'

And then he sold her tomatoes and a lettuce which he described as 'the best lettuce in the shop'. I'd almost have believed him myself, but for the fact that I'd already heard the same phrase on about three previous occasions that day.

Gerry Breen was very proud of his shop, but he took a special pride in his displays outside, and he did this expert printing with whitening on the front window. Not only did he fancy himself a bit of an artist, but also as a kind of poet laureate among fruiterers. He had all these bits of cardboard – I think they were backing cards out of shirts – and on them he printed, not only the names and prices of the fruit, but also descriptive phrases meant to stimulate the taste buds of the reader. Grapes might be described as 'deliciously sweet' or strawberries as 'the sweet taste of summer' while Comber spuds were always 'balls of flour'. The front window always looked well. Bedded on a gentle slope of simulated grass rested the various sections of produce, complete with printed labels. Each morning when he had arranged it he would go out on the pavement and stand with his hands on his hips, studying it like an art critic viewing a painting. Inside he had other signs saying things like 'Reach for a peach', 'Iceberg lettuce – just a tip of the selection' or 'Fancy an apple – why not eat a pear?'

After the first week or so we started to get on a little better. I think he realised that I was trustworthy and prepared to pull my weight. He probably thought of me as being a bit snobbish, but tolerated it so long as he got good value for his money. I in turn became less critical of what I considered his defects. Gradually, he began to employ more of my time on less menial jobs. After three weeks I had progressed to serving customers and weighing their fruit, and then a week later I was allowed to enter the holy of holies and put my hand in the till. I still had to chop sticks and brush up of course, but whenever the shop was busy I served behind the counter. I almost began to feel part of the business. The continual wet weather stopped me from missing out on the usual activities of summer and I was increasingly optimistic that my father would reward my industry with a motorbike. Mr Breen didn't much like the rain – he was always complaining how bad it was for business. According to him, it discouraged passing trade, and people didn't buy as much as they did in warm weather. He was probably right. Sometimes, when a lull in trade created boredom, I tried to wind him up a little.

'Mr Breen, do you not think it's wrong to sell South African fruit?'

'Aw, don't be daft, son.'

'But do you not think that by selling their fruit you're supporting apartheid?'

He swapped his pencil from ear to ear and did what looked a bit like a tap dance.

'I'm only supporting myself and the wife. Sure wouldn't the Blacks be the first to suffer if I stopped selling it? They'd all end up starving and how would that help them?'

I was about to provoke him further when a customer appeared and I let him have the last word.

'God knows, son, they have my sympathy – don't I work like a black myself?'

The customer turned out to be Mr Breen's wife. She was all dressed up in a blue and white suit and was on her way to some social function. She had one of those golden charm bracelets that clunked so many heavy charms I wondered how her wrist bore the strain, and while she hardly looked sideways at him, she made an embarrassing fuss over me, asking about my parents and school, and gushing on in a slightly artificial way. When she finished whatever business she had, she said goodbye to me and warned Gerald not to work me too hard. I smiled at the name Gerald, and I could see him squirming behind the counter. A heavy shower came on and we both stood in the doorway watching it bounce off the road. He was unusually silent and I glanced at him a few times to see if he was all right. When he spoke, his voice was strangely colourless.

'Never get married, son – it's the end of your happiness.'

I didn't know whether he was joking or not, so I just went on staring at the rain.

'My wife's ashamed of me,' he said in the same lifeless voice.

I uttered some vague and unconvincing disagreement and then turned away in embarrassment. I started to brush the floor, glancing up from time to time as he stood motionless in the doorway. In a minute or so the rain eased and it seemed to break the spell, but for the rest of that afternoon, he was subdued and functioned in a mechanical way. He even closed the shop half an hour early – something he'd never done before.

Nothing like that ever happened again, and my first experience of work slipped into an uneventful routine. One day, though, comes clearly to mind. One afternoon when business was slack he asked me to deliver fruit round to a Mrs McCausland. The address was a couple of streets away and I felt a little self-conscious as I set off in my green coat. It wasn't a big order – just a few apples and oranges and things. I followed the directions I had been given and arrived at a terraced house. Unlike most of its neighbours, the front door was closed, and the net curtain in the window offered no glimpse of the interior. At first, it seemed as if no one was in, and I was just about to turn and leave, when there was the slow undrawing of a bolt and the rattle of a chain. The door opened wide enough to allow an old woman's face to peer out at me, suspicion speckling her eyes. I identified myself and showed the fruit to reassure her. Then there was another pause before the door gradually opened to reveal an old woman leaning heavily on a walking stick. Inviting me in, she hobbled off slowly and painfully down the hall and into her tiny living room. She made me sit down and, despite my polite protests, proceeded to make me a cup of tea. The room resembled a kind of grotto, adorned with religious objects and pictures. Her rosary beads hung from

the fireplace clock and a black cat slept on the rug-covered
sofa. She talked to me from the kitchen as she worked.

'Isn't the weather terrible?'

'Desperate – you'd never think it was the summer,' I replied,
smiling as I listened to myself. I had started to sound like Gerry
Breen's apprentice.

'Summers never used to be like this. I can remember
summers when the streets were baked hot as an oven and everyone used to sit on their doorsteps for you could hardly get
a breath. If you sat on your doorstep these past few days you'd
get pneumonia.'

She brought me a cup of tea in a china cup, and a slice of
fruit cake, but nothing for herself. She sat down and scrutinised
me intently.

'So you're working for Gerry for the summer. I'm sure that's
good fun for you. You work hard and maybe he'll keep you
on permanent.'

I didn't correct her misunderstanding, but I laughed silently
inside.

'He says if it keeps on raining he's going to start building
an ark.'

She smiled and rearranged the cushion supporting her back.

'Gerry's the salt of the earth. Do you see that fruit you
brought? He's been doing that for the best part of fifteen years
and nobody knows but him and me.'

She paused to pour more tea into my cup and I listened
with curiosity as she continued, her words making me feel
as if I was looking at a familiar object from a new and unexpected perspective.

'I gave him a wee bit of help a long time ago and he's never
forgotten it, not through all these years. I don't get out much
now, but sometimes I take a walk round to the shop, just to see
how he's getting on. He's a great man for the crack, isn't he?'

I smiled in agreement and she shuffled forward in her seat, leaning confidentially towards me.

'Have you met Lady Muck yet? Thon woman's more airs and graces than royalty. She was born and bred a stone's throw from here and to listen to her now you'd think she came from the Malone Road. I knew her family and they didn't have two pennies to rub together between the lot of them. Now she traipses round the town like she was a duchess. You'll never catch her serving behind the counter.'

It was obvious that the woman wanted to talk – she was probably starved of company – and no matter how often I attempted a polite exit, she insisted on my staying a little longer, assuring me that Gerry wouldn't mind. I wasn't so sure, but there was no easy escape, as she produced a photograph album and talked me through a maze of memories and mementoes.

Parts of it were interesting and when she told me about the Belfast blitz I learnt things I hadn't known before. Before I finally got up to go, she returned to the subject of the weather, her voice serious and solemn.

'This weather's a sign. I've been reading about it in a tract that was sent to me. It's by this holy scholar, very high up in the church, and he says we're living in the last days. All these wars and famines – they're all signs. All this rain – it's a sign too. I believe it.'

When she opened the front door it was still raining and I almost started to believe it too. I ran back quickly, partly to get out of the rain and partly because I anticipated a rebuke about the length of my absence.

There were no customers in the shop when I entered and he merely lifted his head from what he was reading, asked if everything was all right with Mrs McCausland, and returned to his study. It surprised me a little that he said nothing about the time. He was filling in his pools coupon and concentrating on winning a fortune, so perhaps he was distracted by the complexities of the Australian leagues. He had been doing them all summer and his approach never varied. He did two columns every week, the first by studying the form and this forced him to ponder such probabilities as whether Inala City would draw with Slacks Creek, or Altona with Bulleen. For the second column, he selected random numbers, his eyes screwed up and an expression on his face as if he was waiting for some kind of celestial message. On this particular afternoon, reception must have been bad, because he asked me to shout them out. Out of genuine curiosity, I asked him what he would do if he did win a fortune. He looked at me to see if I was winding him up, but must have sensed that I wasn't, because, on a wet and miserable Belfast afternoon, he told me his dream.

'It's all worked out in here,' he said, tapping the side of his head with a chisel-shaped finger. 'I've it all planned out. Thinking about it keeps you going – makes you feel better on days like this.'

He paused to check if I was laughing at him, then took a hand out of his coat pocket and gestured slowly round the shop.

'Look around you, son. What do you see?'

A still, grey light seemed to have filtered into the shop. The lights were off and it was quiet in an almost eerie way. Nothing rustled or stirred, and the only sound was the soft fall of the rain. In the gloom the bright colours smouldered like embers; rhubarb like long tongues of flame; red sparks of apples; peaches, perfect in their velvety softness, yellows and oranges flickering gently.

'Fruit,' I answered. 'Different kinds of fruit.'

'Now, do you know what I see?'

I shook my head.

'I see places. A hundred different places. Look again.' And as he spoke he began to point with his finger. 'Oranges from

Spain, apples from New Zealand, cabbages from Holland, peaches from Italy, grapes from the Cape, bananas from Ecuador – fruit from all over the world. Crops grown and harvested by hands I never see, packed and transported by other hands in a chain that brings them here to me. It's a miracle if you think about it. When we're sleeping in our beds, hands all over the world are picking and packing so that Gerry Breen can sell it here in this shop.'

We both stood and looked, absorbing the magnitude of the miracle.

'You asked me what I'd do if I won the jackpot – well, I've it all thought out. I'd go to every country whose fruit I sell, go and see it grow, right there in the fields and the groves, in the orchards and the vineyards. All over the world.'

He looked at me out of the corner of his eye to see if I thought he was crazy, then turned away and began to tidy the counter. I didn't say anything, but in that moment, if he'd asked me, I would have gone with him. All these years later, I still regret that I didn't tell him that. Told him while there was still time.

Four days later, Gerry Breen was dead. A man walked into the shop and shot him twice. He became another bystander, another nobody, sucked into the vortex by a random and malignant fate that marked him out. They needed a Catholic to balance the score – he became a casualty of convenience, a victim of retribution, propitiation of a different god. No one even claimed it. Just one more sectarian murder – unclaimed, unsolved, soon unremembered but by a few. A name lost in the anonymity of a long list. I would forget too, but I can't.

I remember it all. There were no customers when a motorbike stopped outside with two men on it. The engine was still running as the passenger came towards the shop. I was behind the counter looking out. He had one hand inside his black motorcycle tunic and wore a blue crash helmet – the type that encloses the whole head. A green scarf covered the bottom half of his face, so only his eyes were visible. Only his eyes – that's all I ever saw of him. Mr Breen was standing holding a tray of oranges he had just brought from the back.

Suddenly, the man pulled a gun out of his tunic and I thought we were going to be robbed, but he never spoke, and as he raised the gun and pointed it at Mr Breen, his hand was shaking so much he had to support it with the other one. It was then I knew he hadn't come for money. The first shot hit Gerry Breen in the chest, spinning him round, and as he slumped to the floor the oranges scattered and rolled in all directions. He lay there, face down, and his body was still moving. Then, as I screamed an appeal for mercy, the man walked forward and, kneeling over the body, shot him in the back of the head. His body kicked and shuddered, and then was suddenly and unnaturally still. I screamed again in fear and anger and then, pointing the gun at me, the man walked slowly backwards to the door of the shop, ran to the waiting bike and was gone. Shaking uncontrollably and stomach heaving with vomit, I tried to turn Mr Breen over onto his back, but he was too heavy for me. Blood splashed his green coat, and flowed from the dark gaping wound, streaming across the floor, mixing with the oranges that were strewn all around us. Oranges from Spain.

They say help arrived almost immediately. I don't know. All I can remember is thinking of the old woman's words and hoping it really was the end of the world, and being glad and asking God to drown the world, wanting it to rain for a thousand years, rain and rain and never stop until all the blood was washed away and every street was washed clean. There were voices then and helping hands trying to lift me away, but no one could move me as I knelt beside him, clutching frantically at his green coat, begging God not to let him die, praying he'd let Gerry Breen live to build his ark and bring aboard the fruit of the world. All the fruit of the world safely stored. Oranges from Spain, apples from the Cape – the sweet taste of summer preserved for ever, eternal and incorruptible.

NAMING THE NAMES

ANNE DEVLIN

Abyssinia, Alma, Bosnia, Balaclava, Belgrade, Bombay. It was late summer – August, like the summer of the fire. He hadn't rung for three weeks.

I walked down the Falls towards the reconverted cinema: 'The largest second-hand bookshop in the world', the billboard read. Of course it wasn't. What we did have was a vast collection of historical manuscripts, myths and legends, political pamphlets, and we ran an exchange service for readers of crime, western and paperback romances. By far the most popular section for which Chrissie was responsible, since the local library had been petrol-bombed.

It was late when I arrived, the dossers from St Vincent de Paul hostel had already gone in to check the morning papers. I passed them sitting on the steps every working day: Isabella wore black fishnet tights and a small hat with a half-veil, and long black gloves even on the warmest day and eyed me from the feet up; Eileen, who was dumpy and smelt of meths and talcum powder, looked at everyone with the sad eyes of a cow. Tom was the thin wiry one, he would nod, and Harry, who was large and grey like his overcoat, and usually had a stubble, cleared his throat and spat before he spoke. Chrissie once told me when I started working there that both of the men were in love with Isabella and that was why Eileen always looked so sad. And usually too Mrs O'Hare from Spinner Street would still be cleaning the brass handles and finger plates and waiting like the others for the papers, so that she could read the horoscopes before they got to the racing pages. On this particular day, however, the brasses had been cleaned and the steps were empty. I tried to remember what it had been like as a cinema, but couldn't. I only remember a film I'd seen there once, in black and white: *A Town like Alice*.

Sharleen McCabe was unpacking the contents of a shopping bag onto the counter. Chrissie was there with a cigarette in her hand flicking the ash into the cap of her Yves Saint Laurent perfume spray and shaking her head.

She looked up as I passed: 'Miss Macken isn't in yet, so if you hurry you'll be all right.'

She was very tanned – because she took her holidays early – and her pink lipstick matched her dress. Sharleen was gazing at her in admiration.

'Well?'

'I want three murders for my granny.'

I left my coat in the office and hurried back to the counter as Miss Macken arrived. I had carefully avoided looking at the office phone, but I remember thinking: I wonder if he'll ring today.

Miss Macken swept past: 'Good morning, ladies.'

'Bang goes my chance of another fag before break,' Chrissie said.

'I thought she was seeing a customer this morning.'

Sharleen was standing at the desk reading the dust covers of a pile of books, and rejecting each in turn: 'There's only one here she hasn't read.'

'How do you know?'

'Because her eyes is bad, I read them to her,' Sharleen said.

'Well, there's not much point in me looking if you're the only one who knows what she's read.'

'You said children weren't allowed in there!' she said, pointing to the auditorium.

'I've just given you permission,' Chrissie said.

Sharleen started off at a run.

'Popular fiction's on the stage,' Chrissie called after her. 'Children! When was that wee girl ever a child!'

'Finnula, the Irish section's like a holocaust! Would you like to do something about it. And would you please deal with these orders.'

'Yes, Miss Macken.'

'Christine, someone's just offered us a consignment of Mills and Boon. Would you check with the public library that they haven't been stolen.'

'Righto,' sighed Chrissie.

It could have been any other day.

Senior: *Orangeism in Britain and Ireland*; Sibbett: *Orangeism in Ireland and Throughout the Empire*. Ironic. That's what he was looking for the first time he came in. It started with an enquiry for two volumes of Sibbett. Being the Irish specialist, I knew every book in the section. I hadn't seen it. I looked at the name and address again to make sure. And then I asked him to call. I said I thought I knew where I could get it and invited him to come and see the rest of our collection. A few days later, a young man, tall, fair, with very fine dark eyes, as if they'd been underlined with a grey pencil, appeared. He wasn't what I expected. He said it was the first time he'd been on the Falls Road. I took him round the section and he bought a great many things from us. He was surprised that such a valuable collection of Irish historical manuscripts was housed in a run-down cinema and he said he was glad he'd called. He told me that he was a historian writing a thesis on Gladstone and the Home Rule Bills, and that he lived in Belfast in the summer but was at Oxford University.

He also left with me an extensive book list and I promised to try to get the other books he wanted. He gave me his phone number, so I could ring him and tell him when something he was looking for came in. It was Sibbett he was most anxious about. An antiquarian bookseller I knew of sent me the book two weeks later, in July. So I rang him and arranged to meet him with it at a café in town near the city hall.

He was overjoyed and couldn't thank me enough, he said. And so it started. He told me that his father was a judge and that he lived with another student at Oxford called Susan. I told him that I lived with my grandmother until she died. And I also told him about my boyfriend Jack. So there didn't seem to be any danger.

We met twice a week in the café after that day; he explained something of his thesis to me: that the Protestant opposition to Gladstone and Home Rule was a rational one because Protestant industry at the time – shipbuilding and linen – was dependent on British markets. He told me how his grandfather had been an Ulster Volunteer. I told him of my granny's stories of the Black and Tans, and of how she once met de Valera on a Dublin train while he was on the run disguised as an old woman. He laughed and said my grandmother had a great imagination. He was fascinated that I knew so much history; he said he'd never heard of Parnell until he went to Oxford. And he pronounced 'Parnell' with a silent 'n', so that it sounded strange.

By the end of the month, the café owner knew us by sight, and the time came on one particular evening he arrived before me, and was sitting surrounded by books and papers, when the owner remarked, as the bell inside the door rang: 'Ah. Here's your young lady now.'

We blushed alarmingly. But it articulated the possibility I had

constantly been pushing to the back of my mind. And I knew
I felt a sharp and secret thrill in that statement.

A few hours later, I stood on tiptoe to kiss him as I left for
the bus – nothing odd about that. I often kissed him on the side
of the face as I left. This time however I deliberately kissed his
mouth, and somehow, the kiss went on and on; he didn't let
me go. When I stepped back on my heels again I was reeling,
and he had to catch me with his arm. I stood there staring at
him on the pavement. I stammered 'goodbye' and walked off
hurriedly towards the bus stop. He stood on the street looking after me – and I knew without turning round that he
was smiling.

'Sharleen. *Murder in the Cathedral* is not exactly a murder story,'
Chrissie was saying wearily.

'Well, why's it called that, then?'

'It's a play about' – Chrissie hesitated – 'martyrdom!'

'Oh.'

'This is just too, too grisly,' Chrissie said, examining the
covers. 'Do they always have to be murders? Would you not
like a nice love story?'

'She doesn't like love stories,' Sharleen said stubbornly. 'She
only likes murders.'

At that moment Miss Macken reappeared: 'You two girls can
go for tea now – what is that smell?'

'I can't smell anything,' Chrissie said.

'That's because you're wearing too much scent,' Miss
Macken said. She was moving perfunctorily to the biography
shelving, and it wasn't until I followed her that I became aware
of a very strong smell of methylated spirits. Harry was tucked
behind a newspaper drinking himself silly. He appeared to be
quite alone.

'Outside! Outside immediately!' Miss Macken roared. 'Or

I shall have you forcibly removed.'

He rose up before us like a wounded bear whose sleep we had disturbed, and stood shaking his fist at her, and cursing all of us, Isabella included, he ran out.

'What's wrong with him?'

'Rejection. Isabella ran off with Tom this morning, and didn't tell him where she was going. He's only drowning his sorrows,' Chrissie said. 'Apparently they had a big win yesterday. Eileen told him they'd run off to get married. But they've only gone to Bangor for the day.'

'How do you know this?'

'Eileen told Mrs O'Hare and she told me.'

'What kind of supervision is it when you two let that man drink in here with that child wandering around?' Miss Macken said, coming back from seeing Harry off the premises.

We both apologised and went up for tea.

There was little on the Falls Road that Mrs O'Hare didn't know about. As she made her way up and down the road in the mornings on her way to work she would call in and out of the shops, the library, the hospital, until a whole range of people I had never met would enter my life in our tearoom by eleven o'clock. I knew that Mr Quincey, a Protestant, from the library, had met his second wife while burying his first at the City Cemetery one Saturday morning. I knew that Mr Downey, the gatehousekeeper at the hospital, had problems with his eldest daughter and didn't like her husband, and I was equally sure that thanks to Mrs O'Hare every detail of Chrissie's emotional entanglements were known by every ambulance driver at the Royal. As a result, I was very careful to say as little as possible in front of her. She didn't actually like me. It was Chrissie she bought buns for at tea time.

'Oh here! You'll never guess what Mrs McGlinchy at the

bakery told me –' She was pouring tea into cups, but her eyes were on us. 'Wait till you hear –' She looked down in time to see the tea pouring over the sides of the cup. She put the teapot down heavily on the table and continued: 'Quincey's being transferred to Ballymacarrett when the library's reopened.'

'Och, you don't say?'

'It's the new boss at Central – that Englishwoman. It's after the bomb.'

'But sure that was when everybody'd gone home.'

'I know but it's security, you know! She doesn't want any more staff crossing the peace line at night. Not after that young – but wait till you hear – he won't go!'

'Good for him.'

'He says he's been on the Falls for forty years and if they transfer him now they might as well throw the keys of the library into the Republican Press Centre and the keys of the Royal Victoria Hospital in after them.'

'He's quite right. It's ghettoisation.'

'Yes, but it's inevitable,' I said.

'It's not inevitable, it's deliberate,' said Chrissie. 'It's exactly what the crowd want.'

'Who?'

'The Provos. They want a ghetto: the next thing they'll be issuing us with passes to come and go.'

'Security works both ways.'

'You're telling me.'

After that Chrissie left us to go down the yard to renew her suntan. Mrs O'Hare watched her from the window.

'She'd find the sun anywhere, that one.' She turned from the window. 'Don't take what she says too much to heart. She's Jewish, you know. She doesn't understand.'

I was glad when she went. She always felt a bit constrained with me. Because I didn't talk about my love life, as she called it, like Chrissie. But then I couldn't. I never really talked at all, to any of them.

The room overlooked the roof tops and back yards of west Belfast.

Gibson, Granville, Garnet, Grosvenor, Theodore, Cape, Kashmir.

Alone again, I found myself thinking about the last time I had seen Jack. It was a long time ago: he was sitting at the end of the table. When things are not going well my emotions start playing truant. I wasn't surprised when he said: 'I've got an invitation to go to the States for six months.'

I was buttering my toast at the time and didn't look up.

'I'm afraid I'm rather ambivalent about this relationship.'

I started battering the top of my eggshell with a spoon.

'Finn! Are you listening?'

I nodded and asked: 'When do you go?'

'Four weeks from now.'

I knew the American trip was coming up.

'Very well. I'll move out until you've gone.'

I finished breakfast and we spoke not another word until he dropped me at the steps of the bookshop.

'Finn, for God's sake! Get yourself a flat somewhere out of it! I don't imagine I'll be coming back.' He said: 'If you need any money, write to me.'

I slammed the car door. Jack was always extremely practical: if you killed someone he would inform the police, get you legal aid, make arrangements for moving the body, he'd even clear up the mess if there was any – but he would never, never ask you why you did it. I'd thrown milk all over him once, some of it went on the floors and walls, and then I ran out of the house. When I came back he'd changed his clothes and mopped up the floor. Another time I'd smashed all the dinner dishes against the kitchen wall and locked myself in the bathroom, when I came out he had swept up all the plates and asked me if I wanted a cup of tea. He was a very good journalist, I think, but somehow I never talked to him about anything important.

Because Mrs Cooper from Milan Street had been caught trying to walk out with sixteen stolen romances in a shopping bag and had thrown herself on the floor as if having a heart attack, saying: 'Oh holy Jay! Don't call the police. Oh holy Jay, my heart', Chrissie forgot to tell me about the phone call until nearly twelve o'clock.

'Oh, a customer rang, he wanted to talk to you about a book he said he was after. Sibbett. That was it. You were still at tea.' She said, 'I told him we were open to nine tonight and that you'd be here all day.'

For three weeks he hadn't rung. I only had to pick up the phone and ring him as I'd done on other occasions. But this time I hoped he would contact me first.

'Is something wrong?' Chrissie said.

'I have to make a phone call.'

After that first kiss on the street, the next time we met I took him to the house, about ten minutes' walk from the park.

'When did you say your granny died?' he asked, looking with surprise around the room.

'Oh, ages ago. I'm not very good at dates.'

'Well, you don't appear to have changed much since. It's as if an old lady still lived here.'

He found the relics, the Sacred Heart pictures and the water font strange. 'You really ought to dust in here occasionally,' he said, laughing. 'What else do you do apart from work in the bookshop?'

'I read, watch television. Oh, and I see Jack,' I said quickly, so as not to alarm him.

'Good Lord. Would you look at that web; it looks like it's been there for donkeys!'

A large web attaching itself in the greater part to the geraniums in the window had spread across a pile of books and ended up clinging heavily to the lace curtains.

'Yes. I like spiders,' I said. 'My granny used to say that a spider's web was a good omen. It means we're safe from the soldiers!'

'It just means that you never open the curtains!' he said, laughing. Still wandering round the small room he asked: 'Who is that lady? Is she your grandmother?'

'No. That's the Countess Markievicz.'

'I suppose your granny met her on a train in disguise – as an old man.'

'No. But she did visit her in prison.'

He shook his head: 'The trouble with you –' he began, then suddenly he had a very kind look in his eyes. 'You're improbable. No one would ever believe me.' He stopped, and began again. 'Sometimes I think' – he tapped me on the nose – 'you live in a dream, Finn.'

And then he kissed me, and held me; he only complained that I was too quiet.

It was nine thirty when I left the building and shut it up for the night: Miss Macken had offered to drop me home as she was leaving, but I said I'd prefer to walk. There were no buses on the road after nine because a few nights before a group of youths had stoned a bus passing Divis flats, and the bus driver was hurt. The whole day was a torment to me after that phone call and I wanted to think and walk.

When I got to the park I was so giddy that I didn't care whether he came or not. My stomach was in a knot – and I realised it was because I hadn't eaten all day. The summer was nearly over – I only knew that soon this too would be over. I had kept my feelings under control so well – I was always very good at that, contained, very contained – so well, that I thought if he even touched me I'd tell him – Oh run! Run for your life from me! At least I didn't tell him that I loved him or anything like that. Was it something to be glad about? And suddenly there were footsteps running behind me. I always listened for footsteps. I'd walked all through those streets at night but I had never been afraid until that moment.

I suddenly started to run when a voice called out: 'Finn! Wait!' It was his voice.

I stopped dead, and turned.

We stood by the grass verge.

'Why didn't you ring me?' I asked, listlessly, my head down in case he saw my eyes.

'Because I didn't think it was fair to you.'

'Fair?'

'Because, well –'

'Well?'

'I'm in England and you're here. It's not very satisfactory.'

'I see.'

'Look, there's something I should tell you. It's – Susan's been staying with us for the past three weeks.'

'I see.'

I couldn't possibly object since we were both supposed to have other lovers, there was no possibility of either of us complaining.

'But we could go to your place now if you like.'

I was weakening. He stooped to kiss me and the whole business began as it had started. He kissed me and I kissed him and it went on and on.

'I was just getting over you,' I said, standing up.

'I didn't know there was anything to get over. You're very good at saying nothing.'

And before I could stop myself I was saying: 'I think I've fallen in love with you.'

He dropped his head and hardly dared look at me – he looked so pained – and more than anything I regretted that statement.

'You never told me that before,' he said.

'I always felt constrained.'

He began very slowly: 'Look, there is something I have to say now. I'm getting married at the end of the summer.' And more quickly, 'But I can't give you up. I want to go on seeing you. Oh don't go! Please listen!'

It was very cold in the park. I had a piercing pain in my ear because of the wind. A tricolour hung at a jaunty angle from the top of the pensioner's bungalow, placed there by some lads. The army would take it down tomorrow in the morning. The swings, the trees and grass banks looked as thoroughly careworn as the surrounding streets.

Lincoln, Leeson, Marchioness and Mary, Slate, Sorella and Ward.

I used to name them in a skipping song.

The park had been my playplace as a child, I used to go there in the mornings and wait for someone to lead me across the road, to the first gate. Sometimes a passer-by would stop and take my hand, but most times the younger brother of the family who owned the bacon shop would cross with me.

'No road sense!' my grandmother used to say. 'None at all.'

In the afternoon he would come back for me. And I remember –

'Finn, are you listening? You mustn't stop talking to me, we could still be friends. I love being with you – Finn!'

I remember standing in the sawdust-filled shop waiting for him to finish his task – the smooth hiss of the slicing machine and the thin strips of bacon falling pat on the greaseproof paper.

I began to walk away.

'Finn. I do love you.' He said it for the first time.

I pulled up the collar of my coat and walked home without looking back.

It should have ended before I was so overcome with him I wept. And he said: 'What's wrong?' and took me and held me again.

It should have ended before he said: 'Your soul has just smiled in your eyes at me – I've never seen it there before.'

Before, it should have ended before. He was my last link with life and what a way to find him. I closed my eyes and tried to forget, all vision gone, only sound left: the night noises came.

The raucous laughter of late-night walkers; the huddle of tom cats on the back-yard wall: someone somewhere is scraping a metal dustbin across a concrete yard; and far off in the distance a car screeches to a halt: a lone dog barks at an unseen presence, the night walkers pause in their walk past – the entry. Whose is the face at the empty window? – the shadows cast on the entry wall – the shape in the darkened doorway – the steps on the broken path – who pulled that curtain open quickly – and let it drop?

I woke with a start and the sound of brakes screeching in my ears – as if the screech had taken on a human voice and called my name in anguish: Finn! But when I listened, there was nothing. Only the sound of the night bells from St Paul's tolling in the distance.

I stayed awake until daybreak and with the light found some peace from dreams. At eight o'clock I went out. Every day of summer had been going on around me, seen and unseen, I had drifted through those days like one possessed.

Strange how quickly we are reassured by ordinariness: Isabella and Tom, Harry and Eileen, waiting on the steps. And Mrs O'Hare at the counter with her polishing cloth, and Miss Macken discussing her holiday plans with Chrissie. Externally, at least, it could have been the same as the day before, yesterday – the day before I left him in the park. But I saw it differently. I saw it in a haze, and it didn't seem to have anything to do with me.

'The body was discovered by bin men early this morning,' Miss Macken said. 'He was dumped in an entry.'

'Oh, Finn, it's awful news,' said Chrissie, turning.

'It's the last straw as far as I am concerned,' Miss Macken said.

'Mr Downey said it's the one thing that turned him – he'll not be back to the Royal after this.'

'We knew him,' Chrissie said.

'Who?'

'That young man. The one who looked like a girl.'

'The police think he was coming from the Falls Road,' Miss Macken said.

'They said it was because he was a judge's son,' said Chrissie.

'The theory is,' said Miss Macken, 'that he was lured there by a woman. I expect they'll be coming to talk to us.'

'Aye, they're all over the road this morning,' said Mrs O'Hare.

At lunch time they came.

'Miss McQuillen, I wonder?'

A noisy row between Isabella and Eileen distracted me – Eileen was insisting that Isabella owed her five pounds.

'Miss McQuillen, I wonder if you wouldn't mind answering a few questions?'

'How well did you know..?'

'When did you last see him?'

'What time did you leave him?'

'What exactly did he say?'

'Have you any connection with..?'

Osman, Serbia, Sultan, Raglan, Bosnia, Belgrade, Rumania, Sebastopol.

The names roll off my tongue like a litany.

'Has that something to do with Gladstone's foreign policy?' he used to laugh and ask.

'No. Those are the streets of west Belfast.'

Alma, Omar, Conway and Dunlewey, Dunville, Lady and McDonnell.

Pray for us. (I used to say, just to please my grandmother.) Now and at the hour.

At three o'clock in the afternoon of the previous day, a man I knew came into the bookshop. I put the book he was selling on the counter in front of me and began to check the pages. It was so still you could hear the pages turn: 'I think I can get him to the park,' I said.

Eileen had Isabella by the hair and she stopped. The policeman who was writing – stopped.

Miss Macken was at the counter with Chrissie, she was frowning – she looked over at me, and stopped. Chrissie suddenly turned and looked in my direction. No one spoke. We walked through the door on to the street.

Still no one spoke.

Mrs O'Hare was coming along the road from the bread shop, she raised her hand to wave and then stopped.

Harry had just tumbled out of the bookies followed by Tom. They were laughing. And they stopped.

We passed the block where the baby-clothes shop had been, and at the other end the undertaker's: everything from birth to death on that road. Once. But gone now – just stumps where the buildings used to be – stumps like tombstones.

'Jesus. That was a thump in the stomach if ever I felt one,' one policeman said to the other.

Already they were talking as if I didn't exist.

There were four or five people in the interview room.

A policewoman stood against the wall. The muscles in my face twitched. I put up my hand to stop it.

'Why did you pick him?'

'I didn't pick him. He was chosen. It was his father they were after. He's a judge.'

'They?'

'I. I recognised the address when he wrote to me. Then he walked in.'

'Who are the others? What are their names?'

'Abyssinia, Alma, Balaclava, Balkan.'

'How did you become involved?'

'It goes back a long way.'

'Miss McQuillen. You have a captive audience!'

'On the fourteenth of August 1969 I was escorting an English journalist through the Falls: his name was Jack McHenry.'

'How did you meet him?'

'I am coming to that. I met him on the previous night, the thirteenth; there was a meeting outside Divis flats to protest about the police in the Bogside. The meeting took a petition to Springfield Road police station. But the police refused to open the door. Part of the crowd broke away and marched back down to Divis to Hastings Street police station and began throwing stones. There was trouble on the road all night because of roaming gangs. They stoned or petrol-bombed a car with two fire chiefs in it and burnt down a Protestant show-room at the bottom of Conway Street. I actually tried to stop it happening. He was there, at Balaclava Street, when it hap-pened. He stopped me and asked if I'd show him around the Falls. He felt uneasy, being an Englishman, and he didn't know his way around without a map. I said I'd be happy to.'

'Were you a member of an illegal organisation?'

'What organisation? There were half a dozen guns in the Falls in '69 and a lot of old men who couldn't even deliver the *United Irishman* on time. And the women's section had been disbanded during the previous year because there was nothing for them to do but run around after the men and make tea for the ceilidhs. He asked me the same question that night, and I told him truthfully that I was not – then.

'On the evening of the fourteenth we walked up the Falls Road, it was early, we had been walking round all day, we were on our way back to his hotel – the Grand Central in Royal Avenue – he wanted to phone his editor and give an early report about events on the road. As we walked up the Falls from Divis towards Leeson Street, we passed a group of children in pyjamas going from Dover Street towards the flats. Further up the road at Conway Street a neighbour of ours was crossing the road to Balaclava Street with his children; he said he was taking them to Sultan Street hall for the night. Everything seemed quiet. We walked on down Leeson Street and into town through the Grosvenor Road: the town centre was quiet too. He phoned his paper and then took me to dinner to a Chinese restaurant across the road from the hotel. I remember it because there was a false ceiling in the restaurant, like a sky with fake star constellations. We sat in a velvet alcove and there were roses on the table. After dinner we went to his hotel and went to

bed. At five o'clock in the morning the phone rang. I thought
it was an alarm call he'd placed. He slammed down the phone
and jumped up and shouted at me: "Get up quickly. All hell's
broken loose in the Falls!"

'We walked quickly to the bottom of Castle Street and began
to walk hurriedly up the road. At Divis Street I noticed that five
or six shops around me had been destroyed by fire. At Divis flats
a group of men stood, it was light by this time. When they
heard that Jack was a journalist they began telling him about the
firing. It had been going on all night, they said, and several
people were dead, including a child in the flats. They took him
to see the bullet holes in the walls. The child was in a cot at the
time. And the walls were thin. I left him there at Divis and hurried up the road to Conway Street. There was a large crowd
there as well, my own people. I looked up the street to the top.
There was another crowd at the junction of Ashmore Street –
this crowd was from the Shankill – they were setting fire to a
bar at the corner and looting it. Then some of the men began
running down the street and breaking windows of the houses
in Conway Street. They used brush handles. At the same time
as the bar was burning, a number of the houses at the top of the
street also caught fire in Conway Street. The crowd were
throwing petrol bombs in after they broke the windows. I
began to run up towards the fire. Several of the crowd also
started running with me.

'Then I noticed for the first time, because my attention had
been fixed on the burning houses, that two turreted police
vehicles were moving slowly down the street on either side.
Somebody shouted: "The gun turrets are pointed towards us!"
And everybody ran back. I didn't. I was left standing in the
middle of the street, when a policeman, standing in a doorway,
called to me: "Get back! Get out of here before you get hurt."

'The vehicles were moving slowly down Conway Street

towards the Falls Road with the crowd behind them, burning houses as they went. I ran into the top of Balaclava Street at the bottom of Conway Street where our crowd were. A man started shouting at the top of his voice: "They're going to fire. They're going to fire on us!"

'And our crowd ran off down the street again.

'A woman called to me from an upstairs window: "Get out of the mouth of the street." Something like that.

'I shouted: "But the people! The people in the houses!"

'A man ran out and dragged me into a doorway. "They're empty!" he said. "They got out last night!" Then we both ran down to the bottom of Balaclava Street and turned the corner into Raglan Street. If he hadn't been holding me by the arm then that was the moment when I would have run back up towards the fires.'

'Why did you want to do that? Why did you want to run back into Conway Street?'

'My grandmother lived there – near the top. He took me to Sultan Street refugee centre. "She's looking for her granny," he told a girl with a St John Ambulance armband on. She was a form below me at school. My grandmother wasn't there. The girl told me not to worry because everyone had got out of Conway Street. But I didn't believe her. An ambulance from the Royal arrived to take some of the wounded to hospital. She put me in the ambulance as well. It was the only transport on the road other than the police vehicles. "Go to the hospital and ask for her there," she said.

'It was eight o'clock in the morning when I found her sleeping in a quiet room at the Royal. The nurse said she was tired, suffering from shock and a few cuts from flying glass. I stayed with her most of the day. I don't remember that she spoke to me. And then about six I had a cup of tea and wandered on to the road up towards the park. Jack McHenry was there, writing it all down: "It's all over," he said. "The army are here." We both looked down the Falls, there were several mills that I could see burning: the Spinning Mill and the Great Northern, and the British Army were marching in formation down the Falls Road. After that I turned and walked along the Grosvenor Road into town and spent the night with him at his hotel. There was nowhere else for me to go.'

I was suddenly very tired; more tired than on the day I sat in her room watching her sleep; more tired than on the day Jack left; infinitely more tired than I'd ever been in my life. I waited for someone else to speak. The room was warm and heavy and full of smoke. They waited. So I went on.

'Up until I met Jack McHenry I'd been screwing around like there was no tomorrow. I only went with him because there was no one else left. He stayed in Belfast because it was news. I never went back to school again. I had six O levels and nothing else.'

'Is that when you got involved?'

'No, not immediately. My first reaction was to get the hell out of it. It wasn't until the summer of '71 that I found myself on the Falls Road again. I got a job in the new second-hand bookshop where I now work. Or did. One day a man came in looking for something: "Don't I know you?" he said. He had been a neighbour of ours at one time. "I carried your granny out of Conway Street." He told me that at about eleven o'clock on the night of August fourteenth, there were two families trapped at the top of Conway Street. One of them, a family of eight, was escorted out of their house by a policeman and this man. Bottles and stones were thrown at them from a crowd at the top of the street. The policeman was cut on the head as he took the children out. The other family, a woman, with her two teenage daughters, refused to leave her house because of her furniture. Eventually they were forced to run down the back entry into David Street to escape. It was she who told him that Mrs McQuillen was still in the house. He went back up the street on his own this time. Because the lights in our house were out he hadn't realised there was anyone there. He got scared at the size of the crowd ahead and was going to run back when he heard her call out: "Finn! Finn!" He carried her down Conway Street running all the way. He asked me how she was keeping these days. I told him that she had recently died. Her heart gave up. She always had a weak heart.

'A few weeks later Jack took me on holiday to Greece with him. I don't really think he wanted me to go with him, he took me out of guilt. I'd rather forced the situation on him. We were sitting at a harbour café one afternoon, he was very moody and I'd had a tantrum because I found out about his latest girlfriend. I got up and walked away from him along the harbour front. I remember passing a man reading a newspaper at another café table, a few hundred yards along the quay. I saw a headline that made me turn back.

' "The army have introduced internment in Belfast," I said.

'We went home a few days later and I walked into a house in Andersonstown of a man I knew: "Is there anything for me to do?" I said. And that was how I became involved.'

'And the man's name?'

'You already know his name. He was arrested by the army at the beginning of the summer. I was coming up the street by the park at the time, when he jumped out of an army Saracen and ran towards me. A soldier called out to him to stop, but he ran on. He was shot in the back. He was a well-known member of the Provisional IRA on the run. I was on my way to see him. His father was the man who carried my grandmother out of Conway Street. He used to own a bacon shop.'

'Did Jack McHenry know of your involvement?'

'No. He didn't know what was happening to me. Eventually

we drifted apart. He made me feel that in some way I had disappointed him.'

'What sort of operations were you involved in?'

'My first job was during internment. Someone would come into the shop, the paymaster, he gave me money to deliver once a week to the wives of the men interned. The women would then come into the shop to collect it. It meant that nobody called at their houses, which were being watched. These were the old republicans. The real movement was re-forming in Andersonstown.'

'And the names? The names of the people involved?'

'There are no names. Only places.'

'Perhaps you'll tell us the names later.'

When they left me alone in the room I began to remember a dream I'd had towards the end of the time I was living with Jack. I slept very badly then, I never knew whether I was asleep or awake. One night it seemed to me that I was sitting up in bed with him. I was smoking, he was writing something, when an old woman whom I didn't recognise came towards me with her hands outstretched. I was horrified; I didn't know where she came from or how she got into our bedroom. I tried to make Jack see her but he couldn't. She just kept coming towards me. I had my back against the headboard of the bed and tried to fight her off. She grasped my hand and kept pulling me from the bed. She had very strong hands, like a man's, and she pulled and pulled and I struggled to release my hands. I called out for help of every sort, from God, from Jack. But she would not let me go and I could not get my hands free. The struggle between us was so furious that it woke Jack. I realised then that I was dreaming. He put his hands on me to steady me: 'You're having a fit. You're having a fit!' he kept saying. I still had my eyes closed even though I knew I was awake. I asked him not to let me see him. Until it had passed. I began to be terribly afraid, and when I was sure it had passed, I had to ask him to take me to the toilet. He never asked any questions but did exactly what I asked. He took me by the hand and led me to the bathroom, where he waited with me. After that he took me back to bed again. As we passed the mirror on the bedroom door I asked him not to let me see it. The room was full of mirrors, he went round covering them all up. Then he got into bed and took my hand again.

'Now please don't let me go,' I said. 'Whatever happens don't let go of my hand.'

'I promise you. I won't,' he said.

But I knew that he was frightened.

I closed my eyes and the old woman came towards me again. It was my grandmother; she was walking. I didn't recognise her the first time because – she had been in a wheelchair all her life.

She reached out and caught my hands again and the struggle between us began: she pulled and I held on. She pulled and I still held on.

'Come back!' Jack said. 'Wherever you are, come back!'

She pulled with great force.

'Let go of me!' I cried.

Jack let go of my hand.

The policewoman who had been standing silently against the wall all the time stepped forward quickly. When I woke I was lying on the floor. There were several people in the room, and a doctor.

'Are you sure you're fit to continue?'

'Yes.'

'What about the names?'

'My father and grandmother didn't speak for years: because he married my mother. I used to go and visit him. One night as I was getting ready to go there, I must have been about seven or eight at the time, my grandmother said, "Get your father something for his birthday for me" – she handed me three shillings – "but you don't have to tell him it's from me. Get him something for his cough."

'At the end of Norfolk Street was a sweet shop. I bought a tin of barley sugar. The tin was tartan: red and blue and green and black. They wrapped it in a twist of brown paper. I gave it to my mother when I arrived. "It's for my daddy for his birthday in the morning."

' "From whom?"

' "From me."

' "Can I look?"

' "Yes."

'She opened the paper: "Why it's beautiful," she said. I remember her excitement over it. "He'll be so pleased." She seemed very happy. I remember that. Because she was never very happy again. He died of consumption before his next birthday.'

'Why did you live with your grandmother?'

'Because our house was too small.'

'But the names? The names of the people in your organisation?'

'Conway, Cupar, David, Percy, Dover and Divis. Mary, Merrion, Milan, McDonnell, Osman, Raglan, Ross, Rumania, Serbia, Slate, Sorella, Sultan, Theodore, Varna and Ward Street.'

When I finished they had gone out of the room again. Only the policewoman remained. It is not the people but the streets I name.

The door opened again.

'There's someone to see you,' they said.

Jack stood before me.

'In God's name, Finn. How and why?'

He wasn't supposed to ask that question. He shook his head and sighed: 'I nearly married you.'

Let's just say it was historical.

'I ask myself over and over what kind of woman are you, and I have to remind myself that I knew you, or thought I knew you, and that I loved you once.'

Once, once upon a time.

'Anything is better than what you did, Finn. Anything! A bomb in a pub I could understand – not forgive, just understand – because of the arbitrariness of it. But – you caused the death of someone you had grown to know!'

I could not save him. I could only give him time.

'You should never have let me go!' I said, for the first time in ten years.

He looked puzzled: 'But you weren't happy with me. You didn't seem very happy.'

He stood watching for a minute and said: 'Where are you, Finn? Where are you?'

The door closed. An endless vista of solitude before me, of sleeping and waking alone in the dark – in the corner a spider was spinning a new web. I watched him move from angle to angle. An endless confinement before me and all too soon a slow gnawing hunger inside for something – I watched him weave the angles of his world in the space of the corner.

Once more they came back for the names, and I began: 'Abyssinia, Alma, Balaclava, Balkan, Belgrade, Bosnia', naming the names: empty and broken and beaten places. I know no others.

Gone and going all the time.

Redevelopment. Nothing more dramatic than that; the planners are our bombers now. There is no heart in the Falls these days.

'But the names? The names of the people who murdered him? The others?'
    'I know no others.'

The gradual and deliberate processes weave their way in the dark corners of all our rooms, and when the finger is pointed, the hand turned, the face at the end of the finger is my face, the hand at the end of the arm that points is my hand, and the only account I can give is this: that if I lived for ever I could not tell: I could only glimpse what fatal visions stir that web's dark pattern, I do not know their names. I only know for certain what my part was, that even on the eve, on such a day, I took him there.

THE WAY-PAVER

ANNE DEVLIN

I rang my sister on the morning the baby was due and said:
'How are you feeling?'
'Bored.' She said.
I wondered then if I should tell her.

My sister has the habit of sadness. She was the second-born. The first-born child was me. My mother said the births were difficult – my third sister was left too long in the birth channel and suffered... they didn't have the equipment, they locked the forceps in a cupboard and couldn't find the key... was kept too long – that's when the brain damage occurred.

We were driving to the hospital, between the prison and the hospital, when I said: 'I must get some flowers.'

'Try Kennedy's at Carlisle Circus,' my mother said. 'We get all our wreaths from there.'

'I don't think that's quite the right place, is it?'

'It's still a florist.'

I tiptoed through the lily wreaths and told the girl I was looking for a spray for my sister.

'She's just had a baby', but I stood looking round.

'Why didn't you tell Maeve she was one of twins and the other was born dead?'

Eight months in the womb and the other dead. My sister is bitter about that sharing.

'It's none of her business. And it's certainly none of yours.'

My mother is secretive about her births – she has not prepared us.

'But you told Michael McMullen.'

'I told him when I thought they were going to get married.'

'She found out from him! Before he left her.'

'You're not suggesting –'

'No. I'm not.'

'Christine – that's a – stop!'

Red lights don't seem to signal stop.

'If you don't drive more carefully, I'm getting out to walk.'

At the hospital my sister was weeping. Her face flushed and hot. I pulled the curtains quickly round her bed, shutting out the other women in the ward – not their first time – who stared without emotion.

'I'm sorry we're late.'

'I thought no one was coming.'

'We stopped to get some flowers.'

'The baby's been awake all night. Every hour I've fed her.'

'Isn't that too much?' my mother said. 'Why don't you give her a bottle? I never breast-fed any of you.'

I wish she wasn't so triumphant about it.

'It's all right, Maeve,' I told my sister. 'I was just the same.'

'Eamonn's mother was here. She doesn't like the baby's name. She thinks we should have called her after Eamonn's wee sister. She just kept saying: "My Mairead's come back."'

'I wish that woman wouldn't say those things. You can't call the living after the dead; your granny always told me that.'

Eamonn's sister was killed when she was four. The dead child calls the living after it.

'You called the boys after Grandpa and Uncle Pat.'

They died in '46, and after that, in '47, my mother married my father.

'That's different. They weren't killed in an explosion.'

She still talks about that summer, at Malahide, away from the war; when Grandpa walked her up and down the shore collecting shells – his youngest and his favourite daughter. And Uncle Pat, her eldest brother, used to walk her home from dances. Many of them, her partners, she'd leave at the Scouts' Hall door: 'My brother's waiting.' He'd walk her home from dances.

'What did Uncle Pat die of?' my sister asked.

'Tuberculosis.'

'And Grandpa?'

'A heart attack.'

'I never knew that.' More secrets. She puts on weight when she thinks about it. No one ever made it up to her.

'We went on holiday in August – there were German officers at that hotel . . .' My father never believed her. '. . . Ireland was neutral.' She insisted. 'They were both dead by Christmas.'

'Can I look at the baby?'

It was the sister from Waterford who got me through it.

'Use your pain,' she said.

'Push if you want this baby, you have to push it out away from you.'

That voice made me angry.

'You're four centimetres dilated,' they told me half an hour before.

'Let go! Let go of it!'

I remember the stillness of the room in between the calls to push – they thought I'd gone to sleep – but it was only my habit of breathing with my eyes closed.

'Ah, I don't think this is going to work,' I said when they tried to get me to breathe again.

'It's worked for thousands of years,' Sister Paul, a West Indian nurse, said.

My favourite brother is called Paul, so I grabbed her hand for comfort.

'Remember your breathing!'

'I can't do it! I can't do it!'

That's when they brought in the sister from Waterford.

'Now listen,' she said, using my Christian name, 'remember you are an Irishwoman.' I hated her for that. The person I hated most of all was Mother – who was not even there. She had not prepared me. And Frank was helpless and beside himself. Earlier, Dr Hussain, the registrar, said: 'I think I should break your waters now.' I was alone in the room with them and the pains were coming so fast I said: 'Yes. Help me!'

That seemed the worst time of all, because I wasn't expecting it; afterwards when they went out I cried. Frank had gone to phone my mother – when he came back he didn't know anything had happened. I felt so betrayed; he promised he would be with me. I knew then that I was on my own. I thought of my ex-husband and Frank's wife – about whom I had never the slightest remorse: if I have committed any sins I am paying for them now. And God! Can this get any worse? The nurse from Waterford held my hand again and said: 'Now push! Use your pain.'

Another voice, a small nurse, English, I think, said: 'The baby's heart is tired.'

The red pulse on the monitor dropped.

'Her pelvis is so strong.'

'I can see the head,' Dr Hussain said.

'Push!'

'I am pushing.'

'Shush. Shush. There's no need to –'

I was yelling.

'Good girl, now use your pain.'

Again.

'Push harder.'

'Will you let me cut you?'

'The baby's heart is weakening.'

'Push harder.'

(They tried to stop me shouting, but I had to.)

'Yes. Please.'

Each time I pushed the head appeared; each time I stopped the head withdrew. Immediately they swung my legs up into a strap, and placed Frank at the other end.

'Stand there now, and hold her hand.'

'The head's out!'

I cried out in shock. The head's free! And the long seal's back dived after it. Was there so much after the head? All that inside me? A genie uncorked from a bottle. The room was quiet, the baby quiet, only I was wailing. A woman's voice, I can't remember who, said: 'It's a boy.' I knew it would be. And Frank took up the chorus in awe and whispered in my ear: 'Oh love, it's a lovely little boy.'

Frank says, when it was first born, the child blinked, looked again, blinked, looked again, blinked and then stared. I remember only, they held him close to my face, he was folded in a blanket, like a letter peeping out of an envelope.

'He doesn't look very happy to see us!'

Worse. He didn't even look surprised.

And Sister Paul said: 'You've been here before, my lad.'

Once cutting, they pulled the head away from my body, with a stroke they held this head up with its long slippery tail. This seal, is my – son. These are the executioners.

'I don't remember any of that,' Maeve said at the hospital. 'When the doctor said: "It's a girl", I said: "How do you know?" And then I looked and he was holding her.'

'Everybody's different,' my mother said uneasily.

'I'm glad you told me it was going to be awful, though.'

'When did she tell you that?'

'When she phoned up. She said I'd feel like the survivor of a nuclear attack.'

'That's an awful thing to say!' My mother was livid. 'Why did you say that?'

'Because it's the most shocking thing that ever happened to me.'

Heart pain. Head pain. And after all these years – this: I went into hospital a proud, ambitious, talented professional, and I came out a snivelling schoolgirl, a crushed face in the mirror, a moveable feast with leaking breasts, I felt suicidal at every suck. I didn't even like cats before. I was eight and a half stone when I found out I was pregnant; when I got past eleven I stopped counting. Angry? I am raging. It breaks out in gusts and I have to be restrained.

Yesterday, Oona and I took the baby for a walk. We could see the post van coming for miles. We pushed the pram into the hedgerow to let it pass; and caught up again at the next house along the road. He passed us and we passed him again and again during the walk, until, finally, we caught up with him when he stopped at the crossroads postbox.

'Good morning.' We smiled.

'It's well for the women,' he said, getting back into his

van and moving on to the next house.

Angry? I opened my mouth and shouted down the lane: 'Then let men have babies!'

Oona, the third-born, looked nervous, she's very wise in her way: 'Oh don't, Christine! Mr Delaney's a friend of my daddy's.'

A nurse came and pulled the screens back.

'These flowers have just arrived for you. How's Maeve today?' She placed them on the bed. They were delicate, not brooding like the flowers I'd brought.

'She's nice,' Maeve told my mother. 'It's the night nurse I don't like.'

'They're from my sister,' my mother said, touching the corner of her glasses as she reads the card. Touching the corner of her pride.

'No cards from his side?'

'Mother!'

Nobody is good enough.

'I couldn't help noticing.'

She insists that she married down; my sister did as well. She scrutinises my brothers' friends, delights in Paul's promiscuity and in Pat's timidity. Oona, the third-born, moves heavily around my great-grandmother's mahogany with a duster and the noise of the TV in her head. 'Oona will always be with us,' Mother says.

No one is good enough. I had to run away.

'Can you bring me a vase?' The nurse didn't hear.

'I must get water for these –'

'Mummy, leave them. The nurse will do it later.'

'The ward's too hot to leave them. I'll just go and get a vase from the kitchen.'

'Let her go. She likes hospitals. She knows what to do,'
I said.

My sister and I have not been friends. The distance between
us is too great to cross. Maeve once described it as not dislike exactly, more indifference. Only this confraternity of
motherhood keeps us talking.

'How's England?' she says.

'I like it more and more.'

'Mammy says you have a lovely house.'

'We spent some time doing it up.'

'She seemed to enjoy herself that time she was over
with you.'

'She was very good. I couldn't have managed without her.'

'Though she said the neighbourhood made her nervous.'

'We live in a red-light district.'

'Oh.'

'It was the only place we could afford to buy a house
that size.'

'You know she lights a candle every night to Saint
Martin' – hopeless cases? Or is that Saint Jude? – 'that you
and Frank will get married.'

When the baby was ten days old, my mother answered
the door.

'There's a lady in a sari and a boy. They want to come in,'
she said.

'It's my neighbour.' Asha and Sultan; she has never called
on me before. Asha looked into the cot and spoke in Urdu to
her son.

'How big is it?' the boy translated.

'He's eight pounds,' I said.

'Would you like a drink?' my mother asked.

'A cup of tea or a glass of orange juice,' I explained.

'No thank you. I too fat. Too much sugar.'

'My mother has diabetes,' Sultan says.

'How many children have you?' my mother asked.

'Eight. How many you?'

'Five.'

I made friends with them when we arrived – Sultan and his sister Tswera were playing at the gate.

I said: 'Hello. I'm Christine and this is Frank.'

'Have you any children?' Tswera asked.

'I have a child in here,' I said, pointing. I was five months pregnant. They fled indoors laughing.

'For baby,' Asha said.

Sultan handed over a gift-wrapped parcel and a card. They had printed the names of all the children.

'Thank you. It's very kind.'

'She wouldn't have visited you, if you'd had a girl,' Maeve said when I told her.

Perhaps. At Ramadan, they sent us in a feast of chicken, rice, chapattis and pakhora. At Christmas we return the gifts. We don't know them any better than we did at the beginning. Asha makes my son laugh; when she sees him she always asks the same question: 'Baby all right? You all right?' She does not ask about Frank. And I have never seen her husband. Occasionally a ball comes over the fence or food is offered. We carefully wash and return all her dishes. She speaks in Urdu to her children. She comes from northern Pakistan and she says abruptly 'Goodbye' at the end of a conversation. She goes along the hall and disappears indoors for another six months. She has eight births to consider and I have one. This is not her country, either. My mother picks up the gift she has left: a white woollen jacket and pants. 'It's expensive,' my mother says, surprised – the neighbourhood we live in is rather poor. The council owns the house next door.

'When are you going back?' Maeve asks, as my mother comes along the ward with two vases of water.

'Not for another week.'

'Where's the baby?'

'Oona's looking after him.'

The third-born. The one and the locked door. My father kicking the door, the cupboard door, throwing the whole weight of his body against it, he told me – swearing, punching, the dull metallic cupboard banged like a drum against the wall. 'Open the fucking door!' Oona. That's when the brain damage occurred.

'Oona loves him. She watches all his little ways and tells us everything he does,' my mother says, arranging her sister's flowers.

'She's going to look after the baby when I go back to university. I didn't ask her to. She offered.'

'Yes, she told me.'

'You've got an au pair?'

Renate. 'Yes.'

At two and a half months I unhooked him from the nipple, gave him a bottle and handed him over to Renate. 'I have to work!' Occasionally I pass them in the hall or on the stairs – like two playmates, both new to this house; he's beaming, she talks to him in German – he's become '*mein Schatz*' – while I watch and hope he'll remember something of me at the end of the day. And think of my own mother picking her way through her children's lives with her lighted candles and her prayers.

'Would you ever have another?' Maeve says.

'Another what?'

'Another baby.'

The prostitutes stand on the corners of the streets on the road to the maternity hospital, shivering in the sunlight in twos and threes. A few hundred yards away a group of Asian men are waiting outside the ante-natal clinic. They do not look at the prostitutes. They do not see them. The waiting room is full as Frank and I enter.

'Number twenty-two next!'

'Where's your co-operation card?'

'I'm post-natal.'

'Oh! You've had it,' the woman said. 'I still need a urine sample.'

I was peeing into the neck of a small bottle when she opened the hatch above me and called out: 'Are you Irish?'

'Yes.' I handed her the bottle.

'I'm from Tyrone myself.'

'I'm from County Down.'

'You had a difficult time?'

'Yes.'

'A boy, too?'

'Yes.'

'Well, the boys are always the worst. They've bigger heads than girls. Next time it will be easier. He stretched you, you see.'

'I'm not going to have another one.'

'Ah, go on. They all say that. You'll be back in two years from now. It's much easier. The first one always paves the way.'

I went in to see the consultant and had a coil fitted.

The nurse came back: 'Excuse me – but you'll have to go now. Visiting's over.'

My mother looked around the ward to protest.

'Only fathers can stay,' the nurse said.

'Where is Eamonn?' my mother asked.

'He has an exam today,' Maeve said. 'Here – did I show you

the photos? The baby ten minutes old. I bought Eamonn a camera for Christmas so he could take pictures of the birth, but we haven't got any – he fainted.'

When I looked up the three of us were laughing.

The woman next door weaves the names of her children on antimacassars in Urdu: my mother does not understand the country I have chosen.

'We thought you'd come home and have your baby here,' she says as we leave the hospital. I decided then that I should tell her.

'Mammy, Frank's just lost his job.'

'When?'

'Three weeks ago.'

'Why didn't you say so before?'

'Because I was hoping it wouldn't come to this.'

'But he seems so well set up,' my mother says. 'I don't understand this.'

'The grant to his department has been cut. He's the newest member of the staff so he's got to go.'

'Is his the only job that's been affected?'

'Yes. I think so.'

'You don't think he's been victimised because of us?'

'Because of us?'

'Your daddy's an ex-internee.'

'Mammy, that was in 1943.'

'Yes, but in '51 –'

In '51 . . . they came back.

'That time I went to visit you when the baby was born, and I didn't have any identification, I forgot the family allowance book and your daddy had to send it on.'

'I remember.'

'Well, I told the plain-clothes policeman when I got off the boat that Frank was coming to meet me. And he asked who Frank was. All I could say was he's my – he's my – I couldn't find the right description and that made them suspicious. They weren't going to let me go until I said: "Frank's a professor of poetry." I think I even gave them his work address. Your daddy said I shouldn't have told them, they'd put Frank's name on the computer.'

'For what? Because he lives with an Irishwoman!'

'But your daddy said –'

My father joined the IRA when he was fourteen, was interned at seventeen, released at twenty-one and met my mother at a swimming gala in 1947. He stopped seeing the republicans after that. They lived above a doctor's surgery in two rooms for a while and then Grandma took them back to live with her – when Mother's elder sisters' opposition died down, or was too far away to matter. Aunt Eileen had gone to South Africa and Auntie Mamie to the London Civil Service. In 1951, when the King and Queen were visiting Belfast, they came back for him again.

'He's on night work,' my mother said – 'he's not involved.' I go back to that moment many times in my dreams, in the womb and on the stairs my mother stood, two hearts waiting, unable to move up or down to answer the pounding fists of the police on the door. Or was that sound her heartbeat and mine, in that safe dark place next to her breast? He was on night shift, so they went to his work looking for him. She did not see him for a week after that until the royal family were safely back in London, and they released him. My father lost his job.

'I'm innocent,' he told his employers. 'My wife's expecting our first child.'

I was born then. I can hear that pounding yet.

'That was held against your father all his life. Only Catholics would employ him,' she says on the way back in the car.

'England is different,' I insist.

'Not at all. Everywhere's the same. Sure my sister Mamie was worried when I married your father that it would block her promotion in the London Civil Service.'

'And did it?'

'No. I don't think so. She did very well. But things have changed for us in England since the Troubles.'

I knew she would say all this. Bring out the old stories, the old suspicions. That's why I wouldn't tell her.

'The new job didn't have tenure. The grant was cut. That's all. It's happening all over. There is no financial security any more.'

'What will you do?'

'Sell the house, send Renate back to Germany, go and live in a council house somewhere... how should I know!'

'Maybe something will turn up,' my mother says. 'It always does – and then you won't have to sell your lovely house.'

Habitat curtains and cork tiled floors.

'Mammy, Frank pays for everything. I have no money at all.'

'But you work!'

'Aye. The odd poetry programme on Radio 3 isn't going to pay the mortgage.'

'Well, I think it's time you gave up that writing and got yourself a proper job. You've a family to think about now, you've got to give your children some dignity.'

'I'm a poet. I don't want a proper job. Oh, I could work as a shop assistant, but I had rather hoped to use all my intelligence.'

'You could teach somewhere. You've got an English degree.'
I was waiting for this.

When my mother's eldest sister Mamie died in London, I was
twelve, the money stopped coming to pay for Granny's big
house. Aunt Eileen came back from South Africa to bury
Mamie and bought her mother a two-bedroomed house in a
quiet non-Catholic part of the city, two buses far for us to visit.
We moved to a new housing estate on the lower slopes of the
Black Mountain, Belfast West. Aunt Eileen gave us plenty of
warning of her intention: she said for years we were too much
trouble for her mother. My mother remembers it all. It was the
first time we'd had to live on my father's income. The boys
were born there, my mother had to give up her job, besides
there was a rent to pay. For the first time we had to live on
Father's income and of course we didn't. My mother remembers
it all. It was three miles to the nearest bus. It took five years
before the city boundary was extended – before a red bus passed
our front door. My mother didn't like the housing estate. My
father promised he'd look around for something better. She
wanted a nice house on the lough. My mother remembers it all.
She pinned her hopes on her first-born finishing school and
getting a proper job, so they could buy a house at the sea. I
couldn't take the responsibility of it. After six years I ran away
to university – England – and I never came back. Me. The first-
born. The way-paver. The one who ran. I married a man who
was careful with money, a teacher, with a house of his own. I
was so desperate to marry that man. I wrote and told them I was
getting married and could they lend me two hundred pounds
to pay for the wedding. I kept him away from my family until
it was too late. I was so desperate. And I was successful. They
found the money. We were married in England: only my
father and mother came. They got off the plane at Heathrow

on the day before the wedding and left by the following day's flight. I remember how they hurried away at the airport.

I never took him back to see the house, on the side of the Black Mountain, with the battered front door – my brothers kicked it when they wanted in – the brunt of so many small tantrums. Andersonstown, my mother lived there for eighteen years. I put the Irish Sea between me and that memory. And I wanted so much to be a poet. Except once when Maeve was getting married, seven years after my own, we went back for the wedding. And he saw it all. The house, the battered door and torn garden. The estate graffiti, the flags and emblems of resistance. The wedding was massive. My mother saved her family allowance for years, for the peach two-piece she wore, the orchids, and the singer at the Mass; the two hundred sit-down in a local hotel. I knew it was going to be like that. My husband said: 'Your father doesn't spend his money on the house, does he?' He'd expected so much more. I had not prepared him. When we went back to England, I gave up my job; I'd been threatening to for years. I want to be a poet, I said. I invited him to abandon me. Which is strange, when I was once so desperate to marry that man. Desperation runs in generations in my family.

I never wanted to marry Frank. He was my lover. I wanted to live with him sometimes and then I found I was pregnant and everything changed. Frank was a professor of literature and the editor of a poetry review. I walked into his office, when he'd read some poems I sent him, and he'd asked to see me. I walked into his office and I thought: No, I am not going to fall in love with this man. Frank's wife said, when he left her, I'd hardly made a disinterested choice of lover, a professor and the editor of a review. He published my poems. The accusation stuck. But

I didn't care. He changed jobs when I was five months on, to get away from the gossip. We moved to another part of the country. And he gave up the review. I didn't expect or hope anything would last. We always seemed to be just minutes ahead of destruction before the baby was born. But I went on writing and then everything changed. When he came home late that Friday night three weeks ago and told me he'd lost his job, I knew when he got out of the car in the rain, two hours late for supper.

I once asked Asha where her husband was; she had a year-old child on her knee. He goes out, she told me, every morning early, he takes his bicycle and he comes back after dark. 'What work does he do?' I asked.

'No work,' she said. 'He no work.'

The journey from the hospital in Belfast takes about an hour along the coast. The road runs past the cottage a little onto pebble, then grass, then rock; below, the waves of the Irish Sea wash the ridge of the peninsula – the first vanguard of the land into the sea. On this unofficial headland the house stands.

'You can see Scotland on a clear day and just over there the Isle of Man,' the estate agent told my father three years ago when they retired to the cottage on the point. He kept his promise. My sister Oona is waiting at the door with my son in her arms when we drive up. They are watching the gulls. He cries out when he sees me. His new voice catches me unawares.

'That's a strange sound.'

'He thinks he's a gull,' Oona said.

My mother looks depressed by this sudden insecurity. I didn't tell her about the tax assessments for more than the price of our house; or the appeal we won in the spring; or the burglary – not surprising in our neighbourhood ... always minutes ahead of destruction . . . I didn't tell her . . . England is the country I have chosen for my son – and like Asha and Sultan, I need to believe in it.

Then I say: 'I'm thinking of getting married – when Frank's divorce comes through.'

She looks out across the water.

'I like Frank,' she says.

Fifteen years ago I put more than the Irish Sea between myself and my family.

Further up the estuary on the other side of the peninsula is a seal colony. Once in a while one or two swim out and make for the open sea; we watch for these from the rocks in front of the cottage.

'They look so human,' my mother says, as a head breaks the water, paving the way. We concentrate on that stray seal.

BIOGRAPHICAL NOTES

LINDA ANDERSON was born in Belfast and educated at Queen's University. An award-winning short story writer, she has written two novels, *To Stay Alive* (1984) and *Cuckoo* (1986). She is currently teaching at the University of Lancaster.

FIONA BARR was born in Derry. She has had a large number of stories and articles published and broadcast, and has worked as a television critic for the *Irish News*. 'The Wall-reader' won the 1979 Maxwell House Women Writers' Competition.

MARY BECKETT was born in Belfast and taught in Ardoyne for many years. Her stories first appeared in *The Bell*, the *Irish Press*'s 'New Irish Writing', and *Threshold*, and were broadcast by BBC radio. 'The Master and the Bombs' dates from 1963 and appears in her fine collection of 1980, *A Belfast Woman*, published by Poolbeg Press. More recently she produced an acclaimed novel about the North, *Give Them Stones* (1987).

SHANE CONNAUGHTON was born in Cavan and raised in a police station on the border with Fermanagh, where his father was a sergeant. His first collection, *A Border Station* (1989), draws upon these childhood experiences to powerful effect. A highly regarded screenwriter, his credits include the Oscar-winning film, *My Left Foot*.

ANNE DEVLIN was born and brought up in Belfast. A distinguished playwright and screenwriter – her plays include *The Long March* (1984), *Ourselves Alone* (1985), and *After Easter* (1994) – she was awarded the 1984 Samuel Beckett Award for Television Drama and in 1985 the Susan Smith Blackburn Prize. 'Naming the Names' was memorably adapted for BBC television and appeared in her short story collection, *The Way-paver* (1986).

MAURICE LEITCH was born in County Antrim and educated in Belfast. After some years as a primary school teacher, he became a BBC radio producer. His novels include *Liberty Lad* (1965), *Poor Lazarus* (1969), which won the *Guardian* Fiction Prize, *Silver's City* (1981), which was awarded the Whitbread Novel Award, and *Gilchrist* (1994). 'Green Roads' is a story taken from *The Hands of Cheryl Boyd* (1989).

BERNARD MAC LAVERTY was born in Belfast and worked for many years as a medical technician before studying English at Queen's University. A full-time writer who has lived in Scotland since 1974, he has won great acclaim as a novelist, short story writer and screenwriter. His first book, *Secrets and Other Stories*, was published by Blackstaff Press in 1977, and later collections include *A Time to Dance* (1982) and *The Great Profundo* (1987) (available from Penguin Books) and *Walking the Dog* (1994). His two novels, *Lamb* (1980) and *Cal* (1983), were made into highly successful films.

MICHAEL McLAVERTY was born in Carrickmacross, County Monaghan, in 1907 and worked for most of his life as a teacher and headmaster in Belfast. Highly regarded as a fiction writer in the 1930s, he achieved a resurgence of popularity in the late 1970s and 1980s with the publication by Poolbeg Press in 1978 of his *Collected Short Stories,* with an introduction by Seamus Heaney, and the reissue of his 1939 novel, *Call My Brother Back*, a year later. In 1989 *In Quiet Places: The Uncollected Stories, Letters and Critical Prose of Michael McLaverty* appeared, edited by Sophia Hillan King. Michael McLaverty died in 1992.

JOHN MONTAGUE was born in Brooklyn, New York, but moved to County Tyrone in 1933, and was educated in Armagh and at University College Dublin. He is best known as a poet, as one of the foremost voices of the North, and amongst his collections are *Poisoned Lands* (1961), *The Rough Field* (1972), *The Dead Kingdom* (1984), and *New Selected Poems* (1989). 'The Cry' was written in 1963 and appeared in his short story collection, *Death of a Chieftain* (1964). A new prose volume about his school days, *Time in Armagh*, is due for publication in the near future.

JOHN MORROW was born in Belfast and, after leaving school at the age of fourteen, worked in the shipyards, and as a navvy and furniture salesman. His short stories began to appear in magazines and on BBC radio in the late 1960s, and were published in *Northern Myths* (1979) and *Sects and Other Stories* (1987). His novels include *The Confessions of Proinsias O'Toole* (1977) and *The Essex Factor* (1982).

BRENDA MURPHY was born in Belfast and has been writing since the age of seventeen. Her stories have appeared in the first *Blackstaff Book of Short Stories* (1988) and in *The Female Line: Northern Ireland Women Writers* (1985), edited by Ruth Hooley.

FRANK O'CONNOR was born in Cork in 1903 and moved to Dublin in the 1930s. Generally acknowledged as one of Ireland's foremost writers in the short story form – W.B. Yeats compared his gifts to those of Chekhov – his most celebrated collections include his first, *Guests of the Nation* (1931), and *My Oedipus Complex* (1963). His anthology of *Modern Irish Short Stories* (1957), reissued by Oxford University Press in 1985 as *Classic Irish Short Stories*, has been repeatedly reprinted ever since its first publication. He died in 1966.

DAVID PARK was born in Belfast and lived there until the mid-1980s. A teacher in County Down, he has published one collection of short stories, *Oranges from Spain* (1990), and a novel, *The Healing* (1992).

ANNE-MARIE REILLY was born in Belfast and now works as a teacher in Strangford, County Down. Her story 'Leaving' first appeared in *The Female Line: Northern Ireland Women Writers* (1985), edited by Ruth Hooley.

WILLIAM TREVOR was born in Mitchelstown, County Cork, and is one of Ireland's most distinguished living writers. Amongst his books are *The Old Boys* (1964), which won the Hawthornden Prize, *The Ballroom of Romance* (1972), *Angels at the Ritz* (1975), which won a Royal Society of Literature Award, *The Children of Dynmouth* (1976), which won the Whitbread Novel Award, *The Distant Past* (1979), *Fools of Fortune* (1983), which also received the Whitbread Novel Award, and *Two Lives* (1991), which was shortlisted for the Booker Prize. In 1977 he was awarded a CBE for his services to literature and he is a member of the Irish Academy of Letters.

UNA WOODS was born and brought up in Belfast, and as a singer of traditional songs was very involved in the folk music scene around Queen's University in the late 1960s. She lived in Hertfordshire and London for a while before returning to Belfast. Her first collection of stories, *The Dark Hole Days*, was published in 1984 by Blackstaff Press.

ACKNOWLEDGEMENTS

Grateful acknowledgement is made to:

Linda Anderson for permission to reprint 'The Death of Men';

Fiona Barr for permission to reprint 'The Wall-reader' from *The Female Line: Northern Ireland Women Writers* (ed. Ruth Hooley, Northern Ireland Women's Rights Movement, 1985);

Jonathan Cape for permission to reprint 'Father and Son' and 'The Daily Woman' from *A Time to Dance* (1982), and 'Walking the Dog' from *Walking the Dog* (1994), all by Bernard Mac Laverty;

Faber and Faber for permission to reprint 'Naming the Names' and 'The Way-paver' by Anne Devlin from *The Way-paver* (1986);

Hamish Hamilton for permission to reprint 'Beatrice' by Shane Connaughton from *A Border Station* (1989);

John Johnson for permission to reprint 'The Distant Past' by William Trevor from *The Distant Past* (Poolbeg Press, 1979);

John Montague for permission to reprint 'The Cry' from *Death of a Chieftain* (MacGibbon and Kee, 1964);

Brenda Murphy for permission to reprint 'A Social Call' from *The Blackstaff Book of Short Stories* (Blackstaff Press, 1988);

Peters Fraser and Dunlop for permission to reprint 'Guests of the Nation' by Frank O'Connor from *Frank O'Connor's Short Stories* (Pan in association with Macmillan, 2 vols, 1990);

Poolbeg Press and Christine Green for permission to reprint 'The Master and the Bombs' and 'A Belfast Woman' by Mary Beckett from *A Belfast Woman* (1980); and Poolbeg Press for permission to reprint 'Pigeons' by Michael McLaverty from *Collected Short Stories of Michael McLaverty* (1978);

Random House UK for permission to reprint 'Green Roads' by Maurice Leitch from *The Hands of Cheryl Boyd* (Hutchinson, 1989);

Anne-Marie Reilly for permission to reprint 'Leaving' from *The Female Line: Northern Ireland Women Writers* (ed. Ruth Hooley, Northern Ireland Women's Rights Movement, 1985);

Sheil Land Associates for permission to reprint 'Killing a Brit' and 'Oranges from Spain' by David Park from *Oranges from Spain* (Jonathan Cape, 1990);

Transworld Publishers for permission to reprint 'Lonely Heart' by John Morrow from *Sects and Others Stories* (1987);

Una Woods for permission to reprint 'The Dark Hole Days' from *The Dark Hole Days* (Blackstaff Press, 1984).

The publishers have made every effort to trace and acknowledge copyright holders. We apologise for any omissions in the above list and we will welcome additions or amendments to it for inclusion in any reprint edition.